AMERICAN REVOLT

Volume I of THE PACIFICATION OF EARTH

By Dean Warren

This is a work of fiction. Names, characters, places and
incidents either are the product of the author's
imagination or are used fictitiously, and any
resemblance to any actual person, living or dead, events
or locales is utterly coincidental.

This book was printed in the United States of America.

Chapter 1

2090
San Angeles--the merged cities of San Diego and Los
Angeles in California

Eighteen year-old Benjamin Bjorn remembered that morning's dawn, when the northwestern ghetto began to awaken with the unbarring of tenement doors, the patter of reconnoitering feet, and the rustle of disturbed homeless. Later, with the sun, the stench of rotting garbage and excrement rose above the steps upon which he stood.

He'd sworn to himself that he'd escape the ghetto--the hopeless millions, the filth, and the gangs. He'd escape to the beautiful world out there. Somehow he'd make this chance work.

He headed a line of four hundred other Welfie kids that stretched down two flights of stairs and along the government block on Pico Avenue.

Now he stood at what he thought was military attention before a female marine lieutenant and made that promise to himself once more.

"Can you read and write?" the recruitment officer asked. She extended a hand. "Your proof of education, please."

Only recruiting drive in years. And she asks me for paper I don't have! Couldn't have.

He swallowed. "We moved a lot, Missus. The few public schools are always full. Doesn't matter. I've zipped on-line through all the courses required for a voter's certificate."

"Not 'Missus,'" she corrected. "'Ma'am.'"

"Sorry...Ma'am." He jerked his gaze from her curves to the strongly boned face framed by black hair. "I did more, actually. Whipped math--calculus was tough--and studied physics and engineering. I can pass any test you throw at me."

The Achiever lieutenant shook her head.

She figured he was lying, he guessed, and hadn't liked his once-over, either. Bjorn rubbed cropped, yellow hair and nervously stretched his muscled six feet dressed in a worn, gray, short-sleeved shirt and pants.

Then he caught himself not standing at attention and stiffened again. *I'm desperate, lady!*

Bjorn and his fellows were surplus. Brilliant, talking computers had stolen most service and lower management jobs, while exploding populations down south had taken simple factory work.

The lieutenant motioned for him to leave her office.

He had to use his fallback plan!

"People around here screw the Corps," he said quickly. "You ought to do something."

The woman's face hardened. "What are you up to?"

"Trying to show you I'm worth recruiting!" Bjorn blurted. "Don't you want people who will look out for the Corps?"

"Yes, but not adolescents who spill the first nonsense that comes to their minds." The lieutenant stared at him and then shook her head as if reprimanding herself. "All right. Tell me in two sentences."

"The Corps set up James's Rest & Recreation Cabaret for marines," he answered. "The wanna-be Achiever who operates it also runs an illegal dream skin business."

"Why should I believe you? Messing with people's nerves via a dream skin is a capital offense. And on government property? He'd have to be pretty stupid."

Bjorn took a deep breath. "Go tonight, Ma'am. The body skins and their stimulators are on the fourth floor. Long way up. The operator will acid-bathe the skins if he hears even a mouse squeak. However, I can make sure you reach James's office on the second floor quickly. You can tackle the computer before he wipes his books."

She tapped the desktop with a finger. "Once you take the oath, you die if you mislead an officer." She drew the finger across her throat. "No expensive trial either. Did you know that bit of reality before you opened your mouth?"

He swallowed and nodded that he did know.

She slid an enlistment chip toward him. "Go to the next office and prove basic education to the testing program. Enter the medical machine for your physical. If you pass everything, come back. I'll swear you into the Corps."

She stared up at him. "Then you will repeat your accusations and your promise about tonight."

"Yes, Ma'am."

He felt her blue eyes stab at his back as he turned away.

#

At noon, when Bjorn told Uncle Will of his bargain with the recruitment lieutenant, his only relative shrugged. "Too late to argue about your scheme," he said. "Let's make it work."

Bjorn relaxed at that assurance of help and glanced around the tenement cubby. He sat on his uncle's small bed and leaned against his own bedroll. In the corner the water tap dripped and he smelled urine from the neighboring toilet through the closed corridor door. No windows, only an ancient Escher print that his uncle loved. Men climbed a castle's battlements but stayed on the same level through tricks in perspective.

Two ration bars of compressed grain and algae

lay on the small table in front of his uncle's chair.

"Eat your lunch, boy. Aquifers are drying up all over the world. Food production is down. We're lucky to have anything at all."

Olive-skinned Will Maestri possessed a cold grin that Bjorn had learned to pay attention to. In the violent 2060s, poor food, skimpy health rations from automated clinics, and poisons in the water and air had stunted the older man. Sickness had removed all hair from his head. But, when you dealt with him, you felt a force you weren't prepared for by his size or looks.

Government had done better in the nephew's childhood. The state rebuilt Welfie ghettos and eliminated pollution sources. The administration's monitoring wiped out infectious disease and local councils regularized rations.

Uncle and nephew didn't look alike, except for dark blue, almost black eyes.

His uncle once explained Bjorn's yellow hair. "You're a throwback to the Gauls who invaded Italy long, long ago. Recessive genes carried by my sister and Scandinavian ones of your father, I guess. Not many blonds in the ghetto here. Nor elsewhere."

"I don't know how you stand this life," Bjorn now said, disdaining the rations. "Especially after working in Health and Human Resources, in Washington. Good food and quarters. A meaningful job. We've got nothing!"

"You're quick, strong, and clever, Benjamin, but you must learn self-discipline. You know I don't like reminders."

Bjorn winced. "Sorry." Then he took a deep breath. "I should never have eyed the lieutenant during the interview."

"Lusts trip you too often. Discipline!"

Uncle Will hit a ration bar on the table to dislodge possible weevils as well as to provide emphasis. "About 'standing this life,' I blew my one chance because I wanted more than an exit from the ghetto. I tried to increase the milk ration of Welfie children, and stupidly screwed up. Take my fate as a lesson—as I do. Think carefully before you act."

"Sorry," Bjorn muttered again. "But I <u>must</u> take this chance to get out of the ghetto. And, I must do what I promised, or I'm dead meat. Lieutenant Morrison won't be as easy on me as your boss was on you."

Uncle Will snorted, probably at the word "easy." "You're lucky for the opportunity to join up, all right. In the service, you can maybe work yourself into officer school and join the Achiever class."

"But why do I have to pull a con to put my life on the line?" Bjorn pretended to spit. "If I ever gain any power, I'll wring the goddamned injustice out of this world."

Uncle Will turned the ration bar in his hands. "You've my do-gooder genes", he replies. "Mask them."

Bjorn leaned forward and picked up his own ration bar. "How will we open James's computer?"

"You didn't promise that, did you?"

Bjorn thought back over the interview. "No. Just quick access. But she'll expect more."

Uncle Will shrugged. "You can only do so much." He smelled the bar. "Your new marine status will let you into the cabaret. As for me, Angel, the madam, hates James. She'll ease me in if I promise to fix things."

After a pause, he shook his head. "I'm told that waves of energy shoot through a customer's nerves from the dream skin. The waves exercise every known pleasure center. But you pay for anything extreme, like that. Customers pay; Mr. James will pay, too." He stared in Bjorn's eyes, and then glanced down at the ration bar. "Anyway, I'll join you in the cabaret tonight. As you probably figured, we'll have to create an uproar that will grease the lieutenant's way to James's computer."

Uncle Will smiled sparely and set down his bar of

compressed grain and algae. "Now, let's hear your ideas for the disturbance."

#

Mr. Roland James' R&R Cabaret filled the bottom three floors of a gray tenement near the corner of Pico and Sepulveda. The building sat behind two trashy palm trees that shaded a stop of the hydrogen-powered bus service.

In early evening, Bjorn walked under a red, white, and blue, blinking sign and through the door. A marine ID coin hung around his neck, but he still wore washed-to-gray ghetto clothes. A bouncer checked the ID and waved him into the cabaret's main room. "You better have a good money disc, kid."

A five-meter high, cream ceiling extended twenty meters, all the way from above the door to a gray composite, back balcony on an abbreviated second floor. Stairs climbed to the balcony alongside a blank wall that, Bjorn guessed, hid an automated kitchen and bar. Offices opened up from the balcony. Spruced up tenement cubbies, where the girls lived, filled the third story, he knew. Up another floor, an Achiever customer who came in the back way and up the fire stairs would find "meditation" rooms, in one of which he could happily writhe from nerve tickling.

After a month or so of such joy, housemen would have to carry the customer up. And the last session…

Bjorn shook his head.

In the cabaret, round tables bordered an oval dance floor. A rainbow of colors cycled through the air from recessed ceiling lights. Bjorn smelled billows of incense drifting downward. Both the colors and the incense blurred his view of a few early parties of marines and of the three burly housemen who lounged along the wall near the stairs.

Soon Uncle Will, in his usual black coat and trousers, entered and joined Bjorn at a table to the right of the entrance. Bjorn felt admiration for his relative's ability to seem insignificant. Loose clothing hid fit muscles. Phony stiffness covered a catlike balance. Small size, baldness, and a bland expression disguised cool deadliness.

Every time the door crashed open to let marines enter, Bjorn jumped up and held out his hand. He introduced himself as a new recruit. The men shook his hand, pounded his back, and offered him a drink. But, after fixing the new identity that he would need later, he always returned to his uncle.

Brass and woodwind simulators played "Stealing Apples," an ancient classic that Bjorn had heard now and again through the flat, web access screen in his tenement's rumpus room. More sweet incense drifted from the ceiling. Girls in short skirts with low-cut tops filed down the open stairway, hips wiggling to the jazz's beat.

Angel, the slender madam, slid into a chair next to his uncle as couples stepped onto the dance floor. Her bright, orange hair framed an olive face. "Mr. James came in the back way," she whispered. "He's upstairs checking yesterday's receipts against his business model. Looking for cheats."

"May I have your drink orders?" a synthetic, baritone voice said from the pneumatic tube platform in the middle of the table. "Appetizers?"

Angel waved off the table computer's program. "We're staff." When the speaker clicked acknowledgement of a registered voice, she added, "And don't record."

"James has to go," she told Uncle Will. "Not just because his other business, upstairs, will get us into trouble. My girls signed up to party with young marines like Bjorn here. Now, they're told to snuggle with smelly gang bosses and old Achiever-types. And James lets the housemen treat us like sluts." Her ample breasts protruding from the top of her black dress jiggled with the force of her words. "The girls talk about running back to their home tenements, even giving up pensions."

Uncle Will patted her wrist. "Patience, love."

She peered at him. "You promised. We're going to fix James, aren't we?"

Uncle Will smiled. "We'll see."

Suddenly, the front door slammed open, banging against the wall. Three tough-looking civilians in their forties pushed aside the door guard. Bjorn recognized one as Consalvo, the Pico gang boss. A white scar crossed from the squat tough's brow to the corner of his cheek and across his beak of a nose. He wore a blue suit over a gray, open-necked shirt.

The Welfie gangster strode over, flanked by his two burly, Hispanic bodyguards. "I heard you'd be here, Maistre," he said to Uncle Will through thick lips. "I still haven't seen the commissions you owe me."

"Ah, my friend, when did I ever promise protection money?"

The low vibrato in his uncle's voice made Bjorn shiver. He edged his chair back.

"You'll pay now, you little bastard!"

"Meet my nephew, Ben Bjorn. As of this morning, he's a marine."

Bjorn stood, glad to be on his feet. His muscles felt tight.

Consalvo ignored the introduction and slid his hand into his suit coat. "Outside!" he ordered Uncle Will. "Now!"

The larger bodyguard, a heavy man with a pocked, fleshy face, lurched in front of Bjorn.

A houseman who stood nearby dashed upstairs. Uncle Will slowly *stood from behind the table.*

Where the hell is Lieutenant Morrison?

The crowd quieted. Housemen straightened against the stairwell wall. Girls and their marine customers rose from nearby tables. Couples stopped dancing.

Then, as if on cue, the front door flew open again. Lieutenant Morrison entered, accompanied by two marines with chevrons running down their uniformed sleeves, one of the men with a briefcase in his hand. The lieutenant wore blue slacks and an insignia-full marine officer's jacket—contrasting with the filmy, deep-cut blouses and short, tight skirts of Angel's girls.

For a moment, Bjorn thought everyone seemed paralyzed. Both the gangsters and the lieutenant's party had paused at the edge of the tables. The gang boss stared at the lieutenant and her men, while his bodyguards stood still. The lieutenant, her NCOs at her back, surveyed the cabaret. A few meters from Bjorn, Uncle Will touched his chin, his hand near the hidden knife that hung under his shirt and between his shoulders. He watched Consalvo. Angel stood up, too, and looked as if she might bolt.

Suddenly, a man with iron gray hair sped down the stairs behind the messenger. The two men paused at the bottom. An arc of tables, the dance floor, and more tables stretched between them and the tense confrontation.

Uncle Will nodded.

Bjorn pointed to the right of the big bodyguard. "What's that?" he asked. When the hulking man turned, Bjorn quickly kicked him in the groin.

His move had pulled the lieutenant's eyes to him. "Look out!" she yelled. .

Landing on both feet again after the kick, Bjorn pivoted. Ducking under the knuckle-duster of the second bodyguard, Bjorn rammed his fist into the man's stomach.

Bjorn saw the gang boss jerk out a nine-millimeter pistol from under his suit coat. Uncle Will held his knife poised.

I'm supposed to leave Consalvo to him!

Some woman screamed.

"Hands up!" yelled a houseman. "Up, you

bastards!"

"Put away the hardware," another shouted. "No shooting or knifing!"

Bjorn raised a chair over his head and brought it down in a powerful sweep. He smashed the second bodyguard just as the man straightened.

"Cream that marine in civvies!" Mr. James shouted. "He started this!"

The three housemen beside the stairwell barreled through tables and across the dance floor toward Bjorn. They brandished clubs. "Second door on the right, upstairs!" he shouted to the lieutenant and then turned to meet his new adversaries.

"Help the civvie marine!" shrieked Angel.

"Yes!" the lieutenant shouted to the troops. "Do it!" Then: "Make way!" She leaped forward, heading for the stairs with the two NCOs behind her.

No gunshot yet.

Half a dozen young marines pushed back tables and kicked aside chairs. "Let's destroy the bastard bouncers," one shouted. "They push us around."

Two smaller marines threw themselves in front of the housemen and then were joined by shouting comrades. "You dirty shit! Help me, Jose! Ugh!" A body crashed into a table with a groan. A triumphant, "Got you!" echoed from above the falling body.

Bjorn didn't dare take his eyes off the bodyguard he'd kicked. The big man now straightened.

Girls jumped on three more housemen who charged through bordering tables. "Bastard!" Angel screamed. With long red fingernails she clawed a bouncer's face, raking blood from his cheek.

Bjorn decked the bodyguard he'd kicked.

Then one of the new housemen shook off a woman who gripped his arm. He smashed a fist into Bjorn's jaw. Bjorn reeled across the dance floor, his face numb. Another bouncer burst from the kitchen and slammed a billy club off his head in a glancing blow.

Bjorn tasted warm blood. He'd bit his tongue. From his knees at the edge of the dance floor, he touched a wet lump on the side of his head. He heard the thud of blows on flesh, yells, and scuffling. Nearby, two of the original housemen lay still, floored by marines.

"We're done!" he heard the big bodyguard say. Both of Consalvo's thugs, on their feet again, staggered away from the dance floor toward chairs.

Bjorn gingerly stood.

"All over!" yelled a gray-haired houseman from the stairs. "Everyone back off."

A young, oriental marine with a stripe on each sleeve steadied Bjorn. "Nobody left on the other side, buddy. I guess you're with the lieutenant. Great fight you started."

Uncle Will walked over to a body sprawled on the floor near their original table.

The gang boss lay as if all his tendons were cut. His gun rested near an outstretched, limp hand. Uncle Will's knife protruded from the man's right eye socket, and bloody fluid leaked down a cheek and draped like a tiny shadow on the floor.

Bjorn's head ached and he breathed hard. He walked toward his uncle.

They'd hoped for only a brawl. Well, the law didn't reach into the ghetto. And the Marines wouldn't care about the fate of a gangster who invaded a government owned facility.

"Your lieutenant arrived barely in time," Uncle Will commented. "For a minute, I thought we'd have the fight for nothing."

He bent and yanked his knife from Consalvo's eye, then wiped the blade on the dead man's suit coat.

Bjorn glanced toward the second floor. "She up there?"

"Yeah. James, too. He panicked when she dashed for the stairs."

Bjorn collapsed in a chair and fingered his bruised cheek and ear. "I hope she found his computer open."

Uncle Will reached up with both hands and replaced his knife in a small scabbard that he pulled from the back of his neck. Then he sat, too. "Doesn't matter. "You got her up there while James was absent."

"She needs the books."

Bjorn wished they hadn't had to kill anyone. Damn! And just to wedge him into the Marines! He guessed Uncle Will had expected it. Solved a problem for him.

He heard Angel order the cabaret's master program start the music again. Bouncers retrieved the gang leader's gun. Accompanied by the badly bruised bodyguards, they dragged away the corpse. Marines and girls huddled while housemen mopped the floor and reset tables and chairs.

Twenty minutes later, the lieutenant came down the stairs, followed by her two non-coms. One carried nasal wires and an electrical device. The master sergeant stuffed them into his briefcase. The other sergeant led a handcuffed, crying Mr. James.

Bjorn's ambition had put James in a deadly fix.

"Think of consequences before you reach for something you want," Uncle Will might say. Well, Bjorn had guessed James would pay. But coming up against the reality turned his stomach.

The lieutenant nodded at Bjorn. "Be on the Marine bus in front of the recruiting office at seven tomorrow morning."

Uncle Will stepped forward. "I'm Will Maestri, Lieutenant. May I have a moment to discuss the future of this establishment?"

Chapter 2

Two weeks later, Bjorn ran around the marine base's parade ground, the "grinder." Deep breaths of evening air stung his lungs; shallower ones tasted foul and oxygen-poor. Damn the pollution!

"Recruit Benjamin Bjorn!"

Earlier, he'd seen Lieutenant Morrison walk from the O Club. Now she stopped at the edge of the grinder. Her black hair was gathered at her neck and shone in the sunlight.

What the hell? He braked, marched a few steps, and saluted.

She wrinkled her nose.

Well, he'd exercised all day, hadn't he?

Sweat had soaked his tee shirt and moistened gold chest hair that protruded from the vee. The muscles of his bare arms and legs glistened. "Ma'am?"

She peered at him. Her eyes were moist and she leaned slightly. A little drunk?

"I'm told you scored high in the technical courses," she finally said, careful with the last two words. "How are you doing in the rest?" She tugged at her black tie and touched her meat-pie hat with the Administrative Service's insignia of two crossed feathers. Her officer's blue jacket bulged over a white blouse, narrowed at her waist, and hugged her hips.

"What are you staring at, recruit?"

"You, Ma'am. You're beautiful."

He stiffened and sucked in his gut. The sergeant ran him around the grinder for threatening guys who messed with his gear. He'd hang Bjorn upside down on a rifle target if he caught him smarting-off with an officer.

Lieutenant Morrison slid her tongue across her lips and left them wet and glistening. "I asked how you were doing!"

"Fine, I think, Ma'am," he answered. "Except maybe in the foreign relations course."

"You're an unusual Welfie."

Get your mind off the sex track! He coughed. "I don't suppose you could tell me why the Corps is recruiting assault infantry. And there's lots of rush."

"None of your business."

That was very much his business. His life, maybe. The Marine enlistment campaign had been sudden. The lieutenant hadn't recruited women. Something was up.

Bjorn knew there was a lot he didn't know. But, he wasn't dumb! According to the marine website back in his old cubby, the Corps performed special operations duty for the services. The Administration also deployed its three Marine divisions or parts thereof when foreign police actions were necessary. Maybe he was set up to be inexperienced cannon fodder.

The lieutenant glanced at Bjorn's wet chest and glistening arms and then took a deep breath. "Just to be democratic, I'll guess at the r-reason y-you'-r-re here." She swallowed and then spoke more precisely. "Too many people slosh around the world. They threaten to flood us because we have rations and order. Our government may want to build a few dams."

"I don't understand, Ma'am." He smiled. His arms and legs tingled. "Can we meet some private place so you can explain?"

Uncle Will would have a fit if he knew what Bjorn just proposed! The suggestion had come out without warning, involuntarily.

The lieutenant's face, a smart and racially mixed face, flushed. "You're presumptuous," she said, stumbling on the big word. "Technical brains and good looks don't give you the right to favors."

He stared at her. *God damn my gonads!*
"What do you suggest, recruit?"

Hello? No tongue-lashing? No call to his company sergeant?

He let the urge take over. "Write an order on your micro-printer," he suggested. "I'll report tonight to the ground floor conference room at your BOQ."

He kept his voice calm and remained braced. Until now all he'd done was brainwork--the classes seemed endless--and stupid exercise. His heart would be beating faster.

With a glint of calculation in her eyes now, she reached into the purse hanging from her shoulder. She spoke into her electronic personal assistant, pulled out a strip of paper, and handed it to him. "Come, then."

Turning, she stumbled and finally gained the sidewalk. She marched away, her head held high.

Nice butt, he thought.

The order gave the date and time, and instructed Recruit Benjamin Bjorn to report to the conference room in Officers' Quarters number Five at seven thirty that evening. "Voice print of First Lieutenant A. Morrison, Recruit Supervisor."

Bjorn started running again. He hadn't finished the required laps. For all he knew, Sergeant Sennet checked.

As he ran, he replayed the exchange. Had a rush of excitement from risk-taking overcome the self-discipline Uncle Will urged? The lieutenant's agreement could be an Achiever trap. Had she decided to weed out a pushy Welfie recruit? He was an idiot.

Bjorn remembered the way Morrison touched her figure and the way she'd moistened her lips. Lust, not challenge, had driven him. He was a hormone-drugged idiot. If he kept up this kind of behavior, he didn't have a chance to make it in this new world of his. All of his hopes, all of Uncle Will's hopes for him...

He told himself he couldn't back out now. He'd

received an order to report to her.

His stomach aching, he forced himself to keep running. He'd take what precautions he could.

Bjorn finished the assigned laps at dusk, studied the edges of the parade ground, saw no one, and then ducked between two low, gray buildings. He trotted to the Electronics Training Lab, hid in the shadows, and forced a window.

The poor security on the base had amazed Bjorn. None of the windows in any of the buildings were wired. Many, like this one, had broken hasps.

Bjorn slid inside and let his eyes adjust to faint light that entered from a street lamp. The long tables and straight, composite chairs were as clean and orderly as when he and his fellows left that morning. The normally red and blue wall posters that read "Obey or Die" and "Assault Marines, America's Toughest" now appeared in shades of gray. At the side, recruits had stacked waist-high integrated packs of infrared, sound, and motion sensors.

He moved to the instructor's desk and picked a sensor and recorder cube out of the sample bin. After making sure the device was loaded and charged, he put it in his pocket.

Bjorn climbed back through the window and ran like hell for his barracks. He stopped outside and dropped the recorder cube in a bush. He'd pick it up when he left for his appointment.

Sweat drenched his clothes down to his underwear when he walked into the barracks lobby fifteen minutes late. His breath wheezed in his chest. Sergeant Sennet stood under the big digital clock, his slight body stiffly arched and his face red with anger.

He looks like the little prick he is, Bjorn thought.

"Report!"

Bjorn assumed attention and tried to control his breathing. "An officer stopped me and chewed me out for not doing better in foreign relations class," he said, his words punctuated by gasps. She gave me this." He held out Lieutenant Morrison's order.

Sergeant Sennet took the paper strip from Bjorn with two fingers, as if the printout might be infected. As he read, his face turned into stone.

"Did you know the lady before?" he whispered.

"Yes, Sir. She enlisted me and then negotiated the change in management of James's R & R Cabaret with my uncle."

"You're related to the new operator of that whorehouse?"

Sennet turned, forcing Bjorn to turn his face into a better light.

Bjorn wanted to hit the sergeant. He knew what "whorehouse" usually meant in the ghetto--a place for quick, cheap sex, where madams imprisoned and whipped their girls--which Angel didn't. Instead, the cabaret provided other entertainment of various kinds, and the girls were free to say no or quit.

"Yes, Sir," he answered.

Sergeant Sennet smiled and then turned and went into his office.

He's only copying the order, Bjorn thought. The man's too smart to check with Lieutenant Morrison. Enlisted men did not question officers.

Sennet marched back and held out the order. "Hurry and clean up, recruit," he said. He smiled blandly. "You have half an hour."

#

Dressed in clean fatigues, Bjorn walked into Officers' Quarters Number Five. He was relieved to see no watch stander at the desk in the entry, but unhappy not to find the lieutenant in the small conference room. Would she punish him if he didn't contact her somehow?

After he picked out Morrison's apartment number from a directory, he climbed the stairs. He held the sensor and recorder cube in the palm of his hand, ready to throw it in some dark corner if the Marine Shore

Patrol showed up. If this were a trap. If not, he had no doubt that Morrison was prepared to sacrifice him if someone interrupted their off-limits entertainment. He must have proof he didn't break in or touch her without encouragement.

Despite a fifteen-minute shower earlier, he was sweating again now.

He should <u>not</u> be doing this.

Bjorn listened at Lieutenant Morrison's door for a moment, and then knocked.

"Go away."

Ah, hah! A rush of excitement stiffened him. "Please let me in, Ma'am," he answered in a low voice. "If your neighbors get nosy..."

A bar slid back and the door opened a crack. He saw that her face was flushed and her body wrapped in a cream bathrobe.

"You were supposed to report to the conference room, not here!"

She smelled fresh and clean. Had she showered to sober up, or prepare for him? Maybe both.

"Since you weren't there, I figured I'd find you."

She stared at him. Then she backed away.

The room was crowded with a sofa, an armchair, a holovision platform, and a bureau. Two doors occupied the far wall. On gray walls hung commercial lithographs of Adams, Hamilton, and Washington, the law and order Founders. Typical right wing, Achiever crap.

"This is stupid!" Lieutenant Morrison said. "I could be broken and you killed."

"Yes, Ma'am."

Excitement tingling his muscles and skin, he strode past her, opened one of the doors, to the bathroom, and peered in. No one. The other room, the bedroom, was empty, too. He quietly slipped the recorder into shadows on a bureau.

She hadn't moved, but simply stood, watching

him.

He walked over, pulled her to him, and kissed her. She was stiff for a moment, then wiggled close.

Picking her up, he buried his face in the opening of her bathrobe, between her heavy breasts. With a shudder she clasped her hand behind his head and guided his lips to a nipple.

#

When she slipped out of bed and strode into the bathroom, he caught a glimpse of her figure. She must have realized that, because she straightened and pulled in her stomach.

He lay on his back, the blanket and top sheet curling at the foot of the bed. Air conditioning spread coolness on his naked body. None of that in the barracks.

The lieutenant returned wearing a nightgown. She stood at the foot of the bed in a model's pose, one foot in front of the other, and stared down at his nakedness.

"Lieutenant Morrison, Ma'am," he finally said, "Who are we training to fight? They've sped up our cycle and doubled the battalion's size. The scuttlebutt says there'll be war. I thought we only sailed out of port occasionally and boarded illegal immigrant boats."

"Get up! Put your clothes on. Leave my order on the bureau and return to your barracks."

Bjorn slid out of bed and walked over to her. She drew a breath and stumbled back a step.

"I'm sorry," he said. "Talking about war and The Corps was dumb. I should have known better."

The lieutenant still frowned.

He leaned close and kissed her cheek. "Thank you," he said.

Her frown smoothed.

When he unbuttoned the nightgown, her breathing grew ragged. She put a hand on his bare arm as if to stop him, but didn't.

He lifted a firm breast and stroked the nipple with a finger.

"God!" she whispered, moved closer and ran her hand up his bare chest to his muscled shoulder. "You're built like an Olympic boxer."

He pulled the nightgown off quickly, fitted his naked body against hers. As they kissed, her tongue coiled into his.

Finally, he led her toward the bed with his arm around her, his hand stroking her soft belly.

"I don't know whom you're going to fight," she said quietly. "All I know is that I'm not one of them."

#

Bjorn gently raised her arm, slid away, and then stood. She murmured something and pulled up the blanket.

He dressed in the bathroom. He pocketed his recorder but left the lieutenant's printed order on the bureau, as she had directed.

Sennet had made a copy anyway.

Outside, he walked quickly towards his barracks, the dark, clean streets illuminated by an occasional light. When he came to an automatic post office, however, he paused. He thought of burying the video recorder in a flowerbed until the morning. But the evidence was only a dangerous, last-ditch proof that she cooperated. He didn't need it now.

He inserted the coin of memory in an envelope provided by Marine Corps Services, addressed the missive to his Uncle Will, and sent it. Then the empty cube sailed into a rubbish bin.

He jogged toward his barracks, feeling loose and ready for anything.

#

Bjorn woke with a start. The barracks lights were on and men were yelling. He felt the sting of a cane on his bare feet and heard Sergeant Sennet's nasty shout: "Out of your goddamn rack, pea brain! Stand at attention in the aisle with the rest of the company."

Bjorn sat up and then jumped down to the deck. The clock at the end of the large room read midnight. He'd only had half an hour of sleep!

His gut tightened.

In his boxer shorts and tee shirt, Bjorn stood at attention with his fellow recruits. Master Sergeant Lunga, a chunky, muscular hulk of a man, stood nearby while Sennet and other company sergeants woke the sleeping troops.

Wonderful! A midnight roust-out, a surprise inspection. Bjorn wondered if Sennet had volunteered his recruits for this experience. Because of Bjorn? Did the bastard hope the non-coms would find his bunk empty?

Sennet hadn't wanted to challenge an officer. Perhaps he'd thought of another way to pass along his suspicions.

Behind him, Bjorn heard the sergeant prod a bunkmate into line, then flip open Bjorn's sea chest and rustle through his clothes and belongings. He heard the cover slam. Sennet opened the next guy's chest.

The master sergeant and his underlings called out the infractions: untidy uniforms, missing hats, even an ear amplifier and a music slug. Then the non-coms gathered at the entrance and marched down the center aisle. One pharmacist mate wore a plastic glove. When they came to Bjorn, they stopped.

"Turn around, drop your shorts, and lay your arms on the bunk," Sennet commanded. "I want to see if you hid a love charm in your asshole."

Son of a bitch!

"He's empty, Sennet," the master sergeant said, when the chief corpsman finished.

Sennet slapped a leg with his cane and pointed at Socorro, the man whose music system they had found. This time, the corpsman pulled out a plastic bag of pills.

Bjorn remembered an encounter on the training mats, when he'd barely gained a draw. Socorro had slapped Bjorn on the back afterward and promised to buy the beers whenever they drew leave together. Nice guy.

Socorro's head jerked but he only grunted when the master sergeant struck him.

"Single file outside!" yelled Sergeant Sennet. "Form column of fours in front of the barracks. We're parading to the grinder."

Two big non-coms marched out with Socorro stumbling between them. Bjorn joined the formation.

The three hundred men of his Recruit Company stopped in front of an empty reviewing stand and assumed parade rest. Platform lights came on.

Bjorn shivered in the cool night.

The master sergeant climbed to the top of the stand, stepped forward, and glared at them. "All right, you maggots," he said. "Listen up. The Corps lives, fights, and wins on discipline. We can be tough on outsiders only because we're tough on ourselves."

He then pulled out the notes he had taken during the inspection. "Sheh, front and center."

One after another, he called four men onto the platform. They about-faced and bent over. The master sergeant hit each backside with a mighty swing of his bamboo cane. Each grunted with pain as the blow fell across his buttocks.

When the men hobbled past, Bjorn saw blood running down their bare legs.

The two non-coms then brought Socorro onto the stand. The master sergeant stood next to the recruit and placed a hand on his shoulder. "No smuggled goods in barracks; no drugs anywhere," he said. "Those are the regulations. You will obey regulations in the Corps."

He paused. "Since the ghetto riots and troop mutinies of the twenty-sixties," he continued, "we

Welfies get something called 'summary justice.' Just so none of you forgets, this is how it works."

Quickly, he stepped behind Socorro. He threw a cord over the recruit's head, put a knee to his waist, and leaned back.

Oh, shit!

Bjorn heard three hundred men suck in air.

Socorro gagged. His eyes bulged. He, twisted and turned, reached back over his shoulder, and fumbled for Lunga's hands. Then he tried to fling himself in a somersault over Lunga's body. The sergeant's muscles bulged and he held Socorro to him. The recruit's feet kicked in the air. Finally, Socorro's body sagged and he collapsed.

Bjorn shuddered. No wonder the windows and doors on post weren't locked and wired.

#

Two days later, night inspection teams struck the other training companies. Maybe they had found the empty recorder. Maybe they'd taken inventory in the Electronics Lab. Just maybe, the roustings were only part of boot camp routine.

Bjorn learned from scuttlebutt that two other recruits had gone the way of Socorro. Not so easily, however. They had guessed what was about to happen and fought back.

He'd ask Uncle Will to destroy the recorded memory.

On the third day, while accounts of savage punishments swept the post, Lieutenant Morrison stopped him near the same spot she had before. Sergeant Sennet had him running again, this time for talking about Socorro.

She stood strong and clear-eyed on the dirt border. "I'm surprised you're still with us," she said. "I'm also surprised I'm not up before a Board."

"Sergeant Sennet has a copy of your order, Ma'am. I've told him that your lecture in the conference room was boring."

"You've kept your mouth shut. See it stays that way."

Bjorn knew Sergeant Sennet watched them. He remained at attention and said nothing further.

"You were almost worth the risk," she said and turned away.

Chapter 3

While Bjorn ran again, his Uncle Will answered a summons to the San Angeles Health and Human Resources (HHR) headquarters. After being dropped across the street by the friendly driver of a delivery truck, Maistre dodged through water vapor from the combustion of hydrogen fuel and pushed past prostitutes and vendors. He finally stepped up onto a sidewalk.

I'll walk in, he thought. Will I leave that way?

He must remember to behave as inoffensively as he looked. Keep his neck bent.

Maestri sighed. He missed his nephew. No one to share with. Benjamin's only communication from recruit training had been a heavy-breathing memory slug. The youngster's encounter with some stirred-up female.

Maestri would be lonely in the years to come. Of course he'd operated as a lonely single once before, soon after Jane--Assistant Professor Jane Sewald--had broken with him. That was eleven years earlier, maybe the reason he'd been careless with data and his job about then. Maybe why he'd been caught cheating and almost killed.

Jane had been too wise to continue her liaison with a Welfie. So had ended art history lessons, pillow fights, heated political arguments, and closeness.

He hadn't been really lonely, however, once he found the eight year-old Bjorn, ragged and starving, hanging around his mother's old tenement. His nephew.

He remembered Bjorn's recent question, "What's life got for me?"

Maestri shook his head. The route to an acceptable answer for him as well as for his nephew was <u>discipline</u>, self-discipline. They must bite their lips and wait for chances.

The HHR building was half the height of the eight-story tenements in the surrounding ghetto. Without windows, glistening composite formed its walls, and a jump jet pad occupied its roof. The sidewalk here stayed free of Welfies, who pre-empted pavement spaces elsewhere. No small entrepreneur dared sell trinkets; no homeless ate their welfare packets of vegpro, or spread blankets. Burly HHR guards kept the block clear.

Maestri stepped to the automated gate, gave his name and, after DNA verification, left his hideout knife, donned the provided electronic beacon, and walked inside the fence. He detoured around massive concrete tubs designed to thwart a vehicle attack, approached the building, and passed through open steel doors. A follow-me light glowed in the floor. It led him down a private hallway. The walls were glass-smooth and gleamed in blue and green patterns. From the ceiling, sensor lenses and poison gas nozzles tracked him.

He wondered if Benjamin had learned enough by now to lead a successful attack on this building.

The follow-me light turned red in front of a steel door.

"Yes?"

"Will Maestri, Mr. Plant."

The door slid back and revealed a Spartan office, a show workplace for the San Angeles "Welfare King." That official's real quarters--luxurious ones--would be in the back third of the building.

Maestri bowed and then sat before the laser fence, an invisible barrier that hissed when he breathed moisture into it.

Mr. Peter Plant, the local Director of Health and Human Resources, slumped behind his desk. Brown hair hung in oily ringlets around a puffy, pale face. His jump suit was made of an undistinguished gray material. "What's this I hear about you taking over James's Cabaret?" he asked.

"That's right, Sir. James violated his contract. A Navy prosecutor executed him. The ward residents' council then approved my agreement with the marines to operate the place."

Mr. Plant dismissively waved his hand at the explanation. "You didn't check with me."

"I thought you'd like the new arrangement. James used your name in situations that could cause you trouble. He sold dream skin time."

"And I didn't like your waste of the gang boss. He was _my_ man."

"The idiot pulled a gun on me. I had no option."

"That's the third gang boss you've terminated since you returned."

"Tell the next one to leave me alone."

Plant leaned forward and glared at him.

Maestri shivered. _Where's the bowed neck I wanted to show when I walked into this building?_

Government only cared for college-educated Achievers who remained employed and hadn't started taking rations. Oh, Welfies passed tests that let them vote. A few like James, and now himself, even held fringe jobs. Wanna-be Achievers. But neither the police nor the courts reached into the ghettos to protect those without the correct internal passports. Plant could wipe him.

Maestri wondered if this Welfare King had a family. If so, the woman's affection must have long ago shriveled from the stories of what went on in the back part of this building, the whispers about Welfie women. He wondered if Plant had ambitions—for a Washington job? Did he pile up credits for a bureaucratic run to higher office, or did he only spend his wealth on vice?

Plant's life was perhaps as purposeless as

Maestri's.

He kept his eyes focused a half-inch below the other's muddy pupils. He was too useful to destroy, he hoped. And Plant didn't know whether Maestri's old connections in Washington might still care enough to pass along punishment for not clearing his decision first.

"Angel's Fun House, Sir--we've renamed the place that--doesn't give me the lifestyle of an Achiever. Nor the rights of one. I know my limitations."

In the stillness of his fear, Maestri remembered the crowded, dirty tenements Benjamin and he occupied since he returned. He recalled the cheats he pulled to give Bjorn a better diet than the eternal compressed block of algae and grains. Boredom was the worst part of that life. No wonder generations of ghetto residents concentrated on religion, electronic entertainment, and copulation.

He and Bjorn had concentrated on education. Not a bad way to spend time. And written and spoken books cluttered up the Web.

Plant's glare softened somewhat.

Maestri lived better when he was younger, when he followed the HHR executive, John Striker, to Washington. As the Welfie action man of a rising political star, he actually worked. He didn't earn enough for one of the "in-between" residential compounds, but he'd been getting there.

Those years spanned the two decades after the great riots of the sixties and followed the legislation of the seventies that stabilized the country. HHR in the eighties tore down blighted city centers, built tenements for the homeless, and established feeding stations. It also distributed internal passports, formed HHR punishment battalions, and crushed crime with on-the-spot justice. Lots of misunderstandings occurred requiring face-saving arrangements. Lots of work for a "fixer."

Before his "mistake," he became the "back-line"

contact between Health and Human Resources and Welfie residents' councils. Will Maestri had been important!

When Plant's fingers relaxed, Maestri guessed he'd escaped punishment.

He unclenched his own fist. The poor traded their freedom during that period for housing and regular rations of food and medical treatment. Lousy bargain. Over the years, he began to feel as Judas must have when he realized the Romans would crucify Jesus.

Now Plant smiled. "Perform an urgent action directive for me."

Maestri's abdomen seemed to flood with relief.

"I need a list of potential troublemakers."

"What kind of trouble-making? How big a list?"

"Rebellion, rioting, and disobedience of any kind." Plant mumbled to his computer wand and stared at the read-out. "Say there's ten million people of Mexican descent in the San Angeles ghettos. Give me the names and addresses of the two thousand most troublesome leaders."

Maestri sat up straighter. "You thinking of putting them away somehow? Why?"

"None of your business. I want a preliminary report in a week. I also want a map of the blocks that contain the most recent border-crossers, the least assimilated."

"Are you shutting down the border, and maybe worried about the reaction here?"

"You may go, Maestri."

Chapter 4

After another three weeks of speeded-up recruit training, Bjorn graduated and left for New Orleans in a draft of privates. There, Administrative Services inducted him into a battalion of the 3rd Marine Brigade. He boarded an undersea assault transport with sailing instructions for southern waters.

No liberty at Angel's; no reunion with Uncle Will.

A week later, while the transport was still submerged, he entered a rubber-sealed compartment with his squad and stepped into an amphibious landing craft. Bjorn perspired in his bulletproof corselet--a shell of light composite armor that covered his torso. When he sat on a bench along the side of the underwater vehicle, he leaned the barrel of his assault rifle on plates that hung over his crotch.

Fellow squad members filled the bench and that across an aisle. Bjorn thought that they looked like beetles, with faceted sensor bands on the crowns of their helmets, reflective visors across their eyes that would filter laser bursts, and the armor.

He should have borrowed cash for the poker games they played on the way south from the States, Bjorn thought. If he owed money, his squad, all older and more experienced than he, would have selfish reasons to help him.

Never mind.

He grinned with excitement when he heard water fill the big transport's pressure compartment and saw his boat's thin, metal wall bow inward. The vehicle's sudden ejection from their undersea carrier shook him, however. He held on as the small boat bucked from the turbulent results of its buoyancy.

An hour later, he heard pumps push water out of the landing craft's tanks. The amphibian vehicle angled upward; in minutes, its sides flexed back as outside air replaced water. Treads climbed on sand. Then the craft stopped hard and threw Bjorn forward against the strap around his middle.

"Move out," barked Sergeant Schilling, Bjorn's graying squad commander. "Keep your safeties on until we're in position--so you don't shoot each other. Brigade says this beach looks peaceful. We're not here to fight, anyway, but to scout."

The side ramp dropped. In the faint light of dawn, Bjorn saw small waves and a broad, sandy beach.

He preceded the last man out, a round, black corporal, a ten-year man named Pauling who hailed from Chicago. Pauling owed Bjorn money. Not a lot, though.

The sergeant led the squad along the water's edge. Then, everyone pivoted and strode up the beach toward the tree line. Bjorn thumbed off the safety of his assault rifle. Even at six A.M. the air hung like a hot, damp blanket.

Once clear of the boat, Bjorn saw thatched roofs a couple of kilometers down to the right, where a little cove drew the bay closer to the hills. Mexico!

Suddenly, he heard the quick blat of automatic rifles, the harsh run of a machine gun!

Bjorn threw himself to the sand without thinking, his helmet toward the tree line, his rifle forward. "Targets up!" he yelled to his artificial intelligence.

Bullets whined overhead, but the blue lines of the short-range map on his visor showed no target pip. So much for infrared sensors that detected warmth, and microprocessors that decided a hot spot was human, he thought. Leaves shrouded targets. What should he do now?

His muscles were tense, his armpits wet. Down the beach, a wounded Sergeant Schilling tried to pull himself toward the boat. The enemy had aimed their machine gun low and started with the squad's leader. The burst hit the sergeant below his armor. Two other squad members sprawled without a sound. Head shots?

Bjorn watched squad buddies send whispering flights of heat-seeking flechettes into the tree line. He didn't think they'd hit anything worthwhile. Too much cover there.

Bjorn shrank as heard a mortar launch. He burrowed into the sand. If the mortar shell homed on muzzle blasts...

The warhead slammed down on the men who had fired. The immediate detonation sent up body parts and a big cloud of sand. As wet pieces of a fellow marine fell on him, Bjorn gritted his teeth and shuddered. Other mortar blasts punched at the line of Marines between Bjorn and Schilling.

"Back to the boat," screamed Pauling over the helmet radios. "Hump it."

Bjorn blanked Uncle Will's cautioning image from his mind, rose, and dashed away from the boat toward Schilling, passing a lone other survivor.

Another mortar launch.

As he ran, he wondered which would be worse--a shell hit on Schilling or on the boat. The first would kill Bjorn too, now; the second would leave him alone, in front of an army of angry Mexicans.

No blast reached him; maybe the warhead had been a dud.

He ran in a cloud of sand, through the depressions formed by the earlier mortar shells detonations. He found Schilling. The poor bastard's legs lay in broken, but connected segments, the flesh at each break chewed into a bloody mess.

"I'm trying," the sergeant mumbled. He dug with his hands and inched toward the landing craft. "Help me."

Bjorn grabbed the lip of Schilling's corselet. Bending, he dragged the sergeant toward the boat, disregarding his screams. By now, only very fine sand from the mortar shell's explosion filled the air. Soon Bjorn would be clearly visible from the tree line. He accelerated until he half-ran, crouched over, pulling a finally quiet Schilling.

The landing craft loomed up through the grit when Bjorn reached a shallow shell crater. He saw bright flashes from the cabin. The boat captain fired his heavy laser at the trees.

Thankfully, the landing ramp stayed down, protected from enemy fire by the armored prow of the boat. Pauling and the squad mate who had also survived the mortar hit stood in the opening. They waved at Bjorn to hurry.

The machine gun fired bursts again! Bjorn dropped to the sand. Bullets hummed over his head.

Some Mexican soldier emptied an ammunition can in his direction, but had started too far to the left, now held too high.

The volley over, Bjorn stood and grabbed Schilling again. The last three meters before he entered the lee of the boat were the worst of his run. At every splashing step, he expected a bullet. Then Pauling and the other man jumped into the water, grabbed the sergeant, and they all waded back to the access ramp.

The apron slammed closed when Bjorn was only partly in. It threw him across the aisle and into the seats.

He righted himself, breathed deeply, and heard a rain of bullets hit the armor out in front. Pauling had Schilling's corselet off and the sergeant's pants in pieces. He worked over the wounded non-com with the med. kit.

I'm too tired to help, Bjorn thought. He'd learn how Shilling was soon enough.

About a mile out and safely underwater, Corporal

Pauling looked up from the floor where he tended Schilling and grinned at Bjorn.

Bjorn squirmed, and then decided he might as well admit it now. "Sorry, Corporal," he said. "I left my assault rifle on the beach."

Pauling's smile widened. "That's all right, Bjorn," he said softly.

Chapter 5

Bjorn's Uncle Will woke; he heard something unusual. Pushing aside Angel's arm, he sat up. Outside, trucks roared down Pico Avenue and stopped at intervals. They kept their engines running.

Mexican Welfies filled unruly, crowded tenements across the street here. They were recent immigrants, mostly illegals to whom the authorities gave rations and cubbies in return for obedience. They fled the misery of their own country and joined their unemployed predecessors who made up fifty percent of the San Angeles ghetto population.

Maistre glanced at the glowing clock face. Four o'clock in the morning! He quietly slid out of bed, dressed, and then muted his electronic personal assistant when it beeped. He carried the two-way communication device into the hall. "Yes?" he whispered.

"Guzman here. You were right. HHR punishment companies have entered the Three Sisters section. Power's down in the A tenement blocks."

"They'll seal off five wards over here also, I think," Maistre said. "I hear personnel carriers and trucks along the Avenue. Other Welfare Kings must have loaned Mr. Plant their HHR troops to supplement the locals. They'll repeat the isolation in the newly Mexican neighborhoods all over the megacity, I'll bet. Comb-out is next."

"Velasquez picked up reports that the marines have invaded the old country."

"Not surprised. Where?"

"Down south, at Veracruz."

Maistre stretched. Angel's was nearly empty this

morning, except for the girls. Few marines stayed over these days. Hell, they'd all gone to war.

"Were you ready for the round-up?" he asked.

"Our leading people took your advice," the phone voice said. "They hide with friends over in China City or Black Town. HHR will catch only the hot heads."

"Well, that's who Plant wants, anyway."

Maistre started down the stairs to the automated kitchen. One of the many delights of Angel's was the animal protein in the cold room and the hot chic-coff kept on a counter.

Suddenly, the holovision in the big entertainment room turned on with an official snap.
"EE-YEE-EEE-YEE," screamed its sound system, again and again. The alarm summoned everyone nearby to watch an upcoming broadcast.

Maistre went for his hot, wake-up cup. When he came back, Angel had shepherded her beautiful charges and a few male customers to chairs in front of the holovision platform.

Maistre watched the scantily dressed women chatter among themselves and flirt with the few men who clustered around the dispenser of hot drink. He wished Benjamin were there, not because his nephew would enjoy ogling the women--and he would, of course--but because he probably risked his life down south.

Maistre sat next to a tall redhead in a sheer negligee. She had an interesting face, he thought. Laugh lines. She flashed a brilliant, full-lipped smile at him.

Angel shooed the young woman away and took her chair.

The holovision siren stopped bleating and a three-dimensional figure materialized on the platform. Floating specks of dust reflected laser light. The resulting bright spangles detracted from the image's believability, but soon the dust settled.

The image resolved to a standing Mr. Plant. The rotund HHR executive wore a blue Nehru coat, buttoned at the neck. A gold-embroidered HHR seal shone from his breast.

Maistre thought Plant's fat face and oily ringlets a public relations nightmare. Didn't the people at the top of HHR care anymore for the good opinion of Welfies?

"Last night," Mr. Plant said, "in executive session, the United States Congress approved a declaration of war against the Republic of Mexico. Our leaders decided to stop the disorganized but flagrant invasion of our country by waves of hungry people!"

Plant smiled as if he expected his watchers to approve. He moved back, apparently picked a glass of water out of thin air, drank from it, and then set the liquid down out of camera range.

Lazy shit.

"Our Marines march toward Mexico City from Veracruz," Plant continued, "while other units cross the Rio Grande and the Colorado."

Angel placed a concerned hand on Maistre's knee. Maybe she worried about Benjamin, too, he thought. No. This place and her power in it meant more than any man did. Angel feared for Angel's. War could mean the end of marine visits.

Now Plant leaned forward. "The President has declared a national emergency," he said. "Everyone must support the government." His face formed a stern frown; his fists were clenched. "We'll expel San Angeles people who give their loyalty to the Mexican dictatorship and execute leaders who incite to riot!"

HHR goons shoved possible troublemakers onto buses and trucks, Maistre guessed, and would soon escort them to the border.

"HHR has a good grip, I think," he reassured Angel. "The emergency measures won't affect you. And the Administration won't want a protracted war. Our business will return."

HHR's grip was largely Maistre's own doing, of course.

Despite his calming words, Bjorn's Uncle Will felt excited. With population's inexorable growth, the planet showed more and more signs of overburdening. Civilization's downward slide that had started in the 2030s accelerated. Most urgently, the availability of food decreased. Starving foreign populations rebelled by migrating north to where large continents grew grain. The U.S. reacted now with a single, what could only be temporary, measure, while he knew that other northern hemispheric nations defended bordering seas with navies. Blood stained the Mediterranean and the seas around Australasia. This was maybe the first violent convulsion of a new sort. All developed governments might soon face land invasions.

Somehow, there might be an opportunity for him in the coming chaos!

Mr. Plant leaned back. "I declare a three-day curfew in the Mexican wards. Don't leave your tenements without approval from the HHR appeal circuit." He frowned heavily. "Commanders on the streets will kill anyone who disobeys."

Here in San Angeles, maybe one hundred thousand would die, Maistre thought. Homeless people first forced off the street, then violently expelled from tenements they invaded, and finally shot by HHR punishment squads when found huddling in the open. Sufferers who couldn't stand the anoxia of even more crowded tenements would commit suicide. The old with health emergencies would die in the arms of their loved ones. And the wild, bottled-up emotion that now filled the Mexican wards would cause men to murder anyone who got in their way.

The authorities wouldn't care, of course. There were too many Welfies, anyway.

Mr. Plant shifted his feet and assumed a sorrowed look. "I appeal to my friends of Mexican ancestry. Remember where you live, where your welfare benefits come from." The sorrow changed to sternness. "We shall continue to treat you with kindness only if you behave."

The Welfare King nodded, his image dissipated, and then the column of light disappeared.

Angel waved at her people to remain seated. "What will happen, Will?"

The others turned. They wanted reassurance, he supposed.

"The Marines will probably seize a big swath of Mexico along the border," he answered. "They'll build a death strip there."

When Angel stirred questioningly, he shrugged. "The Veracruz operation is a diversion, I think. Cortez, Winfield Scott, and Maximilian conquered Mexico by that route, you know. The capital is close. As a result, the Mexicans will put most of their army there."

He poured a cupful of chic-cof. "Our big move will be at the border. Construction battalions will build an immense minefield from Texas to the Pacific, and then install robotic sensors and guns. Meanwhile, bus convoys will head south, through the belt, to the soon to be smaller Mexico. HHR will dump a lot of our neighbors into the Baja California desert."

And afterwards, he thought, because of his warnings, the Mexican wards would accept Will Maestri as a true friend.

Chapter 6

"This task force's mission is to land, climb to the plateau that holds Mexico City, and take the capital."

Second Lieutenant Louis Lefko was a lean, sandy-haired, hawk-nosed man, almost as young as Bjorn himself. He perched on a box and stared down at Bjorn and the twenty other assault marines clumped on the hangar deck. "Sergeant Cisco, tell us why we're to do that," he ordered the slim sergeant who stood below him.

Cisco had olive skin, short-cropped, black hair, and as large a mustache as regulations permitted. Bjorn and Pauling now reported to him.

"So we can put in a government that will keep the bastards in their own country, Sir."

Bjorn guessed Lefko didn't know whether he should trust Sergeant Cisco down here, among the latter's cousins. But the non-com spoke Spanish, of course, and, if trustworthy, was a useful subordinate for an officer charged with reconnaissance.

"You're right," the lieutenant replied. "And it shouldn't take the task force long. Here's the situation for us." Lefko gave his platoon a hard-edged smile. "The fleet is bombing the hell out of the Veracruz harbor entrance. It explodes the mines the enemy laid in the water. Mexico declared Veracruz an open city, so our force won't have any trouble once the ships sweep the mines that survive the bombardment. But the Navy will take at least a week to secure the port, land everything, and set up defenses.

"Our assignment is to by-pass all that, start feeling our way up to the central plateau from the other side of Veracruz."

The lieutenant glanced at Cisco again. "What's the Mexican Army got, Sergeant?"

The dark non-com frowned. "A few long-range, search-and- destroy missiles, Sir. Lots of cheap, short range, man-portable ones, too. Anti-air and anti-hard target."

"And old-fashioned rifles, Sergeant. No assault rifles or personal armor. Their army's pretty primitive, doesn't have most of our high technology gear."

"We'll stomp it, Sir."

Lefko pumped his fist in agreement.

One thing both of them forget, Bjorn thought. The Mexicans will be pissed-off.

The lieutenant nodded at the platoon. "Okay. The rotor bird will drop us in a plaza on the outskirts of town. We'll set up a perimeter and wait while our transport goes back for the armored personnel carrier and one of the regiment's tanks. While we're waiting, Sergeant Cisco and his squad will reconnoiter the road ahead."

Lefko stood silent for a moment, frown lines on his young forehead. He probably wonders what more he should say, Bjorn thought.

Lefko swept Bjorn's platoon with his hard glance. "That's the mission and the tactical plan. Any questions?"

Bjorn felt sorry for the lieutenant when no one accepted his invitation. "Yes, Sir," he said. "What's the chance that the Mexicans launch something big at us--a nuke say, or germs, or gas?"

The officer sighed. "What's your name?"

"Private Benjamin Bjorn, Sir," he answered, snapping to attention.

"One of the scouts we picked up. Tell me, how come you're so ignorant?"

Bjorn felt himself flush. When he realized that he had to answer, he almost said, "Because people don't answer my questions," but caught himself. "I score poorly in international politics, Sir," he answered instead.

"Fix that, Private. Quickly."

Lieutenant Lefko turned back to the rest of his platoon. "In case we have other boneheads here, no one uses weapons of mass destruction nowadays because everybody has them. It's called deterrence, and it works as long as nobody presses the other guy too far."

He glanced at Bjorn. "In case you're worried about anything else, rest easy, Private. This operation will be more professional than the one you guys screwed up the other day."

Bjorn kept quiet now. He marched with the others into a saucer-shaped, medium-sized air transport, strapped himself in, and sat still while their undersea carrier lifted toward the ocean surface.

After five minutes, the gigantic submarine shuddered. Bjorn saw rivulets of seawater pour to the deck nearby as the panels of the submarine's top shell retracted down the hangar's curved walls. The aircraft's engines throbbed, rotors bit into the air, and the jet transport lifted. Bjorn watched the hangar bay drop below; then the blackness of night blinded him.

The rotor transport deposited Bjorn and his platoon in the western outskirts of Veracruz half an hour before dawn. Bjorn helped guard the landing area and then watched others unload the ground effects mule that carried their guided missile battery. Its big fans held the tube structure and its load of ten missiles two or three centimeters off the surface on a cushion of air. Still, the mule's inertia gave the artillery corporal problems.

The battery would be worth any trouble, Bjorn thought. Back in basic training, an instructor bragged that each precision guided missile could do as much damage as three thousand dumb artillery or anti-aircraft shells.

Then Pauling and Bjorn trotted out to scout the

area. Bjorn was the point man because he, like Sergeant Cisco, spoke Spanish. He led Pauling in a circle, on silent, dark streets, between dilapidated, four-story tenements where people stared at them from every window. When morning's light filtered between the buildings, he found a table in front of a closed café. Pauling soon joined him.

Bjorn wished he had some of the beer he could now see advertised everywhere. "What do you think?" he asked Pauling. "Would the women be safe here?"

"In what way, Bjorn? In the disease or in the poison aspect?"

"Do you really think they'd kill a man? Women like sex as well as we do."

"I don't think they all do. At least my wife says so." The corporal grinned. "Not all the time, anyway."

Pauling's command speaker squawked and they both reluctantly rose.

"Bjorn, listen to me."

"Yeah."

"I did not put you in for a medal, for what you did on the beach. You know why? I would have set you up for a garrote instead. You disobeyed my order to fall back."

Bjorn turned as he trotted, wished he could study the helmeted face of the corporal. "What are you talking about?"

"I could be disciplined, too," Pauling replied. "I made the boat's coxswain wait. I endangered our reconnaissance mission."

"You've got to be kidding!"

"No. No. We're going into action again, I think. Don't disobey anyone, understand?"

Disgusted, Bjorn led them to Sergeant Cisco. Then all six of his new fellow squad members, Pauling, and he piled into a commandeered local truck and roared down the deserted highway toward the mountains.

What a heartless outfit the Marines were, Bjorn thought. He probably sat on chicken shit, which matched the service's rules.

He leaned his back against a slatted side and stared at the reflective visors, the composite armor of his three-squad mates opposite. Hadn't Achiever officers ever heard of fighting better because you trusted your mate to look after you if you went down?

Yeah, answered the spirit of Master Sergeant Lunga, who had garroted a man in front of Bjorn's company back in basic training. We believe in all that, but obedience to orders comes first. First and last.

Bjorn watched as the truck passed fields full of big fruit that protruded from the ground. Pineapples, maybe, not that he'd ever seen any. The farmers would pick whatever the fruit were soon, he guessed, if war didn't get in their way. The Corps had invaded in early December, after the rainy season and before harvest.

The Mexicans didn't waste a square inch. Already, young corn stood between the rows of pineapples. Every piece of rocky ground seemed to hold a hut, also, although he saw no people.

Bjorn had never breathed such fresh air. But then, he thought, he'd never been in farm country before. A hell of a lot better than the ghetto.

The truck whizzed along the road. He rose to his knees and craned his neck around the cab. The foothills seemed a lot closer.

He moved over behind the passenger seat in the truck cabin and put his mouth near the broken, back window. "Hey, Sarge," he said, "aren't we taking a hell of a risk running full speed like this? We could hit mines or an enemy blocking position before we knew it. I thought we were supposed to go slow, scout the sides."

"Who do you think you are, Bjorn, an expert in war already?" the sergeant replied, his dark face turned toward him. "I got an objective I don't plan to walk to."

"But..."

The sergeant's voice rose. "As we all heard this morning, brains don't go with bullshit. Shut up and turn around." The non-com faced forward again.

"But you're violating the book of tactics," Bjorn replied. "The lieutenant won't like it if--"

"I'm in command here." Cisco's voice was cold; he didn't turn back again. "Sit down."

Bjorn wondered why the sergeant was so anxious to dash through the countryside. Maybe he was afraid. If real Mexicans ever got hold of him...

"I may not know what's going on in the world," he said, "but I know the tactics book. Chapter ten, page 113, says..."

The sergeant screamed something. Bjorn held on as the truck violently shuddered to a stop, throwing his teammates up against him.

"Get out, Bjorn! Get out! I don't want no damn sea lawyer in my squad."

Bjorn began to protest, then backed away from the window as he suddenly stared into the muzzle of a 45-caliber pistol.

"Shit, Sergeant," he said, "We're all in this together, aren't we?"

Bjorn's visor display reported that the sergeant's communications circuit was busy. Maybe the bastard was reporting him to the lieutenant.

The nose of the sergeant's gun jerked commandingly as his communications line opened again. "Out, you yellow belly," Cisco said. "I'll give you fifteen seconds."

Bjorn slid off the back of the truck and glanced at Pauling.

The pudgy corporal shook his head sadly and moved back to his prior position in the truck.

Standing on the asphalt road, watching the truck accelerate away, Bjorn forced himself to stay calm. He knew he was in big trouble. He moved to the drainage ditch at the side of the road and pulled off his backpack.

Kneeling, he adjusted the control screws on the communications transceiver so his helmet radio would access the lieutenant's command circuit. Then he paused, absently watching the truck as it approached a curve about half a mile away.

If this meant a garrote party, he wouldn't attend. He'd cross the country on his own and try to slip across the border into Texas or New Mexico, hike to California, then scoot under Uncle Will's wing. But first, he would feel out the lieutenant, see if the officer was another disciplinary fanatic.

He had to be careful, damn careful.

On the curve, the truck seemed to hit something. Its motor exploded and then the vehicle cartwheeled over on its back. A great red and yellow ball of fire immediately blanked Bjorn's view of the vehicle.

"Three," he said to the visor. "Emergency priority."

"Shut up, Bjorn," the lieutenant answered. "I'll talk to you soon enough."

Bjorn glanced at the large-scale map he called up on his visor. Through the helmet's magnifier that protruded in front of his right eye, he noted the lieutenant's command symbol on top of a personnel carrier. The square of a tank followed. Infantry clung to the top of both vehicles.

"Emergency priority," he repeated.

"I'm listening."

"Something took out the truck. No survivors possible. I'll see what's up. Bjorn out."

Poor Pauling.

Chapter 7

Bjorn ran back down the highway. Once he couldn't be seen from the continuous curve behind the still-burning truck, he crossed the road, climbed through the ditch, and scrabbled up to the field. He quietly stole down rows of pineapple plants toward the fire, careful not to disturb the tops of crowded-in maize.

His visor clock reported ten A.M. The air was windless and humidity grayed the sky.

Stopping for a moment, Bjorn peered over the rows of plants. His back and front corselet acted like a covered baking dish, he thought and turned up the chemical cooling unit. He drank water from the bottle behind his pack.

Up ahead, he could see thatched roofs of the village that had been Sergeant Cisco's objective.

He ducked as a missile screamed overhead, a big one. "Three," Bjorn shouted in his helmet's microphone. "Cruise missile scooting toward you, low!"

All he heard from the lieutenant was a curse. Explosions burst out behind him, toward Veracruz--sharp cracks in the air and muffled thuds against the ground.

Then, through a lane in the plants, Bjorn saw heads moving in the ditch beside the road. He collapsed to the dirt.

Soon he decided the Mexicans hadn't seen or heard him. Crawling closer, he counted four men and a boy. The Mexicans wore wide, straw hats over gray uniforms. They carried small missiles in launchers and rifles on straps over their shoulders. After pausing to talk, they started stamping down weeds for places to hide. The boy trotted fifty meters further down the road, where he bent and examined the surface.

He's probably seeing if there's a pothole big enough to take another mine, Bjorn thought.

The god dam flies were awful. What in hell did they spread on the crops, anyway?

Bjorn backed away and continued his quiet scout through the field toward the village. He spotted the smoldering wreck of the truck, turned over so its belly steamed. Big, black birds circled overhead.

"Okay, Bjorn, report."

The lieutenant breathed hard, bit off his words.

"Aye, Sir. The enemy's set up a five-man ambush just behind the start of the curve, where your sensors will pick them up too late. They're in the ditch to the south."

"Destroy the ambush from the rear."

Bjorn sighed. "Aye, Sir."

He came up behind the Mexicans, via the ditch. Crawling the last thirty meters, he found cover behind a pile of cuttings.

The enemy excitedly pointed at road dust in the distance. They stacked their rifles, dug shallow pits for themselves on the lip of the pineapple and maize field, and lay out the missile launchers. Two assembled a light machine gun.

Bjorn pulled back behind cover and sighed again. Then he switched a control on his assault rifle to "AIR BURST, FIFTY METERS." He gritted his teeth, aimed the rifle over the Mexicans' heads, and pulled the trigger.

He vomited when he saw bodies burst open and human parts fly in all directions. The damn heat-seeking flechettes separated in the air at the designated distance, homed on hearts, and exploded when they touched the soldiers' chests. Poor bastards.

He stood, only to be knocked down as something hit his chest a terrible blow that drove out all breath. Dazed, he looked up and saw the Mexican boy running toward him, rifle outstretched and tears on his face.

The corselet had saved Bjorn.

He waited, his chest damn sore. When the boy came close, Bjorn rocketed off the ground, wrenched away the kid's rifle, and then was in close enough to kill.

The boy was female!

Instead of breaking her neck, he twirled her around, gripped her in a Half Nelson, and shoved up his visor. "Que nombre?" he breathed into a small, well-shaped ear.

The young woman screamed an obscenity and struggled. She cried out in pain and stopped moving when he increased pressure on a shoulder socket.

"Bjorn, report."

He held the young woman pressed against his corselet. "Acknowledge, three. Ambush destroyed."

"Well, surprise, surprise! Stay put."

Another big missile screamed toward Veracruz, but this time it exploded not far east of Bjorn, and an American one thundered back. It lifted toward the foothills.

Bjorn twirled the girl so she faced him, but gripped her shoulders. She was cute, with straight black hair, brown skin, reddish lips, and a tight, young figure. Her face contorted with fear; tears trickled from her eyes.

He held her away from him with one hand, and then reached into the medical pack at his waist. He pulled out a "Buddy Hurt" stick-um beacon and palmed it.

"You wouldn't like a prison compound, sweetheart," he said in Spanish. "Our worst men run them. Run off to your people; stay out of this war." He turned her around, slapped her butt hard enough so she wouldn't feel the beacon going on, and pushed her away.

She staggered. Then, adopting dignity, she walked slowly to the remains of one of the soldiers and leaned over to touch the man's lips. She turned to stare at Bjorn. "Beast!" she said, and ran down the road toward the village.

A cursor on his visor map showed her progress.

Bjorn stood still for a moment, breathing hard. He felt the dimple in his corselet. His whole chest would be black and blue from bearing the distributed impact of the rifle bullet.

The dust cloud approached. He shook himself, strode down to the shelter of the wrecked truck and made sure his gun's safety was off. He hadn't forgotten the possibility of discipline and moved so he stood protected by thick metal.

Only one vehicle arrived: the personnel carrier that was supposed to become almost invisible in a war zone. Normally, optical cabling transferred what one side of the vehicle saw to the opposite side's skin. A viewer wouldn't realize a military transport moved in front of him. Now, however, the carrier bore a terrible rent that had stopped the transmission of images.

The lieutenant stepped down from the cab. "Where was the ambush?" he asked.

Lefko carried a short, semi-automatic shoulder gun, but didn't point it near Bjorn. The seven soldiers, who also dismounted and took positions on the lips of the fields, didn't seem threatening either. Bjorn saw no hostile sergeant, no sergeant at all, in fact.

He walked beside the lieutenant and showed him the ditch abattoir. Standing on the road above it, waving off the flies, Lieutenant Lefko gestured at Bjorn's dented corselet. "From the front, I see."

"Yes, Sir."

"Well, we'll forget Sergeant Cisco's wild report. I don't have enough men to waste one now, especially a soldier who's shown he can scout and fight smart."

Taking the girl's round had been stupid.

"What happened to the rest of your platoon?" Bjorn asked.

"If you're not a bonehead, or yellow, you are insolent," Lefko commented. "Better learn not to challenge sergeants or cross-examine officers."

Lefko shook his head, turned and walked back toward the personnel carrier. Bjorn stepped along with him. "The cruise missile took out the tank," the officer said. "It arched up over us and then shot down guided bomblets. The tank exploded most of them with its shotgun defense. Not all, unfortunately."

He stopped and toed a small stone. "The carrier sheltered under the tank's defense, but one munition hit, cut the skin, and took out the system that sucks up dust. Everyone on this damn shelf of jungle can see us coming."

Now he kicked the stone off the road. "I lost all the men who hung on outside, including my artilleryman--and his mule, which trailed us on a leash. I've only a small squad left."

Bjorn hardly had time that morning to meet his new platoon's members, much less get to know them. Still, he shuddered. He'd awakened lucky this day. "What are you supposed to do, now?" he asked.

Lefko frowned. "You really are going to have to shut up, Private."

The lieutenant started walking toward the carrier again. "We're to take the village and wait there until reinforced," he said. "Go scout it."

Bjorn supposed he couldn't complain. But weren't warriors supposed to rest after battle? His hands still trembled.

He mentally kicked himself into action and stepped carefully down the ditch toward the village. Then, thinking of mines and maybe bore-sighted machine guns, he climbed the ditch and drifted through the maize and pineapple field again. It was afternoon now, and he wasn't hungry, but stopped to sip at his water bottle.

Could he avoid the dangers of the village?

Maybe a long semi-circle around the buildings, back to the road, might satisfy the lieutenant.

"What are you doing, Bjorn? Why've you stopped?"

Damn the high level sensors and the real-time, automated communications from the upper atmosphere to the soldier! Damn the global positioning satellite system that located almost everything on an officer's helmet map!

"You've stopped too, Lieutenant."

He heard a long-suffering sigh. "I won't move until you report what's going on in the village."

The cursor, which reported the beacon the girl wore, blinked on his map at the end of the settlement, where the road crossed a stream. It had remained there for at least five minutes.

Bjorn advanced again, straight for the village now. Soon, he passed thatched huts and whitewashed houses, crossed dirt paths, and paralleled pigsties and piles of cornstalks. He stopped every once in a while to listen, his rifle held ready. Sweat dripped inside his helmet--no matter its artificial cooling. He saw and heard no one.

A doorway curtain swayed, personal effects lay scattered around outside. He heard a rustle behind a hut, prepared to shoot, and then grimaced at three small pigs rooting in an upset handcart.

At the last line of houses, he crawled up to the ditch and peered back down the curve. "No one near the road, Lieutenant," he reported. "No one in the early part of the village, either. Be careful, though. I think there's hostiles in a building near the bridge on the other side of the village."

By now, his trembling had stopped. He was good again.

Bjorn drifted away from the road, weaved through the village toward the stream. Looking back, he saw a tail of dust over low roofs. The lieutenant came.

On one empty patch of dirt that led to the road he found tire tracks. A lot of them.

Finally he lay behind a hut, exposed only his helmet and visor. Across a wide yard stood a two story, stone building bearing the Mexican flag. The cursor blinked on its bottom level.

"Three. Bjorn here."

"Go ahead."

"I figure we caught them before they moved everyone out. The leftovers are holed-up in a stone government building near the bridge. They probably hope we'll screw around, let them break out tonight."

"How many? Do they have heavy guns? Missiles?"

"No idea. Why don't you drive your carrier down here and find out?"

"Private, watch your attitude."

The cursor went out! Somebody else must have patted her ass.

"How about calling in the orbital bomber," Bjorn suggested, "or a missile with a global positioning satellite connection? Why risk our necks?"

He heard that sigh again. "We're not supposed to blow up government buildings just for the sake of blowing them up. 'Minimize civilian casualties' is the operative phrase. We have to live with the bastards afterwards, remember?"

What was he supposed to remember? Some officer briefing that never trickled down to the troops, Bjorn supposed. The real reason the lieutenant wouldn't use an easy way to take out the stone building might be money. One of those fancy missiles cost several million dollars. The government had invested only twenty thousand or so in Bjorn.

"Can you try to talk them into surrendering?" the lieutenant asked.

What a stupid idea! Then he saw movement. "Hold on."

Someone in the building waved a white cloth. Soon the girl who had shot him walked outside with it. Kept walking too. Up the main road, toward where the lieutenant and his men would be.

Bjorn stood, pushed up his visor. "Over here, Mi corazon," he shouted.

She turned, strode closer, and stopped about three meters away. She had opened the second button of her shirt and now carefully kept her hands visible.

"I've never seen your face," she said.

Bjorn took his helmet off and grinned.

"A blond beast."

He didn't say anything, but held the helmet open side up, so the lieutenant could listen.

"That beacon was a low, disrespectful trick. Typically American."

"What's your name?"

"This is not a social occasion."

She stepped closer, however, so he could admire the swell of her small breasts. He smelled a faint perfume.

"If you attack, we have fighters who will kill many of you, despite your missiles," she said. "Let us leave."

"What's your name?"

Her lips tightened; her foot tapped the ground. "Angelina Salinas." Then she smiled and leaned forward. "What about my suggestion? We have many women and children here."

By name, another Angel. Different silhouette, though. Different temperament, too. Bjorn donned his helmet again.

"Women and children, my ass," Lieutenant Lefko said. "You killed uniformed men, didn't you? They knocked off Cisco's squad, didn't they? We can't let whoever's in there leave to fight another day."

"If they don't go this way, under a flag of truce," Bjorn responded, "they'll break out of the building by the back. That'll tip them off about how small a force you have."

The lieutenant didn't reply.

"There's probably more of them than us. You have to decide whether <u>we</u> fight another day. And whether occupying the village quickly is important."

Another long silence. Then, "All right."

At least Lieutenant Lefko wasn't a waffler.

Bjorn raised his visor, bowed slightly to the girl. "My commander doesn't fight women and children," he said. "You are all free to go. Out this front door and then over the bridge, please. All guns to be carried muzzles down."

Bjorn wondered whether Angelina understood the capabilities of his assault rifle. A ball of flechettes could, <u>would</u> kill fifteen people within a radius of thirty meters of where it detonated. Once out of the stone building the Mexicans were at his mercy, even if some carried guns.

She stared at him, and then bit her lip. "Word of honor?"

"Word of honor."

She nodded, smiled more genuinely this time and then turned and trotted back to the stone building. He had to chuckle when he noticed her buttoning her blouse as she climbed the short steps.

Soon, a group of ten uniformed fighters, who scowled in his direction, left the building and strode to the bridge. They stopped behind its buttresses, ready to defend their people.

Bjorn stepped forward, turned, and made quieting motions, as if he commanded a line of American marines.

Women and children followed the initial group of warriors, then old people, more soldiers, and unarmed men who carried bulky boxes on their backs, including a radio, probably. Perhaps a hundred Mexicans walked across the yard, along the road, and over the bridge. Bjorn frowned at all the weapons, the military goods. Still, this was a truce, not a surrender.

He picked out Angelina in the rear guard and waved at her. He received no reply.

#

That evening, Bjorn lay in the warm water of the stream, above the village and let it cover everything but his face. He supposed bacteria, leeches, and other ugly things feasted on his body, but he trusted the implanted health-helper. It already tamed the bruise that covered his chest.

The lieutenant allowed him four hours. At midnight he'd be out of the water, among the mosquitoes and flies again.

He pulled out his hands and stroked the small scabbard that he had found, with its sharp knife, in one of the larger houses. He worked the leather, reaching over to the bank and scooping up grease. He could fasten the scabbard to the chain that bore his military ID coin and hang the knife at the back of his neck. His open shirt collar, then the corselet lip, would hide the weapon, yet let him quickly slip it out.

He had fallen in love with the knife. It was made of old, slightly rusted iron that he could sharpen easily, and was balanced just right for throwing. Uncle Will had something fancier and newer, but no better.

He heard a high whistle, glanced up, and saw fireworks against the western sky, now slightly red from the sinking sun. Surface to air missiles, he thought. He noted a sparkling glob dance amidst streaks of condensation. Probably an airplane fired its defensive suite at those missiles. Then he saw a spectacular explosion.

Scratch one American bomber.

He heard a soft roar close by and felt, first, a stir of air, then a rush of wind. A transport copter landed in their little perimeter. He stood and water cascaded off him and over the stream's banks. It tipped the little clay pot of grease. His R & R had ended.

After dressing, Bjorn found a sergeant and ten

new men huddled in the dusk around Lieutenant Lefko and a map. Three other marines helped an artillery corporal unload a mule full of missiles. Bjorn walked toward the rotorcraft. He noted stacks of ammunition and provisions still in the hold.

A man came up off the dark ground in front of Bjorn, as if out of a tunnel. He was big, too, bigger than Bjorn, and coordinated. He moved like a cat after a rat.

Bjorn leaped backwards and crouched.

The man wore three stripes with a mailed fist above them on the short sleeves of both arms. He was special cadre, an Enforcer.

"What's your name, Private?"

Bjorn straightened, stood at attention. "I'm Benjamin Bjorn, Sergeant."

The big man drifted up close, examined his un-armored figure. "Where's your rifle?"

"Back by the stream. So's my corselet."

A big fist appeared to rush toward his face, but at the last instant, opened to slap.

Bjorn squelched his instinct to duck. He staggered from the blow and then returned to his position. The whole side of his face stung; his brains felt loose.

"He's off duty, Sergeant Poll," the lieutenant called and then left his new men and walked over. "He's the recruit who did such a good job today."

A big, ugly face thrust itself inside Bjorn's breathing space. "You never leave your rifle when you're in enemy territory. Understand? Fuck being off duty."

"Yes, Sergeant."

"That tickler at the back of your neck is ghetto shit. It won't take out a man firing at you."

This Sergeant Poll must have eyes that went with his cat quickness. Still, he didn't pull out a garrote. The Enforcer might have tried to kill Bjorn if Lefko had related the early part of the day's events. If he had repeated Cisco's story.

"May I return to the stream and pick up my rifle and corselet, Sergeant?"

The big man sniffed, turned away. "Go ahead."

Chapter 8

The next morning, in the faint light of dawn, Bjorn sat on his heels before Lieutenant Lefko, his assault rifle on the ground near his hand. He wore his dented corselet and held his helmet.

The lieutenant sat, leaning back against the wall of a stuccoed house, his arms around his knees. The commander's clothes appeared dirty. His face showed caution now, and tiredness. He seemed to Bjorn a lot older than he appeared back on the submarine transport.

"The road starts to climb once you cross the bridge here," Lefko said. "After four or five kilometers, it winds and runs up a ravine. Our intelligence drones report that people cram the edge of the plateau two kilometers above us and fill the switchbacks in the road all the way down to the next bridge. Go as far as you can."

"What's happened with the rest of the company and the battalion?" Bjorn asked.

"Why can't you only obey orders and do as you're told?"

"You want to send me out stupid? I'll be a lousy scout, maybe a dead one if I run into trigger-happy marines. I need as much information about what's going on as you've got."

After a moment, Lefko stared over Bjorn's head. "The enemy ground up the rest of our company yesterday," he said. "Long range missiles, like the one that hit me."

He sighed. "The captain's no more, most of the headquarters squad is gone, too. The first lieutenant and I split the rest of the third platoon. He'll join us sometime today."

He glanced down. "Don't spread those glad tidings, Private First Class Bjorn."

A promotion! How absolutely wonderful.

"What will we gain by blundering up into the hills by ourselves?" Bjorn asked.

"We'll learn more. This is the main road to the capital. The rest of the battalion follows us."

Bjorn chewed on the information. "Who's this Sergeant Poll?" he asked, referring to the Enforcer. "Is he your platoon sergeant now?"

Lefko glanced at Bjorn again, a resigned expression on his face. "No," he answered. "Poll's from Brigade, here to encourage us."

Tough to fear an enemy in front and a fellow marine behind.

Bjorn stood, put on his helmet, and sketched a salute. "See you, Lieutenant."

He kept to the road the first kilometer or so and took time to admire the soft sunrise, unstained by pollution. Then he stepped into the right hand ditch and forced a way up, through the thick foliage of the bank. He entered a grove of tall trees, each trunk only four or five centimeters in diameter. The leaves were silvery, thinly spaced, and on long stems. He could see sky when he looked up.

He walked parallel to the road, shifting from one rigid forest lane to another. Full daylight arrived. Small birds fluttered high up. Fallen leaves gave off a pleasant, acrid odor when crushed. Bjorn supposed all this would be familiar to a rich Achiever, but was a wonderful surprise to him.

The land climbed more steeply after an hour. The columns of trees undulated; rising ground closed off open forest lanes to his right. His audio sensor brought the sound of far-off water trickling over stones.

Working back toward the road, he smelled smoke and heard voices. Crawling now, he forced his way through the bordering brush and gained a view of the road. It crossed the stream again here and then climbed up next to the running water into the foothills. A small, one story, stone building guarded the crossing. Shelters made of branches occupied a large parking lot and also sat in scars on the hills forested with scraggly trees. Mexicans of all ages and both genders wandered around.

"Three?" he said to his helmet mike.

"Okay, Bjorn. What've you got?"

"Civilians. They're camped on the road, on every clear space, up as far as I can see. Must be a thousand; maybe more around the bend."

"Soldiers too?"

"Not that I can see, Sir."

"Stay put."

Shortly, Bjorn heard the feathery slap, slap of giant fans. A stealthy rotor transport landed on the empty road to his left, back out of sight from the bridge. It disgorged the lieutenant and the rest of Bjorn's platoon.

At the same time, he heard off to his right the sizzle and pop of water fried from vegetation. A laser burned a landing place in the tree grove, he guessed. That transport would deposit the rest of the company, maybe the battalion brass.

Bjorn stared overhead. He couldn't see air defense drones, but hoped they'd be there, American ones.

An artillery corporal Bjorn didn't know blazed a trail up the ditch wall with his heavy laser. Then, the lieutenant joined Bjorn, after waving his other men to the ditches on each side of the road. "Nice spot to observe from, Private."

Bjorn wondered if a Mexican officer might agree and order a soldier to fire a short-range missile carrying flechettes over the site.

But he still hadn't seen any enemy soldiers.

At a sound, he glanced to the north. Two men in complete composite armor clomped toward him down a tree lane, probably talking to his lieutenant through their command circuits as they strode. One had a lieutenant colonel's silver leaf stenciled on his helmet. The other was a major.

After the folderol of saluting ended, the other officers kneeled next to the lieutenant for a time, studying the scene. Then all three moved back, removed their helmets, and sat.

Bjorn crawled off a few meters and tried to appear busy at guarding.

"How are we supposed to get through this crowd?" asked the battalion commander. "Laser them, then walk over their crisped bodies?"

"Intelligence says the Mex general keeps ordering more civilians down and shoots those who don't obey," the major--probably the battalion's exec--replied. "The bastard's forming a human barrier."

"What does brigade say?"

"Our long range missile company will bombard the defenses up there, try to punch holes the refugees can use to seep west. We're to apply pressure down here."

The lieutenant colonel shook his head, ran a hand over his face. "Slaughter pressure, you mean. We'll have to move slow, be cruel, for the message to travel up and work. We'll spend days at it."

The command group sat silently and sipped water from their bottles.

"Three."

The lieutenant heard and donned his helmet. "Yes, Bjorn."

"Why not tell the refugees to go home, let them through behind us? Once they know we don't plan to kill them, they'd empty the road faster than a Welfie woman will agree to marriage."

A sigh. "Shut up and watch the bridge."

Lefko removed his helmet and shook his head at his curious superiors. "Just a nervous trooper, gentlemen."

When the battalion commander made motions as if to stand, the lieutenant held up a hand, "Let's send in a flag of truce," he said. "Maybe we could record names, confiscate guns, and then let them return to their homes. We'd chance guerrillas at our back, but would avoid the reputation of butchers, something that might hurt on the plateau. And, we'd save time."

#

Bjorn strode unarmed and bareheaded beside Lefko toward the bridge. Neither carried a white flag. Lieutenant Lefko figured that waving a sweat-stained T-shirt was undignified.

"I still don't understand why you need me, Lieutenant," Bjorn said. "You're the guy with the formal education, the smoothie language. And you have the communication screws that let you talk to the lieutenant colonel. I'm extra."

Lefko glanced at him and smiled. "Don't wriggle, Private. It's too late, and it's uncharacteristic. You're quite brave, actually."

Up ahead, young boys ran back toward the camp.

"I'm learning about war," the lieutenant continued. "One lesson is that good ideas can come from the ranks. You've had several, Bjorn. Maybe you'll have another."

He figures I'll reduce his risk by fifty percent if some nut takes a shot.

Men collected on the opposite side of the bridge, a few armed with guns. Most carried hoes, shovels, and wicked-looking hand scythes. From the top of the span, Bjorn saw women, children, and older men clot behind the few fighting-age males. Further back, the shelters had emptied. Hundreds collected at the edge of the parking lot, or beside the stream, under the steepening bank of the gully. More tried to move up the road, meeting fierce protests from those who had established housekeeping there. Others sat on their heels among their fellows and stoically waited.

Bjorn's armpits ran with sweat. He didn't dare reach around to turn up the chemical air conditioning lest someone think he went for a weapon.

"Good day, gentlemen," Lefko said from the bridge's high point, where they stopped.

Castilian Spanish irritated ghetto Mexes, Bjorn remembered. The accent made them think about the conquistadors and centuries of Indian slavery.

"I come in peace. See? Neither I nor my companion bear arms."

Lefko pirouetted and motioned Bjorn to do the same.

He did have his sneak knife, Bjorn thought. He wondered if the lieutenant had caught Poll's reference the previous night.

"Hola, Beast!"

Damn if Angelina Salinas didn't push her way through the foremost men! She stared up at Bjorn, the cleft between her breasts well shrouded by her dark dress. "Did you herd us here so you could kill a bigger number?"

He glanced at the lieutenant.

"Find out what you can," Lefko ordered.

"To kill you would be a terrible waste, beautiful one," Bjorn said in his border vernacular. He grinned. "Who's the boss around here?"

Angelina shrugged with a lack of friendliness. "No one. The administrative types ran the fastest up the road. The troops are above, too. They prepare a barbecue fire for you."

"Pick someone to represent the crowd, lady. The lieutenant wants to let all of you go home."

Bjorn said that loudly.

Members of the crowd repeated his words.

She stared up at him. A frown marred her smooth, brown forehead. "Word of honor?" she asked under the crowd's noise.

"Word of honor," he answered.

Chapter 9

"When the order comes lead your squad up that slope," Sergeant Poll, the marine Enforcer, said several months later. "Do it fast. Remember, I have a clearer shot at you than the enemy will have."

Bjorn removed his helmet and wiped at the late afternoon sweat that trickled from his hairline. *What an asshole this Poll was!*

Bjorn kneeled in a low jungle of creepers and stumps and stared at the side of yet another steep hill. On the top was the latest switchback of the highway to Mexico City. The members of his squad, who in turn were remnants of three squads, crouched nearby. They'd all be uneasy at being under the orders of a young, acting corporal.

Hell, he was uneasy too. He hadn't asked for the two stripes. But if his men were smart Poll would scare them more.

He turned on his knees and glanced at the sergeant. The lined face and black eyes showed no sympathy, no worry about other men's well being.

"Why don't you lead us, Sergeant?" Bjorn asked. "I'm new at charging machine guns."

The sergeant crouched too far away in the scrub to respond with his fist. They glared at each other.

Lefko, a first lieutenant now, spoke through the speaker in Bjorn's helmet. "You have five minutes. We're going up the gully on this side; you go up the face."

To climb would be fucking suicide, Bjorn thought. The hill, almost a sixty percent slope, held only a stump here and there to hide behind and plenty of vines and

logging trash to trip a man. Yet to the left, a stream
tumbled down a ravine. Bushes, then high banks,
sheltered the ascent and rocks provided firm footing.

The stream was too distant, the lieutenant had
said, and led away from his gully to a high waterfall.
He'd set his mind on Bjorn being the diversion, rather
than accept the distracting role for himself, and wouldn't
listen to argument.

Lefko was under a lot of strain, Bjorn thought.

"Hey, Sarge," shouted Private Julio Capodonno,
down the line three men. "I heard what Bjorn
suggested. Great idea. I'm not climbing unless you
lead." The little man spat.

Poll jumped to his feet, turned toward
Capodonno. Bjorn rose with him and swung the butt of
his assault rifle at the sergeant's strip of neck that
showed between corselet and helmet. The blow
knocked the Enforcer senseless.

"Up," he ordered, and didn't spare a glance for
the prostrate Poll. "Let's get out of here."

He turned and shouted in border Spanish toward
the Mexicans, "We quit, Senores. Keep your fucking
road." Then Bjorn stomped downhill through the
undergrowth. His men stumbled behind him.

"Where are you going, Bjorn?" the lieutenant
asked through the helmet phone. "Your beacon moves
in the wrong direction."

"Talk to you in a bit. Hang on."

When Bjorn guessed he passed beyond the
range of the enemy's sound retrievers, he angled over to
the streambed and led his squad into the cover of
bushes on its bank. He commanded his
communications system to open again, keyed it so his
squad could hear too.

"You running away, Bjorn? Come on, man.
Don't let me down."

Bjorn heard the lieutenant's artillery missiles
thrust up the hill, exploding on whatever targets they

could find. He also heard air-launched ordnance
scream down to hit the slope he'd just abandoned.
Supposed to prepare the way for his assault, he
guessed.

"I'm climbing the stream bed, Lieutenant. With
my squad apparently bugging out, I figure the Mexes will
move their men to face you. They're as shot-up and
short of good people as we are. That'll give me a
chance to break out of the chute near the top."

"You're deliberately disobeying me."

"Yeah. I've also taken out the Enforcer. I'm
mutinous because I don't have what it takes to be
stupid."

He ducked down the bank, low here, and led his
men over rocks near the thin stream of water. All had
their visors up and talked among themselves. But no
one put a bullet in his back on behalf of the lieutenant or
continued Bjorn's original route and took off for
Veracruz. Decking Poll was popular, apparently, as was
his decision not to charge the hill. But would they obey
in battle a corporal who'd showed that he, himself,
wouldn't obey?

Bjorn climbed hard up the almost vertical rock
chute, the water splashing down beside him. He slung
his rifle over his shoulder and used his hands in the
climb, glancing at the short-range map on his visor
occasionally. The satellite couldn't show him his
location under this cover, of course, but he used its
picture of the overgrown stream and of the bare hillside
on his right to orient himself.

"Take it easy, Lieutenant," he said at a stop to
rest, breathing hard. "Don't press up the gully until I get
in position. That'll take me fifteen minutes or so."

After another ten minutes, he stopped. He saw a
pool, white with the splash of a waterfall. Cliffs, twice
his height, rose above the little ledge of rock on which
he stood.

While his men gathered, he studied the right

bank. The brush on top looked dense. He'd make a hell of a noise, forcing his way through.

He raised his visor and grinned. "Okay, boys," he gasped. "Last man up is likely to get blasted by the goons we wake. Pick your handholds; let's all arrive together."

Bjorn leaped and grabbed a root sticking out of the bare bank, found another, then clawed his way up. A big stump held the bank here; he climbed around it, came to his knees, and unslung his assault rifle. Sweat poured down his face, neck, and belly.

Brush blocked any view. Private Billy Hone, a big black marine from Atlanta, pulled himself up the same way Bjorn did and slid around to the other side of the stump. He seemed in good enough spirits.

Bjorn pushed through brush until he could see the devastated hillside. Ten meters below were signs of a camp in a sheltered pocket of ground. Ponchos, packaged vegpro rations, and flat ammunition pouches lay around beds made of leaves.

"Okay, we're clear," he whispered in his helmet mike. "We'll move along the hill. I'll take the top; Capodonno takes the bottom. The rest of you spread out between us. Walk easy and don't ask whether you should shoot. Just do it."

"It's about time," the lieutenant said in his ear. "I can see your marker now. The colonel has been on my ass."

"Don't take risks until I flush them, Lieutenant. You're too sensible to lose."

"I'm not as sensible as I am unemotional, Bjorn," Lefko replied after a silence. "What counts for me is success. That's why you're still alive."

Dusk now, Bjorn saw a glint overhead from an otherwise invisible aircraft. He walked carefully on the steep, grown-over hill. Grasshoppers and beetles flew up from underfoot. Capodonno had it easier, he thought; the little man traveled a trail from the pickets' camp.

The hillside curved. Ahead lay the slope Bjorn had been ordered to climb. He walked even more carefully now, entering shadow as he turned north. Below and a little in front of him, Capodonno's trail disappeared in a tamped-down swath of bare earth.

The little man crawled up, poked his rifle into the ground, and pulled the trigger.

A ball of heat-seeking flechettes was more fearsome than the old-fashioned hand grenade, Bjorn thought.

Capodonno's shot aroused no reaction.

Bjorn moved slowly, the highest man of his squad. Hone eased along two meters below. Capodonno clambered up toward him from the apparently vacant fortification below. He collected Hata and the rest as he climbed.

Then Bjorn stepped before recessed glass. Curved, it would provide a wide view to any inside video watcher.

He immediately fell to the ground. This was a second line of defense that overwatched the first. After a moment with no enemy reaction from the optical sensor, he rose. The Mexicans had deserted this line of fortification, also.

"Hone, you come up behind me," he broadcast. "The rest of you follow us."

Bjorn led his big squad mate up the hill another five meters, found a heavily worn trail that probably snaked down from the highway above. He followed it around and then faced another piece of optics placed at an open entrance. Bjorn heard a shout from inside. He smashed the glass with his rifle butt, yelled, "Engaging, Lieutenant," and dived into the tunnel.

Blind from the sudden change in light, he fired his assault rifle in the closest setting possible, heard screams. Then a bullet knocked him down. Hone walked over his body, cursing and firing.

Bjorn stood, felt for a second dimple on his corselet, and found it where his shoulder met his chest. His left arm was sore already; his upper body would be black and blue tomorrow. If there were a tomorrow.

He picked out Hone's beacon on his helmet display and followed him, wishing that he wore a senior officer's complete set of armor. You didn't know where a bullet or knife would land in this kind of melee.

Then Hone was down, although his vital signs, when queried through his helmet, were still good.

By now, Bjorn's eyes adapted to the dimly lit tunnel. Its curve followed the surface of the hill, he supposed. On his right, enemy engineers had dug two-meter deep embrasures and reinforced them with one half-meter square timbers. Heavy machine guns sat behind steel accordion slits, mortar muzzles projected through slaved valves in the roof, and missiles filled launchers fitted into the wall.

The nearest embrasure contained fallen men, taken out by either his or Hone's flechettes. Farther on, men turned away from viewing screens and emplaced weapons. They lifted light guns.

He fired another burst of flechettes, nudged Hone with a toe. "Up, friend," he shouted into his microphone. "That was just a love tap."

He moved on. A man leaped at him from the reverse face of an embrasure. The enemy stepped inside the arc of Bjorn's rifle and raised a short, semi-automatic hand weapon.

Without thinking, Bjorn reached to the back of his neck and threw his knife. The man took it in his eye, like the gang boss had, at Angel's.

Bjorn leaned over to retrieve the knife and wipe the blade on the soldier's uniform. He squelched an urge to vomit.

Hone backed him now. And Hata followed. Bjorn fired a flechette burst every five or six meters, while his squad members watched the rear for still dangerous wounded. Soon, Bjorn heard enemy run ahead of him. Like rats, he thought, when a ghetto-trained ferret entered the sewer.

The tunnel quieted, except for the scuffle of fleeing soldiers. From outside, however, came an explosion of sounds; the tunnel shook from direct hits. Sensor screens blanked out, small lights along the side blinked. Dust filled the air.

No sense trying to stop the barrage by attempting to contact the Lieutenant, Bjorn thought. The earth blocked radio waves, too.

He came to a huge embrasure that possessed four outer sides, each filled with missile launchers or heavy machine guns. Here, he found bodies of faithful men who manned their weapons despite enemies at their back. He looked through optics protected from lasers by color filters, saw Marines charge up the ravine wall and over the deserted fortification in the line that Capodonno had tested. Firing broke out in front of Bjorn, where the tunnel occupants must have run out into the clear. Then all noise ceased.

Bjorn guessed the exposed Mexicans surrendered.

#

Later that night, after they'd carried Norving, with his destroyed knee, up to the road and the med copter, Bjorn led his men down the gravel track to a rock wall that faced east, toward Veracruz. "I'll take first watch," he said.

He sat ten meters from them, against the rock, and stared toward the lights of Veracruz.

Poll would come for sure.

Bjorn left his assault rifle leaning a meter away, held his little knife in his hand, cutting side up. He had never met a man he hadn't thought he could beat in a fair fight. Poll was special, however, and Bjorn admitted to himself that he was frightened.

After a while, he detected the grind of granite

chips against granite, rose to a crouch, and opened his eyes wide to catch the loom of his enemy.

"Coming on a visit, Sergeant dear?"

That was the high, caustic voice of Capodonno.

"We're jealous of our corporal, ain't we boys? No private meetings while we're around, heh?"

Someone flicked on a light cube and set it on the gravel.

Bjorn's squad was on its feet. Hone led Hata and Smith, all from his recruit draft, up the road's margin. They cut Poll's escape route. Capodonno stood easily below Bjorn.

"No firing," Bjorn commanded.

The sergeant seemed like a dark mountain. He wore no corselet, carried no gun, but held a large Bowie knife. He turned in a slow circle to examine each man, the weapon pointed forward. Finally, he wiped his brow with his other hand, stopped so he faced Bjorn, and shrugged. "I'll kill that one," he said, pointing at Capodonno. "After I cut off your balls, Bjorn. He mouthed-me, too."

Poll glanced over his shoulder in the direction of Hone and the other men, who now stood outside the light. "Walk up the road to Lieutenant Lefko's camp," he ordered. "I'll forget you followed this bastard."

Bjorn thought of throwing his knife. But Poll was very quick and had a lot of meat over vital parts.

A rock flew out of the darkness. It struck Poll on the head. "That's in gratitude for forgetting we followed Bjorn, you shit." Then the thick voice continued. "I'll never forget."

Hone, Bjorn thought.

Capodonno chuckled when Poll spun around, crouched, and pointed his knife up hill. "Bloodied you, didn't he? How does an Enforcer feel with enemies at his back?"

Poll didn't say anything and turned toward Bjorn again.

Another rock slammed out of the darkness and struck the big man's shoulder.

"We'd all be dead on that slope if it weren't for Bjorn," Hata said in his deep voice. "So would a lot more of the lieutenant's men than we buried. You're a maniac."

Poll turned suddenly and dashed for Bjorn's assault rifle. Capodonno hit him low; Bjorn struck him high, ripped his enemy's chin line with the little knife and then gripped Poll's own knife arm with both hands.

God, but the man was strong!

Poll tried to stand and shook Bjorn like a man does a child. Then he grunted and fell to a knee. Capodonno had hamstrung him.

Hone finally crushed Poll's head with a brutal swing of a sharp-edged rock.

As they stood around the body in the faint light, breathing heavily, and swearing, Bjorn heard another grind of loose rock. He spun and saw the lieutenant walk toward him, holding a pistol in his hand.

Lefko surveyed the scene, and then holstered his gun. "Take him down to the tunnels," he said. "I'll name him a hero in my report tomorrow."

The lieutenant stared a long time at Bjorn. "There are more ghetto males than we Achievers will be able to feed," he finally said, "but it's stupid to waste a useful one."

Then he turned back.

Chapter 10

In late May, Bjorn led Captain Lefko's skeleton company into the town that they conquered months earlier. He figured that ten members from his original company still lived. Medivac had lifted two of those to the submarine hospital. Most of the sixty-two men who followed him came from other shattered units, were drafted from rear area logistic posts, or had joined them here direct from recruit barracks. They wore torn, patched uniforms, limped, and had red eyes and the shakes.

The three chevrons of a sergeant decorated the short sleeves that poked out from his dented corselet now.

"Bivouac next to the church, Bjorn," Lefko directed through the radio link from somewhere up front. "Administration put up poles, covered them with tarpaulins. You'll have shade, anyway."

The goddamn Achiever officers flew down here and left the enlisted men to make it on foot. Lefko's one good lieutenant supposedly was in Veracruz with the battalion's executive officer to see about replacements and re-supply--even rotation back to the States, if he were conniving enough. The other company lieutenant was probably off quivering somewhere.

Lefko had no top sergeant anymore, nor four stripers, either, only jumped-up corporals and privates like Bjorn. Death was often the cost of non-coms "leading from the front," Bjorn had learned.

"Shit," Corporal Capodonno said from behind Bjorn, his helmet also hanging from his corselet. "They've put us in a graveyard."

He was right. Bjorn had led them off the highway, marched them across the town's small parking lot that now contained marine vehicles, to a large cemetery temporarily roofed with canvas. Marines slept, played cards, or stared into the distance among tall, concrete grave markers. Some monuments portrayed angels; most were ornate, Catholic crosses.

Well, Bjorn thought, the only alternative would be to take over farmland or move into houses. Either might seriously irritate the locals. Impolitic.

"The dead make way for those en route," Capodonno said.

"Over here," shouted Lefko from the side.

The captain stood next to the church, where a lane led to the rear of the graveyard. He turned and limped in front of Bjorn and led them to a vacant area, twenty-five meters square. A resting unit had stayed in it before them, obviously, and hadn't policed the place when it left.

Lefko appeared pale and drawn. Bjorn suspected the dysentery bothered him more than the laser burn from a Marine attack copter. Lefko's new implant that released disease counteragents hadn't taken well.

The captain leaned against the church wall, watched the non-coms settle everyone, and finally wiggled a finger at his acting top sergeant. "There are three bars here that serve beer and a local white lightning," he said when Bjorn sat on his heels in front of him. "The booze will make you sicker than drunk." He smiled sparingly. "The women will have nothing to do with us. Don't force them; you know the penalty."

Lefko pushed away from the wall. "Conserve the men in their ghetto frolicking," he said. "Brigade's sending us another draft of recruits. We need every veteran we've got."

He nodded and walked away, to the stone office building, probably, Bjorn guessed. It would be officers' quarters, now. He wondered if Lefko's pad had air conditioning, refrigeration, and maybe decent liquor.

#

Late one evening, Bjorn sat at a table in Mama's cantina with Capodonno, Hone, and Hata, the three men who had helped him kill Sergeant Poll. These marines were friends, proven fighters who would die for him, as he would for them. Despite that, he still insisted on the seat that backed against the adobe wall. Old precautions became iron rules in a combat area, he mused, and sipped from a warm bottle of beer. He'd learned a lot of new rules, too. If he lived through this fucked-up war, he'd be a changed man.

"How about music, Jose?" Hata asked Mama's rat-like, crippled husband. "Your beer's lousy, the food explodes in my innards, and you've no women. But I like Mexican music. Bring out your guitar. We'll sing about the sadness of war."

Hata was about Bjorn's size and well educated for a ghetto kid. He claimed three generations of American ancestors.

Almost ten in the evening, humid heat made Bjorn think about wallowing again in the stream down at the bridge. Greatest pleasure he'd found here.

Mama's was full of marines who drank, talked in quick bursts, and then, for something to do, put a fist in the face of a comrade. Earlier, Bjorn suffered through a man's long crying jag, grateful when his sergeant finally led the marine back to a graveside bed.

What a lousy rest stop! The officers should do better for their troops.

"How do we keep our men from getting runny brains?" he asked. "The captain says he's got no recorder cubes, so they can't send messages back to family and friends. There's no holovision, either, nor music slugs and ear players."

"I bet Veracruz has good slugs, even porno stuff," growled Hone. "The Achiever officers will have whore houses there, too. Rear area people never suffer."

"Maybe the States want to forget us," Capodonno contributed in his girlish voice. "We've three brigades here, now, almost a third of the Corps. All we've won are casualties and a stalemate. Our troubles maybe made voters change their holovision channel."

However, Lefko told Bjorn that construction battalions had almost completed the Sanitation Zone along the U.S. border. A violent Mexican Army test of the automated fortifications already proved their quality. Maybe the Veracruz expedition had done its job, even though the Marines hadn't taken the Mexican capital. Maybe the lack of support provisioning meant re-embarkation soon.

"I heard a rumor from one of our neighbors today," Hone whispered. "Tenth Battalion of the Second Brigade mutinied Friday. Troops killed the Enforcers and top officers."

Bjorn knew what would happen to the mutineers. Command would turn back from the task of climbing toward Puebla. Achiever officers would direct the capture of the rebellious and then nail them to large, wooden crosses planted along Marine parades. The mutineers faced a slow, painful death.

He hoped they'd die with guns in their hands instead, but didn't dare voice his wish, even among friends.

He could have ended that way, if he hadn't been lucky and drawn a wise officer. Shit, he could still end that way. Quiet obedience was not his specialty.

Lucky for his mood, Jose returned with his guitar. The music brought memories of Bjorn's days in the Mexican part of the San Angeles ghetto. Damn if he didn't even become teary.

About eleven, fat Mama with the mustache came out from the kitchen to whisper in Bjorn's ear. "Senorita Salinas would speak to you, blond one."

Bjorn jumped to his feet and then waved his

curious friends down. But before he ducked through the beaded kitchen curtain, he stood still and checked himself. His knife sat comfortably at the back of his neck and he felt coordinated, despite the beers.

He wished he could brush his teeth.

The steaming kitchen smelled of garlic, peppers, and onions. Angelina waited near the outside door. She wore a frilly, white blouse and a dark, flaring skirt. Most importantly, she showed a smile.

Bjorn passed Mama, strode close to the girl, and bowed his head. "Hola, mi amante! I decided not to ask for you, thought you hated me."

Her smile disappeared. "I am not your sweetheart. Nor will I be, ever. Your people are the enemy of my people."

He straightened, watched her carefully, and smiled still.

She sighed. "But I have thought about you much. You are very handsome and I have been lonely." She looked down. A pert tongue moistened her lips.

He reached out, caught her hand. "Is there somewhere we can go, Angelina? A place where we can talk?"

A strange, spicy smell rose from between her small breasts. God, she wore no bra! Maybe she didn't know what one was.

She pulled her hand away, almost violently. "Don't touch!" she exclaimed.

"Mama is my aunt," she then whispered. "She believes I carry a message to you from my grandfather. Don't make her think otherwise."

She smiled and swayed toward him. "Come, my beast. It's not far."

He held out his hand. "No trap?" he asked. "Word of honor?"

"Word of honor," she gravely repeated.

Outside, a slight rain fell. It marked the start of the wet season, Bjorn guessed. The water would further bog down their attempt to climb up onto the plateau that held Mexico City. The moisture brought coolness, a welcome relief, however.

Angelina led him down a barely lit, narrow street lined with two-storied houses set close together. Then they turned into dark alleys bordered by adobe houses and thatched roof huts--the part of town he had scouted that first day so long ago. He barely saw three meters in front of him because of the night and light rain.

Was he stupid to go into a dark, enemy town with a girl who had once tried to kill him? Then, he grinned. Faint heart never won fair maiden, or some such shit.

Finally, Angelina stopped. "We are here, beast," she said and walked into a dark doorway.

Bjorn followed her, but sensed the presence of other people and tried to jump back. Two huge women seized his arms and practically threw him into a large room.

People lit flickering wicks, and he heard murmuring.

Dazed by the light and the surprise, he straightened and glanced around. Five old men sat behind a wooden table. Maybe thirty other people, mostly women, lined the walls.

A perfect ambush, Bjorn thought. The crowd didn't make a sound until he stepped through the entry.

Thatch walled the hut as well as roofing it, the brown leaves woven over a framework of long, narrow poles. Pounded raw earth composed the floor.

"Grandfather," Angelina said to a gray-haired, thin Mexican who sat in the middle of the old men, behind the table, "this is the man who killed Antonio. He has influence over the marine soldiers and some officers."

Bjorn snapped into parade rest in front of the table. What a fool he'd been!

"When will you leave my country, Sergeant?" The leader's voice was gravely, his face hard.

"I don't know, Sir."

"We need our strong men to plant the fields. We want our graveyard in which to plant our dead."

Sweat gathered under Bjorn's arms. "We both have the same enemy, Sir. Your government. We invade your country to stop your people from invading ours."

The old man's eyes were cold and black; small lines ran from their corners. Shallow, long creases bordered his nose, and then flared to the corners of his mouth. Bjorn recognized nothing that reminded him of the attractive Angelina.

"You use your warriors' strength to fight for your land," the old man said. "We use more than our young men. To tempt the enemy with a woman is an old trick of our people."

While standing next to the table, Angelina pulled back her hair and knotted it. She glared at him, now, and looked careworn, like the other hostile women who filled the hut, only younger.

Had he followed her because he had once saved her life, thought his own thus protected? Because of honor mutually sworn? No. No sense fooling himself. Lust led him here, had fogged all caution. Like before, like with Lieutenant Morrison back in training. Once again. "Am I on trial?" he asked.

Two large, heavy women jumped forward to grab Bjorn's arms when he brought them forward from the locked position behind his back. He did not struggle.

"No trial, Sergeant. We held that an hour ago."

The grandfather motioned at the impassive faces around the walls. "We are of Indian stock, only slightly contaminated by Spanish blood." A grimace contorted his thin lips and leathery cheeks. "Both old races knew how to treat opponents. After your fellows inspect your body tomorrow morning, they will no longer think of this village as a rest area."

He nodded at his granddaughter.

A club struck Bjorn behind his knees. Once on the ground, his arms free for a moment, he twisted his head, decided he could kill either the grandfather or Angelina with a toss of his knife. But that would kill all hope, too. The mob would tear him to pieces.

A knee rammed into the small of his back. Then, one of the women pulled back his arms and tied together his wrists with leather thongs. Angelina kneeled beside him. She held a small pot, offered a ladle full of a steaming, brown concoction. "Drink this, beast," she said. "It will make what is to come easier for you."

He rolled his head away. "Men will fear you," he said. "No one will dare love you."

She spat in the pot and dumped its contents on the ground. "I won't miss love," she whispered. "All you men want from us is sex, children, and work. You rarely give anything."

Other women forced his mouth open, shoved between his lips a long, corncob gag, and tied the ends together with a thong around the back of his neck. Then they were up and so was Bjorn, hauled to his feet by the two burly, women guards.

The time was about midnight, he guessed, when the women jerked him out of the hut. He sucked-in around his gag a breath *of moist air.*

Oh, Uncle Will, why aren't you here to save me?

The women marched him through a silent town, to the plaza in front of the church--and in front of Bjorn's sleeping comrades. There, Angelina showed him a large, sharpened pole that her confederates had planted between flagstones. Protruding more than a meter above the ground, the white, recently shaved point gleamed through the rain.

Two big women kneeled next to him and grasped his ankles, matching the two who held his arms. Angelina punched him in the groin and paralyzed him with pain.

She pulled a sharp little knife from her belt and pretended to shove it in his stomach but, instead, cut his belt and waistband. She sliced his shorts too so scraps of underwear fell on his pants. His buttocks and groin were bare now.

"Ho, beast," she whispered in his ear. "Do you shudder inside your skull, in your cave there?"

He decided not to wait any longer. His testicles hurt, but his asshole would hurt more if the women impaled him on the damned stake. He convulsed in a wild attempt to throw off those who held him. Then, he planted his left foot and kicked with his right. When that didn't free his ankle, he kicked backward, then forward again. As he did, he turned his body back and forth, thrashed so the women holding his arms couldn't help those at his feet. He bit down hard on the corncob that ran lengthwise through his mouth, sawed at one end, pushed it out with his tongue until his canines could tear at it.

He would not let them do this to him.

His heart beat wildly. He felt the veins at his temples stand out. His face would be red. He continued to lash out, now planting his right foot and kicking with his left. His teeth were down to the core of the cob.

"Hit him in the cojones again, hard!" commanded Angelina, darting around Bjorn.

"He fights like a netted cougar," gasped a woman.

When a big harridan swung at his crotch, Bjorn lurched so her club hit the woman who hung on to his left ankle. For an instant his foot was free; he used it to kick the woman who held the other leg. She didn't let go.

God! His teeth broke the corncob. He pushed the small end out and mouthed, "Marines, to me!" Then he spat out the larger half and bellowed, "Lefko Company! Help."

The club whistled at his head. He ducked and took it on his shoulder. "Help! To the Plaza. Marine in trouble!"

The women pulled him to the ground and lay on his legs. One jammed shut his mouth with a hard hand under his chin. They gasped and swore.

After a moment, Angelina poked her head between two of them, her head over his bare crotch. She still had that damn knife. "They come, beast," she said. "You saved yourself from the stake, but not from my knife."

She pushed up his shirt, reached for his testicles.

He rolled maybe ten centimeters, heaved, wriggled back and forth. The women on his chest and legs couldn't stop all movement. Tears ran out of his eyes.

Angelina's hand fumbled for him, the knife made an arc over his groin.

He heard shouting. Heavy marine boots ran toward him. He forced his exhausted muscles to more contortions.

"Beast of a man!" Angelina gasped and then plunged the knife into his abdomen.

She stood and held a strangely bloodless knife. "Vamanos," she said. The other women rolled off him and stood. They all ran.

The pain wasn't great; he felt only a looseness, a liquid spreading. He raised his head to look at his wound. A small slit showed above his belly button. Blood oozed from it.

I now have a ticket out of this damn war, he thought, and then shuddered.

Chapter 11

Five years later, in May of 2096, Will Maestri followed pudgy Mr. John Striker, Executive Director of Health and Human Resources, into a San Angeles Achiever restaurant. Bjorn's uncle admired the mother-of-pearl lobby, the flowing color on the dining room walls, and the silver and white of the tables. When Maestri stepped into the table space reserved for the HHR executive and his guest, he smiled at hearing Mozart.

The luxury reminded him of old times.

Mr. Striker's returning smile slid down at one corner into a boy's mischievous grin. Wide-spaced, blue eyes, framed by bushy, black eyebrows, invited Maestri's confidence. "Take your seat, old friend," his one time boss said.

The Achiever's charm almost made Maestri forget the events of their last meeting, sixteen years earlier. After listening to an auditor, Striker almost had Maestri killed, fired him instead, and then exiled him back to the San Angeles ghetto.

Now, Mr. Striker slipped a card into a slot that would direct canceling sound waves from the manifolds around their table. The conversation would be private. "Don't bother ordering," he said. "I remembered what you like."

Waiters hovered, their service more satisfying, Maestri remembered--from an earlier incarnation, it seemed--than the automation of most restaurants.

He watched a wave of many-shaded blue crest on the wall near him. It fell in cascades of teal and turquoise to a pool of shifting pastel colors that, in turn, gave off a rainbow mist. Then the blues surged up the wall again. He shook his head. He'd missed Achiever beauty.

"Well, Maestri," Mr. Striker said, "I wasn't totally wrong years ago when I picked you for an assistant. You've scrambled to a position of some power again. You advise the San Angeles Residents Council, and others too, I hear."

Maestri waved a deprecating hand and sampled a white wine that came from Achiever fields exempted from food growing. It had a lovely, brilliant taste and smelled faintly of cloves.

A waiter brought hors d'oeuvres.

"I understand your nephew recovered nicely from his wound in the Mexican war and is a trusted member of the Corps Special Services," his host said. "His record is a credit to you also."

"He misses three centimeters of intestine but has a more realistic view of women now."

Maestri had learned that his nephew's buddies found the Indian girl and hanged her. Bjorn had written that he regretted the punishment.

"Do you expect to be the next President, Sir?" he asked.

Mr. Striker shook his head and smiled again. "The current President wants another term," he answered. "My HHR council says I must wait."

He shoved back his empty hors d'oeuvres plate. "I understand you control the Welfies of California."

Maestri raised an eyebrow. "You control those Welfies, all Welfies as a matter of fact."

"My methods are digital. I can starve or feed; kill or ignore; abandon or house. As a result, I set boundaries to behavior, but I can't fine-tune. That's why I need you."

Waiters delivered salads.

Maestri hadn't eaten delicate, fresh greens for years. He savored each leaf. "I do have links to residents' councils, in Southern California especially."

In his past, as Maestri improved his effectiveness with the ghettos, HHR promoted Mr. Striker. So, in a way, Maestri was responsible for Striker's earlier success. Of course the bastard had provided his own ruthlessness.

Today he held the biggest job in the country, short of the presidency. Weird to have this powerful man wine and dine Welfie Will Maestri.

Waiters now brought the main course and switched the wine to a red cabernet.

"Do you want me to ignore the HHR council's decision, and work for your election anyway?"

Mr. Striker leaned back and affected a laugh. "Of course not, of course not. I'm not fighting my own council."

Maestri shrugged. "Forty percent of the voters are Welfies," he said. "They plus a few others could elect you if given reason to."

"Do you actually believe I could beat HHR?" Mr. Striker shook his head. "The idea's ridiculous. If you and I went around the Welfare Kings, those petty despots would have their punishment battalions kill anyone who listened. And, central HHR would send assassins after me—properly so, too.

"I can wait," the Achiever continued. "You guessed wrong. My personal ambition is not the reason for this dinner."

The wall next to Maestri changed from flowing hues to altering patterns. Starbursts and colored pentagons expanded, then folded into each other, even pronounced soft chords that underlined moments of Mozart.

Mr. Striker cut into his blackened filet mignon. "I liked the way you and Plant kept the ghettos calm during the war with Mexico and want more of the same."

"Crowding is worse," Maestri answered. He leaned forward. "Can't you increase the dried milk in children's packages and build more tenements for families? That would calm everyone."

"God damn it, there you go again!" Striker shouted. He put down the knife and slapped the table. "Policy is none of your business."

"Sorry, Sir."

"Don't forget what your last seizure of conscience brought you."

Red slashes on his passport and a dangerous drop off to the ghetto were what it brought, Maestri remembered. He'd been lucky, at that.

He'd never stop caring, though, despite the danger of demanding more welfare. An image of his frail mother crying as she fed him crusts was etched into his memory.

"You never understood the big picture," the HHR executive said. "I'll try once more."

Something nasty is coming, Maestri thought. That's why this dinner.

"Since the start of the twenty-first century, food production has declined as population has increased," Mr. Striker stated importantly. "That's world-wide."

He waved a bloody hunk of beef. "The U.S. lost topsoil from erosion every year since we took up intensive farming in the nineteenth century. The mid-west has less than a quarter of what it once had. Did you know that?"

Maestri shook his head.

"The Ogallala aquifer under the Great Plains has been pumped dry. And petroleum-based fertilizer is now unaffordable." Mr. Striker sighed. "We've done everything we can think of to increase food production," he said. "For instance, we've cleared towns off good land and assembled small farms into large, automated ones."

In the process, dumping more people into the ghettos, Maestri thought.

"We converted a lot of grazing land to grain fields,

also. That forced the cut in milk rations, which you protested years ago and now want restored." The HHR executive smiled coldly. "We produce more calories per square meter of ground with grain."

Maestri pushed his plate away.

"We must cut Welfie rations," Mr. Striker announced. "We must reduce all forms of Welfie support, as a matter of fact."

God! Now Maestri's upset stomach had turned into a sharp ache.

His host tapped the table. "We're placing a cap on what food we provide, as well as on what money we spend for medical treatment and housing."

Maestri was sure his face had turned white. His hands trembled. "But rations are marginal now," he protested. "And women still have babies."

"There's waste and abuse in the administration of rations. I'm told the ghettos still boast fat people." Mr. Striker struck the table with his fist. "Maybe cuts in support will make Welfies stop breeding so fast!"

Maestri's muscles had stiffened; his face now felt flushed. "Surely we still produce an agricultural surplus."

"Yes, but we must export more of it instead of less."

Mr. Striker's tongue worked on a strand of meat caught between his teeth. "After repeated devaluations, our money isn't worth anything overseas," he explained. "We can't bring in the foreign commodities and minerals we need to keep our factories going."

"You'd starve people in order to export grain?"

Striker glowered at him. "Economics may be too complex for your Welfie mind, but yes. We can't let our civilization die."

Maestri lowered his eyes to hide disgust. Other Achievers were eating like Striker and he were at the present time, while they discussed cutting Welfie rations!

"Our grain is like gold. More precious, in fact."

Maestri fought his urge to shout the hate that surged through him. He thought of the girls who flocked to prostitution for the food it brought, of the young men who stole ration packets from the sick and old and how they fought each other, and of their death rate. He remembered the squalor and the plain nastiness of the ghetto. How could the Achievers, as a class, even consider imposing further suffering?

They never entered a ghetto, never met a Welfie. That was the reason.

"Don't take this new policy so hard, my friend," the HHR executive said. "Your Welfies will still consume more calories per head than the poor of the Southern Hemisphere."

"You could ration everyone," Maestri said. "Achievers, too."

Striker's mouth drew back in a snarl. "You have the same stupid, moralistic point of view as before. You want equality in this country when it's undeserved and undesirable. Change your point of view if you wish to survive."

Maestri knew enough economics to guess that worldwide price inflation accompanied the growing scarcity of food. Achievers would be hurting, too. More would become Welfies--to starve like their new neighbors.

"Why cut medical and housing support too, when food is the problem?" he asked, and then guessed the answer. "To fund additional HHR punishment battalions that will squash protests when rations decrease?"

"Yes," Striker growled. "But we'll build an army, too."

"What will the President do with an army, for God's sake? Mexico has been paralyzed by civil war ever since we left."

"We'll threaten the Canadians," Mr. Striker answered. "Since global warming has moved a lot of our rainfall north, we have a legitimate claim on their grain. We'll also loan regiments to our trade partners in Europe in return for products we need. The world has grown restless."

Maestri had control now. He'd forced the rage into a tiny ball in the pit of his stomach.

Striker studied him and smiled knowingly. "The President hates the necessity to cut Welfie rations and support, but he has agreed. What else can he do in the face of facts?"

"I thought better of him."

"He will place a nice, liberal patina on the announcement by saying the cuts are only temporary." Striker grinned. "True, but later we'll increase the reductions instead of restoring them."

He leaned forward. "We're not alone in facing worsening times. The European Union sinks North African boats in the Straits of Gibraltar and around southern Italy. The Iranians and other Moslems press up against Europe on both sides of the Caspian and Black Seas. Chinese armies collect in Mongolia, and prepare to march into Siberia, then westward. Every nation is hungry."

Thinking of his nephew, Maestri asked, "Why an army rather than more marines?"

"The latter compose our elite, high technology force. We don't have the equipment to expand the Marines and won't dilute it."

Maestri looked at the lovely broccoli without hunger. He felt weak now, as if he'd taken a terrible beating. "What do you want from me?"

"Work more magic," Striker answered. "Make the San Angeles Welfies bear reductions without complaint. Use what influence you have in the nation's other ghettos for the same end."

Don't let Welfies riot and invade Achiever suburbs, in other words, Maestri thought.

He wondered how the new generation of ghetto

leaders would react to the coming cuts. Con Wagoner, for instance. The son of a Welfie radical, Con now ran the previously boneless San Angeles Residents' Council. The man was bright and a fighter.

The coming reductions would move leaders like Con in ways Maestri couldn't combat. Maybe wouldn't want to combat.

"Your new divisions will need officers with experience, Mr. Striker. My nephew..."

"No. Achievers will fill all leadership ranks."

"Benjamin is intelligent. At the hospital, he started to repair the holes in his education. He now reads a book a week."

Maestri's host slammed his fist against the table. "No, God damn it! A man doesn't enter the Achiever class, whatever his skills, unless he's the third generation of talent. Then he must graduate from a university. We must protect our high mental and energy genome."

Maestri stared at Striker. He supposed his expression was unfriendly.

The HHR executive leaned forward. "You're an ungrateful, stupid, Welfie bastard." He leaned back and sighed. "I tried to let bygones be bygones, even explained the necessity of our new policy. I hoped you'd use your mind instead of primitive emotion, but that's too much to expect from a Welfie, I suppose." He sighed again and then frowned. "Remember your place and my ability to destroy both you and your nephew. You will do my bidding in the western ghettos. Assure peace there, or I'll squash you."

Mr. Striker threw down his napkin, rose, and left.

Chapter 12

Sergeant Benjamin Bjorn sighed. His gut ached, even though five years had passed since he left the hospital. Five long, difficult years. He'd stayed alive, despite his wise-ass, independent nature, only by taking nerve-wracking assignments like this one.

He had baby sat a frail explosive specialist and a computer hacker with old fashioned, thick, contact lenses in a glider drop from high altitude. Now he must manage a personnel extraction.

The stomach pain wasn't from the old wound, of course. From fear, rather. Bjorn wished he sat back in San Angeles at Angel's Fun House. Instead, he lay on dark, Argentine ground in body armor. He'd romp on R&R a week from now, though, he promised himself.

Private Frenny Smith finally moved the building-buster rocket back far enough for it to build velocity before hitting the target.

"Remember, Smith," Bjorn whispered into his helmet mike, "stay where you are. No stud demo, or I'll find time in my busy schedule to rip off your balls."

"I hear you, Sergeant."

"Shenso?"

"Right behind you, Sergeant," whispered his communications specialist.

Fortunately, the target building sat alone, off the road from town, near the river. The action would be a nighttime set piece, with little chance for interruption, and the escape boat waited, submerged nearby. Two kilometers of open ground, dotted with only a few, feathery trees, lay between him and the prison, however. Long run.

"Fire," Bjorn ordered.

A roar drummed his ears as a rocket with a microwave generator payload arched over the prison. The motor quit suddenly and then Bjorn heard a blast. The warhead had detonated in the air, as programmed.

The microwaves it produced would induce high voltage currents in wiring that should short out all the enemy's electrical equipment.

Bjorn heard a second roar when a flechette dispenser took off to shake out heat-seeking warheads over the perimeter. The red exhaust and shrieking whine of the building-buster followed.

Bjorn stood and ran, but stumbled when the big warhead blew a hole low in the side of the concrete building.

Half a minute later, he stumbled again when bullets, which collectively must have emptied a semi-automatic clip, swept by him, chest high, a round flicking off the convex frontal plate of his special, layered armor.

Not enough mass to slow him, though. Lucky the shooter had fired the burst chest high; Shenso, who ran behind Bjorn, wore only a corselet, his legs unprotected. The stream of bullets probably knocked down his lightweight communications specialist, though.

On the infrared underlay in Bjorn's visor a white blotch extended out of the hole that the building-buster had made. Hot breath.

Can't see the gunner's body, he thought. *He's pulled back, maybe to reload.*

Bjorn fired with a single, heat-seeking shot into the wall's new cavity. Lots of opportunity for ricochets there. If nothing else, noise would give the shooter something to think about for a second.

He dropped to his knees and dived into the hole. He paused, then pushed a naked corpse with a shattered, bleeding skull before him, crawling over busted masonry and skewed reinforcing rods. His comm. expert followed, breathing noisily over the helmet phone.

"Mi corazon! Mi corazon, que pasa?" a female voice shrieked.

When Bjorn exited the hole with his weapon's muzzle slowly moving from side to side, pieces of concrete sliding from his armor, he crawled over the body. He stood. "The man's dead," he said.

The shrieks stopped.

He could see what must be the Ambassador's infrared signature on his visor screen--blotches of white from her hot heart and warm breath.

"I'm over here on the sofa, you murdering bastard!" she cried. "You damn near killed me, too."

The rocket warhead's blast had pushed fragments of concrete before it, carving a gigantic, follow-on hole through the bedroom farther wall into the lighted guards' area beyond. Bjorn poked his gun and head through the inside wall and saw no one.

What was an enemy gunner doing in the Ambassador's rooms late at night? Without clothes. Where was the guard detail?

Shenso stepped past and dived headfirst through the new hole into the guardroom. At least they wouldn't have to blow a door and kill more Argentines.

Bjorn turned and stomped toward the woman. He flicked up his visor. "Sergeant Benjamin Bjorn, Ma'am," he said. "The crap from the wall wouldn't have been dangerous if you'd been in bed."

"How dare you tell me where I should have been?"

He pressed a cube light at his belt and set it on the floor. The Ambassador was a young forty-five, even better looking than in her photographs. She was lush, brunette, and totally naked.

Her eyes were wet, and her body trembled. That surprised Bjorn. Poor nerves didn't go with her profession.

She straightened instead of covering herself. "You had no business shooting him, Sergeant," she said, her voice shrill. "He had emptied his gun. You must have known that."

True. And, Bjorn had been ordered to minimize enemy casualties. But he hadn't lived this long by leaving enemy gunners alive. He couldn't shrug in his armor, so stood stolidly.

She sighed, pointed to the hole into the guardroom, and then wiped at her face with a shoulder. "Leave the light and go do something military."

When Bjorn located Shenso, he found that the four-eyed genius didn't need help. The expert quickly connected his box to the guardroom information terminal and pushed aside security safeguards with hacker sweet talk.

Optical cable carried photons of light, of course, not electrons. The MMW detonation didn't damage the enemies' data transmission lines as it did their electrical systems. The Argentine leaders in town, at the local airfields, and at army headquarters would soon feel Shenso and start wriggling.

Bjorn listened at the door to the rest of the prison. He heard alarmed voices.

He climbed back into the Ambassador's quarters. "To hell with your clothes," he told her. "Put on shoes and wrap a sheet around yourself."

She had donned panties, and now fastened a bra behind her back. "You're a lech, aren't you?" she asked. Her breath caught and she coughed. "All you psychopaths are." She wiped her eyes. "Couldn't stay away; had to have an eyeful? Feel free, but I shall finish dressing."

She was the President's sister, of course; arguing his authority would be pointless.

"Shenso, as soon as you start the tape, slide back out," Bjorn whispered in his helmet phone. "On your belly. Talk to Smith when you have line-of-sight so your radio works. Tell him we're coming."

After Shenso passed, Bjorn stood next to the hole in the guardroom wall and watched the steel door to the rest of the prison. Not one to reject a superior's generous offer, he turned to sneak a look at the Ambassador occasionally.

She was pulling the dress over her head when he heard the sound of a short-range missile launch outside.

Damn!

"Get your ass in gear!" he yelled at the Ambassador as he clumped toward the hole in the outer wall. "Now!"

He pulled himself over busted concrete via broken reinforcing rods. His visor covered his face again, and he picked up Shenso's "down and hurt" symbol immediately.

"Behind the corner to your right, Sergeant," Smith whispered. "I can't get off a cluster shot from here. Too far."

At least Smith had obeyed orders and stayed in position.

Bjorn switched his gun to CLUSTER, TEN METERS, and fired toward the corner. Then he stood and sprinted, dived to the ground again, and slid along on his armor until he could poke his head around the corner.

The acrid smells of Argentina got to him. The dirt around the prison seemed tired and drained of energy. It had supported too many people for too long. Around the corner, however, blood and shit overpowered the old scents and the dry dust. Dislike changed to revulsion.

He had nothing to do there.

He clumped back to Shenso, felt heavy now, and tired. Damn it! If only the hacker...

Surprisingly, the Ambassador knelt beside his expert.

Bjorn whispered in his helmet phone, "You conscious, Shenso?"

"Yeah, Sergeant. I stood only for a second, but the bastards got me." The communications tech breathed raggedly. "Chest hurts bad."

"Can't you see that his armor's caved in?" hissed the Ambassador. "Do something!"

Bjorn opened his visor. "I suppose your rank gives you the right to run your mouth," he growled, "but mine lets me run my team."

He closed his visor. Shenso could be worse, he supposed. The oriental talked rationally, and his fingers and toes worked, according to the transmitted vital signs. Bjorn knelt and shot the man with a "songs and ecstasy" dose, then grabbed both feet and dragged him toward Smith.

The tech moaned and bit his lip.

The horizon was dark as an Achiever's heart.

"Carry him!" the woman ordered.

Bjorn couldn't carry another one hundred and seventy-five pounds, and Shenso slid smoothly enough on his armor corselet. He said nothing and kept moving.

"You carry him, Ben Bujorn, whatever your name is. Bent Brain!"

As he stayed silent, she shouted, "When we get home I'll see you get no independent action bonus!"

"How bad?" asked Smith through the helmet phone.

"He busted ribs but ought to be okay once he reaches the medics. Dangerous to make him walk, might puncture a lung. Empty the artillery mule. We'll litter him to the boat."

Bjorn wouldn't have volunteered, wouldn't have talked Shenso and Smith into volunteering except for the bonus. His neck warmed with anger.

He dragged Shenso near the mule and carefully let the marine's legs down together. He heard the Ambassador stumble and swear softly as she followed him.

He patted Smith on the helmet and leaned

against a tree.

The woman stood for a moment, and then sat. "Why don't we move?" she asked.

Bjorn waved toward the main road and the river beyond. "Coastal defenses over there. Guns and infantry all along the bank. We need to make them open a space for us."

"Well, why aren't you getting to it?"

"Things have to happen first."

"Will you spread a dirty story about Manuel and me back in the States?"

She thought only about herself, didn't give a damn for Welfie soldiers who shoved their lives out on the gambling table in order to rescue her. "I admire someone with a body like yours sharing it with others," he answered. "My friends will feel good about you, too, when they know."

He heard Smith swallow.

"I'll break you if you spew that poison, Bent Brain, bounce you back to the Welfie ghettos, maybe worse. Hear me?"

Shenso began to babble through the helmet speaker. Bjorn switched him off. He could see a line of trees along the road now.

"Let's load him, Smith," he said. "Then scatter personnel mines behind us and block the prison driveway. I don't want messengers to report what's happened. While you do that, I'll set up the hologram lasers."

He straightened and then pushed the woman down as she tried to stand. "Stay here. You'd be in the way." Then, slowly: "I'll come back for you, despite your mouth."

#

When he returned, Bjorn began to feel a little friendlier toward the woman. She held his hurt communications tech's hand and maybe even cried. Now she sat beside Bjorn under the trees, properly quiet, and watched the road and the far-away buildings near the river. She wouldn't see much, though. The pale, early dawn fought river fog.

He jutted his head forward. Yellow lights blinked on, motors roared. About time! The phony information and orders his comm. expert had fed the enemy finally brought results.

Truckloads of Argentine infantry poured out the gate opposite the luxury prison. One stream of vehicles drove toward the city, the other to the headlands where the river met the sea. Towed artillery and heavy machine guns on flatbeds roared east.

Fog filled the holes the last vehicles made near the ground, the mist dirty from exhausts. South America still had cheap oil, Bjorn thought, or at least their military had. No hydrogen-powered equipment yet. Didn't need it.

He had one hundred meters of visibility now. Patches of clear air showed only part of the military road and the guard shack at the entrance to the military reservation.

Bjorn commanded his backpack computer to turn on the hologram lasers via his tactical radio. He strode out, while his party trailed behind. He felt kin to the armored knights of the Middle Ages he had read about in officer-books. He wore protection from most anti-personnel weapons, could kill any man not dressed like him--and carried a launchable limpet mine for those enemies who bore armor.

He quietly moved behind the trees, along the driveway, and suddenly heard a voice from ahead. "Jose, will you look at them? Caramba!"

A partial view of the main road opened up, to the right of the guard shack. In that space, Bjorn saw the work of one of the lasers he deployed. Even from the rear and in the colorless light of dawn, the hologram figures were enticing. Angel's image showed a fine, firm rump and those of her assistants had the tight, hourglass shapes of youth.

"Hello, senoritas," said another voice. "Dressed for games already?"

"You mean undressed." A bray of a laugh followed.

"Bring your bottles and food," said the first voice. "We can party in the guard shack."

The Ambassador knocked on Bjorn's armor. "What are they raving about?" she whispered.

He pointed to the gap in the trees.

She stiffened. He held up his hand for Smith to wait. Let the enemy collect a bit better, he thought. Poor bastards.

Bjorn had to grin, despite the awful murders he was about to commit. He'd a great time shooting the scene, two scenes actually, since the frolic on the other side of the gate starred different women. Lots of red wine, salsa, chips, and mariachi music helped each girl relax and enjoy herself.

Bjorn walked forward, dogged by the Ambassador. He motioned Smith toward the middle of the driveway when he saw the guard shack. Ten enemy soldiers hung on the gate, whistled and yelled. A sergeant slid back the bar.

"I never thought I'd see the Corps use porn as bait."

Bjorn pushed up his visor. "What should I have done, run fake tanks at them?"

He was fed up with her. Sometimes he wanted to treat his Achiever superiors like he did enemies. Sometimes they deserved it more.

He nodded at Smith, who then launched a flechette area weapon.

Bjorn thought more than one flechette tore apart each guard.

Grimacing at the exploded chests and abdomens, at the bloody flesh he stepped over, Bjorn led his party through the gate. He walked into deep fog. "Stay close," he said to the woman. He grasped her arm. "I'd have liked coming through here better just before dawn, in clear air," he said. "Use the holograms all the way in to hypnotize anybody we ran across. This damn fog shrouds my infrared sensor, could lead to accidents. But if we stay a little off the military access road..."

"Don't hold me, Bent Brain."

He sighed but didn't let go. "What makes you so ornery?"

She tore her arm away.

"Frustrated? Did I interrupt at a crucial moment?"

She stomped alongside him in silence. "My feelings are none of your business, Sergeant," she finally replied, icy cold. "Just do your job and get me out of here.

"You murdered a fine man," she then blurted. "One I cared for. You didn't have to wipe him. But you're a killer who likes his work, that's clear." She walked silently for a moment. "Welfie animals like you need punishment training to make you think before you kill. You're lucky I'll stop at withholding the bonus."

"Who was he?" Bjorn asked. He touched her arm to gain her attention and angled off to the left.

"The Argentine President's brother," she answered from his side. "Manuel was our only hope for a successful, self-supporting alliance down here."

She stumbled, but Bjorn didn't reach out to steady her. No wonder the guardroom at the prison was deserted and her room's sensors unmonitored. He'd burst into a secret conference that became something else.

"What irony," she said. "My brother employs a high-technology killer to rescue me, to show the Latinos his arm is long. The bastard then kills the person we need if we're ever to solve the problems that flow from South America."

"Keeping you in a prison doesn't seem like a promising start to negotiation," Bjorn said. He pulled down his visor.

Smith trailed along and pulled the mule. Bjorn flicked on his unconscious Marine's sound. Shenso didn't talk now, but still breathed.

Then the warm exhaust of a bunker that guarded the river showed on Bjorn's sensor strip. He reached out and grabbed the Ambassador's arm again, pulled her close and flicked up his visor. "Quiet and sit," he whispered.

He didn't give her an option, but pushed her down.

Bjorn lowered his visor. "Okay, Smith, take this side. We blow the doors together. I'll call."

He had little fear of radar. The more powerful enemy dishes would scan the river and cover the sky. High power and a damn good signal processor were needed to make sense of his suit's edges and cracks. Also, his armor chemically absorbed his heat, kept him cool for at least twenty-four hours. It revealed no infrared image.

His sound was the main danger.

As he quietly neared the bunker, he saw that the door he had assigned Smith to detonate was ajar. The Argentines made it easy, he thought.

One trouble with automatic intelligence systems was that they let men relax. Come at the target in some unexpected way, like from behind, from inside the enemy's own perimeter...

A soldier darted out of Smith's door, stared at Bjorn's artilleryman, and raised a gun.

Bjorn had been as over-confident as the Argentines! Smith's damn corselet didn't do anything about the heat coming from below the smaller man's waist, didn't hide moving legs from high frequency, small radars.

Smith popped the soldier with a flechette, darted forward like a cat, switched his rifle to SHORT RANGE CLUSTER, then poked it in the open door and fired.

Bjorn turned and walked back toward the woman. Only dead and cripples remained in the bunker now. No one would threaten Bjorn's party as they passed.

"Okay, Smith, set up the beacon."

#

The stealthy landing boat came to the surface, streamed water over its top and sides all the way to the riverbank. Bjorn guessed the fluid layer would make enemy sensors believe the broached underwater vehicle was a wave.

He helped the Ambassador follow the mule and wade waist-deep out to the boat's midsection. "Have you still got your jaw set about not giving me the bonus?" he asked.

At the gunwale, she turned and looked hard at him, hard as anyone ever had.

"That'll cut out Shenso and Smith, also," Bjorn said. "Officers reward team members together."

"Go to hell."

She climbed on the step-upper, ducked under the transom, and slid through the seal and into the cabin.

He sighed and then boarded and hung on while the pilot backed out. When below the surface and headed for their submarine transport, Bjorn bent over the mule and unbuckled Shenso's helmet.

"How about giving the money to a Corps charity, then?" he asked. "In our names. That way, the officers won't blacklist us. Shenso and Smith didn't do anything to you.

"I'll swear not to talk about you screwing the Argentine," he added.

Smith had already unbuckled his helmet and had his corselet off. He squatted on the other side of the pilot.

Bjorn leaned back against a bulkhead. "I'm not pulling off Shenso's armor," he said. "Maybe it's all that's holding him together."

"He may never walk again," Smith contributed.

"The brave bastard."

Smith was a smart little ghetto rat. Bjorn might get him promoted to Private First Class.

From where she sat in the co-pilot's seat, the Ambassador sighed and picked up a memo pad. "All right," she said, "I'll bend that much. Give me your charity's name."

"Angel's Rest House," Bjorn said. "It's in old San Diego."

Smith coughed.

Chapter 13

A week later, Bjorn's skin tingled--his body limp from a bath and the subsequent encounter with giggling masseuses. He leaned back on the long sofa of the number two suite in Angel's Rest House, pulled the bathrobe over the gap between his bare legs, and sipped chic-coff. "I'm here because I'm better than them," he said softly to himself.

"You sound smug, Benjamin," his Uncle Will commented from across the room. The little man sat in front of a screen driven by the words he spoke to his thumb-sized personal assistant. Now, he rolled back his chair and cradled his own cup.

"I'm fed up with the Achievers who run everything," Bjorn replied. "I had the better of the President's sister on my last assignment. Makes me feel I showed them all."

"You don't like the Corps?"

"I can't stand the officers and other Achievers I must cower before, is all. Many of them haven't seen the wrong end of a gun or sweated out a missile strike. Their only qualifications are an Achiever accent and a college degree."

He remembered his stint on a division staff in the operations directorate after leaving the hospital with his Mexican wound cured. He'd learned logistics and administration there but hated the diplomatic crawling required by his low rank. His disgust showed, he guessed.

His officers hadn't liked his habit of improving on orders, either.

So they sent him to a battalion on the Strip.

Supposedly an operations expert now, he supervised support expeditions to the killer machines placed along the Mexican border. In that job he arranged fill-ups for laser burners and short-range gassers, installed replacement parts in automated guns and missiles, and lay down new jumper and hopper mines for ones detonated by wanna-crossers.

He became as good at battalion matters as he had at division staff, Bjorn thought. Both his officers and senior non-coms liked the extra time he gave them in their air-conditioned quarters. And, he learned to keep his mouth shut--usually.

Then battalion command changed and a need for boot-licking became the every day rule. As a result, he applied to join Special Action Services, which smashed and grabbed in sensitive foreign places, dropped spies, and generally used brains and stilettos rather than big battalions. His medal from Mexico and experience got him in, although the colonel warned of carping niggles on his record.

"You've walked a pretty fine line, Bjorn," the officer had said as Bjorn stood stiffly at attention before his new commander's desk. "Don't forget the caning stakes we erect for smart ass Welfies and the crosses we use when they turn irretrievably dumb."

Anyway, he had a decent job now that kept him away from most horseshit. He sipped from his cup. Except when he ran into someone like the Ambassador. She had called him an animal that needed punishment training!

"You may dislike the Achievers even more soon," Uncle Will said, his olive, bald head cocked to the side. "The Administration is cutting ghetto rations. Some idiot's likely to lead a revolt that an HHR punishment battalion can't handle. The Corps will go in. You won't enjoy killing fellow Welfies."

"Can't we do something about the rations?" Bjorn asked. "What about the election this fall?"

Uncle Will shook his head. "The current President is as liberal as we'll get, and his re-election's a sure thing. HHR has come out for him."

"No opposition?"

"Oh, yeah. But that party will nominate someone even more outraged by us non-productive Welfies." Maistre gestured at his monitor. "You'll see historic natural selection raised again. According to Achievers we're all genetically doomed to inferiority. Maybe there's some truth in that since most ghetto-heads don't even vote."

"So, what's the answer?"

Uncle Will shrugged. "There is no answer that I can see. We'll get screwed all of our lives. Increased scarcity, more and more violence, starvation, disease, and early death." He slammed his hand against his knee. "Shit!"

"I've been reading modern history," Bjorn replied. "At the turn of the century we were progressing. The world was getting richer, more secular, and unifying. Education was reaching the poor. Equality of opportunity. Now, everything's going downhill. The guys in charge really fouled up."

"Yeah. The southern hemisphere didn't get rich fast enough. Surplus people spilled over into up here, and in Europe, everywhere. As a result of crowding, water dried up, pollution multiplied. Food got scarce, housing too expensive. Riots resulted. After trying fairness for a while the answer of individual countries was to turn down the screws. Bosses put their budgets into border patrols, police, and jails. That only increased pain and disorder. Now we got the ghettos locked down. We need a world program that cuts population, saves the environment, and rations resources fairly. We need someone to wave a wand."

"Maybe we ought to help any revolt, eh?"

"No, Benjamin, no. You know the Corps. I know HHR. We couldn't win. Discipline yourself. Keep your frustrations for Angel's."

At that, the door popped open and Private Frenny Smith, Bjorn's explosive specialist on the Argentine jaunt, pushed a scantily dressed Oriental girl into the suite, and then pulled a Mex beauty in behind him. All three were in partial stages of undress and weaved a little from stimulants. The driving blare of an old Dixieland slug wafted in from the rumpus room across the stairwell.

"Hey, Sarge," the artilleryman said, "watch us dance the sandwich." He pulled the Oriental to him while the Mex squealed and wrapped her arms around both. They began to stumble in an irregular circle.

They look like a revolving bruise, Bjorn thought. Yellow, black, and brown.

"May I come in?"

He had hardly heard Nita's voice against the noise, but now stood to grab the hand of the young woman he paired with for his leave. She wore belted poly, slick and stamped with rose and yellow patterns. A red sash advertised her "taken" status.

She snuggled her body up to his, guiding his hand to the back of her waist, then stood on her toes to kiss his jaw line.

Bjorn breathed her faint perfume, felt her high breast press against his arm. He hugged her close and gently nuzzled her auburn hair. "Hi, sweetheart."

She grinned up at him. "How was your bath and massage?"

"Exhausting. I thought the girls drained me of all ambition, but now that you're here, I'm not so sure."

"Dinner and the show will start in about an hour. Are you going formal, in your dress uniform?"

"What about you?"

"I hoped you might help me decide what to wear."

As they walked to her room, he thought how unfair it was that the complexities of modern life made formal education so important. Achievers ignored determination, ethics, humor, and social ability when they passed out resources. Bjorn hugged Nita. And they didn't care about <u>charm.</u>

Chapter 14

In the early summer of 2096, while Sergeant Benjamin Bjorn enjoyed his leave in old San Diego...

"I won't change my mind," Mr. Peter Plant said to young Con Wagoner, chairman of the San Angeles megacity's resident's council. "I'm de-certifying the ghetto government you run."

Con held his big frame still in the show cubicle of the HHR building, but his lean face would display unfriendly lines, he knew. "You'll run your wards through that corrupt killer, Segund?"

The Achiever caressed his long, oily hair. "He'll keep you Welfies quiet, that's all I care about. Neither Washington nor I want to hear any more squeals about your problems."

"But women and children starve!"

Plant only shrugged.

The laser fence between the two of them sparkled with reflections from the moisture of their words.

Con bit his lip to force back rage. HHR had squeezed all the food-float from the ghetto. A vegpro packet could buy a married woman for a night, maybe a murder; vegpro brew was almost unobtainable. An epidemic of deficiency diseases had started.

"Food's not the only problem," he said. "The homeless kill to empty a cubby. Power outages keep-in the midwives at night. The ghetto's new shadows give happy hunting to our bad men. You must provide more resources."

"Your complaints only bore me," Plant calmly replied. "The solution is not more rations and money, but less people. Since the residents' council won't eliminate undesirables so others can eat and find shelter, I must find alternative leaders."

He slid his rear back so he sat straight. "Now, if you tell that cloud-walking girl friend of yours to slide down my rainbow, I'll see that Segund lets you personally alone."

Con forced himself to sit still. He didn't have time to recover from a punishment.

Mr. Plant shrank back against his seat at the hatred he apparently saw in Con's face. Then he smiled, perfect teeth glinting in the harsh light of the interview cubicle. "See?" he said. "You aren't friendly. Yet I am an Achiever boss!" Plant heaved forward quickly, like a fat duck about to peck a slug. "Don't worry about what I should do, Welfie. Worry about yourself."

Con's seat rose and the bottom rotated down to vertical. He had difficulty gaining his balance.

"Leave!"

In a moment, Con limped into the hallway, and then paused to let leg pain subside. He used the time to curse the cap on medical rations. After Segund and his gang's brutal visit to their cubby a month earlier, Con saved his father's life by transferring to him his own medical quota. He'd have this crippled shank forever.

"Move along," the wall monitor commanded.

Jami and Dad looked questioningly at him outside the HHR building's security perimeter. They both carried full bags.

He shook his head.

He wished Will Maestri were in town. The smart little vote-buyer had Washington connections. But Con couldn't wait for him to return from the Mexican wards, from the party at the end of his nephew's leave. Con believed that ghetto gangs would eliminate those on HHR's "dissident" list very soon. Dad and he, and most of the current residents' council would be on that list.

Jami walked beside him. Her high-breasted figure, strong nose and chin, smooth olive skin, and glossy black hair drew glances, as always. She passed her bulky bag to him.

His father gripped Con's arm with his free hand, squeezed, and then let go. Now a shadow of the imposing man he'd once been, Dad Wagoner weaved as he walked away. Yellow-white hair splayed off his head and heavy brows sheltered sunken eyes.

Con wished Billy Joe had turned out more like their dad, inside especially. His brother was a druggie, however, whose moods swung between high and low, from dangerously hyper to self-pityingly depressed. Mostly the latter, these days. Drugs were in short supply, too.

Billy Joe had told him he was crazy, wouldn't help.

Con led Jami across the street, breathing mist spewed by hydrogen-powered delivery trucks. He weaved through a mob of aimless Welfies, then stepped up over the curb and confronted Segund's eight-story headquarters. Flush with its neighbors, graphite mesh covered the doorway and the few lower windows. Only the absence of people sitting against its wall made the structure unusual.

He nodded at the men who set up a red plastic fence and warning signs around a nearby utility manhole.

"I leave you here," Jami shouted in his ear. "You know what I think of this madness." Her slick, blue blouse rose and fell rapidly, and she kept her eyes focused several inches below his.

Con reached into the bag and made sure the small crossbow was still cocked.

Jami had rejected him as a poor mating risk. Now she damned him for starting something that justified her judgment. Illogical.

"Mr. Plant asked about you," Con said.

She raised her arm as if to strike him, then pivoted and strode away.

He thought she might be crying. If he hadn't more pressing things to do, he might cry also.

Con walked up to the door mesh, peered at the heavy-set female guard behind it. "Segund in?"

"Not for you."

The woman wore a waxed mustache that lay above thin, dark lips. She cut her black hair man-like. People called her No-pity Rose.

The guard grinned and moved closer to the screen. She pursed her lips to spit.

Con poked the rod he'd tipped with a knifepoint between the mesh and pulled the crossbow's trigger.

"Ah-gh-gh!" No-pity grasped the shaft that protruded from her breastbone, tried to scream around the torrent of blood that gushed from her mouth, and fell writhing to the floor.

Dad stepped from where he stood flat against the building's side and pushed Con away. He stuck the open side of the can he held to the lock, then leaned back and kicked it. A puff of smoke accompanied the bang from the homemade explosive. Neither the plume nor the sound was significant enough to attract bystanders.

Con pushed the bent screen door open and entered. He found No-pity's multi-purpose army gun behind the door and turned on its targeting system. He nodded and Dad limped hurriedly away.

Inside, Con turned at a noise to his left and saw a man exit into the hall.

"What happened to your vital signs on my read-out, No-pity?" the dial-watcher shouted. Then: "Jesus Christ!"

Con shot him with a precision guided round that would impact the hottest spot, his heart.

He glanced up the empty stairwell as he limped toward the man he'd just killed. In most tenements, people would sit on the stairs, play with children, and maybe buy and sell. However, air conditioning, unusual in the ghetto, kept the residents in their apartments in Segund's building.

He skirted the dead guard, stepped past the man's indented sensor station, and opened a door. A holovision platform dominated the room he looked into. Around it, Con recognized many of Segund's gang members. Obese, bearded, middle aged men and heavy, ugly women ate fried potatoes as they watched a pornographic drama. Many carried guns slung over their shoulders or weapons leaned beside them on the floor. An aisle led to a handleless door in the rear.

Smoke and incense filled the air, coarse grunts and sighs assaulted his ears, and revulsion nauseated his stomach. Did he really have to do this?

Con backed into the hall and flicked his gun's control to "SHORT RANGE AREA WEAPON." Breathing hard and frowning at his stupid feeling of guilt, he stuck the short gun into the room, pointed its muzzle at the ceiling, and pulled the trigger.

His shoulder hurt from the recoil and his ears rang with the loud bang. His stomach was tight.

Con waited a moment and then entered the room again. A roar of screams and groans greeted him. Straining mouths and thrashing limbs filled his eyes.

He vomited, spewing mostly stomach acid against a flat-screen workstation near the door.

"Puke your guts out, Con," a voice shouted. "Know fear, you ghetto idiot!"

By now, Segund must have sealed the entrance to his private office. The bastard cowered in an armored box, while he started a broadcast conversation.

The gang boss would also be shouting through his command circuit at thugs in other rooms and ordering them into the hall.

The holovision platform in the middle of the blood-spewed room emptied of media drama. Segund's standing, three-dimensional image appeared instead. A wide, yellow mustache cut his bald head by a third, while slitted yellow eyes and scraggly brows cut it into another third. He wore red velveteen, maybe the chameleon kind that fit color to emotion. Achiever clothes, anyway.

"Don't go, Con." His voice now was smooth, almost syrupy.

Con stood quietly.

"The raid on you a month ago was supposed to be a learning experience," Segund said. "You took education badly." His eyes slid back and forth, never fixed for long on anything.

Con wondered whether the bastard had anyone else in the room back there. Or in the cells below.

The gang boss shook his fist. "You're stupid, Con. Stupid. Welfies trust you and your father. That's useful. You could do okay, if you only cooperated with the king and me."

Jami also thought him stupid--to try to change ghetto conditions, first as head of the residents' council and now through violence. And Billy Joe called him an idiot.

"Say something, Con."

Segund tried to keep Con here, while Con stayed to keep Segund there. Ironic.

Con heard four, loud, sledgehammer blows to the building's outside wall. Dad's men had broken through to Segund's holding cells, cut the sixteen inch, high pressure, hydrogen gas main, installed a timed igniter, and sealed the entrance they made.

They figured that the steel flooring under Segund would act like a giant hydraulic ram when the hydrogen detonated.

He changed his weapon's setting to "ANTI-PERSONNEL CLUSTERS, VARIABLE RANGES." Grimacing at the need to commit more murders, he stuck its muzzle through the hall door and fired four times, waited ten seconds, then hobbled out.

Con exited the building as it heaved in a tremendous explosion. He fell, stood, and then fell again, after mistakenly putting weight on his bad leg. Tired, he thought. Wrung out.

His shoes were red with blood and smelled of the shit that dying men released.

Dad and his two helpers joined him in the torrent of people escaping the blast site. As he crossed the street in the crush, Con wondered whether Mr. Plant would be smart enough and act soon enough to save himself.

Con expected the Welfare King to stay in his headquarters after his fellow Achievers left their presumably invulnerable offices by jump jets for the suburbs. He would want to coordinate the hunt for Con.

#

"We ought to take our fake internal passports and ramjet out of here," Dad said after they reached their "safe" cubby.

Neither of them could travel fast anywhere. Dad's knee was badly bruised from the recoil of the lock-opener. Once the adrenalin had worn off, the old man limped as badly as Con.

"Don't get nervous on me now."

The squalid little cubby in the tenement seemed crowded with only the three of them. He and Dad occupied the armchairs in front of the holovision platform, while dark Toby sat alongside its controls.

Toby couldn't turn away from his appended data screen. Relief that Segund was gone and reports of HHR counter-strikes flooded-in from residents, as did queries for information from other ghettos up the coast.

"A punishment company hits our old block," Toby reported. "A millimeter wave clanger shut down all electricity. Armor with laser blinders cordons the surrounding streets."

"I was born nervous, son," Dad answered Con,

"and became more so when I saw how you were turning out."

Con grinned at that. Punishment teams publicly whipped his father maybe twelve times in the man's fifty years. Most people didn't really blame them. Other men's acts that earned punishment--robbery, rape, and murder--were normal, but spitting on Achievers or demonstrating in front of ration centers? That was crazy. He had asked for trouble.

Jami slid in, past a hallway guard.

"General curfew," Toby announced. "Everybody off the streets. Mobile laser blinders will fire jolts at eyes."

The holovision flickered on as central authority bypassed the off switch. That authority appeared in the pudgy person of Mr. Plant. Standing with his fists clenched, he gravely damned the ghetto violence started by the chairman of the residents' council and placed a reward for all of its members, big ones for Con and his father.

Con watched Jami. She was stiff-faced, but her eyes darted to his and then fled back.

"I'm glad you made it," she whispered.

He felt remarkably good. Others wouldn't realize the significance of Segund's execution yet, what it had started, but...

The holovision platform emptied.

He stepped up to where Plant had strutted, stopped in the focus of the laser and its split beam. "Okay, Toby," he said. "Tag on to Plant's transmission; put me into ghetto cubbies."

He'd have to make this quick.

"Good evening, fellow Welfies," Con said. "I'm Con Wagoner, Chairman of the San Angeles Residents' Council. HHR has cut rations below the minimum on which we can live. Since many of us will die anyway and the rest of us may wish to if the Achievers have their way, we're rebelling. Help us fight the bastards.

Check with your tenement bosses. They'll soon know what you can do to help."

He nodded at Toby. "Terminate," he ordered.

"Not pretty," Dad said, "but it ought to do."

"I'm sorry," Con said to Jami, "but I must continue to take risks. Tonight."

Jami pulled the door open. "Why pretend?" she whispered. "You don't care what I think. You can't win, but will destroy yourself and everyone who loves you." She strode out, crying again, and slammed the door behind her.

#

"I now believe you're serious, Con," Fifty-two Smith said.

The Welfie leader was black, bearded, and ringed in ears and nose. Small, too, like most Welfies.

"Dad and I will go in," Con answered.

"Don't need to. Squashing Segund showed us what you've got between your legs. Who'd take over if anything happened to you?"

Con surveyed the members of the Black Demon gang who milled around in the tenement lobby. The gang, about thirty in number, carried knives, clubs, and home made cross bows like the one he had used. "We have to do this," he said to them all when they quieted. "We can't stop now. Mr. Plant will put people through the mind vomits to find those who've supported me. He'll give you a spineless Residents' Council. Whoever he puts in charge of the streets will spread your women, murder the homeless, and slaughter gangs that don't tithe."

Violence had an inevitable escalation, Con thought. If he hadn't taken the first step and killed Segund... But the men here didn't blame him. They demanded change, too.

"Dad's worked on Billy Joe," he said. "My brother's willing to risk the big send-off and has convinced some of his pals to go along. A matter of wiring them just high enough and pointing. Toby will tell us when Dad's ready."

His stomach knotted. He moved his mind off his brother.

This was the third gang he'd talked to, all now positioned in a tenement arc before the HHR building. He'd go in with Fifty-two and his men.

Someone's daughter danced from one of the rooms, "Toby says our druggies go to the entrance," she reported. "He hears only orders from machine guards so far."

Con picked up the white, reflective shield of paper, fitted it over his left arm and followed Fifty-two out.

#

"The Rollers wouldn't let me go in with Billy Joe," Dad said, his face wet. "He was my son; he needed to know I loved him enough to die with him. Christ, I talked him into taking the risk!"

"You know the Rollers were right," Con said, crying too. "We need you."

They stood in shadows before the entrance to the HHR building, periodically wincing at the shriek and glare of red strobe alarms. Billy Joe and the other druggies had used home made bombs and careless valor to clear the guard gate and open the entrance. Burned and bleeding bodies lay on the cement walkway around a smashed, stolen truck. The interrogation booth leaned over, ripped apart by an explosion, and the dented steel gate had collapsed.

Beyond the destroyed gate, more dead sprawled near the concrete vehicle barriers. Automatic guns firing from the building's facade had taken out these Welfies, Con guessed. Their bodies were torn and stinking and their abandoned, laser-reflecting shields flickered under the red strobe flashes.

Explosive stuck to the steel doors had blown them open, while brave men darted in to neutralize the guns that poked through the outside wall.

Dad sighed and wiped his face. He nodded at Billy Joe's body at the entrance to the guard shack. His son's lower skull was shattered, his jaws gone, arms torn and broken by the impact of hollow-pointed bullets. He apparently carried explosive in his mouth for his last charge. "Before Billy Joe led the attack," Dad said, "he told me he gave you a hard time 'cause he was jealous. But he loved you. Said to tell you."

The Chinese gang held the streets, although its members would initially hide from armor that returned from enforcing curfew. They would kill any HHR punishment squad member who dismounted and tried to help Mr. Plant, however. And Welfies had ways to get at stationary vehicles while the armored cars paused to reload shotgun batteries emptied from long range at Welfie bands. Daring individuals would paint over vision blocks, drop explosives into vents, or set off charges placed between wheels and axles.

Con knew he could count on an isolated battle. At least until HHR aircraft appeared.

Fifty-two's men had followed the Holy Rollers. The little leader ordered two warriors to guard but keep Con back.

Billy Joe rested. *He'd been a mess ever since Mother died.* Con wiped his nose with the back of an arm.

Con walked forward now. Bodies littered the halls. Rollers and Demons. Con's men had smashed sensors while computer-controlled guns killed their fellows. Others held their breath while stuffing a gas port, then contorted in agony on the floor. Each wave gained a corridor, and new warriors kept coming forward.

The lights went out; the alarm strobes and siren shut off. Con stopped in blackness.

"Hot damn!" Dad exclaimed. "We've reached the central power tap. That finishes the automatic defenses."

Both Holy Roller and Demon protectors kept them there until torches came in from the rear. Certain of success now, Dad went back for the rest of the Residents' Council.

Con picked his way forward through dead and wounded until he arrived at the grand, two story lobby to the Achiever executive suite. Jonesy, the Rollers' second in command, held a light overhead. Maybe fifteen men watched the perimeter, half of them dripping blood. The facing wall would be steel, the door composite armor.

Fifty-two walked through a door in the right wall. He carried a multi-purpose infantry rifle, same as the gun Con took from No-Pity and used in attacking Segund's lair. His men crowded behind him, some with torches, others carried weapons seized from the HHR armory.

"Put the big rockets as far back as you can," Con said to Fifty-two. "Distance will give them the velocity they need to punch through."

"Stupid, stupid Welfie." Plant's voice resounded from speakers hidden in the lobby's corners. Apparently the Achiever quarters held a back-up generator. "You're even more stupid than I thought. You'll go down in books as an example of the culling the human race needs."

Con still was wet-eyed over Billy Joe. Now he trembled.

"The government will send in the Corps," Plant continued. "The Marines will hang you all from streetlights."

"We have weapons now, Plant," Con answered. "Tomorrow we'll have your armor, since their drivers won't find clear streets for escape. In a week we'll be in all the Achiever offices in the megacity and control all communications. We'll put up barricades and start the manufacture of weapons. Your little, high technology

Marine Corps will get a nose bleed if it tries to climb over a pile of forty million people."

Con hoped he was right about that. He knew little about military matters. "Better tear down some of these offices," he told Fifty-two. "Get the rockets back a good thirty meters."

"We control the food, water, and power!" screamed Plant. "You can't deal with the vegpro companies in the mid-west or the water electrolyzer combines on the coasts!"

"Why do you think the Achiever government will let us starve and do without for long?" Con shouted back. "Why let us develop a fury that'll slop into their suburbs? Why start a civil war that might expand to all the megacities? You're the one who's stupid, Plant. Someone smarter than you will negotiate rather than order in the Corps. In a month we'll eat better and run our own affairs."

I hope I'm right about that, Con thought. If I am, we'll then force some unpleasant decisions on the Achievers. Like shipping meat to the ghettos for the first time in years. Like merit schools that let bright children leave the ghetto. Like identical medical ceilings for both classes. Like funding new tenements.

He would need Will Maestri's negotiating smarts badly if he survived the next critical week.

Dad showed up with the Council and nearby apartment house bosses. He also had Toby in tow, busy with a battery-powered, cannibalized camera. The self-taught comm. expert had contacted a media network and now transmitted pictures of the invaded HHR building and of the Welfie men who bore guns and missiles.

"I've got Jami," Plant said, after a long silence.

Con said nothing; his mouth had become too dry.

"Just a harmless interrogation, Wagoner," Plant shouted. "I didn't get to chemicals, even. But I won't be so nice if you come in after me. I'll kill her."

Fifty-two and Jonesy stood beside him, with Dad. "He doesn't get off, Con," Fifty-two murmured. "Too many scores."

"What do you suggest, Plant?" Con yelled.

"Go back! You've made your point. Let me and my two bodyguards climb up to the grid. I'll call for a rescue jump ship."

"No good," Con answered, not bothering to check with the others. "We're setting up the building-buster rockets now."

Con heard panting, slaps, and a swallowed scream.

"She's here, Wagoner, even if she's too stupid to beg for her life. Think again."

Con bared his teeth and then sighed. "All I can do is maybe make sure you live a little longer, Plant. You can hope that our emotions cool, that your bosses bargain for you."

Jonesy shook his head.

"Open the door," Con shouted. "Let me in. If you throw down your weapons, you can walk out with me."

Fifty-two put his hand on Con's arm.

After a long silence, Plant shouted, "Just you," and the thick door opened, light spilling out in a wedge.

Con turned to Fifty-two. "The past, with his crimes, is gone," he said. "This is now. Let me save her."

His eyes were wet; his chest pumped air into his lungs; he crouched.

Fifty-two released him. "I guess a leader has to be pig-headed occasionally," he said. He turned to spit on the floor.

Jonesy, a big, older man with a lined, dark face shrugged his shoulders. "You're taking a chance to trust him."

When Con walked through the door, he entered another two-story lobby. One wall swam with apparently living butterflies that swooped over wind blown flowers.

A second shone with tiny lights and reflectors and poured out a changing kaleidoscope of color. Mr. Plant stood against the third, the facing wall, which held a door surrounded by concentric, expanding rings that flowed through the color spectrum. Above it moved a frieze of figures, the greats of human history, Con guessed. The sculpture spiraled up to the ceiling and flowed around the sides.

Plant gripped an electric stinger.

Con's girl stood between two guards, who held her lightly. She shook her arms free, walked over to Con, and then stood on her toes to kiss his cheek. "I give up," she said. "'For better or for worse.'"

Con put his arm around Jami and turned her until they both faced the Welfare King.

Plant smiled and a wisp of air signaled the closing door. "Stupid," he said. "I diagnosed a bad case of it before. This time your gullibility is almost terminal." Plant's normally sallow face showed patches of pink in the cheeks.

"I thought we had an agreement."

"Did I ever say I'd walk out with you? Now I have a hostage whom everyone out there cares for." He waved his free hand in the direction of Dad, Fifty-two, Jonesy and the rest. "Tell them to move out of the building. They can hear. I've left on the speaker pick-ups."

Con leaned his head back, as if he shouted for distance. "Dad and friends, shortly I'll attack Plant and his guards." He glanced at his girl. "Jami will go after them, too."

He eyed the Achiever HHR boss, felt contempt replace his fear. "I will not give in to him," he continued. "Plant will have to put me down. Go ahead and shoot the rockets with the big warheads. When you get in, what you find will tell you what to do."

Con hugged Jami, then pushed her away, towards one of the guards. "I love you, honey. I'm sorry there'll be no 'better.'"

He walked toward the other guard. Jami swore and stepped forward with him. Her face was pale, but she hunched over, apparently preparing to leap.

"Wait!" shrieked Mr. Plant.

Chapter 15

"The audit people are after you, Bjorn," the staff captain said from behind his desk a few days later, at the Marine base outside of San Angeles. "They've heard you had too good a time on your recent leave: three weeks at one of the most expensive Rest Houses in the country. You and your artilleryman. Since we gave you no action bonus from your Argentine adventure, where'd you get the money?"

"Civilian generosity, Sir," Bjorn answered. He kept his body in military "at ease" but felt his guts spasm. The damned audit ankle-biters could call in the Marine Corps Adjutant General!

He felt defenseless in his soft dress blues. Authority could take away his rate, put him in a penal company, maybe even bust him back to the ghetto. Not the garrote, though, he thought. He had the medal.

"It isn't my business, I guess," the officer said. "But I'd hate to lose you."

The captain was a typical Achiever son of a bitch. Didn't care what happened to a Welfie enlisted man, just worried about his own inconvenience.

"But that's for later," the man said, and waved a print-out. "Now, I've an escort job. A Washington heavy-weight wants to go into the San Angeles ghetto and negotiate with the residents' council. There's a rebellion going on in there."

That's not news, Bjorn thought. "What's wrong with an escort by the state police?"

"The politician will have her own bodyguards. She wants a uniformed rep from the Corps, though, and asked for you by name."

"She the President's sister?"

"Yeah. You must have wowed her when you pulled her out of that hostage fix." The captain gave him an easy smile. "The colonel says you're to reconnoiter while there, in case we get ordered in."

"Special action bonus?" Bjorn asked, wondering at his own nerve.

"No. This is diplomacy, not war."

At least I'll be close to the Ambassador, Bjorn thought. My sex drive made me hunger for Angel's and got me into this fix; my smart-ass mouth has to get me out.

#

"Hello, Bent Brain," the Ambassador said as she descended from the government ramjet in the late afternoon. "Have you spent all the bonus I thought I gave to charity?"

"Yes, Ma'am," Bjorn answered.

She wore a dark brown suit, a string of red beads, and a folded red handkerchief she was too important to ever use for its designed purpose. She'd pulled her black hair tight into a bun and wore no make-up on her hard face.

Two White House security men accompanied her, both squat Latinos.

"Walk beside me," she ordered.

He stepped out at her left. "Why me?" he asked and gestured at the two men who moved ahead of them, hands loose at their sides, eyes roving restlessly. "I'm a marine, not a bodyguard."

"I needed someone who wore your pretty suit. You'll remind the Welfies of their alternative. And, you had the better of me once. You've a certain low cunning I might find useful in here."

"Yes, Ma'am."

Or did she want to punish him--for the killing of her lover and for his subsequent con job? Did she think she owed him something?

They stopped at the hydrogen-powered van that awaited them. The vehicle's hydrogen fuel tank clung like a giant black leech to its back.

"The damned HHR has our country on the edge," the Ambassador said while they waited for her bodyguards to check out the vehicle. Finally, Bjorn joined her in the back. A state police sergeant climbed in behind the steering wheel.

Dusk, the ghetto appeared relaxed and full of the usual aimless people. Only the maze of wrecked trucks that their van threaded through and the captured armored personnel carrier at the first checkpoint were strange.

The people in the San Diego extension of this ghetto had spoken out for the rebellion but there'd been no fighting down there. At least Uncle Will and Nita were safe.

"Will you marines come in to kill your own kind?" asked the giant escort whom they picked up at the checkpoint. Armed Welfies there called him "Dad." He sat in the front seat, now turned and stared at Bjorn from under bushy, white eyebrows.

"Because we enlisted men came out of the ghettos doesn't make us anybody's kind," Bjorn answered. "Marines are a kind of their own."

He held the old fart's eyes until the escort turned forward again.

Night arrived while they drove. The van pulled into a lighted parking area and stopped in front of a big building. Bjorn saw signs of a fight everywhere: bullet holes gaped in a crushed guard shack, laser burns scarred the building's composite walls, and dark, dried blood stained the concrete in long streaks.

When the Ambassador stepped to the pavement, her two bodyguards stayed close. Bjorn followed her and felt water disgorged by the hydrogen-powered vehicle flooding his shoes. Dad grinned at him as he hopped from the front seat and carefully avoided the puddle.

Without warning, pain blanked Bjorn's brain. All nearby lights went out. At the same time, he heard a high-up explosion and felt a shove on his shoulders that made him stagger.

The Ambassador swore as she pushed herself off the concrete. "What the hell was that?"

"Microwave bomb!" Bjorn answered. "Someone's overhead, coming down." He pivoted. "Take us under cover," he ordered Dad. He grabbed the man's arm. "Not into your headquarters, but over there." He pointed to a dark tenement. "Now!"

"Go to hell."

Bjorn spun Dad, wrenched a spindly arm behind the man's body, and marched him across the street to the block of ghetto buildings. The Ambassador and her two bodyguards followed.

"This is a set-up," Dad said in front of a barred entrance. He turned his head and snarled at Bjorn, "HHR must have timed the attack for your arrival, when the bastards knew Con would be inside and you could help."

"Being the trigger doesn't make us party to the scheme," Bjorn replied. "If you were right about me scheduled to help, I'd be in your headquarters right now, taking out door guards."

He knew an officer up above had their heat signatures on his infrared scope. He would estimate the danger that they posed for the assault team. Maybe he listened, too.

"They'll chew us up with heat-seeking flechettes if you don't stop screwing around, old man," he whispered in Dad's ear. "The man in charge will want to clear his operating table. Get us inside!" He shoved the bastard toward the locked, mesh door.

More curses, more struggling.

Bjorn finally let go of Dad and leaped for the nearest bodyguard. He struck the nape of the man's neck and then held the limp body as a shield between himself and the other member of the White House detail while he slipped the guard's automatic from a shoulder holster.

He pointed the weapon at the free bodyguard. "You've got a count of two to drop your gun."

"Do what he says," shrieked the Ambassador. "He's a psychopath. Do it!"

The Latin let his weapon slip and looked away.

Bjorn dropped the man he held, tripped the Ambassador, and then kneeled to push her flat.

"You do what I say, too, if you want to stay alive," he told her. He gripped her arms, leaned close. "Lie on your hot belly, head down. Let these bodyguards protect you. That's what they're paid for."

He moved the limp guard so the man covered one side of her. Bjorn stood, and then shoved his gun into the other guard's ear, brought him to the pavement, too. "If she dies and you don't, I'll kill you," he whispered and pulled the bodyguard so both he and his partner completely shielded the Ambassador.

"Tough duty, friend," Bjorn added and then turned.

Dad had shoved off. Past time for Bjorn to do the same.

He sprinted for the van, slid under it as he heard a low explosion, then the patter of flechettes when they hit the vehicle's top and surrounding pavement. Only a few detonated. Those had found and torn apart the hot engine compartment.

Fabric rustled in the night, control surfaces creaked. Bjorn imagined a glider stall above him, slide backwards and then fly forward again. Finally, a high-winged people carrier coasted to a landing not five meters from the van.

Good pilot, lousy tactical commander, Bjorn thought. According to doctrine, the man in charge should have sanitized the entire area before landing. To take out the van and Bjorn wasn't enough. The Achiever officer should have launched a cluster at the entrance to the tenement, where heat signatures showed live targets. And done it earlier. Bjorn was damn lucky he wasn't dead.

Maybe the officer picked up the Ambassador's title with sound magnifiers, though. The officer might then want instructions from higher up before he killed the President's sister.

Bjorn heard another glider land on the roof of the headquarters. The jump jet platform up there would make that operation easy.

A squad of eight men in composite armor corselets stepped out of the glider near him. They wore no insignia and carried no lights. One attacker nodded his head as if receiving radio instructions, and then turned to aim his assault rifle across the street, in the Ambassador's direction.

Bjorn shot the man in the knee with his appropriated handgun, scooted behind a tire as another attacker leaned down to point his assault rifle under the car. The man he'd wounded dropped his gun, crouched on one knee, and held the other. "Shit!" he whined.

"Shoot the other armored bastard below the waist!" Bjorn yelled back toward the prostrate but conscious bodyguard. He tried to bring his gun around the tire without exposing his head.

The White House bodyguard would be antsy. He'd have picked up the gun he'd dropped and might be ready for action. Maybe Welfies in the apartment houses, hanging around in entryways, watching, might help. Bjorn's stomach cramped.

No one interfered and the attacker fired his assault rifle.

The flechette cluster skidded under the car and detonated ten meters on the other side. "Whoof!"

Bjorn perspired as he aimed his gun and then lifted the muzzle when he saw the attacker run to join his unit before it entered the shattered headquarters. Bad training. Never leave alive at your back an enemy who's armed. The attacker with the shattered knee now curled up in a fetal ball. He cried. These guys weren't marines.

"Come, Sergeant," the Ambassador called from in front of the tenement block across the street.

Bjorn picked up the downed man's assault rifle as he passed. He was the last one inside the tenement's now opened door and stopped in the entry hall.

The Ambassador strode in the wavering, shadow-filled light of hydrogen torches to where Dad used a wall phone. "Hang up!" she shouted. "I must talk to Washington!"

Bjorn breathed hard and glanced around. "Here," he said, and handed the handgun to the dazed bodyguard he'd taken it from, then backed against the wall next to the doorway. He held the assault rifle with its butt on the floor.

After the Ambassador tore the phone away from Dad, she had trouble getting through. "There's a priority message to you from Marine Corps headquarters that blocks me in the local military communication exchange," She yelled at Bjorn. "Something about reporting to the adjutant general's office immediately."

"That's spider droppings from the other deal," he shouted back. "Tell them to quit the investigation, or you'll never get through."

She glared at him and then snapped orders into the phone.

A scraping, sliding sound outside signaled that another glider landed.

Welfies trickled into the entry, from the back. They were warriors, some armed with first class weapons they'd probably seized from HHR dead.

A slight black man with ear and nose rings and tight black curls that hung down to his shoulders jumped in front of Bjorn when he drifted toward a clump of men around Dad. "What you doing here, Marine?"

The man had an assault rifle too, but Bjorn feared more the pared-down kitchen knife in his belt. The Welfie would know how to use the latter.

"He came with the President's sister," Dad said, turning. "More important, he shot one of the bastards. That's why I told the door guard to let them in."

"The gate-crashers aren't Marines," Bjorn said.

"He's right," the Ambassador said and pushed her way into the group. "My guess is they're a private venture of Health and Human Resources. The President is about to melt down with anger. He told me he had no warning that violence would replace negotiation."

"How long before he can do something here?" the black asked. "The bastards must figure to take our leaders to Washington, then squeeze till their backbone jelly runs."

"My son Con won't give in," the old man said. "He's already proved he's stubborn."

"If they take him, this place comes apart," the black man told the Ambassador. "You won't negotiate nothing."

"My brother's screaming at HHR headquarters."

"If you're not in this, Marine, why don't you save Con?" the black asked Bjorn. "Let's see what you can do." He grinned and his men laughed.

"Come on, Fifty-two," Dad protested. "It's Con in there, and the Residents' Council. Jami, too. Be serious."

"We don't have surprise this time, like we did when we took out the Welfare King," the black answered. "Saving Con and the rest of our people won't be easy. I'll lose a lot of warriors, probably lose the council, too."

"Do you know Will Maestri, the vote buyer?" Bjorn asked.

They all stared at him.

"I'm his nephew from down south."

The tension eased.

"Maybe I can help as a military advisor."

"What do you say we do, then?" the black asked.

"Send men to the roofs around the building with enough firepower to take out reinforcements coming in by glider," Bjorn answered. "Put people and your captured armored personnel carriers on the streets around headquarters. Let the assault party know there's no way out of here on the ground."

Fifty-two turned away and waved to messengers.

"Ask the President to order in fighter cover, Ma'am," Bjorn told the Ambassador. "Fast. Don't let someone extract these guys and their prisoners via attack aircraft and the jump jet platform."

She stared up at him, her eyes narrowed, her thin lips tight.

"Someone high up in HHR ordered one of them to shoot you out there," he said, "in case you're thinking of letting the bastards negotiate from a torture chamber back east."

"The kill order was probably a mistake by an intermediary," she said. "And sometimes closed-fist negotiation works."

"Won't work, here," Bjorn replied. "Too much emotion on the ground. The ghetto will write-off the prisoners and fight whoever tries to take over. I'll bet the rebellion spreads, too."

"Don't try policy, Bent Brain. I don't want your input." Then she smiled. "And you didn't get me to cancel the adjutant general's investigation while I was on the phone."

Bjorn looked away while he regained control. *Bitch*!

He supposed Uncle Will would tell him to back off, that the Welfies as a class hadn't a chance of bettering their situation. But he was one of them, damn it! And, maybe he could wiggle out of his current fix.

"You owe the HHR something," he finally told the Ambassador. "Also, if Washington successfully yanks out these people's leaders, the Welfies here might squash you as pay-back."

She glared at him and then stomped over to the phone. "I'll see what my brother says."

Bjorn lay down near the doorway and inched around until he could see the headquarters entryway across the street. Hydrogen gas from the gutted van burned like an Olympic torch, casting light over the side of the guard shack, on the large concrete tubs that kept vehicles from coming close, and over the discarded gliders.

He guessed that invaders from the follow-on glider had knocked out their wounded man and dragged him into the entryway. He saw what could be a foot there.

No perimeter. The enemy would fight from the building. Welfies had destroyed or lifted HHR's original defenses, but the assault force would have brought semi-automatic weapons, anti-vehicle missiles, and sensors. No apertures in the higher stories provided overwatches that he had to worry about, however. Snipers on the roof could be a problem if he took too long.

Fifty-two kneeled behind him. "What now?" he asked.

"We wait," Bjorn said. "If the President orders local Air Force units here before the enemy pushes a transport jump jet through--it'd take two loads to get everybody out--then we starve them into surrendering."

"We'd be fucking insane to depend on anyone in Washington."

Bjorn turned his head to look at the black man. They stared at each other. "I'll think about how I'd get in," Bjorn said. "Why don't you ask the Ambassador for my help?"

#

The President's sister finally squatted beside him. Strands of hair had come loose from the bun and her expensive, tailored suit was spotted with dirt. Still, in the wavering, yellow light she looked as hard and controlled as ever.

"The Air Force wants consensus with HHR before it will interfere," she said. "My brother's going through hell, even with his political supporters in the Pentagon. None of them want to give a Welfie rebellion a chance."

"The HHR transport will come soon," Bjorn said. "Attack planes will clear nearby roofs. There's not much time."

The Ambassador pressed her lips together for a moment. "If this ghetto stands firm even without its leaders," she said, "my brother says the hard people will take over in Washington. They'll move him and me out, one way or another, and send the Corps into San Angeles. God knows what will happen, then. People in the ghettos are more ready to die than they were in the sixties."

Her operative phrases, Bjorn thought, were "move him and me out, one way or another." This rebellion had opened a crack between the President and the rest of the government, one that frightened the Ambassador.

"He says we can't risk civil war," she continued. "We must negotiate a deal that'll disarm both sides. The Welfies won't even talk to me now, though. Except to say they want your help."

Bjorn sighed. "I don't know whether I can do any good," he said. "I'm as good as arrested because I spent the special action bonus I deserved but you kept from me. That makes me insecure. I'm like a recruit in a minefield. Any move I make might be wrong. I don't think I could fight well."

She glowered at him.

Bjorn tried for his dumb-ass, innocent smile.

"All right, you simpering snake," she finally said.

"I'll tell Washington to okay the transfer of your bonus to Angel's, no matter that the place is a moral abscess instead of a charity."

He made sure not to strut as he walked beside her to the phone.

"Thank you, Ma'am," he said, as she hung up. "Now, if I'm to lead an unsupported war party here, I'll want another special action bonus. Could you call them back and authorize that too, please, Ma'am?"

#

The captured armored personnel carrier was a police type. The turret that fired the missiles and automatic weapons gave it a high, bulky profile. But the chemical, mid-power laser had a half-full tank and an automatic mode.

The APC wouldn't last long, but long enough, Bjorn thought. He put it in gear and drove around the corner. He braked when he had a clear view of the headquarter building's fire-lit entrance.

He flicked on the laser that would sweep the side of the building and send blinding pulses when it detected a reflection from eyeballs or glass, then punched off a building-buster missile, grabbed a handful of flares, and dived out the open hatch.

"Haul ass," he yelled at Dad. He yanked the assault rifle from the old man's hands and sprinted toward the entryway, now dust-filled from the missile's detonation.

Fifty-two and five of his men joined him as he passed the burning van.

Bjorn fired a short-range flechette cluster through the blasted-open doorway, then fell on his stomach and slid to the side. Fifty-two and his men, and Dad finally, crashed down behind him.

Bjorn quickly scrabbled in, grabbed a foot of the armored body, and pulled the soldier back out.

"Send a cluster in every ten seconds," he directed Fifty-two, who had moved up beside him.

"That'll keep the look-outs in their side rooms."

Maybe that wasn't necessary, he thought, as he stripped the enemy's body of its corselet and helmet. The screams from laser blinding and the poor firing on his run-in showed that he had hurt the defense.

Machine gun bullets ricocheted off the pavement from a weapon inside.

His assault rifle's flechette cluster quieted the gun.

The wounded attacker's corselet felt loose on him--dangerously so if he took a missile round--and didn't protect his arms and legs. A full set of fitted armor was the right gear for this type of combat.

He pushed Fifty-two aside, fired in a ten-meter range cluster, lobbed in a flare to attract any loose flechettes, stood, and dived through the door.

All the way back to the cross hall, he could see only bleeding, armored torsos. And scraps of flesh.

He slid by each door, while Fifty-two waved his fighters into the rooms. Dad followed three meters behind Bjorn. He carried flechette reloads the Welfies had picked up in their original assault on the Welfare King.

The old man was slow, a big target, and would find no armor to fit him. "You're not keeping me out of the action," he said back in Bjorn's planning session when Fifty-two pointed all that out. "Con's the only family I have left!"

At the corridor's end, Bjorn looked back. With the entry cleared, reinforcements now filled the corridor. Fifty-two and a few others donned captured corselets and helmets.

He motioned Fifty-two forward, gave him flares, fiddled with the man's assault rifle. "We fire around the corners at the same time," he said. "Then, you take the left; I'll go right. Use the flares. Put a flechette cluster into each room."

Bjorn held Fifty-two back, waved his gun in the

opening.

An anti-armor missile shrieked by, chest high, followed by the explosion of a flechette cluster on the right.

Bjorn fired, lobbed flares in each direction, let go of Fifty-two, and launched himself into the hall. He flattened on the floor.

Fifty-two fell half on him, but that was okay with Bjorn. The more protection, the better.

After he sent new clusters to detonate in front of doorways, he sprinted down the hall and fired around the next corner.

Agonized screams told him he had finished the poor bastards.

#

Soft music, moving wall colors, the smell of gunpowder, and a dozen of Fifty-two's men filled the two-story lobby in front of the Achievers' offices. Bjorn watched as the black gang leader supervised the placement of launchers back from the wall. The devices used small tripods that could be rotated. The hard target missiles themselves were short, a half a meter in length, but they were Marine issue and packed a warhead that would tear apart almost anything. Earlier, someone cleared out partitions and opened the lobby back a good fifty meters. At its two-story height, the room looked cavernous.

"Armored enemy soldiers on the roof have taken out the APC and now keep anyone else from joining us," Dad said from a communication center in the corner. "The Ambassador wants to talk to you, Sergeant," he added. "She says the enemy's in touch with her from the Achiever center here."

"Shut off your receiver, Dad. Hear me? Now!"

Bjorn started toward the scarred module but stopped when he saw the old man obey.

"If the HHR men can't speak with us, they can't give us a choice, right?" he explained. "If they take to torturing their prisoners, it'll be for their own kicks, not because we won't do what they want."

"We still have to move fast," Fifty-two said, as he stomped up to Dad and Bjorn in a corselet at least two sizes too large. "But I don't like a frontal attack through the wall. The bastards will use our people as shields."

"Yeah," Bjorn said. "How about pointing those missiles at the ceiling instead? Over the communication module here."

Fifty-two stared at him. Then he grinned. "Screw up the jump jet platform first, eh? Then go up through the holes, come down at them?"

Bjorn felt the building tremble, heard a roar from aircraft engine's nozzles. He pulled Dad by the arm and ran back while Fifty-two shouted to his gang.

From the corridor, Bjorn saw the missiles blast off, one by one, and felt shock waves from the warheads that detonated above and in front of him with increased power as each missile's velocity grew with the distance it traveled. His ears rang; dust clouded the far end of the lobby. In a second, though, he could see a crumbling, large hole in the tile and block ceiling, seven meters up, then, through it and further back, a gaping circle in the steel bulkhead that partitioned the Achiever third of the building. Beyond, he viewed only structural scraps of the third floor, and finally, along the slanting path of the missiles, starlight. The last warhead's explosion must have pushed big chunks of concrete before it through the roof.

He heard thrusters pulse, as if a pilot desperately tried to maintain his jump jet's balance. The noise was ragged, uneven. Maybe some of the nozzles didn't fire; maybe concrete spawl had damaged them.

Bjorn heard and felt a thunderous, shaking crash on the roof. The aircraft apparently rolled, scraped forward on its side, its jets roaring. Blue flame belched through the holes.

Then silence.

In a few minutes, Bjorn sat on a parapet with both Dad and Fifty-two. He surveyed the tipped-over jump-jet that protruded beyond the roof. It might fall in a strong wind, he thought. Welfie reinforcements pulled themselves through the ceiling holes and watched the doorway down to the Achiever private offices.

"You guys want to run everything in the ghetto?" he asked. "If so, you need your own military to give you muscle."

"Washington would never agree," Dad growled.

"Don't be so sure," Bjorn answered. "Officer a battalion with ex-Marine Corps non-coms. Put a dumb Welfie sergeant in charge. That might seem safe enough to the Chiefs of Staff in Washington. They'd figure they had more brains than your officers and had a string to them, too.

"Now's the time to try," he said. "While the hard men can't protest too much because of their attack on the President's sister. They'll be too busy apologizing and making excuses to take a strong line. And a peaceful agreement will look good to most of the country."

The President was a compromiser, Bjorn knew; that's what made him a successful politician. And he wanted re-election. He might give on this to gain ten million or so Welfie votes in San Angeles. More elsewhere.

Then Bjorn wondered what Uncle Will would think of his proposal. That "acting without thinking" business had worked okay in tough spots recently. His instincts had been honed by danger. But this... He had no feel for politics.

Bjorn's stomach tightened.

"Sergeant, the Ambassador's on the screen," came a shout. "She says the enemy inside gives up. She wants you to bring her over here."

Bjorn sighed and stood. "I surely am tired of that woman," he said.

#

"I'm glad you succeeded," the Ambassador murmured out the side of her mouth. "You may have saved the country from a civil war. This time I won't screw with your bonus."

He stood aside to let her precede him into the headquarters conference room. She had pushed into her bun the errant strands of hair and brushed the dirt off her suit.

"Thank you, Ma'am."

"Despite your unprincipled demands when you had leverage," she added, giving him one of her hard looks.

He squelched a desire to slap her nice butt as it paraded past him.

The Residents Council, five men and two women, sat on one side of the table, along with Fifty-two and Dad. A good-looking young woman sat against the wall behind the Council's leader.

The Ambassador took one of the chairs opposite them and pointed Bjorn into another.

Soft Achiever music filled the air, and wild beasts that used to occupy western parks gamboled on the walls.

"The attack has made us lose trust," the Council's leader told the Ambassador. "We talk only because of the outstanding help of your sergeant here."

This Con Wagoner was a big, young man who had limped when he walked past Bjorn and had multiple bruises on his right cheek. Bjorn liked his looks.

"Our hacker speaks with the rest of the megacity," the Welfie leader continued. "He says our people prepare for invasion. And, the nearby Achiever suburbs form militia, hire retired military. San Angeles is about to explode."

"Both sides need a quick solution," the Ambassador said. "What's your bottom line?"

"Old ration and budget levels. Formation of a

city-state. Federal subsidies to be processed through the offices of that state."

"Why do San Angeles Welfies deserve control over our charity?" the Ambassador asked.

Wagoner leaned forward. "Listen!" he said. "Automation is like a deadly fungus that sickens more of the work force every year. Welfare isn't charity; it's a measly acknowledgment that you could become Welfies too."

"Never. Machines can't create, nor can they set objectives."

This was an old argument.

Wagoner flung up a hand. "Call welfare tribute, then. Consider us a horde of barbarians you have to pay to keep outside of your suburb frontiers."

"There's still the option of sending in the Corps," the Ambassador replied.

"You don't want that," Wagoner said. "Neither does your brother. We know. Besides, HHR couldn't get something that nasty past Congress right now. And it might set off the other megacities. Anyway, if you want a civil war, better start soon. We're forming our own fighting force here."

He pointed at Bjorn. "And we want him to run it."

Bjorn straightened and sat at attention.

"You must transfer the sergeant and the equipment for a battalion before we'll finally settle. We want to feel safe from hit and run attacks like this last one."

The Ambassador, who sat next to Bjorn, quivered but didn't glance in his direction.

"Call his force a Marine reserve unit, Ma'am," Dad interposed. "The sergeant would be on detached duty for recruitment and training."

The Ambassador turned and stared at Bjorn now. Her face was flushed.

"I don't know whether I'd want to accept that," he said. "I like the special actions I'm assigned, especially the people I meet. But I'll obey orders, of course."

  "Shut up, Bent Brain!" The Ambassador's face was deep red now. "I know you've put them up to this."

  "I'll make my headquarters in old San Diego," Bjorn replied.

Chapter 16

A week later, Will Maestri sat in the broadcasting focus of a beam-split laser at Angel's Rest House while a surrogate Mr. Striker, his image similarly produced thousands of miles away, leaned back in an armchair facing him. Bjorn, his girl friend Nita, and Angel, manager of the Rest House, sat at the side.

The Achiever executive pointed a long finger at Maestri and stared down it as if over a gun barrel. "I expected you to at least control the Mexican wards. Yet they joined this San Angeles rebellion! Was that direct disobedience?"

Maestri threw up his hands. "I'm an advisor to Residents Councils, not their boss."

The HHR chief glowered. "And what advice did you give?"

"I gave none. The Mexes down here are desperate, too. They jumped in with both feet when Wagoner asked for support."

Con was a damn hero in the ghetto, Maestri thought. So was Benjamin, for that matter.

"The idiots! They'll be sorry." Mr. Striker tapped a finger on his knee. "Where were you, anyway? My search program couldn't reach you for a whole week."

"I took time off to relax."

"You never relax. I know you well, remember?" Mr. Striker leaned forward. "I'll tell you what you did. You decided to let events evolve."

He couldn't have stopped Wagoner, even if he'd known the man's intent, Maestri thought. Plant and Segund squeezed Con too hard, would have soon squeezed him dead. Nor could Maestri still the enthusiasm of the Mex wards; he'd have become a traitor if he tried. Then, he anticipated HHR's immediate, violent response, although not Benjamin's successful intervention. Safety lay in distance, he'd thought.

Maestri held himself very still. This was a critical conversation. A kill order might go out at the end of it.

"Criticize me all you want," he finally said. "With Plant gone, however, and with all local HHR workers either dead or hiding in their suburbs, you no longer have reliable representatives in this megacity. You need timely information about what the Welfies think and do. I'm prepared, of course, to serve as your agent."

Mr. Striker snorted.   "Forget it. I know you oppose our current policy and suspect you would help Wagoner if you thought it safe."

Maestri said nothing.

"I don't appreciate your nephew helping the President's sister, either, and his destruction of an HHR punishment platoon enrages me. He must have known whose force he fought."

"He merely obeyed the Ambassador's orders."

"He should have known better."

"Benjamin's only a Corps sergeant, Mr. Striker. He's not political."

"He now commands a Welfie battalion that's only purpose is to oppose HHR intervention." Mr. Striker held up a hand. "I won't argue more. Listen to me. We're at a political watershed. The President agreed to release additional rations for San Angeles ghetto-heads. That agreement, if applied to the rest of the country, will draw down our grain stores so badly that we'll have to either reduce Achiever supplies or cut exports and close factories."

The HHR man looked down at his hands and whispered, "Worse, by agreeing to the local Residents Council's control of rations and a tame military force the President has created in other ghettos a demand for

similar powers. "These arrangements must not stand!
They will ruin our country."

"But what alternative did the President have?"

"Confrontation! He should have sent in the Corps
and slaughtered the Welfies who killed Achievers
performing their duties. He was weak, and he
temporized." Striker leaned forward. "Hear me, now.
The power structure of this country will not let a failure of
internal discipline turn us into a riotous, populist
disaster."

Mr. Striker's lips and cheeks contorted in a snarl.
Then he sat quietly for a moment.

"Surely you're not planning to overthrow the
President?" Maestri asked.

The Achiever sat back and shook his head. "A
coup is not necessary. I'll run against him in November.
We've initiated new control measures in the northern
Californian and eastern ghettos to quiet the agitation.
They'll get me elected."

Although his stomach was tight and his neck
muscles ached, Maestri kept his face bland.

"I'll avert my hand this last time for the sake of old
services." Striker finally said. "Don't try me again."

He glared once more before his image
disappeared.

"Wow," exclaimed Benjamin.

Glancing at his nephew, Maestri thought the
naive look had almost disappeared. "You must hurry to
train your battalion," he said.

Benjamin absently hugged his girl.

Nita had auburn hair and an alabaster body, at
least as much of it as Maestri could see. Young and
vibrant, she acted thrilled with his nephew and appeared
to make every effort to keep him faithful.

"What should we do?" Angel asked.

"Nothing." Maestri replied. "The Corps won't let
HHR mess with your Rest House." He hesitated. "You
might set up a few hide-outs for Benjamin and me,

though. Pick out-of-the-way cubbies in destroyed buildings or old cellars. Supply them."

"I cut a great deal with the Ambassador," Benjamin said. "I've brought over from the Corps the best non-coms I know. They like the officer ranks--even though the privileges aren't the same--and are working hard as hell. The light arms, the vertical take off and landing transports are coming in. And, of course, we've got more recruit applications than we need. The battalion will be pretty deadly by election time. We'd hurt the Corps in a ghetto melee."

One battalion wouldn't be enough to change the Welfie fate, of course. Benjamin and he must develop a strategy to confront a future that now appeared terribly dangerous.

Chapter 17

Major, once Sergeant, Benjamin Bjorn's old Veracruz buddies had a grip on their commands; the exercise at least proved that. Billy Hone's company had penetrated Tommy Hata's perimeter around the old HHR headquarters, but hadn't progressed beyond the first cross-corridor.

There's an unproductive melee inside, Bjorn thought, as he stood outside in the gray, oxygen-poor dawn of the ghetto.

"Okay, Captain Hone, try forcing the entrance from the jump jet grid now. See if we've preoccupied the defense."

Almost immediately, a scout plane careened overhead and spewed flares and chaff, while a transport copter tried to sneak onto the roof. Low power laser beams reached out from the top of the building, however, and triggered beacons that declared on Bjorn's visor the death of each air vehicle.

Third Company fired grapnels from the ground that sailed over the roof's parapet. Then men climbed up the smooth sides of the old HHR building. Thrown bundles of plastic strips that mimicked balls of flechettes fluttered down beside them. Once again, Bjorn's visor declared kills.

A squad tried another explosive concoction on the armored building. The detonation produced a sharp crack that made the crowd of onlookers wince but left no great impression on the material.

"Defense wins again, Major," Master Sergeant Julio Capodonno said.

Bjorn remembered when the wizened little man, a long term private then, led a few men down the stairs of

a defended Mexican farmhouse after silently breaking
through the thatched roof. On that occasion, Bjorn lay
behind an iron table, pinned down by low velocity rifle
bullets. A tricky offense won that time. No maneuver
capable of similar success occurred to anyone now.

Their present defeat would infuriate the men in
the attacking force and make the officers think again
about the tactics of entering defended city structures.
During the next exercise, of course, when they reversed
roles, Captain Hata's men would try to show how they
could do better.

They must do better, Bjorn thought.

He glanced at Capodonno, who stood nearby in
his deceptive, gray helmet and tunic. The master
sergeant carried a single shot missile launcher over his
shoulder. The skinny weapon protruding from it boasted
a radar seeker and three warheads, one directly behind
the other. Detonated in sequence, the explosives could
penetrate even a special suit of armor. Capodonno's
defensive chaff and flare launcher hung over the other
shoulder, while the sheet of sensors and automatic
controls that fed his visor folded down his chest and
back. A handgun and a large bowie knife, plus a pack
of missile reloads at the small of his back, completed his
armament.

Good equipment for urban combat, Bjorn thought.
Most people around were supporters you didn't want to
massacre with heat-seeking flechettes, while your
enemies would have armor of one kind or another. Still,
his men needed armor of their own and small transports
that could drop into ghetto alleys or stick to high stories,
over windows, and long-range aircraft that would let him
project his growing power.

"Sound recall, Capodonno. We can have
breakfast. Then I want a battalion-wide analysis.
Umpires will input before the intelligence program talks
to us. Pick at my plan and how I carried it out. Work
down each unit to squad level. All officers and senior

NCOs."

He turned to greet Dad as the big man moved through the mob that obediently stayed behind a tape. "Has Con squeezed what he wanted out of the Ambassador?" he asked.

The father of the city-state President seemed to tower when he came close enough for private conversation. Sometimes he reminded Bjorn of a drained Sergeant Poll, the terrifying, but now long-dead Enforcer.

"She wants to see you privately," the old man said in a low voice. He ignored Bjorn's question. As usual, the bastard did only what he thought worthwhile.

In the old days, the invitation would have excited Bjorn. Now, no. Nita kept his lusts pacified.

He smiled as he thought of Angel's prize pupil, installed in an air-conditioned cubby three streets over. When he moved his command north to this realistic practice target, he resettled her, too. One of the perks of command.

Bjorn remembered Nita's flashing white limbs, the soft, smooth skin of her abdomen, and the eager smile that greeted him when his alarm rang at four that morning. She made him lie back and insisted that they take their time. He fondled her proud breasts as she placed a knee on each side of him, then stretched up to meet her lips, reached around her smooth back to clamp her to him.

He couldn't get enough of her and felt excited when they just talked or ate. She made him laugh. She dealt with his tension.

He grinned, recalling their earlier argument in bed over the relative merits of men and women.

"Men have bigger skulls," he said, "to hold their bigger brains."

"Okay," she answered, her auburn hair falling over one greenish eye. "But the extra brains are only to control your inflated egos. Manipulation is our bag, and we don't need many neurons to get around you men."

"You're full of crap. I'm known as a con artist myself."

She reached down between the sheets and grinned at him. "Are you saying I can't manipulate you?"

He stretched and looked up at the ceiling. "That's unfair."

She flung the top sheet aside and put her long, mobile lips on his abdomen. "Then, there's your second navel here, the one made by Angelina--wasn't that her name? Of course, you got the better of her too." She kissed the scar.

He had shivered.

He saw no reason why their relationship would ever end. As long as she fought off the female need for children and took her pills, they were free to enjoy life and each other. They could live well on his officer's salary, more than well compared to the welfare rations they both were originally accustomed to, and then compared to the modest money income of an enlisted man and an entertainer.

Unless the Corps came in and destroyed their little dream.

"Ask Captain Hata to take over the exercise evaluation," he ordered Capodonno. "I've got business."

When he entered the Ambassador's suite, the President's sister stood, turned off a terminal, and nodded at him. "Good morning, Major Bjorn."

Still the cool, competent executive, she wore a linen suit over a pale blouse. Around her neck, she flaunted a string of deep blue stones set in gold. A coiffure machine had cut her black hair in a boy-like bob, but the strong nose, dark eyes, and thin, controlled lips were all too familiar.

He assumed parade rest near the door. "Ma'am."

She exhaled disgustedly and motioned him towards a chair. "Please don't play the humble savage or the obedient servant. I've had my fill of those acts."

She sat, too. "The Washington establishment has a gas pain about this battalion of yours," she said. "More specifically, my fellow Achievers double over when they think of you Welfies as officers."

"Are they afraid that President Striker will make us Achievers before he sends in the Corps?" Bjorn asked. "If he can't buy us off, San Angeles could put up a fight that'd upset the whole country."

She looked startled and then shook her head with a resigned sigh. "So you believe my brother will lose his re-election campaign, eh? I always convince myself that you're lucky until I talk with you again. Hell, you don't even look smart."

"I learn American politics at the feet of a master, my uncle," Bjorn replied. "What do you think will happen to you and your brother after you lose?"

Her stare wasn't as hard as he remembered it. Speculative, rather. "You have a pagan handsomeness," she said. "I suppose intelligence is genetically correlated with good looks. Over the centuries, smart men won the beautiful women."

When Bjorn waited for his answer, she waved a hand. "I could protest and say he'll win, but I won't. The Achiever class is against him and most Welfies will obey HHR. After the election, HHR won't let consciences who nag live. It'll kill us."

The same fate waited for Uncle Will and himself, Bjorn thought. No matter the deal Striker offered before invading San Angeles.

"Have you talked to Uncle Will this trip?"

"Of course." She toed off one shoe and then the other. "He says the way things are now, he can't guarantee that the Mexican wards will vote for my brother. Ironic, isn't it? The President builds a barrier against an illegal immigration the Achiever right has wanted to stop for a hundred years and supports the ghetto self-government that Welfies have demanded. Instead of pleasing both ends of the political spectrum, however, he's angered everyone."

"Uncle Will believes that the only way the President can win an election is to openly fight HHR," Bjorn said. "The Mexes would swing to him, then. So would the rest of us. Welfies, if they feel strongly enough to vote, plus a few Achievers, can elect him."

"Your Uncle gave me that speech," she said. "But the strategy is so dangerous! We'd break with the whole Achiever class."

"Since assassination is probable, being scared of a method to avoid it seems dumb."

"HHR grips the ghettos," she countered, "and could maybe produce a last minute vote for Striker, despite what each Welfie really wants. If my brother lost after he roused the horrors of class warfare, he'd really be doomed."

"Did the President turn Uncle Will's scheme down?"

"Maestri said you might have a proposal that would make us feel better about it."

He watched her bite her lip and, under her skirt, pull both legs together. Under that calm pose, the Ambassador was wound tightly.

"I'll attack and take HHR's Washington headquarters," he said, very softly.

"Shit!" she whispered.

"I'll move quickly right before the election," he continued, "and capture Striker and the rest of the HHR Council. There'll be no time for the Corps to react."

Bjorn tapped his knee. "Striker's Presidential campaign would become directionless. I'd have everyone who could coordinate the megacities' Welfare Kings. There'd be no discipline to produce the landslide Striker wants. And he couldn't queer the adverse vote tallies that flowed into Washington."

She stood and paced back and forth in her stocking feet, her eyes locked on him. She breathed hard. Her large breasts jiggled under the blouse and suit jacket.

"My battalion and the Welfie militia we'd form from the Washington ghetto would control the area around HHR for the necessary election period," he said. "As soon as the President claimed a popular majority for his re-election, the Corps would have to obey him and support me."

He hoped the Corps would obey the President. Of course, mutiny and civil war were other possible outcomes. But he'd grip the head of the snake and maybe, just maybe...

"Could you actually take HHR and Striker?" she asked. Her eyes gleamed.

Bjorn wasn't so sure after the morning's exercise. But, somehow... He'd put Uncle Will in terrible danger by his rescue of Wagoner.

He stood, too. "That's what I'm training my battalion for."

She moved close, put her hands on his shoulders, and kissed him full on the lips. Then she stepped back. "Welfie or not, you're some package of man."

She unbuttoned her jacket almost casually. Her nipples pressed against the smooth blouse. Hell, he might have saved her life here. Celebration was in order!

And sex might glue him to her.

Bjorn put his hand on her shoulder and slowly drew her close. "I need long range aircraft," he said.

The Ambassador resisted his pull.

"Also, you've heard Uncle Will's demands. The ghettos will only risk voting for the President if your brother shows he's against HHR early. They'll want commitment. Especially the Mexican wards. He must name Uncle Will head of the President's election campaign at once. My battalion's attack will be a secret piece of last-minute insurance that Welfie commitment won't be wasted,"

He unclipped her necklace, tossed it aside.

She stepped closer, ran her hand up and down his groin, wet her lips again. "I've wanted to screw you for a long time," she said.

He should feel guilty about Nita. But then, this was business.

Chapter 18

"Good evening, Major Bjorn--and Nita, isn't it?"

The Ambassador smiled from the White House receiving line. She wore a clinging, silver sheath that made nearby men sneak repetitive looks.

"You've got quite a brawl here," Bjorn said. "We sure appreciate being invited for my Uncle Will's coming out party, or whatever."

With a disgusted grimace--at his bumpkin pose, probably-- the Ambassador turned and introduced them to her brother.

"I like your simple uniform," President Petersen said to Bjorn. "And aren't those our service ribbons above your shirt pocket?"

A tall, Lincolnesque man with his sister's strong nose and thin lips, the President's eyes seemed to pierce Bjorn--the effect of wrinkles from far-sightedness, he guessed. In any event, the Ambassador hadn't briefed her brother very well if he was curious about Bjorn's military record. He apparently didn't recognize the ribbon!

President Petersen didn't wait for Bjorn's answer. He grasped Nita's hand. "Aren't you beautiful, my dear?"

Nita <u>was</u> beautiful, Bjorn thought as they moved on. Taller than the Ambassador, she was as generously endowed--the décolletage showed too much, he thought. Her strongest point was her dramatic coloring: the auburn hair and eyebrows, the green eyes, and the cream-white skin.

Nita had other merits. She seemed always ready to laugh and praise, while she was smart enough. She liked him, maybe loved him, too. Bjorn slid his hand around her waist, gave her a possessive hug.

A marine captain with the braid of an aide-de-camp led them from the receiving line into the dining room, toward one of the small, round tables. The officer didn't introduce himself and kept his stiff back turned toward Bjorn as much as possible.

They'd never met behind Veracruz, Bjorn realized, nor had he run across the aide in the deployments since. The bastard was a headquarters bit-battler.

Bjorn glanced around. Burly waiters watched them from the sides. Old paintings filled the walls and two marble heads sat on pedestals at the entrance. A string quartet played softly from a raised corner. He guessed that ten tables, each set for six or eight guests, filled the room.

The HHR executive with whom Uncle Will had talked via holovision stood as they approached, while a thin, young brunette in a "safe" evening dress examined them with long-lashed, blue eyes. "John Striker's my name," the man said, when the captain didn't introduce them. He offered a hand to Bjorn. "You're Benjamin Bjorn, aren't you? Ginny Petersen, here, is the President's daughter. She's assigned to entertain us lesser lights."

"Come, come, John," the young woman protested. She held out her hand to Bjorn, but looked up at the Achiever. "You're not a lesser light. Word is that you're HHR's candidate for President, and that you'll run against my father. I'll have to forget how much you've amused me the last few months."

She switched a cool gaze to Bjorn. "And you're not a lesser light, either, Major. You command an independent fighting force. That's much more important than the jobs of staff officers around here who haven't yet learned to be polite."

She smiled sweetly at the aide de camp and withdrew her hand from Bjorn's grasp. She offered it to

Nita, who introduced herself with an admiring nod.

Mr. Striker helped Nita sit. The captain whispered to Miss Peterson as he held her chair.

"Oh, I only boss a bunch of Welfies like myself," Bjorn said. "Haven't you heard about the San Angeles 'Bluffers'? That's what the captain here, and his friends, call us, I'm told."

Miss Ginny had a racehorse frame: long, muscled legs and arms; a strong, tight body and ass; and not much frontal development. Her face was long and narrow, too, with lips wide and thick enough to seem passionate. Bjorn thought the girl more interesting than pretty.

She studied him also, as he sat. "Despite your disclaimer, you've impressed my aunt somehow."

Nita dug her fingernails into his thigh.

"And what do you do, Nita?" Mr. Striker asked.

"I keep Ben here happy," she answered and grinned at both the people new to her. She darted a quizzical look at Bjorn. "I also fight-off competition."

Unmarried arrangements were common, unequal unmarried arrangements almost the same set. Bjorn guessed that probably half the pairs in this room included a non-entity.

Miss Ginny grinned and reached over to touch Nita's hand. "He is awfully handsome."

Bjorn felt like growling, then told himself to grow up. If these outsiders thought him only a good-looking, empty-headed escapee from the ghetto, good!

The aide still stood near the table. His face was flushed.

"Oh, go bring my aunt over, Captain Wallace," the girl said. "I'm sure she's tired of the receiving line and anxious to talk to our guests here. Then you may join us."

The aide pivoted and stormed away. The President's daughter sighed. "Do you make all men mad, Major?"

"Please don't rub us against each other, Miss. You'll get heat, maybe fire."

She darted a sharp glance at him.

"I really like your dress," Nita said. "It sets off your black hair."

He patted Nita's thigh in gratitude for the distraction, obvious as it was.

"Tell me, Major," asked Mr. Striker, "do you really believe your Bluffers could take-on one of our punishment battalions?"

"I don't see why not, Sir. There's enough hate there, certainly."

The HHR executive blinked.

"The Mexicans held the Corps off the plateau for eight months," Bjorn continued. "With little more than rage and good defensive positions. My troops would do even better in the cross streets of their ghetto."

As the Ambassador approached, the men stood. She sat between Mr. Striker and Bjorn. Captain Wallace also joined them, taking the chair between Nita and Miss Ginny.

"Major Bjorn," the President's daughter said, "how about doing something with the bowl of flowers between us? As a flat screen addict still in her teens, I believe vision blocks unfair."

Bjorn had other problems. The Ambassador laid her hand on his leg as soon as she settled into her chair. She leaned forward and made sure he could see her breasts in the open oval at the top of the tight dress.

At the same time, Nita moved in on his other leg and whispered, "Make her keep her hands off!" Her breasts were lighter colored, younger, and her perfume an innocent lilac rather than the Ambassador's seductive gardenia.

Bjorn suddenly stood and reached over to lift the flower bowl. "Yours to command, Miss Ginny," he said. He turned and gave his burden to a waiter.

Before he sat again, he moved his chair back

from the table. "If you all don't mind," he said, "I'll stretch my legs until the dinner comes."

God knows what I'll do then, he thought.

"Well, Mr. Striker," the Ambassador said, as if the by-play hadn't happened, "my brother and I are happy you agreed to come tonight. We're particularly interested in your personal reaction to the election strategy you'll hear."

"I understand you're putting a Welfie in charge of a ghetto vote-winning campaign," Mr. Striker answered. "I can hardly believe it. The Achievers who run the country will flee your camp in droves. Your plan destroys any chance for the President's re-election."

"What chance did he have before?" she asked and then glanced at the aide. "What about the Corps, Captain Wallace? Will your superiors revolt at a Welfie campaign manager in the White House basement?"

"Not if you keep him out of military matters," the blond young man answered. He fixed Bjorn with a stony glare. "There's a certain pride that goes with being an officer," he said. "Don't insult us."

Miss Ginny reached over and touched his fist. "We understand, Jimmy," she said.

Waiters poured champagne and put out plates of hors d'oeuvres. Bjorn slid his chair back to the table, gripped Nita's hand as it glided along his leg, and shook his head. When the Ambassador touched his other thigh, Bjorn caught her hand too. He squeezed and then dropped it between them.

"Welfies don't wear horns," he said. "With my Uncle Will, you know for sure he doesn't."

When the President's daughter looked blank, Nita volunteered, "Mr. Maestri's completely bald." She grinned. "He claims he has a curved solar panel that others don't have. It gives him more mental energy."

The Ambassador leaned over and whispered loudly in Bjorn's ear. "I've a bedroom here for afterward. Get rid of her."

Bjorn saw Nita bite her lip at the overheard message.

He believed that what he now ate was prime rib, a dish he'd only heard about on holovision dramas. He had to be careful. Too much rich food could make him sick.

"Why'd you come east?" asked Mr. Striker. "I'd think your post should be at the head of your battalion, protecting that outrageous city-state government of San Angeles."

Bjorn tried to smile naively. "What? And miss Uncle Will's coronation?"

The President's daughter swallowed something wrong, coughed, and then stared at him.

"You're right," the Ambassador said. "He isn't as stupid as he puts on."

"I don't know," Captain Wallace said. "Anyone who sets himself up as a target like he has is bound to have missed a few, higher order, neuron junctions."

Bjorn remembered the transcontinental flight with Nita. They flew on the cattle-car ramjet, stood between straps the whole way. Achievers filled the aircraft and complained of the uppity behavior of ghetto-heads. According to them, inequality was a natural consequence from centuries of poor genetic matches. Even prior Achievers, now taking rations, must have fought inbred inferiority.

He hadn't worn his uniform; both Nita and he avoided talk in order to conceal their accents.

Identification, these days, in a crowd of unsupervised Achievers might be dangerous. More and more seemed to advocate "a firm hand."

Uncle Will, of course, traveled east with the Ambassador, sitting comfortably in a government transport.

"I don't see myself as exposing myself to punishment, Captain," Bjorn now said. "I'm only a jumped-up Marine non-com who serves as ordered.

The Corps will defend me."

"You serve as a shield against the HHR," Mr. Striker said. "The Corps will not defend you."

Bjorn needed to make a personal reconnaissance of HHR headquarters, but now worried that this attention might prevent a quiet reconnaissance. He sat easily and kept a bland smile on his face.

"Your Uncle Will is even more of a target," Mr. Striker continued. "I expect he'll declare war against Achievers tonight--as part of his ghetto vote-winning strategy."

Bjorn leaned forward to draw the man's eyes. "Uncle Will isn't warlike at all," he said. "He wants what is best for everyone, including, of course, the Welfies."

"Maestri will declare war only against the HHR," the Ambassador inserted. "He'll find Achievers like me who support him. Many of us believe it's time to force fairness on you and your Council, Striker."

Her statement pissed-off Bjorn. Why tag Uncle Will as an HHR enemy? Killers were sent to the address of anyone with that reputation.

Striker's eyes half closed; a slight smile controlled his lips and cheeks. "In San Angeles your brother went against us by agreeing to the City-State idea," he said to the Ambassador. "Now, I hear he would swing all the way and make Welfies equal. If true, Mr. Maestri and your brother are enemies of both HHR and the Achiever class."

Bjorn leaned toward Striker again and pushed back the Ambassador's restraining arm. "Listen to me," he said, his voice deep. "You move against Uncle Will, and you better watch out for me." His voice dropped more. "Personally!"

He was rigid, his face stiff. He stared at a surprised Mr. Striker for a long moment and thought of tearing his throat with his teeth, thought of disemboweling the executive with his bare fingers.

"Major, Major, please calm down," Miss Ginny

whispered. Her voice and shiver broke Bjorn's concentration. He sat back.

They all stared at him. He picked up a fork, toyed with his dessert. But he still felt enraged. He knew his pupils would have narrowed; his smile would be a grimace.

"He's not as nice as he seems, either," the Ambassador said.

A tinkle of a fork against a glass caught everyone's attention. The President stood at the center table and smiled at the sixty or so people who pushed their chairs back and pivoted so they could see him clearly.

Bjorn still was tense.

"Thank you all for coming," the President said in a deep baritone.

"Is that Mr. Maestri sitting next to my father?" Miss Ginny asked Bjorn in a whisper.

He nodded.

"I've invited here tonight the most powerful people in the land," the President said. "They include the heads of the four media chains, the chairmen of the food conglomerates, the utility people, the heads of our political parties... Oh, you know who you are."

"Are you one of the most powerful people in the land, Ben?" Nita asked, bending close to whisper in his ear. "I'm impressed."

"The reason for my invitation," the President continued, "is to make sure you're the first to hear about the end of the two nations policy. When re-elected, I plan to nullify the emergency laws of 2066, return this country to the rule of law, even in the ghettos."

Men and women stood. "How dare you!"

Bjorn wondered if the President would also re-introduce fair courts martial to the Corps and eliminate the hated Enforcers.

Mr. Striker sat, stiff as a dead man, on the other side of the Ambassador. A straight gash had replaced the lopsided smile he'd shown most of the evening.

"How will you keep Welfies out of our suburbs?" someone shouted when the hubbub subsided.

"The police will still arrest loiterers who don't belong," the President replied. Slight beads of sweat appeared on his forehead. He nervously brushed back his thick, gray hair. "And, we'll establish joint commissions to handle chronic difficulties."

He lifted his head. "Both nations must learn to become one again, to live together," he declaimed.

"There aren't enough resources!"

The President turned. "Yes there are, if all consume equally. Justice..."

"You'd ration us?" The shriek was a scream of rage. Additional guests jumped to their feet. A few shook their fists at the President.

Next to Bjorn, the Ambassador's hand trembled, but her face stayed strong.

"All right, Ben," Nita whispered. "I'll go back to the hotel alone. I can see that what she wants from you is strictly release. It's business."

"What's HHR's reaction?" was the next loud question.

Mr. Striker stood. "We think he's crazy," the HHR executive exclaimed. "We think you won't re-elect him."

Other men and women now kicked their chairs back. Security people moved along the sides of the dining room.

Bjorn forgot his doubts. He admired the President. Petersen had refused to send the Corps into San Angeles. Now he accepted the derivatives of that refusal and started to fight against defeat and death. He marshaled the Welfies and the more thoughtful Achievers to his side. He was a man of principle. More important, he had guts.

After curses and shouts, a few people returned to their seats. Security men kept others from congregating near the President's table and channeled many to the exits they loudly sought.

The President stooped, whispered in Uncle Will's ear, and helped him rise. "Ladies and gentlemen," he said over the quieting clamor. "Let me introduce you to Will Maestri, a Welfie who I'm naming as co-chairman, with my sister, of my re-election campaign."

Striker still stood. He studied the President and Uncle Will with a cold, calculating expression.

"Remember my warning," Bjorn said in a low voice. "Don't mess with my uncle."

Striker turned toward him. They stared at each other.

Uncle Will didn't speak, just waved to the crowd.

More people left for the exits. Striker pushed his chair away. "Why don't you come to see me tomorrow?" he suggested to Bjorn. "I'd like to know you better, and you need to understand what your uncle faces."

Bjorn hesitated.

"He used to be a protégé of mine in HHR, did you know that? He should understand what he risks and his odds. But you have no reason to know, yourself. I would save a winner of the Navy Cross a humiliating, maybe deadly, experience." Striker smiled. "Come at ten."

The HHR executive nodded at the rest of the table, held the Ambassador's glare for a short moment, and then left.

The President table-hopped to speak with those who remained.

"I must join him," the Ambassador said. "This is an Achiever crowd; they're my portfolio." She sent a commanding look at Bjorn. "I'll see you later."

"Not tonight," he responded lazily as he stood and helped Nita up. "We'll escort Uncle Will to the hotel."

Chapter 19

The next morning, Will Maestri walked down the hotel corridor to his nephew's suite for breakfast and said hello to the secret service detail on the way. Nita, in a loose-fitting robe, greeted him with a big smile, a kiss on his cheek, and a whiff of gorgeous perfume.

He missed female companionship! Even over-possessive Angel.

Maestri sat and poured himself real coffee. Across the table, his spruced-up nephew wore a dress uniform that hid his sneak knife--although Will had warned him he wouldn't get it into HHR.

"Who's there?" Benjamin asked when someone knocked at the door.

"Two Welfies to see Mr. Maestri."

"They'll be members of the local Residents Council," Will said. He raised his voice. "Let them in."

Two black females entered, tight-lipped. A woman of the White House security detail had patted them down for weapons, Maestri guessed. Both Welfies were skinny and short from life-long diets of vegetable protein, and welfare ration quantities at that. "I'm Tracey," one said in a thick voice.

Nita came back from the bedroom after she apparently realized the visitors were women. She offered sweet rolls. The newcomers stared at her with hostility. "Hell," Nita said, "I'm Welfie too, although only a first generation one. My parents came to the States during the Quebec, French riots. I'm Ben's bed warmer."

The visitors shook their heads at offered chairs but relaxed a bit.

"You got bed warmer?" Tracey, the apparent

spokeswoman asked Maestri. "One who can handle assassins?"

Maestri shook his head. "She couldn't leave her job and wasn't handy with weapons, anyway."

Both ladies nodded. They would think a job too valuable to leave for almost any reason. And specialization was all too common, whether it was bed warming or body guarding.

"I send bodyguard who looks like bed warmer," Tracey said.

Maestri thought about that and then nodded. "Okay. The White House security details should be competent. But, thanks."

"You ask on comm. line who runs wards," Tracey said. "Most ghetto here is black town. We and three men are Council. The king and gangs say what happens, though."

Maestri heard another knock.

"Yes?" Benjamin answered.

"The President's daughter, Sir. She wants to see Miss Nita."

Benjamin frowned in puzzlement. "Let her in," he told the outside security detail.

Maestri remembered meeting Miss Ginny the night before, as he was about to leave the White House with Benjamin and Nita. Only her large, inquiring eyes had registered. She wasn't the usual type of woman you met around Benjamin.

Virginia Petersen entered. She took-in the Welfie guests, reached out a hand, and smiled serenely. "I'm so happy to meet you," she said. "Aren't you glad my father will end our two nations' differences?"

The president's daughter wore a green silk suit that appeared "unpatted" by the White House detail.

Their faces sour, the black ladies touched her hand.

"We gotta leave," Tracey said to Maestri. "We talk on didg comm. line."

"Don't go because of me," the aristocratic girl interjected. "Nita and I will huddle in a back room."

"This place too rich. Make sick."

The bright, new colors, the fabrics, the space, and even the conditioned air would be as strange as the sweet rolls, Maestri guessed. "Okay," he said to Tracey. "But your didg address may be known and our communications recordable. I'll come over to your tenement. How about seven this evening? We need to put our heads together about getting out the vote."

Tracey nodded.

"Hi, Miss Ginny," Maestri heard from behind him. "Hi, Nita!" was the response of the president's daughter.

He escorted the Welfie women to the door.

"Can I take you to the Washington tourist spots?" Miss Peterson asked. "We could go shopping."

The girl's probably only eighteen, Maestri thought. A late developer. She has her eyes on Benjamin and uses Nita to get close.

After letting out the three representatives from the local ghetto, he turned to watch.

Nita glanced at Benjamin for permission to sightsee, then, after his nod, smiled widely. "Oh, I'd love to, Miss Ginny. I thought I'd be left here alone today." She ran for the bedroom, and then stuck her head back out the door. "Can we go into a real, live, Achiever dress shop?"

Maestri sat again.

Benjamin pulled up a chair for the President's daughter and poured coffee. "Anything happen after we left?" he asked.

"Nothing, except my aunt chose Captain Wallace as your surrogate. He's walking around with a dazed expression this morning."

Benjamin grinned and studied her. "What makes you tick?" he asked.

"My father," she answered, seemingly not embarrassed at all by the question. "He's a great man.

I fear for him."

"You're right to fear," Maestri said.

When she glanced at him, almost accusingly, he spread his hands. "I'm not the satanic plotter that the Achiever media makes me out to be, Miss Ginny, may I, too, call you that? I'm only a useful man who knows the ghettos. Your father employs me."

He paused and then added, "But I've worked with the HHR much of my life. I know it, too. I know Mr. Striker. It and he can be deadly. Your father and I must watch our backs."

"Does your father really want equality, or does he only need to win Welfie votes?" Benjamin asked.

"He's always hated discrimination and wanted full rights for everyone again," the girl stated, her eyes now back on Benjamin's and not shifting.

You can have ideals, but never risk your all for them, Maestri thought. The President was really on the line now, probably for the first time in his life. And if he won this election, Welfies wouldn't let him relax in the luxuries of the presidency. They'd make him carry through on his promises. His high risk would stay with him for the rest of his life.

"Any bodyguards with you?" Benjamin asked. "Two young women on a spree are prizes."

"They're in the hall with your White House detail," Miss Ginny answered. "And I have this." She reached into her shoulder bag and pulled out a face snare, a baseball-shaped coil of barbed wire tightly wrapped about a gimbal that carried a video sensor, a tiny jet engine, and a microprocessor. The vicious mechanism would seek and then explode into an attacker's face.

"You should be careful yourself, Benjamin," Maestri said.

He sighed as he watched first his nephew depart for HHR headquarters and then the two women leave for shopping. He supposed he should return to his own quarters next door and plan an electoral revolution.

Chapter 20

Later that morning, in the heart of Washington, a long bank of precipitators hummed near the HHR complex and probably pulled tons of particulate matter from the fetid atmosphere. To Bjorn, the gray air seemed little cleaner on the processed side. As he walked toward the HHR complex in a light crowd, he wore no breathing mask, however. He figured it would reduce his oxygen and limit his ability to react.

There was just too much pollution. The prevailing wind in the Northern Hemisphere blew from west to east. Thus, the people here on the east coast lived in the effluent from a continent.

Most of his fellow pedestrians were jobless probably, but still had personal reserves and weren't yet hard-core Welfies. They dressed too well, stood straight, and appeared healthy.

As he approached, he studied the HHR building's slick, unwindowed surface and the interlocking wings that could defend each other from armored blisters. Bjorn noted explosive nets on the roof that would fragment landers. He expected there'd be automated surface-to-air missile launchers and anti-air guns, too.

The building's ground-based defenses were familiar from his days in the sanitation belt, on the Mexican border. He saw composite plates sprinkled around the grounds. Hopper mines and blinding lasers would lie beneath them. Automated turrets also protruded from concrete foundations. They'd hold machine guns or flamers. Long, humped barriers that paralleled walkways could eject devil nettles, the barbed and poisoned, always moving coils of wire.

That building's a son-of-a-bitch to attack, Bjorn thought.

"Are you from one of the new infantry divisions, Sir?" a black man asked. He walked with a military bearing as he fell-in next to Bjorn, but limped. Probably an HHR outside man.

"Don't recognize my uniform, eh?" Bjorn answered. "I'm from the San Angeles City-State Battalion. I've an appointment with Mr. Striker."

"It's hard to believe the Achievers let you bastards live."

The stranger smiled.

"Where'd you get the nick?" Bjorn asked. "Most of us San Angeles officers won our non-com stripes at Veracruz. Were you there?"

The man put his hand on Bjorn's sleeve and slowed him. "What company?"

"Lefko's. I hear he's a colonel now and has one of the new army infantry regiments."

"You Bjorn?"

Bjorn stopped and nodded. "And you?"

"Carlson. I'm not supposed to remember my company. According to the Corps, it never existed. There's nobody else left alive, anyway. I was wounded and shipped-out before it mutinied."

Bjorn began to walk again. The gate was only a hundred meters away. "Give me your didg access number, quick."

After they parted, Bjorn wondered why HHR trusted Carlson. Had he toadied to the Enforcers? Did he gain his "nick" fighting mutineers? Maybe he wouldn't contact the man after all.

He walked through two pairs of open, armored doors. Bjorn noted that the walls of the entry held diaphragms to valve-off shock waves from warheads, thus minimizing the effects of explosive. Armored openings for the muzzles of high velocity guns then ringed a small foyer. Finally, a concrete maze equipped with sensors, automated gas projectors, and burning lasers brought Bjorn to a manned desk and a gnarled guide.

The entrance was as formidable as the outside seemed to be.

He was asked for his hide out knife.

When Bjorn's escort led him beyond the desk, the bottom floor opened to something like an art gallery. Articulated statues set in transparent columns filled with glowing gas paralleled his path and moving panoramas covered an occasional wall, while springy carpet cushioned Bjorn's feet. He encountered only three men. They stood outside a door, probably taking a social break.

"Are there many offices upstairs?" he asked his guide. "Seems to me this floor is largely waste space."

"Most of our big people work at home," the squat escort said sourly. "They order offices here only when they tire of mama and the teen-agers. Or when they don't want to meet shits at their houses."

Bjorn registered the insult.

The squat escort carried himself like a marine, too. He was an ex-Enforcer, Bjorn guessed. "Hell," the guide said, "if the fumble-bum President can work where he lives, so can HHR bosses."

Mr. Striker met Bjorn on the top floor and led him to an office with surrogate windows: electronic screens that showed a view of the Washington Monument and the White House, and of the purposeless crowds that milled around the Reflecting Pool.

Bjorn's chair changed shape as he settled into it, formed a lumbar roll at the right spot in his back, and raised cushioned arm rests. A small shelf, a cup, and a coffee dialer appeared near his hand.

The HHR chief wore a dark blue Nehru jacket and gray slacks. He smiled and his eyes crinkled under heavy, gray brows with ingratiating charm. His skin was rough, his waist thick. A man's man. "This building's a hard nut, isn't it?" he asked. "Surely, you couldn't crack it. You must ask yourself, also, what you'd gain if you did, since my staff usually works somewhere else."

Bjorn hoped he didn't show his shock. There must be a spy in the White House!

The HHR leader swiveled his chair and stared unseeing at the screen that pretended to be a window. "Now that the President will stir up the Welfies, there'll be murders and executions in the ghettos this fall, Major Bjorn," he said. "Lots of both. Will Maestri's people versus ours. But we'll win, we'll win." He turned back. "We won in the twenty-sixties; we'll win now. We have organization and the punishment battalions."

He studied Bjorn. "After I handsomely take the election, we'll tell the agricultural combines, the medical houses, and the utilities people to shut off supplies and services to hold-out ghettos. Suffering residents will then see it's in their interest to put down the militants. If they don't, I'll have the Corps raze the disobeying wards."

Bjorn took a deep breath. "Uncle Will thinks the President can win."

Mr. Striker shook his head. "He's a romantic. That character trait ruined him once before. Will Maestri believes 'good' people--Achievers--will rise up against their own interests, throw us out, and put kinder, but incompetent executives in our places."

"The President isn't incompetent."

"Oh yes he is, Major. You don't see it because we've propped him up. He's all moonbeams and public relations. That's why he approved your city-state in the first place."

"Uncle Will isn't incompetent."

"In little things, no. In the big things... Why, he'd stick his head into a high speed fan if he thought he could help small children."

Mr. Striker stared into Bjorn's eyes. "Welfie children are what we don't need. The United States

can't feed the adults we have. We certainly can't afford
to raise more of those who will never earn their keep."

When Bjorn said nothing, Mr. Striker leaned back.
"You're a military man. You understand the need for
hard choices and the fact that they can only be taken
from a central, authoritarian perspective. Thus, you
should be on my side."

He smiled. "Surplus people threaten civilization
everywhere, Major. Especially in the middle latitudes.
The Chinese, Indians, Moslems, Africans and Latinos,
each need to move hundreds of millions off their farms
to make agriculture efficient. If they do, they would add
to the hundreds of millions of unemployed that already
wander in cities. Think of their problem! At least our
surplus people, the Welfies, are concentrated and
managed."

He paused, sipped from a coffee cup. "We won't
wave away that accomplishment because of the
President's and your uncle's soft-headedness."

"Can't you somehow make us useful?" Bjorn
asked. "Get rid of some automation, for instance. The
President's program..."

Mr. Striker struck his desk. "The nation doesn't
have the resources or the time to re-sculpture our
economy!"

So what will finally happen to us? Bjorn
wondered.

"We Achievers," Striker continued, "have the
power to crush the President's rosy dreams of populist
equality." He paused. "And I have the will."

Bjorn was silent for a long moment. Did this
bastard plan to wipe us all out, he asked himself. If
we're "surplus..."

"What do you want from me?" he finally asked.

"Tell the Ambassador you can't take this building.
Return to San Angeles and push cooperation rather
than confrontation. Sit back and watch the election
campaign progress. Don't use force against us when

we move into San Angeles after the election."

He's terribly confident of winning, Bjorn thought.

"Of course, the San Angeles City-State will have to go," Striker said. His face relaxed into a condescending smile. "If most wards wake up and vote with us, however, we'll put in one of our best people as Welfare King--after our punishment battalions cleanses the city of dissidents."

No mention of larger rations. Instead, a dark, unspoken threat to "surplus" people. No suggested place in Mr. Striker's post-election scenario for Uncle Will, nor for the President and his sister. Nor for Wagoner.

Am I expected to now bargain? With what set of counters?

He must have shown his anger.

Mr. Striker stared at him. "I see I haven't convinced you," he said. The Achiever's face seemed heavier, somehow, its lines deeper, the fleshy cheeks pulling down mouth and eyelids.

"Well..."

"This meeting is over!" the executive whispered.

Bjorn rose when the other man did. "Why don't you bribe me?" he asked, trying to smile ingratiatingly.

"Maybe later," Striker said. "If you survive." All friendliness had disappeared.

As he stepped outside the office, Bjorn shivered at Striker's immediate perception of his guest's reaction, his decisiveness, and what he guessed was the HHR man's present resolve.

.Chapter 21

When Bjorn exited HHR property, he shook his shoulders to settle the returned hideout knife.

Carlson, the veteran of Veracruz, limped alongside. "How about eating lunch with a friend and me?" he asked. "We'll give you the lowdown on this place."

"Can't right now. I need to get back."

"Okay, buddy. Give me a call." Carlson grinned and raised his arm to slap Bjorn on the back.

Bjorn spotted the squat, Enforcer-type approaching from the rear as he grabbed Carlson's arm. "I'm a 'Sir' now," he started to say, and then realized something was wrong and dropped on his knee. He yanked the veteran down too and twisted Carlson's arm, forcing the open hand up.

A sharp little needle protruded from a flat bag taped to the man's palm. A drop of fluid beaded its tip.

The other HHR man charged through the crowd. His hand also held something. At three meters distance now, he seemed to radiate rage.

Bjorn pulled the Mexican knife from its neck sheath with his free hand and flung the sliver of iron at the attacker.

Without time to determine the success of his throw, he turned back to Carlson. By now, the ex-Marine had also scrambled to his knees. Carlson struggled to yank his arm free, lurched for Bjorn's eyes with his other hand.

Bjorn stood and slipped behind as both reached their feet. He gripped the veteran in a half nelson and inexorably forced the open hand ever closer to its owner's heaving chest.

His other opponent was down.

"How do you like your own friendly slap, buddy?" he asked, and then exerted all his strength in a sudden heave that brought the needle hard into the man's body and undoubtedly emptied the contents of the bag into his tissues.

Carlson screamed and thrashed.

Holding his victim in an iron grip, Bjorn glanced at the Enforcer-type on the pavement only a few meters away. Bjorn couldn't see his knife, but blood trickled out of an open mouth. His weapon's hilt must have stopped against the veteran's throat wall, the blade having penetrated the spinal cord where nerves climbed up into his brain.

To recover his knife would be like retrieving a swallowed hook from a fish. He shivered, even under the fierce control he exerted over his body just then.

"You've killed me, you bastard," Carlson moaned. His violence subsided. "Within a minute, they said."

He sagged now in Bjorn's grasp. His body trembled.

Bjorn made one last, convulsive heave to grind the needle in and then flung Carlson away. He watched him fall, face up, over the other body.

Spectators left a considerable space around them. The curious shuffled and spoke in whispers.

Maybe Striker had sent only two assassins, but Bjorn studied the nearest loiterers.

"I have things to do," murmured Carlson. His eyes stared up. His body jerked occasionally. "Booze to drink, and women..." He sighed and his eyelids closed; his voice faded. "It's like sleep," he then said in an ordinary tone. He sat upright, his eyes now wide. "No! I won't die!" He only croaked the words. In a moment, his chest stilled and he fell back.

Bjorn turned to face the HHR building. Striker might watch him this very minute, might focus sound amplifiers on him.

"I warned you, Striker," he said. "If you've gone after Uncle Will, too..."

He turned and ran.

#

"Greetings," Maestri said to his friend, through the nationwide Web. "Will Maestri here. Where's the punishment battalion barracked for the Chicago megacity? How good a grip on the ghetto has the HHR king and his sector gang bosses? Who runs the residents council there?"

He had friends in most ghettos, men and women who knew the local HHR system, who would give him the needed information when asked. Maestri's years with Striker, his job as ghetto political coordinator for the HHR executive, and the subsequent years when he maintained his contacts through the web prepared him for this election fight. But could he win?

The more he explored HHR's empire and understood the weaknesses of his friends, the more he doubted.

He recorded the information he gathered on a memory slug. By eleven thirty he'd covered the major ghettos and started on the smaller cities.

A knock sounded on his door. Maestri looked up and smiled when he realized that he hadn't missed the noise of the San Angeles ghetto, nor the company at Angel's. Benjamin and Nita should be back for lunch soon, too. An Achiever lunch. "Yes?"

"Two Welfies, Mr. Maestri. One's the same as this morning."

"Let them in."

The security detail had patted the women down once more. After all, plastic knives and compressed air guns passed metal detectors and, if carefully sculptured, sneaked by edge-analyzers, too. The Welfies entered, angry.

The new black was even smaller than Maestri

was, and definitely female. She wore a tight, red knit dress that showed everything. A pocket Venus, he thought.

Her pinched lips smoothed as she came closer and studied him. "I'm Madeline, Mr. Maestri," she said. "My mother, Tracey here, tells me you need a bodyguard."

He grinned at her. "You need one more than I do."

Madeline was in her mid-twenties, he guessed. Bright white teeth and pink gums contrasted with dull black skin. Her nose was splayed and her lips thick. She had kinky hair cut into an even hedge that protruded about three inches above her skull all the way to the nape of her neck.

"My dress is camouflage, Sir," she replied. "I'm not in the business of relieving male tensions. No bed-warming shit unless and until I want to. No finger-wandering, either."

Maestri displayed his open hands and grinned again. "My fingers will never leave my hands."

"HHR rates," she said. "Since they're your enemy."

"Of course," Maestri answered. "The election campaign pays for everything." He gestured at the suite. "Why don't you inspect the place? Make yourself real coffee. That's one of our perks."

After Madeline wandered into the back, the older woman nodded at Maestri. "She good. Hates the HHR."

After Tracey left, Maestri stared at the door for a moment, unwilling to return to work.

He couldn't fool himself. Mr. Striker had force and economic leverage. Maestri had only the raw emotion of millions of individual ghetto dwellers.

Neither the President nor he offered a long-range solution to resource shortages, or to threats from restless populations around the world. They could only propose more equitable domestic consumption. And, most Welfies wouldn't believe their promises.

He knew no way to gain enough holovision and flat screen time to even reach his audience. Producers, Achievers all, would refuse to spread what they would call "incitement to riot." He'd receive only limited viewing time, and that would be censored. By agitating on the ground, in the ghettos, he'd probably only cause HHR to squash his agents.

"Captain Wallace is here, Sir. From the White House."

The security detail opened the door without Maestri's verbal permission. Wallace wore his Corps uniform, an aide cord looped under his arm, decorations lined above his blouse pocket.

"Is Ginny here?" he asked.

Maestri shook his head and waved his arm, giving Wallace friendly permission to search the place.

His nephew had heard that the blond, freckled officer was one of the textile Wallaces, a powerful clan that operated automated plants close to their markets all over the world. According to Benjamin, the man had gained none of his decorations in combat.

"Her father's looking for her," Wallace said.

That's a lie! Maestri thought. The White House probably plotted Miss Ginny's position in real time, through a beacon on her person. Her father would learn her location if he asked, could talk to her at any time.

Maestri swiveled in his chair and shook himself slightly to make sure his shirt didn't impede his access to the knife scabbarded at the back of his neck. Out the corner of his eye, he saw a finger tap the dining room doorframe. That would be Madeline.

Wallace pulled out a hand-held phone. "Okay," he said into it. Then, after a long pause and a glance at Maestri, he moved it to his mouth again. "She's not here. I'll try Eaton's tea shop next."

He nodded and turned to go.

Maestri rose, thinking he'd keep Wallace here, as a hostage in what was to come.

Then the door opened. Miss Ginny and Nita burst in, arms full of packages.

"You should have come with us, Uncle Will," Nita bubbled. She flashed a wide smile. "What wonderful clothes; what neat shoes! I bought a negligee Ben will slobber over!"

Miss Ginny set her boxes on a chair and smiled at Wallace. "What are you doing here, Captain?" She didn't wait for an answer. "If you're free, please come with us when we go out again. We could use a strong back and weak mind." She grinned.

"Great, Ginny!" Wallace said. "Turn around. Let's go." He grasped her by the elbow.

"Don't be in such a hurry," she protested and stepped back to free herself. "We need to freshen-up."

"I'll give you three minutes," Wallace said. The captain's hands clenched. His feet moved nervously.

Maestri walked to the dining room doorway and glanced in. Madeline whispered in Nita's ear. The black was good. Somehow, she picked up Maestri's fear or Wallace's nervousness.

"Grab weapons," he murmured.

He glanced back, found Miss Ginny studying him, frown lines on her normally smooth forehead.

"Move away from the door to the hall," he ordered. "Join Nita in the back."

"No!" shouted Wallace. "We must leave now." He grabbed his charge's arm, pulled her toward the door. "Trust me," he said. "As your father's aide..."

Maestri supposed he should let them go. Miss Ginny was an innocent, after all. He palmed his knife instead. "You will freeze, Captain Wallace," he said. "My favorite target is an eye. From this distance, I can't miss."

He pointed with the haft. "Please do as I asked, Miss Ginny. Join Nita. Your father's aide acts suspiciously. I believe we're about to be attacked."

The girl yanked her arm free from Wallace's grip and stepped toward Maestri. "The danger's not from my father," she said, "if any exists." She reached into her shoulder-slung purse and spoke into a transceiver. "Trouble at the hotel. Send back-up teams immediately."

Maestri liked the girl. No nonsense there. "My nephew and myself are your father's supporters," he said. "We would not harm you." He frowned at Wallace, wiggled his knife to hold him still when the girl obeyed his earlier command to join Nita. Maestri then turned and followed Miss Ginny into the dining room.

Wallace kicked at the wainscoting.

Maistre poked his head back around the corner. "Guards," he shouted. "Check to see if Wallace left a package out there. It's a bomb, maybe. Be careful of strangers."

There was no time for an answer. A great glare of light burst through the cracks of the hall door. A powerful punch hit Maistre's head and exposed shoulder and knocked him, spinning, to the floor.

So much for the White House Security detail and Miss Ginny's bodyguards, he thought.

The hallway door hung crazily from its bottom hinge. A smoldering fire lit the outside hall. Smoke poured through his suite's doorway. Captain Wallace's crumpled form lay against the left-hand wall.

Maistre staggered up and glanced at the women. Madeline and Nita held knives, their faces tense, while Miss Ginny grasped her face snare. He turned back to watch the hallway.

"My father had nothing to do with this," the President's daughter said from behind him. "For one thing, he wouldn't endanger me. It has to be HHR..."

Three men darted through the smoke and into the suite. They wore clothes decent enough to bring themselves through the security system of the hotel, but now covered their faces with black stocking masks and held short guns.

Maistre threw and stuck one of them in the neck. Blood pulsed out in a great stream. The man desperately tried to hold his throat together as he collapsed. The other two whirled and pointed guns at the entryway where Will stood.

"Down," he yelled and threw himself inside and to the floor.

The volleys of automatic fire sounded tinny, Maistre thought, probably a sign that the bomb had partially deafened him. Bullets thwacked through the partition and thudded into the solid wall at the rear.

"Man, you've a high-intensity life style," whispered Madeline as she crawled over him and poked her head around the partition. "Stay down, now. You've no weapon."

She rose suddenly, swung a large carving knife from the floor, and caught one of the attackers in the crotch. The man screamed. He fell through the doorway, dropping his gun as he curled up, blood staining his pants, and then shrieked great gulps of sound.

Shots sounded, then a rapid burst from an automatic weapon, from further away now. Maistre couldn't see but guessed that the remaining gunman had moved back and fired through the partition. He didn't seem to care about his fellow.

"Shit!" whispered Madeline as she fell over Maistre. Blood poured from her chest. She moved to cover him better and then lay still.

Her limp body stirred from a bullet. Maistre felt a red-hot streak pass through his buttocks; another hit him high. A bad one. He tried to move, but couldn't.

Then he glimpsed a blood-covered Miss Ginny scramble forward from behind him and grasp the abandoned gun. Her face was cold, graven. She carefully fingered the safety, leveled the gun above the floor, and held the trigger down.

"Rat-a-tat-tat-a-tat-tat..."

Her arms and wrists must be strong, Maistre thought as he began to fade. She sweeps the other room, and the gun doesn't rise on her.

#

Minutes later, Bjorn flung men aside and jumped over pieces of flesh and burning carpet to enter the blood-spattered suite. He identified hotel guards and curious guests but no medical team yet. No White House support force either.

Miss Ginny leaned against an interior entryway, her dress smeared with blood, her hand holding a semi-automatic machine pistol. Tears ran from her eyes.

"I'm so sorry, Major, so sorry."

He felt ice cold and walked carefully, more in fear of what he might do than what he might see.

A body lay against the right hand wall, dressed in a Corps uniform. Bjorn stepped over another man, who wore black and a mask; his shoes squished in still uncongealed blood. Uncle Will's reddened knife lay near the man's clenched hand.

A third body--the final gunner, he guessed--had died from lead indigestion. He curled on the other side of the room, opposite Miss Ginny, and held his belly.

Bjorn touched the girl on her arm as he stepped over a fourth man, who had bled to death from a crotch wound. Gently, he pulled a dead black woman off Uncle Will and felt for a pulse in his neck.

Yes! Weak, but...

"Nita?" he asked.

He knelt down, didn't glance away from the man who meant damn near everything to him. His hands trembled.

"She didn't dive down fast enough," Miss Ginny answered in a weak voice. "A bullet took her in the chest. I could do nothing."

That gay life gone. What a waste!

Now, Bjorn looked up at the President's daughter. "I owe you," he said.

Chapter 22

"You can't back down," Bjorn told the distraught President a day later, in the White House. "Somehow, we'll have to do without Uncle Will."

His gut tightened at the memory of orderlies pushing his uncle out of the Bethesda Naval Hospital operating room. Drained and small, Uncle Will lay on his stomach, a black, glistening apparatus that looked like a large leech strapped to his spinal cord.

"Striker declared war," Bjorn said. "Changing your campaign strategy and swallowing your words will only turn what supporters you now have against you."

"We know, Bent Brain," the Ambassador said. "Don't repeat the obvious."

The President actually moaned as if the bottom dropped out of his stomach. He wobbled from the room.

Later that day, Bjorn flew in a Presidential ramjet back to San Angeles. There, he met with Con Wagoner in the Residents Council conference room and gave him Uncle Will's memory slug.

"I don't know the other ghetto leaders," Con protested. Dad and supporters milled around while Con and Bjorn sat. "Why do you think they'll listen to me?"

"You started this revolution. You're a hero to most of them. They'll listen."

Bjorn bent forward in his seat, so his head was only a half-meter from Con's. "Listen," he said. "You've got to get off your ass and fill-in for Uncle Will. You must persuade ghetto-heads all across the country to vote for the President. A win's the only chance we have."

He sat back. "Tell the other Residents Councils

that we're 'surplus people,' according to Striker. Ask them what they think will happen if we let that bastard win."

Con and the rest seemed stunned by the tale of his interview with the HHR director and of the attempted assassinations.

"The first thing Striker will do when he takes the presidency is to order punishment battalions, and maybe the Corps, into San Angeles," Bjorn continued. "No matter what he does to the other ghettos, we leaders here will all end up dragged into refuse trucks by dead-meat drag hooks."

"Invasion's not for sure," Dad said. He stood over Bjorn now. "We've got signed self-government commitments from the Administration." He took a gulp of air and glared at Bjorn. "Besides, smart ass, what'll you be doing, while Con's pissing off HHR even more?"

Bjorn stood and turned to walk away. "I'm calling on friends in another part of the country," he answered over his shoulder. "I've put Tommy Hata in charge of the battalion while I'm gone."

Bjorn left then. Wagoner was a grown man, and Bjorn's employer. Con didn't need a holovision script to tell him what to do, for God's sake. He'd probably get mad if Bjorn shoved a plan under his nose.

Besides, Bjorn didn't want to start people talking. Let the bastards worry about what they should do rather than spend time chewing about what he planned.

Then Bjorn took off with Capodonno for San Antonio, where the administration trained a new army division. He had contacted an old Veracruz buddy and arranged a secret meeting.

#

His hosts didn't turn on the main lights in the cavernous gymnasium of the 8th Infantry Regiment because they didn't want to attract officer attention. Only illumination from open doors to bordering offices and lavatories reached out, leaving dark shadows along two back walls. Bjorn estimated he had an audience of about sixty non-commissioned officers, who sat in rows, in the lit section. Many were veterans of Veracruz. About half represented other regiments in the division.

The men hunched on the mats used in hand-to-hand combat training, their arms around their knees, while he and the regimental sergeant major occupied composite chairs in front. Two heavy-set first sergeants ticked-off names as more men slid through the door.

The air was dry and the night cool, but Bjorn perspired. He pulled at his officer's blouse in order to increase ventilation near his skin, careful not to dislodge the ironed-on ribbon strip he wore. Waiting to speak reminded him of the minutes before battle.

His San Angeles Company's master sergeant, Julio Capodonno, stood in the gymnasium's shadows somewhere, his scarred face bland, his cynical eyes taking in everything.

Finally, Sergeant Major Lopez stood and the low rumble of conversation ceased. The regiment's senior non-com was a short and wide man with a large nose and bigger chin, his grizzled black haircut close to his skull. "All right," he said. "Let's get started. You've all heard of Major Bjorn, commander of the San Angeles Independent Battalion. Some of you remember him from Veracruz. Myself... Well, Bjorn was the glue that kept most of us in place on San Ysidro ridge. Listen with respect, even if you don't like what he says."

Bjorn stood as the men made last minute moves to become comfortable and then quieted. He walked a few steps to the side and surveyed the crowd.

"Most men of this regiment and in this gym are from Mexican wards in San Angeles," he started. "Have you thought what will happen to your people if HHR wins the election? I'll tell you. Punishment battalions will march into the ghetto and slaughter everyone who helped throw out the Welfare King and ship south anyone who thought of helping."

"I suppose you're for the President," a voice from the darkness shouted. "The bastard invaded the old country, ordered the death strip, and threw some of our people out of the U.S. He's no better than the fucking HHR."

The voice, heavily accented, came from a shadow to Bjorn's right.

"He did the right thing." Bjorn retorted, turning. "You know something? My Uncle Will fingered the guys they threw out. He named the hotheads, located the cubbies of the most recent wetbacks. He did the right thing, too."

He motioned at the sergeant major behind him. "Those of us who fought at Veracruz also helped the President close the border."

Bjorn didn't hear a sound now.

"The operation worked. No more illegal immigration; stable rations until recently."

Shouts rose from the crowd. Men argued with their neighbors. Bjorn stood silently, waiting for his audience to settle down. The quiet, when it came, was partly hostile.

"What's your alternative--let everyone in?" Bjorn shook his fist. "Screw the outsiders. The President did the only thing he could to give those of us who live here a chance."

He stood strong, stared in the direction of the man who'd originally spoken. "Let's move closer to now," he said. "The President okayed the Wagoner government after the revolt. We've got the old rations back. Residents Councils and law courts run the wards rather than a corrupt Welfare King and his gang bosses. The President has promised to repeal the laws of sixty-six across the whole country."

He then turned to the other side of the room. "This world's coming apart fast," he said. "We men have a duty to protect those we love. It's time to forget your ethnic background and remember your families."

Bjorn found himself pacing back and forth, turning every three meters or so. His voice had dropped into a growl. "Do you want to lose them? Do you want to see your relatives die from short rations? God damn it, we must keep this President in office!"

"I tell you, Senores, you from San Angeles are lucky," a voice from near Bjorn's feet said. "The Texas ghettos hurt!" The speaker was a heavy first sergeant, who turned so his voice penetrated to the back of the gymnasium. "The ration sharing groups break up; tenements fight each other. My mamacita spreads the money I send, but family starves. Listen to this man!"

Reluctant nods replaced frowns now.

"I believe this is our last chance," Bjorn said. "If the President loses, HHR will raze a lot of San Angeles and force ghettos everywhere to decide who's to die in order to keep livable rations for the rest. You men must speak out for your people."

"So, how do we do that?" asked Sergeant Major Lopez from behind.

Bjorn picked another man in the back to talk to. "Form an enlisted men's council. Have it tell your officers you want them to obey the President before the election, not the chiefs of staff, HHR, or anyone else. Tell them you non-coms will take over command of this division if Welfies can't vote freely. You will defend the ghettos against HHR. Tell them you will fight the Corps if it interferes."

A hubbub rose, but Sergeant Major Lopez stood and Bjorn turned to him. Everybody quieted.

"That's mutiny," Lopez protested.

"Not quite. Under the old Constitution, the President is our Commander in Chief. Soldiers are supposed to obey him. No one ever repealed that."

"They'll send Enforcers in."

Bjorn felt coldness settle in him.

"Kill them, then," he snarled. "Don't tell me

you've never heard of putting down Enforcers and the officers who back them."

"That's mutiny, for certain," someone said. "Guys in the Second Brigade, Tenth Battalion were crucified for killing those pricks."

"Yes," Bjorn said. He forced his audience to be quiet by saying nothing for a long moment. "You're right. If you shot bastards who tried to make you forget your people, senior officers could order loyal troops to nail you on crosses, maybe try to send the Corps against this regiment and division.

Bjorn took a deep breath. "I think the President can stop anything like that. When people hear that you've declared for him, he'll become stronger.

"Your courage will make others step up, too. I'm hoping that every unit in the two new infantry divisions sends up my message. I'm hoping that our Welfie brothers in the Corps will too."

He surveyed the room and wished he could look into individual sets of eyes. "I'm not inviting you to a game of musical chairs with eager whores," he said. "My party could become a barroom belly-opener, instead.

The crowd grunted.

"There are lots of futures worse than what I've outlined," Bjorn continued. "You could act like men, while other regiments lie on their faces with their legs spread and listen to you scream. HHR could kill the President, leaving us leaderless, and then send in the Corps. For warriors there's always risk," he said. "That's what we're paid for."

He slapped his thigh. "No matter what happens, the San Angeles Bluffers won't lean their heads back for easy throat cutting," he said, "I guarantee that." Bjorn felt prickling under his skin. "I won't surrender, ever!" he shouted.

No one moved.

"What happens if the President loses the

election?" Lopez finally asked.

Bjorn turned to him. "If we lose, you'll see me again. HHR plans to put down hundreds of thousands of people, and then cut the rations of millions. If we don't have balls, our people die."

He took a deep breath.

"You'll have to shift allegiance from the new President," Bjorn continued, "to a ghetto-based government, to the San Angeles city-state for example. We'd have civil war, then."

His audience moved restlessly now, whispered to each other. The sergeant major sat down, frowning thoughtfully. "At least you lay it out," he said.

"There's an officer back here, wearing fatigues," someone shouted. "It's Colonel Lefko."

"Capodonno, check the outside perimeter," Bjorn shouted over the resulting clamor.

"He can't have reinforcements out there," Lopez yelled. "I'd be warned."

Non-coms stood to make way for the straight figure that slowly walked through the shadows towards Bjorn.

"How'd you get in?" someone asked.

"I came early, waited near the boxing ring."

The light voice made Bjorn shiver with memories. "Come along, Colonel," he said. "Don't try to identify those you pass, or a mutiny will start before any of us want it to--with the execution of a commanding officer."

"There's a better alternative to murder," Louis Lefko, Bjorn's old commander in Mexico said, turning his back to Bjorn and addressing the crowd. "I'll forget what I've heard and who I've seen, if you all return to barracks and don't involve yourselves anymore in this dangerous conspiracy."

No one stood to leave.

The slim Lefko strode in front of Lopez. A faint scar marked the officer's cheek, starting from his hawk nose. The wound, and others more serious, Bjorn had heard, invalided Lefko only days after Bjorn himself had been evacuated to the hospital ship.

There was little chance of murder. Bjorn supposed the men thought as well of Lefko as he did.

The colonel turned again and placed his frowning stare on his non-commissioned officers. "Get out of here," he ordered. "Now!"

"Begging your pardon, Sir," Sergeant Major Lopez said. "I think we should vote on Major Bjorn's proposal before we break up. Otherwise..."

Otherwise, clever Lefko would transfer the ass out of this collection of men, Bjorn thought. He'd start with the sergeant major. His old commander was not a bloody man, only very competent. There would be no more chances for a meeting like this.

Lopez stepped forward and stood next to the colonel. He seemed about to speak to the men. But Colonel Lefko preempted him.

"Well then, Sergeant Major, may I contribute to your decision process?" he asked. The colonel didn't wait for an answer, but moved past Lopez so he would not be masked. "What will happen," he asked, "if you take the actions Major Bjorn suggests, and you paralyze the new infantry divisions until after the elections?"

Lefko held up a hand. "By the way, you know the Corps won't mutiny, don't you? Not a chance."

Bjorn had to agree. His abdomen was stiff as a board.

"What happens when the current President loses?" Lefko continued. "As he will, of course. Major Bjorn said you'd fight in a civil war." He pretended to spit. "That's ridiculous, and you all know it.

"You can't beat the Corps," he continued as the men stayed deathly quiet. "It's got high technology weapons, has twice the numbers of your two new army divisions, and is disciplined. Every man in this room would die on a cross, plus a lot of your friends who stand watch for you now. Bjorn tries to talk you into certain death."

"I want my boy to go to the same school you did, Colonel," a man yelled from half way down the floor. "He's good enough. I'm sick of the way HHR keeps us down."

"Yeah," shouted another. "A goon gang killed my brother. Thanks to Wagoner, they're crematorium smoke now. We need to kill all the HHR latrines."

"The President speaks for the decent Achievers," one of the top sergeants at the door said.

"If Striker and the HHR wins, we're all dog food anyway," in man standing up at the back of the mats said in a deep baritone.

"It comes down to rations!" the Texan near Bjorn shouted. "Do you guarantee food for my family, Colonel?"

A torrent of similar observations gave Lefko his answer. The issue was not what Striker might do to them, but what they felt needed doing. Bjorn wouldn't have to make a second visit.

"The ranks wouldn't have reacted like this without you," Lefko said to him under the noise.

"Look at your hole card, Colonel," Bjorn answered. "Do you want to side with the goddamn enforcer types? The President needs able Achievers, especially proven military leaders like yourself."

Lefko stared at him and then shook his head. "The only argument that says I should 'come over,' is you. You've always frightened me, Bjorn; did you know that? Now here you are, surprising your opponents, leaping for the jugular, as always. From past experience, I concede you might win."

Then he looked away. "But, it's highly unlikely."

The sergeant major stood and quieted the crowd. "All for forming an enlisted council say yes," he yelled. A roar made a further dialogue unnecessary.

"I appoint myself chairman," Lopez said when he could be heard. "I'll nominate the others secretly."

He turned to Lefko. "To avoid trouble, Sir, consider Bjorn's message delivered. Pass it on to your superiors. Tell them not to screw with the ghettos in this election. Now go. We've got to discuss how we'll deter you from putting up crosses." That big chin thrust out. "You know, eye-for-an-eye business."

#

"Lopez dreams if he thinks Lefko will let his superiors decide how to react to my message," Bjorn growled later that night. "The bastard's moving! Right now!"

He wore civvies, a one-piece work suit of an undistinguished brown, while Capodonno had donned gray. Lopez dropped them off at midnight near the main refueling station for the automated highway. They stood near a lighted gate.

"The sergeant major thought you had the frights, I guess," the wiry non-com said, "when you insisted on taking this way back to San Angeles."

"My passport number, DNA profile, and picture will be on security screens at all transportation check points," Bjorn growled. "Yours too, probably."

He kicked at the dirt. If only he'd ordered a search of the gymnasium before the meeting's beginning! If only he'd started with some other regiment.

Strange how his first sight of Lefko had told him what the man's counter-move would be. It was what Bjorn would do if the roles were reversed.

Capodonno leaned against the fence like a civilian.

"I've given Lefko an opportunity to star," Bjorn said. "The colonel knows national politics, who the players are. He may have reached Striker already. After this, Striker will know Lefko."

"So what'll Striker do? Why can't the infantry still put pressure on HHR?"

Bjorn felt like yelling with rage. Damn!

"Lefko will talk Striker into isolating the new divisions," he answered. The chiefs will send them out of the country or into the desert, then remove all long-range transports. They'll transfer-out officers like Lefko who are at risk. If the men mutiny, the administration will stop the shipment of all supplies."

He sighed. "After the election, when hope is gone, the chiefs will send in Enforcers. They'll take their time combing-out the independent spirits, but there will be a lot of garroting and crucifixions until the infantry divisions are as disciplined as the Corps."

"Can't you ask the President to stop the chiefs from doing what you say, from shifting the troops?"

"The bastard chiefs all take Striker's anti-Welfie line. They'll tell the President that supply considerations require the moves. He will be easily fooled by senior officers he trusts, while I'm only a jumped up sergeant."

Bjorn clenched his fists and stared at the dry, brown ground. "Anyway, this wonderful strategy of mine is now a loser," he said.

"Man coming."

They stood near a locked gate in a three-meter-high fence that formed the base for another meter of angled razor wire. "Play this meek and humble, Capodonno," Bjorn directed. "Pretend we're in a little trouble in San Antonio, but not a lot. Don't make this bastard look us up."

The "Fixer" was small, fat, and brown. He talked Mex, as probably everyone in San Antonio did. "Who sent you?" he asked.

"Ponce de Leon." Bjorn didn't smile as he gave the password.

"You got payment?"

Bjorn held out his hand. "Two discs on the people-hauler airline. Should be worth more than your price to ride a train."

The Mex examined the discs in a hand-held reader, then smiled, but without friendliness. "You hot, eh?"

"Like all your other passengers, I guess."

The fixer's eyes shifted. He continually wet his lips with a very red tongue.

Bjorn's rage with his own poor planning didn't leave much emotional play. However, he forced a smile.

"Come." The little Achiever unlocked the gate by inserting his finger in the DNA reader and then led them between a large liquefaction station and the old pipeline. The latter now brought hydrogen gas from nuclear electrolysers on the Gulf instead of pumping natural gas in the other direction. "I have the very best carriers for ghetto-heads," the fixer said. "Old fashioned truck-trains whose engines are converted to burn hydrogen."

Lights dotted the landscape. They showed Bjorn a large, low-pressure tank that floated on its pond of water between the pipeline and the liquefier. It would hold hydrogen gas, he knew. Also, a net of guide rails threaded between switches and finally led into the refueling yard.

A long line of flatbed, wheeled vehicles between one of those pairs of rails held big boxes of many shapes, mostly standard containers. The flatbed trucks trailed behind a large hauler engine that now sat under overhead fueling lines. As Bjorn followed the fixer into a small yard that contained maybe forty people, he saw bright flashes from behind the big, aerodynamic shields that hung over the leading edge of each flatbed truck. He looked away quickly.

De-lousers, Bjorn guessed. Automatic laser burners cleaned out people who secretly climbed up to the perches that Bjorn and others paid to occupy.

"The truck-train comes by here after it refuels," the Achiever said. "You will run and climb on. It gains speed fast; you only have seconds."

Sergeant Major Lopez told Bjorn that prior travelers had reported to him after safely arriving in San

Angeles. The hobo route was good if riders jumped off
at each refueling stop before the de-lousers activated
and then on again before the train departed. And if
three hundred kilometers an hour wind caused by the
train's velocity didn't scoop them out from behind an
aerodynamic shield.

"Two more? Carramba, there aren't enough
shields!"

The speaker was a strong-faced woman with
long, gray hair. She wore pants stretched over wide
hips. Two small boys stayed close to her. "You cheat
us, Fixer," she said. "You say I get a shield, myself.
Don't think you can screw me because I'm a woman and
my men are young."

She waved a small knife.

The Achiever stepped back. He now held a
pistol. "You insolent, Welfie bitch!" he shouted. "You
were a stuck-up Residents Council member, weren't
you?"

He waved his gun at the crowd that huddled
against a blank-walled hut. "All of you are Welfie rats
trying to escape to your fancy new city-state, I suppose,
before the pogrom gets really tough. I could probably
make more from rewards than you pay, so don't fuck
with me." He turned and leveled his gun at the woman,
his lips firming.

"Wait a minute, compadre," Bjorn said, in as
meek a voice as he could muster. "Maybe I can solve
this without forcing you to hurt your reputation with
future customers."

Capodonno glided behind the Achiever and made
the man look over his shoulder nervously.

"How about letting us share your shield, senora?"
Bjorn asked the woman. "The boys can sit on our laps.
We'll help them up and down at the refueling. I
understand the vibration is fierce at the train's top
speed; to hold on is a challenge. You could use the
help of two strong men."

The woman stepped forward to stare closely into Bjorn's eyes and then nodded and put her knife away. "I accept."

The Achiever pocketed his gun and smiled thinly. He began to place them along the tracks and assign cars.

Bjorn bent down to introduce himself to the boys.

I've screwed up any chance of winning military help, he thought. What's my plan now?

Chapter 23

When Bjorn returned to San Angeles from San Antonio, Con Wagoner reported to him that the big man made little progress with his fellow Residents Council chairmen in other megacities. "They're scared shitless," Con said. "Curfews everywhere. Burner lasers instead of blinding ones clear the streets now. And machine-gunning. Hesselrein of Pittsburgh told me his people stand in long ward parades--total families instead of individual representatives--waiting their turn for food. They inhale threats."

The DNA-linked ballots of those who did eventually vote would no longer be secret, either, Con suspected.

"We'll have to try something else," Bjorn told him after reporting his own failure. "Wait a week."

#

In the early hours one morning, Con leaned his back against the inside of a jump jet, Dad next to him, and stretched. His previously injured leg wouldn't cripple him anymore. A month earlier, after the revolt, his Council had granted him the necessary medical rations. "Hell," Fifty-two said at the time, "we need you spry so you can lead us into the Promised Land."

A re-break, the biological melt of bad growth, and the use of hurry-up hormones on the bone straightened and evened it again. His muscles were weak from past misuse, that was all.

Past time for him to focus on this move.

Of course, if he couldn't trust Major Bjorn's initiatives, the ghetto cause was damned anyway. Relax, Con told himself.

Bjorn sat forward with his command team, near the cockpit. A primal force field seemed to emanate from the man.

Con bit his lip. Don't be foolish, he told himself. Bjorn's poise was impressive, that was all. Nothing supernatural there.

His military commander apparently reviewed the flight path. A cone of light directed on a map in Bjorn's lap and made his tight yellow curls seem almost gold, left deep pools of darkness under wiry brows. In the foreground, soldiers sat in two dark rows of bench seats that pointed to the major.

Con shivered and looked away.

His future, the future of the people he loved, of those for whom he was responsible, rested on Bjorn's shoulders. Decisive action must replace talk now. All their other hopes had proved empty.

"How come the damn technologists don't shoot us down?" Dad asked in a whisper.

Con shrugged. "Achievers are imperfect humans too, you know," he answered. "Major Bjorn says all the ground radars are at the borders or around the capital, and the overhead ones aren't usually interested in what goes on inside the country. Then, the airplane's stealthy and we're flying low, 'in the clutter,' whatever that means."

The transport suddenly changed heading, causing Con to grab the safety belt around his middle.

"I didn't want you to come on this hare-brained attack," grumbled Dad.

Con thought of saying: "No one asked you along, either. You should have stayed with Jami and your coming grandchild."

He welcomed his father's companionship, actually. And, if this expedition failed, Jami would be better off without an identifiable male Wagoner around.

They left San Angeles at midnight. Four transports carried four hundred men, the whole battalion except for a training nucleus. First, they flew over the southern United States but now abruptly headed north.

Major Bjorn told Con that HHR had a spy in close, that he dare not inform anyone in the White House. Besides, there'd been no need to share the secret. Since the President supplied the transports some time earlier, soon after forming the battalion, Bjorn had everything he needed. And Con had his own doubts about the President's grit at this low time. The man's sister, the Ambassador, had the balls of the family.

Just as well that the Welfies acted on their own.

After flying another ten minutes, Con saw light reflected in the spy screens up forward. The airplane shuddered as it launched missiles and released piggybacked assault craft. The engines vibrated as wings rotated. Airplane structure complained. They sunk.

Con held on tight.

Lights on the forward screens blinked off as he heard dull thuds from exploding warheads. He sensed outriggers extend and unevenly settle onto the ground.

Down! Air defense missiles hadn't intercepted them, thank God.

Bjorn grinned at him in the red light that suffused the cabin. "We caught the Chicago Punishment battalion by surprise," he announced. "We're in their compound."

Men stood quietly.

"Our microwave warheads worked, too," Con heard Bjorn say from beyond the men. "Their electricity's off."

Red lights blinked out. The aircraft side opposite Con folded out and formed a ramp. He sat straight now, held by the seat belt. A quiet struggle of men who left seats and stepped down toward the loom of dark buildings surrounded him.

A shadowy hand reached across and released

the belt. "Up, Mr. Wagoner," Master Sergeant Julio Capodonno said. "Major Bjorn wants you with the command group."

"We know what we're supposed to do," grumbled Dad. He stood next to Con, helped him up. "We don't need no sheep dog."

Con touched Capodonno on his armored arm. "Dad's only ornery when he worries about other people, Master Sergeant. Lead the way."

Outside, Con heard the first firing, mostly at a turreted wall that extended to his right. A small saucer--one of their piggyback aircraft--had lodged on the blister of an embrasure. Sharp explosions of light signaled missile firings from around his transport, a streak of tracers swept the top of the wall.

"Look out!" Dad yelled. Then his father shoved him down, fell on top, his weight making the gravel bite through Con's clothes.

Glancing under the old man's shoulder, Con saw a man sight an assault rifle at them from above, on the wall, while other HHR troops hurriedly mounted a light machine gun in a notch of the parapet. The enemy stood out in the glare of a searchlight just snapped-on from the airplane he had left.

"Shit!" Capodonno exclaimed. He closed his visor.

Con felt two explosions shake his father. The old man groaned, then seemed to hiccup and became limp.

Capodonno, completely armored, winced from a ricocheting round and kneeled next to Con and Dad. He fired a short burst at the men on the wall.

A heat-seeking flechette, no, two, had hit Dad and exploded in him! Frantic, Con tried to heave-off his father's body. He wiggled and started to slide out. Then another weight drove the air from his lungs and pinned him to the ground.

"Stay, Wagoner."

Capodonno must have rotated his visor up again

as he, too, lay over Con.

He heard more shooting up on the wall, but bullets didn't scream his way. "Dad," he whispered. "Are you conscious?"

There was no reply. Now, shouting resounded from the wall.

"Dad," he screamed. "Say something!"

Capodonno stood, slid Dad's body off Con, and rolled it face-up. "His back's a mess," he said. "The flechettes took out everything aft of the ribcage. At least death was quick."

Con rose on his knees and peered in the dim light provided by the overhead searchlight at his father's strong, old face. The bony eyebrow ridges, the white hair, and gaunt cheeks made Dad look like a king. That brave soul who defied HHR, that loving human who cried for a week after Con's mother died from ghetto flu, the wise advisor...

Only an empty hulk now.

Con found himself sobbing; his eyes ran with tears.

"Up, Mr. Wagoner," Capodonno said, as he put his hand under Con's elbow. "You need to move inside, with the Major. I'll have Dad's body brought into our temporary morgue."

Con shook loose the hand, but stood anyway. He wanted to shriek with rage. His body trembled and perspiration wet his skin.

"This way, Sir," said his guide, and moved between Con and the wall. "This door."

After he limped inside, Con blinked and halted, rested on his good leg. Red light showed a command center, no longer operating, and Bjorn's men making room on benches for their own equipment. Screams, shots, and the detonation of missiles reverberated from farther back in the building. Like a scene from hell, he thought, even to the contorted bodies scattered on the floor.

Bjorn's men were used to the loss of friends in combat, he supposed. They went on, knowing grief in action unaffordable. He hadn't their training.

"Hone, if they won't surrender, punch in a thermite warhead. We don't have time to screw around."

Major Bjorn stood in the middle of the room. A helmet covered his face now, but his voice echoed from a speaker set on the floor. A technician hurriedly turned off the broadcast.

Master Sergeant Capodonno brought forward a composite chair and Con sat down. "We've found the fuse stations, Sir," the little man said. "In five minutes, we'll have white light."

Bjorn removed his helmet. "I'm sorry, Con," he said. "You and Dad were targets of opportunity. Bad luck is all."

He's saying not to blame Capodonno, Con thought.

"Dad was about as proud of you as a father could be," Bjorn went on.

The last thing Dad heard from his son was to be called "ornery," Con remembered. He leaned back to relieve the pain in his stomach.

"Put the speaker back on the communications net," Bjorn directed his technician. "So Mr. Wagoner can hear."

"Given surprise," he told Con, "the HHR battalion had no chance. The architect didn't design the installation with the idea that a high technology force might come at the compound from on top. He only worried about a Welfie mob crashing against the walls."

Con didn't allow himself to cover his face or wipe away tears.

"I know this doesn't help you, but we'll have very few other casualties."

"Major Bjorn, Hata here."

"Go ahead, Tommy."

"I've deployed my company in front of the Welfare

King's headquarters, down town. Lights are on inside, but nobody's come out to sniff around. They probably prepare for our attack and call for help. But they've no weapons on the roof as our defensive teams had in our exercises. My building-buster's aimed at the door, my fully armored squad's primed to jump in the hole."

"Make it quick," Bjorn answered. "We want the Residents Council types to come out of hiding--which they'll do once they know the king's gone. There are lots they need to do."

"Wagoner here, Captain Hata," Con interrupted, loudly. "When you talk to Welfies, make sure they know we're friends. This isn't a raid; it's a liberation."

Now he did wipe his face. The worse was over, he guessed, although he would break down again when he talked to Jami.

Con heard a beep, then a different voice. "Hone here," it said. "We've got the barracks--and the fun house, as these bastards call their slave quarters. You ought to see it, Major."

With that, the lights of the command post blinked on. Con shrouded his eyes.

"The place is pretty much secure," Bjorn said. "Let's go for a tour."

That'll get your mind off Dad, Con finished for Bjorn.

Capodonno led, one of the missile launchers held at the ready, while two soldiers with regular, high velocity rifles trailed them. Con limped along with Bjorn. They walked outside and then paused to let their eyes take in the now-lighted parade ground that Bjorn's three transports occupied.

Con knew from the pre-briefing that the fortress measured a kilometer on each side. Walls enclosed the working area, while buildings huddled together in the middle, designed to give occupants a last redoubt.

Dawn's clarity diffused over the compound.

He saw only a few men. They wore his San

Angeles uniforms and entered a turret on the wall,
apparently not under fire.

Con peeked into a large hanger that contained
small assault rotorcraft and several rows of ground
vehicles. Some of the latter flaunted the optics and
chemical tankage of laser blinders. Others carried
building-buster missiles and machine guns. There were
armored personnel carriers, prisoner transports, a
mobile command center, and an unidentifiable variety of
other vehicles. San Angeles soldiers climbed over
several of the laser blinders, apparently prepared to
drive them into the compound.

Bjorn pointed to lines of prisoners who walked out
of the building in front of them. Unarmed, most in
underwear, they sullenly stumbled past Con, and swore,
spit, and sometimes yelled in anger. Their guards,
carrying electric prods, were threateningly silent.

"They'll sit out in the middle of the parade
ground," Bjorn said. "We'll use laser blinders as fences
to keep them in place and turn the beams into burners
when they get desperate. These men are arrogant now,
but will humble-down when they realize they're going to
Welfies for trial. They'll cry and scream with fear, then."

Con questioned trials--he hadn't prosecuted
HHR's men captured in San Angeles. Then, he began
to wonder about something much more important,
something he should have thought about before.

Captain Hone met them at the door to a building
next to the barracks. He was a big man, with shiny,
black skin over a fleshy face. "I'm glad you came too,
Mr. Wagoner," he said. "You need to bring by the local
Residents Council. This'll lock them in to us, if they
aren't already."

A brothel, Con thought, as he limped on plush
carpet past drink and drug dispensers, saw colored,
moving friezes of porn on the walls, and heard lush
music. Even the air smelled jungle-rotten.

Five prostrate men, whose arms were tied behind

them, had been garroted here. They were paunchy, perhaps depraved men, wearers of embroidered HHR patches.

The executions angered Con. But then he walked into the next room, a long hall bisected with an aisle, and came to the cages, forty or fifty of them. Girls, women, boys, and young men stood stark naked behind translucent bars, behind individual panels carrying the kind of finger holes that sampled DNA and confirmed credit. Some of the prisoners wore the yellow marks of electric whips, others seemed dazed with drugs. Beyond the cages a stairway led up, probably to bedrooms.

In the back of the cages, where the occupants couldn't miss them, signs blinked in red and black: "Eagerness Earns Life" and "Provide Joy; Win Food and Rest."

"The prisoners stood when we entered," Hone said. "Their sleeping pads are wired for a current that flows when a customer walks in. By the way, an incinerator behind the building is large enough for bodies no longer useful. We found a dead little boy there."

Two naked, dead males rolled down the stairs. Probably HHR soldiers, Con thought. Two young girls, maybe fourteen or fifteen, staggered down behind them. Their eyes were wide with terror; their bodies bore red welts; and their arms were blue with pinch marks. They tried to cover their genitals with their hands. Three white-faced soldiers in San Angeles gray gently shooed them along.

Con turned away and vomited.

Bjorn stood coolly by his side. He was a professional soldier, of course, and probably had seen worse.

Medics arrived, along with technicians who could open the cages--and a hologram cameraman. Con pushed by them, desperate for fresh air. First Dad; now this horror.

"We must return to the command center," Major Bjorn said from behind, once Con stepped outside. "The President calls."

As he followed, Con glanced around the fortress. Air defense troops erected mid-range anti-aircraft missiles at the corners of buildings; soldiers unpacked portable, short-range missiles and deployed them on the walls.

That reminded Con of his new worry. Despite his general weakness, he limped faster. "We can't repeat this, can we?" he asked Bjorn, when the young officer stopped to let him catch up. "HHR will make sure we don't take any more ghettos by military force."

Bjorn nodded and looked at him curiously. "If you can't persuade other Welfies to revolt," he said, "San Angeles and Chicago will be the only ghettos the President holds going into any election."

"I had hoped this might break the political freeze," Con replied. "But, if HHR has paralyzed everyone in the megacities, why would liberating one more ghetto change things?"

"It's forward motion," Bjorn answered. "We can't stand still or HHR will win." He placed his hand under Con's elbow. "The President waits."

Con cursed himself for an idiot. If he'd known Bjorn had no grand strategy, he wouldn't have come. He'd have preferred to spend his last hours fighting beside his loved ones. And Dad would have lived longer.

When Con entered the command center, he observed that the President, down in Washington, was violently angry. Still wearing pajamas, his hair uncombed, the Achiever's image strode up and down on the holovision platform.

"What were you two thinking of?" the President almost shouted. "HHR has demanded that I order the Corps to hang you."

"In four hours, I'll be dispersed in Chicago," Bjorn said, calmly. "The Corps will have to comb through twenty million people to find me. And they'll lose their shine doing so. I'll give the punishment battalion's weapons and mobile equipment to locals, and will soon have a demi-regiment--plus a cooperative, angry populace. Tell the Corps that; see if they like their prospects."

That's why I'm along, Con thought. To make sure the Welfies here support Bjorn.

"You've lost your mind!" shouted the outraged President. "We have an election campaign, yet you jump around and fight people. Wagoner is with you! People tie me to both of you."

"You can't win an election without Uncle Will," Major Bjorn said, still calm. "Maybe you couldn't win even with him."

"You don't know that!" the President said. "For sure we can't win now!"

Maistre's nephew has a larger purpose than action for action's sake, Con thought now. He's not just a military man, flailing away. I've been wrong.

"Join us for your own protection," Bjorn said. "Bring your family and Uncle Will, if he can be moved. Better hurry."

Chapter 24

When Bjorn, in his major's uniform, met the Presidential jump-jet in the central Chicago square the next afternoon, he remembered HHR Executive Director Striker's description of the President as "incompetent." Under disturbed gray hair, the politician's eyes were wild and his face was flushed.

"They're impeaching me," the President shouted as he stepped to the pavement. "The election's off."

In a mussed, gray suit, the following Ambassador almost hit Bjorn when she apparently detected a smile. "You crazy bastard!" she shouted. "The White House security chief stated he could no longer guarantee our safety in Washington."

Miss Ginny trotted down the aircraft steps in an impeccable, blue silk blouse and pleated cream skirt and gave a quick nod to both he and Con Wagoner. Her expression was curious, rather than desolate or angry. "We couldn't bring your uncle," she told Bjorn in a low voice. "The doctors said no. But I saw him again. He's better. The spinal cord re-growth is working. When I told him I'd be seeing you, he whispered that you were to "use your brains, not your balls."

She grinned.

"Let's go to a cleared facility where we can talk," he said to them all.

#

"You were supposed to attack HHR headquarters just before the election, not some meaningless punishment battalion months earlier," railed the Ambassador that evening. She paced back and forth, an emotional substitute for her brother, who sat, head down and silent, in a red and yellow armchair.

Bjorn disliked the sector gang's opulent headquarters. Glitzy, depraved, it violated Uncle Will's motto of "discipline, order, and restraint." Besides, Bjorn smelled dried blood.

"I couldn't take HHR headquarters," he replied, standing at ease with his hands clasped behind him. "And, I learned that distributed information systems permit distributed offices. I couldn't have killed the HHR snake even if I'd taken its nest."

"We're dead," gloomed the President. He wore a black suit that fit his mood. "The Vice President has taken over. With the agreement of Congress, he has, quote, 'deferred the election until the country settles down,' unquote. He really means until Striker has cleansed the ghettos of rebellion, until someone's eliminated me."

"I agree with Major Bjorn's remark when we talked via hologram earlier," Wagoner volunteered. "You had no chance in an election. The Welfare Kings have named wardens for each tenement--the most popular people available--and made them mortally responsible for the vote. My friends here say that the hostage system is detailed and believable."

The Ambassador stomped over and confronted Wagoner, her chin thrust forward. "Why couldn't Welfies kill the kings and punishment troops like you did in San Angeles?" she asked. "That would wipe out any hostage system. Tell the ghettos it's now or never."

Wagoner's taking the death of his father well, Bjorn thought. Hasn't blamed anyone. He's still effective. And, in his gray jump suit, that leonine head and athletic body are impressive. The President fades in comparison.

"I had surprise," Con replied. "HHR now randomly monitors the comm. lines, answers suspicious acts with raids and executions. Gang bosses have a quota of killings, can you believe that?" He shook his head. "I've come to the reluctant conclusion that my wife was right. There's no way we Welfies can win on ghetto power alone."

"Technology and organization can always beat the masses, don't you think?" asked Miss Ginny, who sat near her father. "As long as those who control the weapons keep their nerve?"

Bjorn thought she sounded emotionally uninvolved.

Wagoner glanced at him. "The major has a plan, I believe," he said. "We should hear it."

Striker had known of Bjorn's intent to attack HHR headquarters. Someone very close to the President or his sister was a pipeline into HHR. Had the President left the spy behind when he fled Washington? "I thought two ghettos were better than one, that's all," he replied.

The Ambassador marched over in front of him, now. "Don't give us your idiot act, Bjorn," she said, her face centimeters from his. "Why, of all places, Chicago?"

Mentally, he shrugged. No sense in keeping his thinking secret, he supposed. Striker would guess his motive soon enough. "Food, of course," he answered. "The mid-west harvests our grain, raises Achiever meat animals, while Chicago processes and ships most of the country's rations."

That silenced all of them. Miss Ginny developed a little smile and cocked her head as she watched him.

"Owning Chicago lets us squeeze the Achiever suburbs almost as badly as they're squeezing Welfie ghettos," he added.

The President sat up. His sister stepped back and stared at Bjorn. She began to smile, too.

"What about San Angeles rations?" Wagoner asked. "Washington can blockade my people."

"What about your uncle?" Miss Ginny asked also. "They'll use him as a lever."

Bjorn shrugged. "The more they squeeze us, the

more we squeeze them." But his stomach turned over at her reminder of the risk to Uncle Will. "Will the Welfies here agree to take over the food factories and stop shipping to Achievers?" he asked Wagoner.

Con stood. "They'll love the idea," he said and limped out.

Competent man, Bjorn thought. And positive, too. Wagoner always looked for a way to do something, rather than whining about difficulties.

"But how will we ever resolve this stand-off?" the President asked. He stood now, jolted out of his daze.

"The Vice President will go directly to the automated farms and ranches," his sister added, her smile now replaced by calculation lines on her forehead. "He'll set up new mills, slaughter houses, and packagers to process the raw food he gets."

"Yes," Miss Ginny countered. "But that will take months. Our 'just in time' inventory policies have resulted in empty local warehouses. Achievers will starve before the administration can build an alternative feeding system."

"We should only cut off the meat," Bjorn said. "After all, we're not out to hurt people, just persuade them."

"Achievers eat animal protein every day," noted the President. "That's almost as bad as starving them."

"Each side has more moves to make," Bjorn said. "We can't foresee what will happen. Let's relax."

The Ambassador pivoted and presented her silhouette to him. "Yes," she said, and wet her lips, then gave him a big smile. "I apologize if I was hasty just now."

The President smiled gravely. "I confess I'd about given up hope," he said. "Maybe we can negotiate a compromise."

"Come up with me to my suite," the Ambassador said to Bjorn. "I'll pour drinks. We can watch the news together."

Bjorn remembered the long lunch he had shared with the Ambassador back in the San Angeles hotel. She had been voracious for sex. The memory excited him.

But, Miss Ginny seemed to droop.

"Not tonight, I think," Bjorn said. "I'm tied up."

The Ambassador glanced at her niece, then back at Bjorn. "This is the second time you've said no, you bastard," she said. "You won't have a third opportunity." Her face red, she strode out of the room.

Miss Ginny sat straighter. "Nice of you," she said, "but negative acts don't do much for me."

"If you both don't mind," the President inserted, "I think I'll see if my chief of staff has set up a command center yet. I need to talk to Washington. HHR will have to listen to me when it realizes I control everyone's food."

He's so preoccupied that he's unaware of the sexual gaming around him, Bjorn thought. And, he lives in a dreamland, politically. Welfies will do the negotiating. The President didn't control anyone's food.

After her father left, Miss Ginny studied Bjorn. "I didn't know my feelings were so obvious," she said.

He liked her. And, for a tall clothespin, she was attractive enough. Good skin and bone structure, wide mouth, intelligent eyes.

He stepped over to her and held out his hand.

She bit her lip and stood. When his hand remained out, she stepped forward and placed hers in his palm.

He gently grasped her hand, stilled its shaking. "We must be friends, too, Ginny," he said. "I need an Achiever friend, God knows."

"Too?" Her smile wobbled. Then, she pulled herself toward him and threw her arms around his neck.

She was exactly his height, he discovered. Her body touched almost every inch of his front, more than touched as she wiggled against him, covered his lips with a long passionate kiss.

He passed his hand down the back of her jacket--she wore no bra—and found her waist only thinly covered by a blouse. His hand slipped under the elastic bands of her skirt and panties. He stroked the smooth rise of her buttocks.

"Oh, Ben," she moaned.

Ginny placed her mouth against his neck, breathed hard as he turned his hand under her blouse and brought it around to free the light material from her skirt. Her stomach was gently rounded, firm yet soft. He unbuttoned her skirt, pushed it and her panties down.

Bjorn found himself breathing fast, too. Urgency replaced analysis.

"Please, please," she gasped after she stepped out of her lower garments, and then returned to press against him. She leaned away so he could unfasten her jacket, unbutton her blouse, and push both over her shoulders. She did have breasts, after all, he found. They were small, but upright, with rosy, hard nipples.

He bent and licked the right nipple then sucked it.

"Oh God!" she whispered, and then leaned against him as if she would fall.

Her hands fumbled as she helped him undress. They fell together to the carpet. Then, she squealed when he entered her, and wrapped her long legs around him.

#

"I accept the invitation for friendship," she said afterwards as she lay beside him on the carpet and gasped for air. "As long as you let me stay with you for a while." She turned on her side and cupped her head in her hand. Her black hair was cut short. Strands did not interfere with her inspection.

Why had she fallen for him like this? Bjorn wondered. Was it his military aura, his differences from Achiever men? Was he only a curiosity? He'd make her an ally, if he could.

"There's more to your plan, isn't there?" she asked and then placed a finger over his lips. "No, you're right to keep mum. I don't need to know."

She grabbed his hand and lay back. "Oh!" she exclaimed. "That was so good." She turned on her side again and stared at him. "I suppose you can have lots of Nitas." Her voice stumbled; she tore her eyes away. "She was so beautiful. I'm skinny and young."

Bjorn turned on his side too and pulled her to him. "I want more than sex, Ginny," he said. "I've been lucky, damn lucky, but I'm alone. Only Uncle Will..."

She wriggled her arms free and flung them around his neck again. "Anything," she breathed. "Everything."

They kissed slowly. She slid a leg over his, clamped her lean body against him. "Will you sleep with me upstairs tonight?" she whispered against his ear, when they broke for air. "Unless you really are tied up."

He stood and collected his clothes. "Let's go," he said.

As they walked upstairs, their arms around each other's waist, their clothes carried under outside arms, she laid her head on his shoulder. "How will all this work out, Ben?" she asked. "I can't imagine Welfies improving their lot much. They'll only build another ruling, Achiever class."

"When you say 'they,' you include me," he answered. "I'm a Welfie and will be part of that ruling class if we win."

She kissed his shoulder.

"That's all academic, anyway," he added. "We're in a fight to the death. I plan to make sure my side lives."

Chapter 25

When the Welfie guards escorted the three
negotiators from the Administration and the two San
Angeles representatives into the conference room two
weeks after the conquest of Chicago, Con Wagoner let
out a whoop. Limping to the door, he hugged Ms.
Evaline Carmel, his deputy on the San Angeles
Residents Council and then shook Fifty-two Smith's
hand while clasping the black man's shoulder.

"I hope this trip is worth your risk," he said, "Make
sure you both talk to the Welfie leaders here. I won't be
going home for a while, and you two must report back."

Ms. Carmel represented many Mexican wards on
the San Angeles Council. She was scrawny, fiftyish,
white haired, and conspicuously intelligent. Fifty-two
spoke for the warrior side of the ghetto. And he acted
now in that role, too, Con thought. The young man
stayed between Ms. Carmel and the Achievers--the
HHR executive, the Attorney General, and the brigadier
general--as the three Welfies now crossed the floor
toward the conference table.

"So you have bigger things to do here than keep
us in order back home?" Fifty-two asked. He grinned
slightly.

"You both come; you return," Con answered.
"That's the deal. No one else, either way. We only
bought your presence by agreeing to leave the
President and General Bjorn out of these negotiations.
The Administration indicted them for treason."

Bjorn's promotion to general was another sign of
who ran things now in the President's camp, Con
thought. With two additional battalions training--in
Chicago and San Angeles--Bjorn had asked the

President for the brigadier rank. He had picked up a fistful of blank commissions for his officers while he was at it.

Ms. Carmel pursed her lips as if she tasted something sour.

"You're right," he responded to her visible doubt. "I was just as happy not to return. We'll decide things here. And Bjorn wants me to stay."

"Sorry about Dad," Fifty-two said.

"Yes," Ms. Carmel contributed. "Someday, if we get through this, we'll put up a statue of him."

Con only nodded.

Leaving the other side waiting, Con led his friends to the Chicago team of three who stood in front of the conference table. He introduced Carmel and Fifty-two to Ms. Ola Kravchuk, a stringy woman with staring eyes and a large tumor on her neck. Next to her stood Bill Loman, a gray-haired, husky man who had connections with the HHR, but was still trusted by his fellow ghetto residents. Finally, Harvey Fay, a balding black whose wards contained the main meat-shipping plants said "Hello."

After they all shook hands, Con called over the administration's team. "I think we know who everybody is," he said. "Our people checked your DNA at the airport. Do you want to check ours?"

"No," answered the Attorney General, an overweight Achiever, who moved to sit in the middle seat behind the table, next to the wall. "You're Wagoner?" At Con's nod, the official frowned. "The stipulations said nothing about you speaking for all the Welfies, or running this meeting."

"Suits us," Ms. Kravchuk said in a gravely voice. She chose a seat next to the Mex woman, Ms. Carmel. "Why don't you take the head seat, Con?"

Mr. Striker placed his hand on the Attorney General's arm and hushed him. He nodded at Con. "Suits us, too, Mr. Wagoner."

Bjorn had whistled when he saw the administration's list of attendees. "Striker tried to kill Uncle Will," he said. "He's brave to come this near me--whatever the guarantees."

Bjorn also knew the Corps representative. "Brigadier General Louis Lefko, my old commander in Mexico," he mused. "Striker thinks to protect himself from my military sleight of hand. He brings someone who knows me."

"Why don't we start, then," Con said. "Go first, Mr. Attorney General."

The jowly man leaned forward to address the Chicago Welfies. "Don't you folks realize you're opposing the national government?" he asked. "We have poison gas, biological agents, and radioactive dust. You name the fright and we've got it. Don't make us wipe out innocent people because of the crimes of these California ghetto-heads. Disown them and distance yourselves from their soldiers' unprovoked attack on the Chicago Welfare King and his Punishment battalion."

Ms. Kravchuk cleared her throat. "As head of the Chicago Megacity Residents Council, I'll answer that." Her sad eyes and tumor probably made the Achievers expect an emotional voice, Con thought, but her words were cold. "The ghetto-heads of San Angeles liberated us here in Chicago and take the lead in saving all Welfies. We honor and support them." She nodded to Con, almost regally. "We'll die before disowning our brothers and sisters."

Now she leaned toward the Attorney General. "Take care with your poisons, Sir. They kill souls as well as bodies. Start that business and you'll find Achiever society rots from within."

She leaned back before continuing. "And we'll attack Achievers wherever we can find them. As uneducated and maybe dumb, as we are, we'll die with our teeth in your throats."

Con found himself teary.

The Attorney General moved uneasily, waved his hand deprecatingly. "An attack's just a remote possibility, Ma'am. I'm sure such a drastic step won't be necessary."

He seemed to regain his emotional balance and placed his palm on the table. "If Wagoner is your friend, maybe he can persuade you to relent on the meat, then. If you in Chicago don't start shipping carcasses to our cash stores again, we'll blockade all food into San Angeles." He slammed his palm on the table and scowled at Con.

"Do that and we'll raid the beach and hill suburbs of San Angeles," growled Fifty-two. "We'll bring back their food and whatever else serves our fancy."

"Don't you like the vegpro?" asked Fay, representative of the meatpacking wards. "We've shipped plenty of it in place of meat. It's made of crushed grain, mixed with dried algae. It's better for you, according to your own dietitians. Or has that been only propaganda all these years?"

Five days passed since Fay's people stopped shipping trimmed carcasses, Con knew. The automatic butchers and dispensers out in the suburbs must be empty. Steaks, roasts, and even hamburger, sausages, and hot dogs would soon be but memories.

"Don't think we're desperate," growled the Attorney General. His cheeks were red.

General Lefko's lean face had become blander, if possible, Con thought. His mess halls must echo with loud complaints.

"I gather we've heard the administration's initial position," he said, "Ms. Kravchuk, could you give us Chicago's requirements?"

"Recall the punishment battalions and the Corps brigades that threaten us," she said. "Then, we'll start shipping meat again. Some."

Con wondered if she were in pain. He

understood from his new friends that her tumor had grown appreciably over the last year. Whether suffering or not, she was a formidable lady.

"And, Ms. Carmel, what does San Angeles want?"

"Abolishment of the `sixty-six' laws. Do what the President promised."

Striker placed his hand on the Attorney General's arm again and took over the response. "Peterson's not the President now, you know," he said. "The nation backed away from his egalitarian policies. They've been tried in the Southern Hemisphere and only impoverished everyone. To produce talent and leadership, you must have a reward system and inequality."

"Lies," replied Ms. Kravchuk. "The nation backed away from nothing. HHR kicked out the President and won't permit a fair election. And, as far as I know, the Southern Hemisphere is full of dictatorships with worse inequality than here. No one has tried fairness."

Mr. Striker leaned forward, clenched his fist, then stopped, and leaned back. "Argument won't convince anyone here," he said. "But maybe it will sway our citizens, in their homes. How about a cooling-off period? You start the shipments again and we'll promise not to send in troops for a while. We'll debate these issues on national holovision."

"That's what the election was for," noted Ms. Carmel. "The President against you, I believe, Mr. Striker. Let's go back to the original plan. Withdraw the troops that circle our two cities and relax ghetto controls everywhere. A fair election would decide the debate."

Striker wriggled in his seat. "Sorry. Our ex-President is barred from running by a special act of Congress. That's not negotiable." He leaned forward and concentrated on the two women across from him. "Be reasonable. If you insist on depriving us, our people will become angrier. Compromise becomes less and less possible. The military may step in. Millions of your people will then die. You must not continue this infuriating denial of meat."

"You can't scare us any more," Fay said. "We're down to the rock. Shut your mouth of that shit."

"I'm surprised we even talk when the chief negotiator on the Achiever side is the HHR executive director," Loman said. "Don't your people in Washington realize that HHR is dead in the ghettos? We'll never, never, let a punishment battalion near our people in Chicago again."

A growl rose from all the Welfies. Even Con found that something deep inside him raised its hackles and bared its teeth. "Not in San Angeles, either," he said.

Holovision images of the Fun House had blanketed the country.

"The Chicago leadership erred," mumbled Striker.

"If you turn over the officers, we'll try them," shouted the Attorney General, his face flushed again.

"We've already tried and punished them, and half their men, too," Loman said.

Con sighed and stared at Striker. "You three didn't come prepared to discuss a long term compromise, did you?"

"I've offered a cooling-off period," Mr. Striker reminded him.

"We might agree to a cooling-off period," Con answered, after a longer pause, "If you permit an air bridge between San Angeles and Chicago."

Striker licked his lips, apparently interested. The Chicago Welfies frowned, however, probably not liking the idea of giving the Achievers meat while the Corp prepared for invasion.

"Bjorn wants the search and destroy missiles that are manufactured in San Angeles," General Lefko said, speaking for the first time. "With those, he could massacre our forces outside Chicago, while his own troops swam inside, anonymous, in a sea of Welfies."

   "Our general wouldn't use them, of course, unless the Corps moved closer," Con said in the following silence. "The arrangement's fair. You get your meat; we gain means to preserve the status quo. No long-term advantage to either side."

   Striker wiped his face and smiled. "No," he said. "I guess we'll have to accept vegetarianism for a while." He stood. "This conference is over."

Chapter 26

"Good afternoon, General Bjorn," Brigadier General Louis Lefko said that afternoon. "I did hope for a private talk before you sent us back to Washington."

Bjorn walked across the bare concrete of the South Side conference room to sit facing his old commander. He bent over the table and offered a hand. "Will you shake with this jumped-up sergeant, Sir?"

Lefko took Bjorn's hand, his eyes crinkling in reserved warmth. His blue, formal uniform, with its red piping, brass buttons, and gold braid seemed pretentious and false. Bjorn remembered Lefko in dirty, green combat issue, his clothes merely a part of him.

"I assume we Washington negotiators don't leave until your San Angeles people make it home?" Lefko asked.

Bjorn nodded. "We don't trust Director Striker," he said. "He may keep to the word of agreements but not to their intent."

Lefko studied him in that distant, reflective way Bjorn had become used to in Mexico. "So, we're both generals, now," he said. "And still in our twenties. Who'd have thought it?"

"Your fellow officers wouldn't lump us together, Sir. I'm illegal. Congress didn't agree to the San Angeles battalion, much less to my increased rank."

Lefko shrugged his shoulders. "I'm only a brevet brigadier, as I was only a brevet colonel. And I'm a staff officer now, while you actually command forces. A fair comparison of status would favor you."

Lefko was always a realist.

"You are responsible for my high temporary rank,

as well," the Achiever continued. "First, by helping make me a hero behind Veracruz. That set me up for promotion when the country needed senior officers for the new army divisions. More recently, I was the only expert on the Welfies' commanding officer."

Bjorn glanced around at the dirty bare walls, concerned how this meeting would go. He'd arranged a long tour of ghetto defense for Striker and the Attorney General, but withheld the same privilege for their military man. He didn't worry whether he'd have enough time with Lefko, only whether he could succeed.

He returned his gaze to the Marine officer, once again admiring the man's apparent detachment. "Well, you earned your high rank today, General," he said. "I couldn't bring a load of search and destroy missiles with me to Chicago. Too few long-range transports. And the Air Force watches me now. If given an air bridge, I hoped to smuggle in surface to surface rockets."

Lefko nodded. "And, you'll ship no meat. Neither side gained anything from this conference."

"The Corps will attack soon, I guess."

"Millions will die," Lefko said. "I grant that."

"Mostly innocents."

Lefko raised an eyebrow. "We're all innocents, really. Death is new to us all."

Bjorn had forgotten Lefko's philosophical turn. "Civil war will harm more than those we kill and maim," he said.

"I may understand the ramifications even better than you," Lefko replied. "In Washington, we've run scenarios against our economic models. If the two ghettos fight as desperately as Ms. Kravchuk said they would, Achievers elsewhere will lose jobs, many permanently. Our economy will regress."

"Both ghettos have plans to destroy your automated factories," Bjorn said. "We'll wipe out the transportation hubs and anything else of value, too."

"And you'll broadcast your agony to the country, I

suppose," Lefko said. "That'll cause more uprisings, despite HHR's new control procedures."

Bjorn tried to keep his face quiet, his eyes undemanding. "Forget regulations," he said, "like you did more than once behind Veracruz. Do what's best for the country."

"You give me credit for too much possible effectiveness. There are thirty or more brigadier generals in Washington. I have little power."

"Fly north to where the chiefs sent your old regiment. Take command of the Eagle and Snake Division in Winnipeg. The non-coms would follow you if you declared for the President. Maybe you could talk other officers, who dread the coming bloodshed as we do, into joining. If reason had a large military behind it, good sense could force justice."

"No."

Bjorn was prepared for that rejection, but his stomach still tightened. "All we ask is for you Achievers to increase rations and give up some power. A generous settlement would be better for our country than a civil war."

"Only in the short run."

"We'd all slide down the next years together, with everyone sharing the decline in food," Bjorn said. "We'd impose a one-child policy, eventually find a population and resources equilibrium we could live with."

Lefko tapped the table. "The slide wouldn't be even or gradual. You Welfies would fight for more. Achiever communities would rebel at rationing, at being treated the same as people who don't work. We'd have an uncontrolled, grappling, thrashing slide, a nasty, unplanned careen to urban wars and local dictatorships."

The Marine general placed a finger below his bottom lip and rubbed an itch. "Our best course," he said, "is to crush rebellion now and begin to structure life without the big city ghettos. That way, we'll control events, instead of the reverse."

"And keep decreasing Welfie rations as Achiever population grows and resources diminish, I suppose. You'd doom millions."

"The Welfies will die off gradually, of malnutrition, disease, and their own violence. It will seem a natural process."

What a cold, unfeeling bastard!

"In another hundred years," Lefko continued, "we'll have a smaller, higher quality population that's in balance with the available resources. Those living then will accept this era's deaths as inevitable."

Lefko and his Achiever bosses would fence out, then gradually abandon, two hundred and fifty million people.

Bjorn looked up over his old commander's head, at the scruffy wall. Life had been fun--punctuated by occasional terror--until the attack on Uncle Will. That offense had given him a fierce anger. This afternoon's rage wasn't as personal as that other fury, but seemed deeper.

"How do you see the near future, then?" he asked quietly.

"We'll soon move into the Welfie-controlled ghettos," Lefko answered. "San Angeles and Chicago. The Corps will tame each, if it has to raze both."

Bjorn held his hands in his lap in order to keep Lefko from seeing them twist against each other.

"We'll fortify our residential areas," the Achiever officer said. "We'll build keep-out zones around the food production areas and factories that are as good as the barrier we've built on the Mexican border.

"This rebellion will be over within a year, Bjorn," Lefko concluded. "And your desperate struggle to keep it alive will be reported in only a losers' history that no one reads."

"Defeating us won't be as easy as you think," Bjorn said, staring into Lefko's eyes again.

Lefko smiled. "I do not underestimate you Welfies, Bjorn, believe me," he said. "Especially, with you as their military leader. The Corps will suffer more casualties when it clears San Angeles and Chicago than it took in the Mexican war."

Then he leaned forward. "Don't think me lacking in personal feelings either. We each have saved the other's life in combat, several times in fact. That ties us together." He smiled and leaned back again. "But I have more important ties: to people like me, without an accent, who've gone to schools like mine, who've argued the philosophers, enjoyed the giants of literature and music, who know what fork to use, what slang to avoid."

You are an aristocratic prick! Bjorn thought.

"I have sympathy," Lefko continued, "for the poor people who must live in the stinking, crowded ghettos. But my sympathy is without depth. Poor ancestry and no culture doom Welfies. People like me have destroyed the Neanderthals, the Australian Bushmen, and the American Indians. Now I shall help destroy Welfies, and shed few tears."

Lefko offered no common emotional rock on which to stand, no crevice of kindness or fear. He was an alien, someone with whom Bjorn couldn't identify. Bjorn felt a terrible, searing pain in his stomach, bent his fingers back against each other until he feared he would break several.

"The shock of our policy wouldn't be as sharp if the two ghettos surrendered now," Lefko continued. "Your innocents wouldn't die immediately in a Corps assault. You'd give them years, maybe."

"No."

"Betrayal is a subjective concept. Welfies would be better off if you and your key men left."

Bjorn breathed deeply and brought his hands up on the tabletop. "Every Welfie I know would be executed, that's all. Con Wagoner, Uncle Will, and all the Council members of both megacities. Nothing subjective about that."

"I could guarantee an airplane to carry you and your list of passengers to any foreign destination you chose."

"No." Bjorn shook his head. "I couldn't live with myself if I turned my back on my people. I must do what I can to defend them."

Then, he let the anger and hate show. He sat there, glared at Lefko, and wished his honor let him kill the bastard right then.

#

"Over time, the Achievers will eliminate all of us," Bjorn told Ginny as they sat in bed. "After gutting San Angeles and Chicago, the Corps will move to the other megacity ghettos, one after another. It will extract every factory, all equipment, and kill anyone who objects. Ghetto survivors will beg and fight over continually reducing rations until there's only a rat population left."

"Well," Ginny said, softly. "Welfies neither sow nor reap. They only consume. Who needs them? I disagree with the present administration's planned method, but not with its goal."

Bjorn's stomach pain came back.

He had returned from the meeting with Lefko, his insides churning, angry. Seeing Ginny reading in the common room, he had swept her upstairs and into bed. Sex restored his sense of power, his feeling of worth. He felt no weakness now, only that hot fierceness.

She pulled up a corner of the sheet, which she had draped over their bottom halves, to mop sweat at her temples. "Your animal vigor has quite worn me out," she said.

Ginny did look drained, he thought. Blue veins made her thin but muscular body appear oxygen-deprived.

"A lack of useful skills is not the Welfies' fault," he growled. "Blame your god dam Achiever ancestors for not forcing birth control earlier and for designing a society around only educated intellectuals."

He glanced away from her and fought down the rage. "I suppose you think I should have taken Lefko up on his offer."

"Would the Corps let Father ride in your plane?" Ginny put a hand on his thigh. "Never mind. He'd still come back in chains. Your potential employers would be Achievers, foreign officials who detest him."

She wiped a trickle of perspiration from between her small breasts. "Yes, I think you should have agreed. War's breaking out all over the world. People will pay good money for mercenaries. You'd land on your feet."

"I have a duty here."

"You want to save the useless," she said, frowning and her lips thinning. "That's stupid. Your people are a collection of genetic commonplaces who should be culled."

"Me, too?" he asked quietly.

"You're one of those superior anomalies that occurs in every wild herd. Your Uncle Will, too."

She wasn't an ally, only a lover. He was surprised she'd been so blunt.

"Why are we still together, Ginny?" he asked. "We have different loyalties, even different values."

They studied each other, neither smiling. Finally, she looked down and sighed. "I'm not the cool, calculating woman I seem, Ben. If I were, I wouldn't have spoken my mind just now. I'm sorry I've angered you. But you keep me at arm's length and must expect snap-backs occasionally."

She looked up. "To answer your question, love has tied me to your war chariot. Why you tolerate my Achieverness is a more interesting question."

His thoughts left her while she apologized. Lefko had made up his mind for him. He must take a large personal risk.

"Are you interested in me because I'm the

President's daughter?" she asked. "Sleeping with me
must give a certain macho satisfaction to a Welfie kid
from the San Angeles ghetto. But Father's no longer
important. You might earn more male admiration from
discarding me. It's not every soldier who can risk
angering an official, a prior President, who once
commanded the Corps and might, possibly, do so
again."

He thought about what he should do before he
left.

"Or am I still in your bed only because I'm
convenient?" She placed her hand over his and
entwined their fingers. "Because I'm good at sex?"

He wrenched his mind back. The pink had
returned to her face and to her upper body.

"Actually, you probably don't like me," she
continued, her voice cool. "I'm too opinionated and
argumentative. You Welfies have a primitive stereotype
of women. They are even lower class humans than
their mates, unable to withstand the stronger males.
Maybe General Bjorn can only 'love' someone he can
dominate mentally as well as physically."

"That's bullshit," he answered. "It proves you
don't know the ghettos or us Welfies. Since rations
don't depend on work, either sex can declare
independence of the other at any time. The pecking
order, whatever it is, develops naturally." He gestured
with his free hand. "You met Ms. Kravchuk and Ms.
Carmel at lunch. They are big sticks in their ghettos."

She didn't argue, but her lips pressed together.

"Who knows what really goes on in our minds?"
he asked. "I don't know why I want to be with you, but I
do."

His need was especially puzzling, considering her
opinions of his people, he thought. "You challenge me,
have never bored me," he admitted grudgingly.

But he never felt close, either. He couldn't show
her the tears for Uncle Will that lay damned inside. He

couldn't jointly commiserate with her over the plight of the crippled beggars that hung around outside the Chicago Residence Council's headquarters. He couldn't share stories of their upbringing; ghetto fights from him and dance classes from her. Laughs didn't punctuate pillow talk. Only sex and politics filled their time together.

She blew air through her lips. "I suppose I ask for too much. Love's mainly a female obsession."

He was silent now.

"There's some question that bars you from the closeness you offered me initially, isn't there?" she asked. "Something nasty occurred to you. Tell me."

He shrugged.

"I can't go on like this," she said. "I reveal myself while you put on armor. Please tell me what's wrong."

He would pull Capodonno aside at dinner and make arrangements.

"You once said you owed me."

He thought about her request. Suspicion that she betrayed his planned attack on HHR headquarters had risen only after his mind chased through the possibilities. Ginny was close to Striker; he'd guessed they were in the middle of an affair that night of the White House dinner. Thus, he doubted her.

"All right, Ginny," he whispered. "Someone told Striker about the plan to hit HHR headquarters. He or she triggered the attack on Uncle Will and me. Someone very close to the President who is privy to the deadliest secrets. Someone who believes in the Achiever cause rather than mine."

She stared at him and licked her lips. "You'd better leave."

Ginny was silent as he dressed. "How do I overcome your suspicions?" she finally asked.

"Show me you're on my side, after all, by saving Uncle Will from your goddamned, superior Achiever friends."

Chapter 27

The Chicago punishment battalion's old hangar smelled of oil and ozone. Master Sergeant Julio Capodonno, in civvies, pushed back a big door that would let the transport aircraft ease out into the night, where, low down, the stenches of a megacity overpowered those of technology.

"Remember," Bjorn instructed Majors Billy Hone and Tommy Hata, as all three sat on their heels near the entrance, "Mr. Wagoner's in charge. To hell with the President. He's not one of us. Con may not want to give orders but will have to if you refuse to obey anyone else."

Their faces told him they felt abandoned.

"Train and fight in Chicago," he said. "Don't let anyone lure you into the farmland."

He stood. Con and the Chicago Welfies would feel abandoned too. Ginny would know she'd been rejected finally.

Bjorn shook hands with both men and walked to the open aircraft. "Let's go," he told Capodonno and the pilot. "No sense giving their spy satellite a long dwell time."

"Winnipeg," he told the pilot when they were airborne. "It's in your navigational data base, seven or eight hundred miles almost directly north."

Capodonno passed him a ballute pack for low-level ejection. The cockpit's red light shone on the master sergeant's cynical, scarred face, revealing no fear or even unusual interest. Bjorn had once probed the middle-aged Capodonno for the man's ground truths and was so shaken by what he learned that he never again became personal. A witness to his mother's rape and murder, castrated by a gang boss, tortured when captured as a runner by an enemy gang, the little man operated by response to challenges, from loyalty to comrades, and with a burning hatred of the day's enemies. "You're smart and lucky," he told Bjorn. "I don't figure to do any better. I'll obey your orders and tell you beforehand if I ever decide to cut loose."

Capodonno was also intelligent and capable. And without dependents who might mourn him.

Bjorn sat next to the pilot and motioned his old Veracruz comrade into an observer's seat.

"Keep close to the ground and try to find a stream of truck trains you can sit above that moving-object radar will think we're part of," he directed the pilot. "We're bound to meet the Air Force before we see Winnipeg; make the dance late rather than soon."

Sergeant Roger Lasker, the pilot, was also single. And a volunteer. A member of the Welfie San Angeles battalion and also middle-aged, he bore burn scars on his face. An Air Force veteran who slipped into maintenance and eventually even test flew repaired transports, the service invalided him out after a crash.

Hata had recommended him, "as long as you keep him away from booze."

The big personnel transport flew like a lumbering truck, Bjorn thought, and glanced into the cavernous, shadowed fuselage behind him. Although fast, it couldn't out-maneuver an Air Force interceptor. Odds were they'd have to come down before they crossed the Canadian border.

"What's our objective?" Capodonno asked in his high voice.

"The Eagle and Snake Division," Bjorn answered. "It sits east of Winnipeg and forces the Canadian Grain Board to ship their wheat south instead of east."

Both of his companions grinned.

Unfortunately, as soon as Achiever intelligence confirmed the direction of the flight, the Administration would guess the destination and maybe the mission.

Bjorn sat back and tried to nap.

In an hour, Lasker woke his commander and told Bjorn that the airplane's sensors detected radar energy: first search sweeps, then narrow beam, IFF interrogations. Bjorn guessed that the Air Force commander behind the radar would seek instructions from Washington. Should he direct the pilot of the unscheduled military transport to land, he'd ask, or quickly end this orphan flight with missiles?

"Fire control lock-on," yelled Lasker thirty minutes later, as he swung the aircraft in a sharp turn and dived lower. The pilot tripped the automatic countermeasures board and glanced to the side at his commander.

"Where are we?" Bjorn asked.

"Northern Minnesota."

The display showed a river, a parallel road for automated vehicles, wide fields, and giant barns.

"Milk factories," Capodonno whispered. "No people cover."

"Eject," ordered Bjorn.

An armored divider slammed down behind them. The cockpit shuddered as it jolted free, created an air stream vortex, and slowed. In the display, Bjorn saw the rest of the aircraft pass over him, its sides opening to provide additional lift stability.

"When we're down," he ordered, "make for the river. Rendezvous there."

He saw missile hits on the transport above him. The cockpit's speed brakes flared, and it curled down and west.

"Twenty meters," yelled Lasker. "Pod burst altitude."

Bjorn bent over the wide safety belt and tensed. A bang signaled the cockpit's breakup. He gave into a downward thrust and his rapidly flying body took the blow of still atmosphere. His lungs emptied and his face and arms tingled. Three thin-skinned spheres shot out of his ballute pack and inflated. In a moment, he poised his feet to meet an uprising field of stubble, then landed and rolled, his seat following him as if connected.

Bjorn unsnapped the ballutes and stood, gazing around him. Fifteen meters away, to the west, a human silhouette broke the night's gloom, and then another figure rose north of Bjorn. His team wouldn't be separated after all.

Something burned off to the east. The transport, he guessed. The yellow trail of an air-to-ground missile sped nearer--aimed for pieces of the cockpit, probably--and a vast, golden hemisphere soon filled the horizon. That would be the detonation of jellied gasoline and an oxidant.

The pilot's escape sequence had been good, Bjorn thought. The higher transport sheltered the separated cockpit from the enemy's sensors until the pod remains curved back north, after it expelled its passengers.

Bjorn signaled to his men and then turned to the west at a trot. Within five minutes, he arrived at a laser fence that bordered the highway. Looking back, Bjorn could see hot tail pipes circling east of him, low. Tough for supersonic aircraft to search the ground, he thought. Their swing-wings would be extended for maximum lift; their engines throttled back. The pilots would worry more about stalling than what their sensors could see.

He moved north now. Capodonno and the pilot followed. He studied the dead pit for a route under the delicate beam that would kill with increased power if a living thing broke its stream of photons. Bjorn finally noted an animal's worn trace on the edge, where a dip in the ditch below also revealed the absence of carrion and old bones. He dropped and slid under the laser's beam.

Bjorn quickly led his men across the empty truck train road, jumping the transponder slots that kept automated vehicles driving straight and true. Then he crawled under the other laser fence and into brush on a bank that bordered a large stream of water.

"The Red River," breathed the pilot. "It runs north to Lake Winnipeg."

Bjorn preceded his men off the steep bank and into the water, which deepened rapidly. He told the pilot to watch for airplanes behind and started north, wading in the shadow of the bank. The sky was partially overcast, but he could see stars in openings between clouds. The air felt cool and smelled fresh. Fall, he thought. Harvest time.

The Achievers might not hunt too vigorously, unless they learned that Bjorn himself had been aboard the transport.

No sense worrying.

"Pier foundations," whispered Capodonno, who walked point now, in the water.

The shore swung west here, formed a bulge that would give protection to a harbor downstream, north of them. But Bjorn saw no light radiate from above the bank. He paused and waited for Capodonno to climb and scout inland.

"Must have been a town once," his master sergeant reported when the little man slid down the bank. "A rubble mound, maybe four kilometers long, keeps back the brush."

The site was a relic of the great town-clearing drive that freed acreage for crops, Bjorn guessed. He wondered what ghetto now held its previous inhabitants.

"Rotor craft south of us," Sergeant Lasker reported.

The three of them might be pinned down soon, Bjorn feared. But right now they were out of passive infrared sensor range.

When the river turned north again, Capodonno stepped up to the gravel foreshore, a flat area left by receding floodwater. The channel would be to the west, on the inside of the curve. The master sergeant ran again.

Bjorn followed, careful to avoid flotsam in the dark, his shoes leaden and his wet legs cold.

Thirty minutes later, when the beach ended, his master sergeant slowed to a walk and then re-entered the water. Suddenly, Capodonno pushed his palm down and collapsed onto his hands in the shallows. Bjorn followed quickly and saw the loom of an offshore island.

"Stone building," Capodonno whispered to Bjorn, who now lay in the water only two meters behind his master sergeant. "More islands and buildings farther along."

"Come over, gentlemen," a voice called as first light began to diffuse from the east. "There's a gravel bar under the water ten meters in front of you."

After a moment, Bjorn stood and motioned his two sergeants up also.

When Bjorn and his men stepped out of the water onto the island, a tall figure in a long, dark cloak rose from a garden chair. Behind their welcomer, a moss bordered, gravel path led to flowerbeds, flagstone walks, and a two-story mansion.

Bjorn turned and glanced across the short span of water they crossed. He saw flat fields and large rolls of hay. The sun was a gold and red wedge at the horizon.

"I imagine you were the cause of the fireworks I enjoyed this morning," the figure said. He stood still as Bjorn's men drifted behind him and then nodded and led them inside.

White hair topped their host's head and also formed a small goatee on his chin, while vertical wrinkles in his face indicated that he'd enjoyed greater bulk once. "I'm Carter Bryant," the Achiever said. He unsnapped his cloak and let it drop to the white-tiled foyer. "I moved here to avoid the crowding that plagues even our suburbs. Recently I've been bored."

A deep, thirty-meter wide holovision platform filled one side of the high-ceilinged room, large enough to hold a surrogate cast of fifty, Bjorn thought. A smaller stage sat in front of an overstuffed chair and against another wall, while varicolored costumes hung in a rack along a third wall.

"My name is Bjorn, Sir. These men are my friends."

The room had been poorly lit. Now light that penetrated from tall windows on the fourth wall gradually swallowed shadows.

"Welfies," Bryant observed. He studied Bjorn. "You run north, like the oppressed in America always have."

Bjorn didn't reply.

"Seats," the man ordered. A piece of wall slid back, and armchairs paraded out.

Bjorn heard a noise behind him, crouched, and swung around. The sound came from only another automaton, however. A robot valet. Extending its talons, the squat vehicle lifted and folded the Achiever's cloak, then turned and rolled away.

"Could you loan us your jump jet?" Bjorn asked. "Please?"

Bryant surveyed the disposition of Bjorn's associates. He shrugged.

"You must come with us also," Bjorn said and smiled.

Bryant also smiled. He bowed and gestured to a small door.

Bjorn walked with their host into a tiny elevator and squeezed back to accommodate Capodonno and the pilot. He soon stepped out into a roof hanger that held a four-seat airplane.

"You must be fleeing the Welfie rebellion," Bryant said, standing stiffly near the elevator. "As I age, I find that my own survival becomes more important than grand generalities. I'll attempt no heroics."

"Well, you won't be bored while we're with you, I guess," Bjorn responded. "I'm sorry but we're in a hurry and can't leave you to communicate with those who chase us."

Lasker hurried to check out the airplane, while Bjorn left Capodonno to watch Bryant. He strolled to a large window with a northern view. Flat land on each side of the river stretched to the horizon, broken only by windbreaks of trees and a few roads. Birds circled behind a line of giant harvesters far to the west. He savored the freshness of oxygen-rich air.

"Please register a flight to Winnipeg with the regional flight controller," Bjorn said, his back to Bryant. "Help him, Sergeant Lasker."

Bjorn was aloft within five minutes. He sat next to the pilot while the other two crowded on the rear bench seat. Lasker flew low, over the truck train road, flew as fast as the pleasure craft could go. This airplane had actual windows. For a time, Bjorn enjoyed the flight.

The communicator started beeping, however, and the pilot's display blanked. Then it showed red stripes and the message: "Land immediately."

"Try to raise the Eagle and Snake Division," Bjorn ordered and craned his head to look up and behind them.

"We're over the border," Lasker reported, "but the damn Air Force won't care." He turned the radio's power to maximum. "Eagle and Snake, friends in trouble. Come in. Come in."

"Broadcast that I'm aboard," the old man said. "The United States Air Force wouldn't dare fire at Carter Bryant. My hologram entertainments have become modern legends."

Bjorn wondered if the old man really believed in his immunity. He probably was so frightened that he scrabbled after any hope.

"The baby that radiates us is within lock-on range," whispered the pilot.

The river still ran straight north between gray-green fields with only an occasional farm building to break the monotony. "Skim the river," Bjorn ordered. "Put the tailpipes into the water if you think a missile is after you. We'll take our chances swimming."

"This is the Eagle and Snake Division communication center. Sergeant Salvador Villasenor speaking. Who calls?"

Bjorn put his hand on the pilot's shoulder and leaned in front of the communication camera. "General Bjorn of the free Chicago and San Angeles Welfies, Sergeant. I've come to visit your enlisted men's council, but the Air Force wants to shoot down my airplane, instead. Please have your air defense people send defender drones along the river."

The sergeant had a round face and a mustache. A moment later, a new face appeared, a young Achiever officer's haughty visage. "Lieutenant Ogilvy, here. Veer away. You are not cleared to..."

Bjorn saw the sergeant again. The man stared at Bjorn. Sweat appeared on his face.

"City's coming in view," whispered Sergeant Lasker. "Shall I turn east to where the division's bivouacked?"

The officer reappeared, stared away from Bjorn, probably at his sergeant. "How dare you override..."

"High speed vapor trails coming up from behind," Capodonno murmured.

"Land on the water," Bjorn ordered the pilot. "Everyone out, swim hard. Stay under water as much as you can."

He heard a shot, then another. The communication screen showed out-of-focus struggling.

By that time, the aircraft flew only twenty meters above the river. The pilot flared the plane so its flat undersurface touched immediately. It skidded in a vee of spray until water quenched its thrust-vector jets. When the airplane stilled, Bjorn saw cracks spider web the hot metal of the engine pods.

The pilot popped the roof and all four men dived out. As Bjorn hit the water he thought of Bryant with respect. The old man hadn't whined, hadn't asked for help or explanation, but only copied them.

Bjorn thrust strongly underwater, downstream. He recalled the Mexican creek he wallowed in when he started this military business, and the Marine pond outside San Angeles where he learned to swim properly. The Red River was colder and much deeper than either of those bodies of water.

He was about to surface for air when he felt a hard shove from above, then three more. Missiles detonated on the metal airplane, he guessed. Then, a bright light flashed above. He felt the water tighten around his body and try to expel the remaining air from his chest. The pressure wave dissipated, but the light persisted, turned gold, then yellow.

He swam up near the surface, his lungs desperate for oxygen. Finally, he bent his head so only his nose and mouth broke the water. He sucked in a little air. Hot but not deadly, he determined, then floated up and let his lungs inhale all his body wanted.

A cloud of fire rose above him, while a cooler breeze rushed along the surface and filled the vacuum caused by the expansion of heated air.

"Will there be another fire missile?" Bryant asked.

The old man had surfaced only a few meters behind him.

Bjorn couldn't see Capodonno or Sergeant Lasker, but the water was rough and the smoke low. "How should I know?" he answered, letting his fear surface, too.

The current carried him north. A gust of wind blew in that direction, also. For a while, Bjorn guessed, the carried-along hot gas cloud would blank out infrared sensors.

"I expected to die when I first guessed what you

really were," Bryant said. "Revolutionaries, not refugees." He kept up with some grace, although appeared tired.

Bjorn lay on his back to rest. "Tell me about the politics of Winnipeg," he asked. "Would the Welfies in the city help me?"

"This is Canada, remember. I'm no expert."

"Winnipeg is American now," Bjorn said. "The pretender President sent a division up here and absorbed the Prairie Provinces."

A wave made him cough and spit. He turned on his belly again.

"He sent one to Vancouver, too, and took the rest of the west," Bryant replied. "The Canadian Maritime Provinces will build an army to take their stolen acreage back. Our conquest of half their country means war."

Bryant rode in the water only a meter away and rotated his head toward Bjorn when he talked. The white hair and goatee lay flat against his pale flesh.

Bjorn slowed to let Bryant keep up. "The Canadians can't make long range missiles, high power lasers, and all the rest of the shit needed to take on the U.S. Marine Corps."

Light flashed behind them. Bjorn turned his head, felt a searing blast of air, and saw two explosions develop into great hemispheres of gold that overlapped in the middle of the river.

"The air commander guesses we're hiding in the brush on the shore," he said. "Maybe that's where Capodonno and my pilot are."

If so, poor bastards.

He frowned at the white-haired man. "What about help in Winnipeg?"

"I'm seventy-two, you know. I can't keep this up much longer."

Bjorn felt particularly bad about his old comrade-in-arms, Master Sergeant Julio Capodonno. The son of a bitch always thought he'd die of a heart attack in a barroom after a round with his friends. Bjorn swore to drink to him when he had a chance.

Soon, rotor aircraft would skim the river, fly below the columns of hot air looking for human signatures. He rolled over and began to swim. He could cut their radiated heat in two if he separated from Bryant.

"Wait." Bryant struck out beside him, his face straining. "Winnipeg has Welfies, but not the sixty-six laws." He gasped. Water from a low wave splashed in his face and choked him for a moment. "You'll find the Canadian poor are anti-American," he blurted. "Your division here has guerrilla problems."

"Thanks, but we'd better separate. That'll give both of us a better chance."

The old man glanced at the blue sky, marked by wisps of black sent up from burning brush behind them. His face was white and his hands splayed weakly in the water. He started to speak and then hesitated. "Any ad-ad-advice?" he finally gurgled.

Bjorn stroked over and pulled Bryant onto his back. "Just kick," he said. "I'll help you into shore."

"Not smart," Bryant whispered. "You surprise me."

The old man looked frail, but his heart and will seemed strong. He flailed away with his left arm and tried to help them move through the water.

"Okay, kneel," Bjorn finally said when they were two meters from the shore. "Keep your shoulders under water, prepare to dunk your head when the planes come."

Stone pebbles that Bjorn guessed had been rounded by ancient glaciers made up the bottom.

Bryant braced himself with his arms; his face hung only two centimeters above the water, and he breathed heavily.

Then Bjorn saw a blur over the land materialize into a large missile that froze in mid-air. It rotated and gradually descended on three, out-folding legs. He saw it first, he figured, half a kilometer above the ground, but it rapidly settled, only twenty meters away, back from the bank. Bjorn heard small engines ripple and observed blue exhausts wink.

He glanced quickly around, saw another missile land across the river, and heard others south of him, too, also along the riverbanks.

Bjorn grinned and stood up in the water. A radar dish rose from the nearby missile's nose and began to nod. The missile's skin pleated back into folds, while an arm rotated from the side. It held a smaller missile.

Enemy aircraft wouldn't kill him today.

Chapter 28

The rotorcraft pilot who lifted Bjorn and Carter Bryant up out of the water told of a sharp firefight in the divisional headquarters. Long-laid plans had exploded into implementation when Sergeant Salvador Villasenor shot his Achiever officer and yelled for help to his fellows in the command center. Then Villasenor buzzed non-com radio circuits out on the parade ground, in training buildings, and in barracks. Men grabbed their guns and arrested or killed their officers.

Thus Bjorn was prepared for the Welfie non-coms who commanded the landing platform and the uniformed, Achiever bodies that lay in the regimental streets.

The headquarters of the Eagle and Snake Division occupied the former offices of the Singh Grain Company. Bjorn, trailed by Bryant, marched into the main building. The man he remembered as Sergeant Major Lopez now wore the single chevron of a private first class. He saluted Bjorn from rigid attention.

Bjorn returned the salute and then nodded at the eight other non-coms who also stood at attention. "What did you do with the officers?"

"About half survived," Lopez answered. "They're in the division stockade."

"Take their insignia, and the brass from the dead, too. Lopez, you're the assistant division commander now and a one-star. Pick non-coms to run the senior staff posts and the regiments, make them nominate the next level down, and so on. Forget brigade commanders. I want the men to feel their new officers--all the way up from the platoon level--by nightfall."

When Lopez appeared frozen, Bjorn walked closer and put a hand on the man's shoulder. "You know everyone. You're the best man to supervise the process. If you make a mistake, we'll fix it later. In the meantime, we must move fast. The Corps will be after us."

As he moved away, he heard Lopez break out of his paralysis, order men to the monitors, and start roaring names. Bjorn toured the room, noted the occasional shattered display and the blood on one officer-seat. "Are you Villasenor?" he asked a man he thought he recognized, a first sergeant who stayed in the communications module despite the furor around him. When Bjorn received a "Yes, Sir" from stiff attention, he gave the non-com a two fingered salute. "Good man."

The communication specialist remained at attention.

"At ease," Bjorn said. "I need smart talking over the commercial network. Do you know anyone better than yourself? Honestly, now."

"No, Sir." An excited grin peeked out of a phlegmatic, fat face.

"Get me the premier of Canada on the flat screen. Tell each bureaucratic filter that the Welfies have taken over the division and that we want to cancel the invasion of Canada, but need the government's help."

Villasenor proved that he thought fast and had guts. But he was also young and a Welfie. Could he brazen his way through the Achiever power structure of a foreign country? Well, never mind, Bjorn thought. He must.

"I'll stay in these offices in case you need me to shout at some bastard," he concluded and pushed Villasenor lightly with the same two fingers he had saluted him with. "Get to it, my friend."

He turned to old Bryant who dripped behind him. "You okay?" he asked.

The retired media executive sat down on the chair that bore dried bloodstains. He picked at his still damp, white lounging pajamas. "I'm fine, thank you," he said.

"How about helping me?" Bjorn asked. "I must talk to everyone back home who has a holovision platform. Seems to me the networks might fight over the opportunity. They'd show the start of Armageddon, maybe."

Bryant stared at him. "What do you want from me?"

"You know the media bureaucracies. Arrange the broadcast. Make sure I get a nation-wide hook up and alert the audience ahead of time." He held the old man's eyes. "Also help me make the pitch as professional as possible."

"Punishment, if I don't?"

"No."

"You're an unusual man. I begin to believe you're a serious do-gooder."

Bjorn shrugged. "I don't know the answer to our predicament, but there has to be something better than writing-off hundreds of millions of Welfies."

Bryant stood. "All right," he said. "Tell the communication sergeant here to give me one of his nodes. I'll try to arrange the show for this evening's prime slot, although it's short notice."

After informing a busy Villasenor, Bjorn interrupted Lopez and met his nominees for the operations, intelligence, and logistics staff. He pulled the grizzled top sergeants into a corner office and sat them down around a conference table.

"We must move out tonight," he said and then grinned as the men swallowed their verbal protests, but frowned at him. "The Corps will be after us by air and probably try a vertical envelopment tomorrow. They can't let this mutiny stand--it gives us Welfies a real military force."

"But, if we move, they'll catch us en route," the new operations chief protested. "They can then slaughter us from the air, stretched out as we'll be."

The middle-aged man's name was Rafael Ochoa, Bjorn remembered. He was half-bald, a slim man who wore scars of optical correction around his eyes.

"If we stay here in your air defense formation," Bjorn responded, "they'll encapsulate us and establish hard points on the ground. They'll fly in tanks, their high power lasers, and medium range missiles. You, we, don't have any of that shit. All we are is light infantry."

Bjorn suspected that the senior non-coms had ruled out mutiny before because of the outcome Bjorn sketched. Still, they had killed their officers when he called for help, and cheerfully obeyed him now. Said something about their state of mind, he thought.

Ochoa seemed to relax. At least this bastard understands the fix we're in, he'd be thinking.

"We can't win a stand-up, one-on-one fight with the Corps here," Bjorn continued. "Hell, doctrine says one Corps brigade can beat a light infantry division."

His listeners bit their lips, but said nothing.

"We won't stay together and wait for some battle we can't win. We'll break into four packages of regiments, instead, and get out."

He studied his audience. All continued to frown. "We have four missions," Bjorn said. "The first is a decoy toward Chicago. Number two is Boston, via Montreal. We need their factories for short range missiles and radar." He held up his hand. "Wait until I finish. The third and fourth missions are to Detroit and Buffalo, both via Toronto. We'll take over half of the division to those last places."

He fixed his gaze on Ochoa. "From Detroit, we link up with Chicago and its food--there are ghettos almost all the way, I think. With Chicago, Detroit, and

Buffalo, and the industrial territory in between, we'll dominate the whole northeast."

Now, Bjorn nodded that he was through.

"I don't know whether your plan is feasible, Sir," said Ochoa, who obviously tried to be courteous to a superior who spoke stupidly. "Winnipeg has plenty of truck trains, but they're slow; there are only a few main highways, and the Corps..."

"What about the Trans-Canadian maglev," Bjorn asked the small logistics specialist who sat next to Ochoa. "Can you seize the empty grain trains that must be stacked up here?"

"Yes, but..."

"Take as many as you need for eight regiments. Put air defenses over the station. Prepare to load fast tonight and, afterwards, kick the trains east. You guys and I will ride on them, too."

He surveyed the stunned men. "I want a plan in two hours. Two regiments south, two to Montreal and Boston, and finally six and the staff to Toronto, initially. Specify the nominated regiments, their loads, and, in the case of the decoy truck trains, their routes once they leave Winnipeg for the south.

"I want the first troops out of here at dusk."

He stood, nodded, and walked out of the room.

#

"Are we on fiber optic cable?" Bjorn asked as he sat before the desk hologram laser.

"Yes, Sir," answered Villasenor. "There's no way HHR or the Corps can pick you up unless one of them has a digital voyeur in the Ottawa switch."

Chromatic bits coalesced in the holovision's focus and became the head of Canada's premier. According to Villasenor, his name was Saltonstall. He was prematurely gray, had a strong face and smooth skin.

"Good afternoon. General Bjorn, is it?"

"Yes, Sir. I have a commission from the President of the United States and, on his orders, have replaced the officers of the Eagle and Snake Division that currently occupies Winnipeg."

The politician touched his lip with his tongue, as if savoring Bjorn's explanation. "You're a Welfie, I gather from your accent."

"Yes, Sir. We admire your tolerant society, Sir."

"You speak well, General Bjorn. Cleverly, in fact. You will forgive me, however, if I have no confidence in the success of your President and cause. But, say I'm wrong. Would you agree, if you survive your military adventure up here and your President regains office, not to seize our food and absorb half of our country?"

Bjorn shrugged. "I can't promise you that, Sir. You wouldn't believe me if I did. I don't have broad negotiating authority. I'm only a general ordered to vacate your land."

Saltonstall waved his hand. "Go then, with my blessing."

"It's not that easy, Sir. If we're not out of Winnipeg soon, the U.S. Marine Corps will bombard us and destroy your city in the process. We need transportation."

Saltonstall studied Bjorn again, this time more thoughtfully. "What do you want from me?"

"A clear maglev line all the way to Montreal." Bjorn answered. "And for the spur line to Toronto. The loan of truck trains at those terminals and clearance south to the U.S. border."

Saltonstall whistled in surprise. "That's a big order."

"Not really, Sir. I'm told there are enough maglev freight trains parked here--grain carriers that had no function once we Americans started shipping south. Montreal and Toronto are megacities. You should have plenty of truck-trains there."

"If we don't help you, the damn American Marine Corps will destroy Winnipeg?"

Bjorn nodded. "You can pretty much depend on

that, unfortunately. Another item you might consider, Sir, is that an effective Welfie rebellion in the States could shield you from further invasions and give you time to build up your forces. You should side with the Welfies."

Saltonstall studied him. "General Bjorn is it?"

"Yes Sir. You might also give our truck trains air cover in the east, where you have interceptors."

Saltonstall held up his hand. "No more requests, please. I need to think over your basic proposal and talk to my cabinet."

"Yes Sir. I'll start loading in three hours, however. If I don't find power to the line's magnets, you'd better write-off the gateway to your prairie grain fields and plan to encounter sixteen thousand angry, armed Welfies hiking southeast through the center of your country."

#

Headquarters was nearly empty, since most of the new officers were at the maglev yards, supervising their troops and the loading process. General Lopez had already left with his two regiments, headed south for Fargo and Minneapolis in truck trains.

Bjorn waited with Sergeant Villasenor and Carter Bryant. He stood on a dais, his newly acquired uniform adorned with a pinned star on each shoulder and a hasty Navy Cross replica dangling from above his breast pocket. Gray canvas covered the wall behind him and ceiling lights shined down on his blond hair and eyebrows. A spotlight at his feet made his eyes gleam with apparent purpose, according to Bryant.

As Bjorn waited, he recalled saying good-by to General Lopez--once Sergeant Major Lopez. The man realized that his assignment was high risk, maybe suicidal. He and his regiments would be driving toward Chicago, which a Corps division had prepared to invade. Lopez knew that the four Marine brigades of that division would now climb into air transports and head for

Winnipeg as he, himself, boarded his truck trains. The marines would fly over the new general's route and surely pick up his truck-trains on their sensors.

Most likely, the enemy commander would think Lopez was Bjorn's vanguard and descend to attack.

"I hope the Marine Airborne Brigade now in Georgia stops to take us on," Lopez said. "That's the Achievers' fastest-reaction force. You need time to win a lead."

Whatever units the Chiefs diverted would be a relief, Bjorn thought. He would bet on them sending assault infantry of the First Division after Lopez, however. The Northern United States had plenty of airports for handling their heavy weapons and a network of roads that permitted easy interception. The Chiefs would want the Airborne first as a reserve and then, when they learned of his dart toward the East, to run up his tail and drop delaying forces.

Amazing, Bjorn thought, how Welfie soldiers would go into mortal danger for the cause that Wagoner created. Lopez had volunteered to command the feint, once he heard the plan and, of course, Bjorn had to agree. The two regiments, if attacked, would have to fight with the ferocity of a whole division. They needed sure leadership.

Bjorn patted the old veteran's arm. "You sure your health is up to a gang bust?"

Earlier, Lopez showed him the crisscross of stripes on his back, the latest caning scars only partially healed.

"I'm okay," Lopez said. "If survivors of my force eventually surrender, Sir, parade on a holovision platform the Achiever officers we disarmed and threaten to kill them if the Corps mistreats its prisoners."

"Good idea, General Lopez," Bjorn said.

Lopez saluted as he boarded the first van of the two-story truck train. "Take care of yourself, Bjorn," he said. "We'd be in a hell of a worse mess if the bastards killed you."

"Time for your holovision broadcast, General," Villasenor now advised.

Bjorn stood straighter on the dais, in the focus of the split laser beam. He didn't feel as ill at ease as he did in front of the non-coms of the Eagle and Snake Division that night in San Antonio. He'd a lot of practice in the political game since.

"Good evening, watchers," he said when Bryant's homemade "On The Air" sign lit. "I'm General Benjamin Bjorn, commander of the Home Guard by authority of the President of the United States. The Guard is a Welfie force, formed to protect people who live in the ghettos.

"Let me show you men of the Guard," he said and then relaxed and stood easy. Bryant had programmed shots of a battalion marching in full gear towards Lopez's truck train. The sight of resolved, tough men as they silently walked down a city street in the dusk, some glancing into the holovision cameras, would sober the audience. The troops would seem to parade along the edge of each holovision platform. They'd tower above the sitting viewers, and the occasional soldier appear to look into a watcher's eyes.

The green, "On the Air" light blinked again.

"You've seen a holovision shot of an army infantry division that has declared for the Welfies," Bjorn said. "The men are on their way to battle."

He leaned forward. "You will soon hear from them, you Welfies who starve in ghettos and you Achievers who sit fat and comfortable in suburbs."

He punched his fist into his open hand and made a slapping sound. "I call on all Welfies to rebel. Throw out your Welfare Kings! Kill the HHR criminals who treat you like slaves. Hook up with Con Wagoner in Chicago."

He waited a moment as he stared into the camera and then spoke more quietly. "Listen to me,

Achievers. Think about your loved ones, for they now
are at risk, as ours have been for years. Tell your
people in Washington to reinstate the President, to
agree to his plan quickly, or start sweating."
He paused again.
"HHR keeps my Uncle Will Maestri a prisoner in
Washington," he finally said. "He was a member of the
President's campaign staff."
Bjorn stepped forward. He expected his gigantic,
threatening visage to now fill each home holovision
platform. "Mr. Maestri speaks for us Welfies. He's our
negotiator. Don't fuck with him, you hear?"
Bjorn spoke his last sentence very slowly,
enunciating each word as if speaking to lip readers, then
waved at Villasenor to close the channel.
"I think your presentation was sufficiently
terrifying, if that's what you wanted," Bryant said from
his seat at the side.
Bjorn saw a flash of light over the center of the
city through the old-fashioned windowpane near him. A
snooper, he guessed. The Corps hadn't time to redirect
a spy satellite and used atmospheric assets, instead.
One of his mid-range missiles snuffed the
reconnaissance drone.
"Let's go," he shouted to Villasenor, and headed
for the appropriated city taxi outside.
He was surprised to find Bryant at the vehicle's
door. "You're free, Sir," he said. "And thanks for your
help."
"I want to come along," the old man said. Then,
when Bjorn shook his head, puzzled, he added, "Every
young conqueror needs an historian." Bryant smiled.
"I've been truly bored until today."
#
A grain elevator burned when Bjorn arrived at the
maglev yards. Yellow light fought with ugly, black
billows of cooked carbohydrate. The other buildings and
the marshaled troops seemed almost invisible in

contrast.

"Our air defense can't kill the long range missiles," Ochoa said when Bjorn walked over to the temporary division command center. "They come down from space with terrible speed. But we can make them miss."

A low-slung train accelerated between grain hoppers and vacuum loaders, past the open spaces that men had used to board. Almost a kilometer long, it progressively lifted on its magnets, gained speed, and curved to leave the yards.

"That's the second regiment," Ochoa said. "Your Boston force is on its way to Montreal."

"Clear track?"

"Yes, Sir. As far as the switching yards in Nakima, anyway. General Lopez put our best master sergeant in charge of the expedition, as a full colonel. He understands your orders."

Nearby, men launched a large air defense drone.

"That RPV carries radar chaff and flares and will dispense at altitude," Ochoa said. "Our radar must have picked up another incoming."

A second train slid into the station. Gull-wing doors opened all along its side. Armed men marched in. They carried heavy loads and pulled artillery mules behind them. Men snapped-in straps that then divided each car into small cubicles and provided support for the standing soldiers.

The logistics non-com, now officer, who synchronized this must be a genius, Bjorn thought. No hesitations anywhere.

To load the train took less than half an hour. As the train's composite sides descended, a man with silver eagles on his shoulders saluted Bjorn from afar and then stepped inside.

The third regiment was on its way, Bjorn thought. At a four hundred kilometer an hour top speed, it would soon travel out of harm's reach. By morning, the regiment should be in Toronto.

"You'll command the four regiments targeted for Buffalo, as I said," he told Ochoa. "In the train, make plans to take the whole Lake Ontario shore and establish smuggling routes to Boston. Link up with me to the west."

He grinned at the man and patted him on the shoulder. "I'll go with the next train. I need to off-load in Toronto early to work the politics of transshipment and maybe air protection to the border." He stared at Ochoa. "And I must make sure some help gets to our people!"

A large missile suddenly detonated in the air a mile away. Bjorn could see a circle of tall buildings collapse under it, as if crushed by a large trash compactor. Then fires started.

Chapter 29

In the first car of the silently rushing maglev train, troops coughed and sneezed. Bjorn, himself, coughed at grain husks tickling his throat. Men spoke quietly as they made room for each other under a curved ceiling that, in the center, gave the tallest barely two centimeters of clearance. Humans made the only noise. Even air that came through the ceiling vents entered quietly.

Bjorn and his small staff had a generous allocation of space: a block five-meters-along-each-side of the car marked off by straps stretched across its width. The train's controls occupied a small cockpit in front of them. It was empty since guidance instructions flowed from Ottawa.

Jose Cardenas, the skinny intelligence master sergeant who now wore the silver eagles of a colonel, had immediately plugged into the train's sensor system. His monitor showed the city slipping by, then dark, open fields. Soon Bjorn's man lifted the focus as increasing speed made near-in scenes disorienting.

"Look backward," Bjorn ordered. "Show me the yards."

"I'd have to use a wide band link to call up Colonel Ochoa's viewer," Cardenas objected. "We're too far away now for the train's optical system. And, the Corps might pick up our radiation and aim a whopper down it."

"Okay," Bjorn replied. "Colonel Villasenor, work the radio and video bands. See what you pick up from broadcasts."

Bjorn stood easily in the center of the train's

command cube. He felt no vibration. The train rarely angled to one side or the other. On the screen that showed what the train saw, he viewed the silver water of lakes pass underneath and noted vast acreages of harvested stubble shimmer under a quarter moon. Further away, dark, harrowed fields waited, probably for seeds of the winter wheat that agricultural corporations would plant.

Near him, Carter Bryant found a half-empty box of vegpro packets, sat on it, and leaned his head against an unenergized, fan-powered mule full of anti-armor missiles.

All he'd done recently, Bjorn reflected, involved abandoning or sacrificing people. He'd deserted his bosses and the San Angeles battalion in Chicago for the chance of major military reinforcements, quickly given up on Master Sergeant Capodonno and the transport pilot in order to take command of a division, and sent as a feint the once regimental sergeant major, Hector Lopez, and four thousand men of the latter's brigade--to their deaths, maybe. Now he fled Winnipeg and many of his new troops ahead of a firestorm.

Had those desertions been really wise? Or only cowardly?

Two military staff members--Cardenas and Villasenor, the two regiments that had left earlier, and this regiment would help him invade the United States if the others back there didn't make it. For instance, if missiles took out the thread of maglev track that he relied on to pull his command after him. When the Corps brigades woke to his move, they'd disengage from Lopez in Minnesota and then surround Ochoa and the left-behind regiments.

In such a scenario, the enemy's attack aircraft would probably figure they'd exhaust fuel in northern Canada before reaching missile lock-on range of whatever trains escaped Winnipeg. They'd return to the States, then move east to anticipate his descent from

Toronto.

Of course, Ochoa still had a chance to follow him. Every regimental train that made it out of the firestorm would be a godsend.

He'd have a good chance to help his people now. Lots of small roads and forest cover at the U.S/Canadian border. He should successfully slide Welfie military forces into northeastern megacities. There they'd find tenement canyon lands to protect them from aerial assault and welcoming Welfie populations.

His actions were smart, but the necessary desertions and probable casualties hurt.

"I've found a news program of the Canadian Broadcasting Corporation, from Winnipeg, Sir," Villasenor said. "Flat screen."

Bjorn stepped close and watched a sweating, middle-aged Achiever point to a map of his city. "The Americans responded to General Bjorn's remarkable speech tonight by bombarding the infantry encampment and our train station," the reporter said. "The quarter of the city south and east of the fork of the Red and the Assinboine is in flames. Grain fires have stopped rescue work and prevent any estimate of damage."

He'd also killed a lot of innocent civilians, apparently.

The announcer flicked to a map of the United States. It carried stylized red flames around many large cities. "American Welfies apparently considered that speech a declaration of civil war," he said. "The poor fight pitched battles with American Health and Human Resources punishment battalions. Great mobs of looters, who commit horrible crimes, have invaded Achiever suburbs."

"Did you see my broadcast on holovision?" he asked Cardenas.

"Heard it, Sir. We put the sound track through loudspeakers down in the train yards. Men cried, they were so glad to hear a Welfie talking back to the sons of bitches."

Well, he'd jarred the system, all right.

"Train's slowing, Sir," Villasenor reported. He studied the control system read-outs. "Trouble up ahead."

Bjorn turned to the comm. specialist.

"All our trains have stopped at Nakima," Villasenor continued after a moment. "Electricity is off to both the Montreal and Toronto lines. No magnet energy."

"Find Canadian Premier Saltonstall, Salvador. He must be waiting to talk down to me. To hell with the risk of interception."

Villasenor found the politician immediately. Saltonstall sat at a conference table with three other old men and two mature women. "General Bjorn?" he said.

"Yes, Sir."

"You misled me about Winnipeg. It's in flames."

"Only a quarter of it, Sir. If my trains all get out, as they should soon, there'll be no reason for more bombardment. And, if you let me through, as I thought we agreed, there'll be no battle on Canadian soil tomorrow."

"Your assurance of no battle is probably as accurate as the scenario you painted this afternoon about Winnipeg. More likely of becoming real are the threats I've received from your government in Washington."

"Have you asked the pretender President to remove his other army infantry division from Vancouver? Do you win anything tangible for not helping me?"

Bjorn received haughty frowns from around the table.

"Please, ladies and gentlemen, to do what I ask is in your interest. My thousands of fighting men will badly cripple the U.S. Marine Corps when we meet in the U.S. The pretender won't even think of punishing Canada after our fight. He'll have no capability."

Saltonstall smiled. "I'm for crippling his forces, all right. We all support that. But we can better afford a battle around Nakima than around Toronto."

Bjorn felt sick to his stomach. "You leave us in a wilderness."

"Good," the tall woman with an acerbic face replied. "That way, you won't infect our Welfies."

"We shall turn off all power to the maglev line from Winnipeg as soon as all your regiments reach you." Saltonstall smiled. "Fight well."

Bjorn repressed his rage, made a cut-off motion to Villasenor, and then walked away. He put a hand to his head.

"An executive cannot let his employees see him discouraged," Carter Bryant said. The old media expert stood and braced himself in the braking train, began to pivot from the force on his unanchored body.

Bjorn gave him a hand. "I was suckered," he said. "Premier Saltonstall tolls me out of his city by giving me magnet energy and then dumps me in the midst of a foodless forest, a target of a high technology army. Maybe Achievers are right to think all Welfies stupid. I was, at least."

"Don't forget you have an Achiever cuckoo baby in your nest," Bryant replied, his blue eyes sharp below his white eyebrows. "I could get killed along with you Welfies. Think of something."

Bjorn had to smile. "Who's parked ahead of us, Cardenas?" he asked.

"It looks like the other two trains, Sir. And, a regiment's coming in behind. We won't crash. There's plenty of shunt tracks here."

Bjorn sighed. "Okay. You're acting chief of operations, until Colonel Ochoa shows up. Tell everyone to detrain and form up. And get me a map of the area, for God's sake."

The map printed from Cardenas's intelligence program didn't make Bjorn feel better. Three train lines fanned out from Nakima. One stretched south to Thunder Bay on Lake Superior, then connected to Duluth and Minneapolis. A second descended from the top of Ontario Province to Toronto and Ottawa. The third traveled almost straight east, through the north woods, before it dipped down to Montreal and Quebec. Roads paralleled the first and last maglev routes, but encountered few towns until they neared the major cities in southern Canada. Lousy options for a march, Bjorn thought.

#

He felt better once on the ground in Nakima, with his men disembarked under a quarter moon and resplendent stars. Colonel Ochoa and the final regiments had made it!

At least he had the full division together, less Lopez's two regiments.

Away from the train yard, he stood in cleared flatland, east of a long, northern-trending Lake. Masses of troops sat wherever he looked. Quiet and disciplined, many chewed on vegpro rations. They were all his brothers.

He turned east to view a black band of forest, a mix of conifers and broad-leafed trees that ran north and south. That was the north woods, an immense forest that extended to the Atlantic Ocean.

Maybe Nakima was a piece of luck, after all.

The town itself consisted of windowless, composite buildings, probably filled with electric and photonic switches. No humans.

Off, beyond the sitting troops and near the lake, however, he saw a yellow light turn on. That'd be an old-fashioned farmer and his family, he thought, people who grubbed rocks from the soil and worked enough food from the short growing season to eke out life. He saw more low voltage lights flick on, all well separated. The farmers had radiotelephones, apparently.

He stood easily next to a makeshift table and

turned his eyes back to the fifteen officers who waited silently before him. They held maps that Cardenas had run off and Ochoa marked up, and seemed grimly resolved. After all, they fought for a cause that was theirs, not the construct of Washington Achievers. Also, they should feel reassured, Bjorn thought. Their new commander had extricated them from a tight fix without casualties.

"Come dawn we'll have at least a Corps brigade on our necks," Bjorn quietly told them. "The Airborne out of Georgia. It's hot on our heels, I'll bet, mad at missing us in Winnipeg. The Chiefs will also tap the nearest division, probably the First that's besieging Chicago. Its first echelon may set down and engage Lopez. That will give us some time to chew only on the Airborne. But the First will let go of Lopez at the first news that we put up a fight here, so we need to get set and learn our roles quickly."

He nodded at Cardenas. "Tell the men what to expect, Colonel."

The slim, balding man--almost a twin of Ochoa--stood to face the other officers. "Yes, Sir," he said, and then took a deep breath. "The Corps will likely hit us where they think we've gone with long range bombardment, as they did Winnipeg. At the same time, they'll secure the cleared area around Nakima for their logistics base. The attack aircraft, their refuelers, and maintenance support, will come down there, finally the transports with infantry, tanks, and blinders. In Phase II the Airborne bombs and strafe where they think we're deployed and then drops in." He smiled sparely. "During Phase II their reinforcements land."

He looked around the circle of ex-sergeants who now commanded the division. "An airborne brigade tomorrow," he concluded. "An ordinary brigade and then the rest of the First Division in the next day or two. That'll be five brigades in total."

Colonel Cardenas sat.

"I didn't choose this place for a battle," Bjorn said. "I hoped to get us into megacities and fight from cross streets and roofs with the support of civvie ghetto-heads. Still, we have advantages here. We've more men than the Corps initially, and have the defensive advantage. We can pick where we fight."

A man spoke up from the back. "How do we know they'll attack tomorrow, General?" he asked. "Why won't they wait for all our food to be eaten or attack when we're strung out, marching somewhere?"

A mumble of disbelieving, disapproving comments rose from the assembled officers. "They'll be after us like rats go after a mouse they've cornered," Cardenas said loudly.

"No, that's a good question," Bjorn said. "The Corps should wait because we'll hurt them bad here if it engages right away. We'll beat them, maybe."

His audience moved uneasily at that. They probably thought he bullshitted about their chances. Well, maybe his growing optimism was only a fighter's confidence, but...

He pressed his lips together. "Achiever officers will want to hit us quick," he said, "while we're disorganized--so they think--and before civilian agitation grows for negotiations. They'll be hot after us because we're filthy mutineers, people who think they can do without Achievers. We'll have killed their friends and defied them."

The regimental commanders and the staff officers mumbled agreement and then stared at him blankly.

"Here's the plan," Bjorn said. "We won't defend the cleared area. Let them take it; let them set up their headquarters here, if they want. We're going into the trees. They'll have to poke around to get us out."

That stirred the officers a little.

"Colonel Ochoa has marked off everybody's sector behind the town. I want you to occupy your whole area, spread out as if you were soft mush. Form no front line, no reserve. I don't want a center the enemy can attack, or any flank he can turn. Keep in touch with your neighboring regiments, but don't bunch into a target."

He walked a meter, then back. "Stay thin so the long range missiles and attack bombers can't get many of you. Spot your air defense squads unevenly; tell them to act independently and to take out anything that flies within range. That'll be first the snoopers, then the airborne burners that try to expand landing zones in the trees made by missile strikes, and finally the vertically-landing transports."

He saw heads nod.

"Once the enemy lands," he continued, "everybody near-by swarms around. Use the trees as defensive armor. Shoot the bastards that make it down, scatter mines, set ambushes when they try to join others. But again, only bunch up close to the enemy."

"This could be a long fight the way you lay it out," another officer said. "What about food and ammunition?"

"Each regiment has its full stores," the logistics officer reported. He sat next to Colonel Ochoa. "Lots of water in this country."

"Don't get into a fire party, for Christ's sake," Bjorn said. "Aim at your targets and hit them. If a group of the enemy forts up behind their vehicles and burns down enough woods to provide a field of fire, let it alone. You'll have plenty of other targets."

"How do we settle the battle?" asked the same outspoken officer from the back. "Could be pretty indecisive and just peter out."

Bjorn shook his head. "Remember Veracruz and the offensive craziness of our officers there? The Corps will send in columns of tanks and infantry from the 1st Division after the drops and try to link up with the Airborne. The commander will order in more and more marines to kill us. He'll bring in Enforcers, for sure, maybe set up crosses to motivate his men. We'll have the chance to bleed them pretty bad."

He paused. "We need to," he then said. "Our people back home are scared the Corps will come into the ghettos."

The officers sighed. This time their noise was a sibilant hiss.

"Once the marines walk into the forest," Bjorn said, "we don't let them back out. Make sure your men remember their families and know what they have to do."

Now the officers growled and some hit an open fist with a closed one.

He supposed he should talk about the chances of winning, but maybe he'd done enough for now. "All right," he said. "Carry out your orders."

#

The command group walked down the maglev line before cutting into the forest. A five hundred-man battalion that pulled mules full of missiles and other supplies plodded ahead of them.

Bjorn put his hand on Villasenor's sleeve. "Keep going down the maglev's laser fence until you find a repeater station for the optical comm. line," he said. "Camouflage a connection and spool-out cable back to our camp. I want to access the net."

"I'll bet the Canadian premier, Saltonstall, hasn't told his people he's marooned us out here," Carter Bryant said from behind. "His own Welfies will give him trouble once we let them know. The bastard."

"We might make you an honorary Welfie when this is over, Bryant," Bjorn said. The comment raised a chuckle from the men walking nearby. "You're sliding into our point of view."

Then he put his hand on Villasenor's arm again. "Try to reach those farmers by radio telephone," he said. "Warn them their homes may be missile targets."

He couldn't think of anything else to do. Once the

regimental commanders located their men and dispensed orders, tomorrow's battle was in the hands of small unit leaders and individual soldiers. He needed to build a nest of leaves and make up some of the sleep he had lost over the last two days.

Bjorn gently pushed Villasenor on his way.

Chapter 30

While Bjorn prepared to sleep before a Corps attack in the north woods, Chairman Con Wagoner of the San Angeles Residents Council and leader of the Welfie revolution worried about his personal life. Con sat up straighter, however, when Ms. Ola Kravchuk, the head of the Chicago Residents' Council, came into the comm room of her headquarters. He'd turned off the picture phone only minutes before.

Near the door she hesitated, put her hand to the palm-sized tumor on her neck and pushed at it, probably reminded of the abomination by its weight. "Sorry," she said. "Have I interrupted something?"

"No. I just finished talking to my wife in San Angeles."

"Major Tom Hata, whom General Bjorn left in charge of our military, is supposed to meet me here. How about sitting in?"

"Sure."

Jami had looked good, still loved him, and cried about Dad's death. Con wondered how people without families coped in frightening times like these. Of course, you paid in fear for the warmth of love.

"Are the Welfies in San Angeles out of control like they seem to be in the rest of the country?" Ms. Kravchuk asked.

"No. But Fifty-two Smith finished-off the Achiever militia, and took over the suburbs. He chose hostages from Beverly Hills and other swank areas and sent them into Black Town and Venice. He shoves the Achievers he doesn't want up and over the Grapevine. Jami says he lets everyone loot, but has stopped rape and murder."

"Does he think the Corps will attack him soon?"

Con shrugged. "Fifty-two found over a thousand big missiles in the Santa Monica and San Diego factories. He's targeted them at the Corps encampments that ring San Angeles now. Jami says he will fire once we detect preparations for an attack."

Of course the Corps had air defenses. Still, their reaction would be at very short range. A defensive missile would hardly have time to pitch over before the offensive weapon was on the target.

"Sounds like the Achievers wait for something," Mrs. Kravchuk observed.

Her fingers were at her neck again.

"Bjorn must still be fighting," Con said. "The high command doesn't want to tie up that California division in a city just yet. In case it's needed up north."

Ms. Kravchuk sat. Her eyes were red-rimmed, her face pale. "He's a tough man, full of surprises," she said. "I'll give him that. But he needs to communicate. He's a Welfie and works for us, after all."

"Soon, I'm sure," Con replied. He studied her. "Why don't you have the growth removed?" he then asked. "You control Chicago's medical resources now. Tell the Achiever doctors to fix you."

"Too late, Con. It has roots all through me."

She touched the tumor again and then put her hand flat on the table. "What's General Bjorn like? I never got to know him."

"His uncle has been his father, best friend, advisor, you name it. HHR made a mistake when Striker tried to murder Will Maestri. Life isn't fun and games anymore for Bjorn. He's serious."

"I don't like the way he treated Miss Ginny, even though she is an Achiever. She's cried ever since he left."

Con was quiet. That subject was beyond him. "I don't know Will Maestri, either."

"Will's the only man we've got who understands Washington and HHR," Con said. "He's got contacts in all the ghettos. And he's smart."

"You think we'll ever get to where he can negotiate for us, like General Bjorn suggested in his hologram broadcast?"

Con leaned forward. "I believe in our general, Mrs. Kravchuk. Look where he's brought us so far." He gestured as if he displayed a map. "The ghettos were terrified; now they attack. He produced a Welfie army!"

"There'd be no General Bjorn without you," the woman answered. "Don't forget that, Con. We in the ghettos look to you, not to some half-Achiever, military man."

Con heard two quick taps, and then Major Hata opened the door and walked into the room. "We've picked up coded Corps radio traffic from North Dakota," the young officer said, "and more from northern Ontario. The Marines also jam somebody's frequency-hopping radio up there."

"What do you guess?" Con asked.

"Fights in both places." Hata shook his head. "And the General tries to contact us."

He's not happy, Con thought. Bjorn was his hero as well as an old comrade in arms and his commander. And Hata knows our survival rests on the man's shoulders. He's afraid.

The door swung open without warning. "So here's where you all are hiding," the Ambassador said. She wore red and black, power colors, but the dress was wrinkled and had a spot on its collar.

She glared at them all. "What is this, a conspiracy? Are you planning something more you don't want the President or me to know? Like the attack on Chicago? Like Bjorn's crazy dash for Canada? Don't forget who gives you Welfie leaders legitimacy." She strode in and slammed the door behind her.

She's had too much to drink, Con thought. And

it's only early evening.

"We're trying to guess what General Bjorn is up to," Ms. Kravchuk replied mildly.

"That's easy," the Ambassador said. She stood on her toes, turned, and slid onto the conference table. "He fights a battle. The Corps has him between its teeth about two hundred kilometers east and north of Winnipeg. Bjorn divided his forces, which even I realize is stupid, and now cowers in a wilderness. We're about to lose a civil war almost before we realized we were in one."

"How do you know all that, Ma'am?" Major Hata asked.

"My brother still has friends in Washington."

"Do these friends advise we do anything?" Con asked.

"Just that we try to help Bjorn." She stared at Major Hata. "You need to attack something and make the Corps divert forces from the north."

"Attack what?" the officer asked.

"I'm not a military person, Hata. I'm not supposed to know those things. You tell me."

The major put his hands behind him and spread his legs in the parade-rest pose. "There's only one possible target, Ma'am," he said. "I could raid the Corps encampments outside Chicago. They're empty since the Marine brigades once there chased after General Bjorn. I could maybe bring back military equipment. But not much."

"Kravchuk, get me a drink, will you?" the Ambassador asked. She kept her eyes on the young officer. "You didn't hear me, Hata. We want a diversion that will pull a lot of the Corps off Bjorn. Start to march east on Washington; do something that'll make the rebel government shout for quick help."

Ms. Kravchuk walked over to the wall communicator.

"General Bjorn already arranged something like

that," Hata answered. "The Corps also fights someone near Fargo, North Dakota."

"More, Major, I want more," the Ambassador whispered and slid forward on the table as if to jump off and attack him. Her dress hugged her thighs.

"I don't think an expedition is a good idea," Hata answered. "It's open farmland out there. We'd be massacred from the air."

"Sometimes it's the duty of the military to die." When no one responded, the Ambassador did slide off the table. "I'll bring in the President."

"Won't do any good, Ma'am," Hata replied. "Before he left, General Bjorn ordered me not to deploy far from the city."

"He has a boss."

Major Hata nodded courteously. "Yes. The general told me to take orders from Mr. Wagoner here if I couldn't contact him."

The Ambassador bared her teeth in a surprised grimace. A Welfie entered with a dark drink. She leaped for it and swigged a third of the fluid.

"We've really sunk low," she said and licked her lips, "when a military man appoints civilian authority, instead of the other way around."

So far Bjorn's initiatives have turned out well, Con thought. But place himself in charge of Hata? It's only because the alternative was so poor. "Both General Bjorn, it appears, and Major Hata have warned against risking our forces in the open," he said. "Let's be sensible and take their advice."

"What would you save your soldiers for?" shouted the Ambassador. She threw her drink at a wall so the glass shattered and the remaining fluid splashed down the unpainted wall. "You God damn, stupid Welfies."

She strode toward the door and then turned. "We're doomed," she said. "Already the smart rats are running from the fumigation tent. Did you know that Ginny went to the airport a couple of hours ago? She's off to Washington, I'm sure. She has a good friend there, who'll protect her from the coming slaughter. I wish I did."

She stormed out and slammed the door.

Ms. Kravchuk broke a long silence. "Your general showed good judgment in making you boss of his little army here, Con. Let's pray for him."

Chapter 31

Bjorn lay on his side under a thin blanket in the cool north woods that night. His head rested among meter-high saplings, while his body curled around a slim tree. Timber machines had cut over this part of the forest a few years earlier. New growth climbed luxuriantly close together in the spaces between the few, left alone, earlier generations of trees.

He stayed awake through the dark hours, not because of the crowded forest, however, or the rocks under the leaves, or the cold. Nor was he alert because others made noise. His staff finished digging shelters for their powered equipment and put up the two-way, electromagnetic radiation shields some time earlier. Then they apparently collapsed from exhaustion.

He couldn't sleep because he agonized over what he couldn't fix. Fears dug such deep ruts in his brain that he couldn't pull out of them. What would happen to Uncle Will if he failed here? What would happen to Con Wagoner and Jami, the Welfie leader's wife? What would be the fates of all the other people who depended on him?

He wanted to turn over, but knew there was no other feasible position among the trees and forced himself rigid.

Poor Ginny. He'd been cold and ugly, yet had no evidence for his suspicions except her familiarity with Striker. After all, she saved Uncle Will's life in the hotel fight. What an ungrateful bastard he'd turned out to be.

In a few hours...

He reached for his old-fashioned rifle and gripped it. Could his men hold under the Corps' first assault?

And under the others that would follow? Could the Welfie soldiers who had given themselves into his hands fight effectively in this forest?

Dawn would come soon, yet he probably hadn't regained an hour of the last two days' missed sleep. How could he be such a hand wringer?

"Incoming, General!"

Bjorn sat up, grateful to the enemy.

Carter Bryant, the old media expert, rose from a similar bed. One of the things that had really pissed-off Bjorn was to hear Bryant's stately snore throughout his own vigil.

"More on their way," advised Ochoa's voice. "Aimed for the lake farms, I think, and the cleared area."

In the gloom, Bjorn made out Ochoa's form beyond Bryant. His operations director squatted in front of a monitor. He must have had the watch awake him.

Bjorn heard a rustle, saw forms rise all around.

Nearby, Cardenas sat on his heels before another device. The officer's intelligence people had planted sensors everywhere. Cardenas would combine automated, short range, broad band radio transmission of data from those sensors to reports sent via the frequency-hopping, narrow beams of Bjorn's regimental commanders. He'd guess at the Corps' plan.

As long as Bjorn didn't broadcast, the enemy couldn't pinpoint where Cardenas sampled the many waves of coded information. Of course, Bjorn and Ochoa did have to send out orders and questions occasionally. And those of his personnel not still shielded by blankets radiated short-range infrared that could be picked up by snooper aircraft.

More hand wringing.

The Eagle and Snake Division had plenty of low cost, short-range sensors, rifles, and automatic weapons as well as anti-air and anti-armor missiles. What it lacked was the sophisticated stuff: personal armor, flechette assault rifles, laser blinders and burners, stealthy tanks and personnel carriers, long range transports, search and destroy missiles, and overhead spy assets. A big list of deficiencies.

Repetitive, strobe-like flashes lit the west, probably along the lake, and were followed by thundering detonations.

He picked up his rifle--after Sergeant Poll's lesson, he'd never left a weapon behind--and stomped over to kneel between Ochoa and Cardenas. He noted on Ochoa's monitor that the Tenth Regiment still hadn't dug in its fragile stores. They'd had the farthest to go, but...

Cardenas looked up through the canopy, where the dark was graying. "I wish we could take out the high snoopers up there," he said.

"Small chance of hitting anything with what we've got," Bjorn growled. "Save the missiles for the transports." He glanced at Ochoa and received a nod of agreement.

"Here comes our ration," whispered Cardenas after another five minutes. His display lit up with the radar traces of missiles arching down from the upper atmosphere, all apparently aimed for the forest this side of the cleared area, aimed at whatever evidence the snoopers had gained of human occupation, aimed at the Eagle and Snake Division. Cardenas crossed himself.

"Spread out; take cover," Bjorn ordered.

He trotted back to his late, unlamented bed and snuggled next to a foot-thick stump, on the theory that it might protect a few degrees of his body. His main hope, of course, was that the moist, thick forest growth would blind end-game sensors and cushion detonations. All the men in the division would hope for that.

The forest lit up as if he were in the midst of flash lamps. Explosions came almost together. A very close one overwhelmed the others, left a trail of dimmer detonations behind it, like after-images. His ears took time to recover from the accompanying thunderclap. An acrid odor of cordite filled his nostrils.

Bjorn clasped his hands and arms tightly around his head, closed his eyelids, and pressed his stomach and groin against the stump.

Suddenly, he lurched into the air and then fell back, his body draped half over the stump. Twigs and leaves rained down. His head hurt like hell, and his vision bore black spots. He said "Shit!" but heard nothing.

Scrabbling with both hands, he finally found his rifle.

Bjorn glanced back in the dim dawn to where Ochoa and Cardenas had set up shop and saw both staring past him. Bryant too. He turned.

He kneeled on the edge of an immense opening torn in the forest. The floor of splintered and compressed wood that started beyond a fringe of bent and broken trees must have a diameter of three hundred meters.

"The snoopers sniffed us," Cardenas said in a tinny voice. "Let's move."

Bjorn shook his head, winced, said "No," and could barely hear himself. "We'd set up an infrared river that the snoopers could lock on. Our men need to keep their blankets over themselves until we're attacked." He tried to walk, found no problem, and moved over to the three staff men, kicking aside broken limbs as he did so. Trees quivered and the earth shook as more missiles landed nearby.

A hundred years of peace almost stopped military research and development, he thought. He was lucky the electronic seekers of long-range missiles still had terminal targeting problems. The enemy had found his general location but their projectiles couldn't home.

The Airborne's attack aircraft and the short take off and landing transports would be landing in the cleared area of Nakima now, and coupling with the tankers. The Airborne would be refueling for a quick strike as soon as the big missile bombardment ended.

He studied the screen of Ochoa's monitor. Regimental command pips blinked everywhere but in the Tenth's location. Then, as he watched, the missing cursor lit.

He hoped--and expected--that there'd be few casualties. Bjorn had sixteen thousand men spread over a wide area, while the Corps possessed only a few hundred long-range missiles in its inventory at the start of this unpleasantness.

Theoretically, America had replaced vulnerable, long-range bombers that carried cheap, dumb explosives with expensive missiles. Gone for good was the carpet-bombing he'd read of. But, the defense factories of San Angeles weren't shipping the Corps long-range anything any more. The Welfie revolution and the new city-state had put a stop to that. In these woods, the Corps couldn't destroy him from afar.

When the bombardment apparently ended, Bryant passed out vegpro packets and motioned to a tiny rivulet they had used as a forest guide to this site. Bjorn wasn't thirsty, but began to gnaw on the food.

"The only large multiple kill was on our officer hostages, General," Ochoa reported. "We grouped them too closely--a natural mistake, I guess. The collection provided a large heat signature." He shook his head.

"The Tenth lost its commander," Ochoa continued, "but the senior battalion Major took over. He changed the communication screws on his radio. Fernando Rodriguez is his name. He used to be the top gunnery sergeant of the Corps' Sixth Brigade. Good man."

"Vertical envelopment will be next," Bjorn growled. "Make sure everyone's ready." He heard the rustle of men moving in the forest now. His headache wasn't as overwhelming.

"Jump jets and rotor haulers land in Nakima,

General," Cardenas reported. "High power radar and radio light-ups."

They all looked up at the roar of aircraft engines that resounded from nearby. All of a sudden, searing white light partly blinded Bjorn and sharp explosions tore at his ears. Munitions dispensers detonated just over the treetops, he guessed, while short-range flatteners compressed small pieces of the forest nearby. Each burst of light and sound was smaller than those that the thousand-mile missiles had produced, but there were a lot more of them. He smelled burning foliage.

"They've picked our location for one of the first landings," Cardenas said. "This is air-to-ground prep."

Bjorn wished he had sent Ochoa off to another sector. Who would command if his little group went down? Another stupid mistake.

Ochoa moved up to within ten meters of Bjorn, to the edge of the squashed saucer in the forest. He carried an air defense launcher and five skinny little missiles.

What the hell! Bjorn thought. A Division Operations Officer didn't have much to do in a static battle, anyway.

He lay down next to his stump and gripped his rifle. Neither did a commander.

A snooper airplane appeared, spread its swing-wings, and wallowed in the air a couple of thousand feet over the large, flattened piece of forest. Bjorn saw Ochoa raise his loaded launcher, but a condensation plume from someone else's missile materialized below the aircraft. The snooper jinked wildly, its wings slid in and its jets pulsed, but not in time. The aircraft exploded.

Stumpy ground-attack airplanes followed the snooper. They flew low to the ground, tasked to erase any targets the sensor-carrier had found, Bjorn knew. Now they dumped fuselage bays-full of little munitions, each equipped with sensors and a ring of tiny, directional thrusters.

As he watched Ochoa take-out an airplane that zoomed right over them, maybe fifty meters high, Bjorn heard a rain of munitions strike the forest canopy. Most exploded on leaves warm from the sun, others trickled to the ground, having expended their energy in the treetops. Bjorn watched a soldier carefully dance around one as it fell.

The transports came in even lower than had the ground-attack airplanes. The first lit braking jets that lined the leading edges of wing and empennage, flared, tilted its engines, and crash-landed like an awkward pelican. Gull-wing doors opened along both sides, and armored marines poured out.

Colonel Ochoa put a missile into the cockpit area. He destroyed the aircraft's airworthiness but didn't kill many marines, Bjorn guessed. Ochoa then lifted his aim to another transport and fired, this time in its transition maneuver.

The fuel tank on Ochoa's target went up with a burst of light and a shock front of pressure. The aircraft fell in flaming pieces that ignited for a moment green rubble on the ground. Bjorn heard a series of other explosions--ammunition and missiles lighting-off inside the fuselage probably.

Marines of the landed transport desperately tried to unload mules while under gathering fire. Bjorn saw a company of a hundred men or more collect under the screams of officers and non-coms. The Achiever officers wore full suits of armor. The ranks boasted advanced corselets that embraced the groin and knee bands that would deflect flechettes.

Bjorn aimed at the main sensor horn on the helmet of the commander, took a shallow breath, and squeezed off a shot. The officer's head jerked back from a helmet impact, but Bjorn had done no damage, he guessed.

A light machine gun opened up from across the

clearing. Marines didn't go down. Instead, bullets screamed off armor and skittered from the crash-landed transport. Too high, Bjorn thought.

But his riflemen aimed lower, and higher. Enemy began to drop, their legs ruined or faces cratered. Bjorn saw an officer explode into bloody fragments by taking an anti-tank missile in the chest.

Then he witnessed the Marine commander point and the enemy split. A platoon stomped as fast as the men's heavy armor permitted toward the machine gun's location. Another came right at Bjorn. A third aimed in between and spread out into a skirmish line. Now the light machine gun tried another clip. The platoon attacking it went down, all but the completely armored officer.

Bjorn concentrated on the twenty-five men or so who strode toward him. He fired at an officer's ankle.

Cardenas yelled over the radio for help. Bryant fell to the ground five meters away and wildly fired a rifle, while Ochoa launched two air-defense missiles that impacted on the company commander's chest armor but apparently didn't have time to fuse.

Well, Bjorn thought to himself, he had a good run.

Several of the enemy launched balls of flechettes from assault rifles. Under the canopy here, Bjorn thought, the little powered and homing darts might find a clear path. Both balls hit broken saplings, however, and sprayed their projectiles into the ground.

Bjorn sweated. His stomach was tight. But he stayed behind the stump.

Another light machine gun entered the fray and put down most of the platoon that charged Bjorn. The enemy command group--two marines and the Captain--kept coming, however. The marines still fired assault rifles uselessly, but the Achiever officer reached for the hand weapon at his waist.

Ochoa and Bryant blazed away at the two enlisted men, while Bjorn let go of his useless rifle and pulled his sneak knife. Damming himself for an idiot, he leapt up and dashed into the forest opening toward the officer.

At least he gained surprise. The armored Achiever turned awkwardly, still fumbling with his short gun.

Bjorn tackled the stiff, hardened figure, throwing his arms around the man's armored body and twisting. He tried to topple him. The officer planted his feet firmly, shook them both and butted Bjorn with his helmet. Bjorn looped his arm around the man's now pistol-carrying arm and fought the enemy's attempt to turn his wrist.

God, but the ceramic-clad man was heavy!

Bjorn shoved with all his strength, finally leveraging the awkward giant off balance so the Achiever crashed over on his back. As he fell too, Bjorn reached up and flicked back the officer's visor. The man was a black. Sweat ran off his face, his forehead was lined with strain and fear. "Stupid Welfie bastard," he grunted and then gurgled as Bjorn's sharp little knife cut his throat.

From his position on top of the armored officer, now, Bjorn saw only his men in the clearing and fringe of timber. He heard fighting in the woods that the line of marines had entered, however. Rifle shots preceded the screams of men probably now disabled by shattered legs and feet. Breathing hard, he shivered and then stood.

Old-fashioned rifles and machine guns had proved superior in thick woods to low velocity, precision guided weapons. That was logical, Bjorn thought, but last night he doubted.

Back in camp, Ochoa helped Carter Bryant to his feet. Both laughed almost hysterically at the stains on Bryant's infantry trousers.

"We must move, General," Cardenas called. "Enemy intelligence will know there's a worthwhile target here from our resistance. And we've taken out a lot of snoopers."

This time Bjorn nodded. Anyway, the Corps would have no more big missiles. He picked up his rifle and trotted over to where men lifted equipment from their holes. "What force hit us?" he asked. "How's everyone else doing?"

He thought the other men stared at him strangely. He supposed they had seen him take down the Achiever armored officer. "Well?" he impatiently asked.

"The single airborne brigade attacked, Sir," Cardenas answered. "They concentrated on this sector and the next one, and have a few major lodgments. My summation program told me before I closed down that we had taken out half an air wing."

The Marines in the forest will be crying for help by nightfall, Bjorn thought. Let's see what the Corps can do with a few beleaguered islands in an enemy-held sea.

He clapped Bryant on the back as the public relations expert approached, walking carefully. "You're one of us now, Carter. You're initiated."

#

By nightfall, a second Marine brigade landed in the cleared area around Nakima junction. And Villasenor hadn't turned up.

Chapter 32

Back in Washington the next morning, Will Maestri waited for Mr. John Striker, the Executive Director of Health and Human Resources and, to all extents and purposes, dictator of the United States. Bjorn's uncle sat in the psychiatric conference room of Bethesda Naval Hospital, dressed in loose, blue-striped hospital pajamas. Maestri felt weak but pretty good, considering what he'd been through. Good enough that, normally, he'd have been sent home to convalesce in Achiever comfort--if he were an Achiever and also not a prisoner. Now he had to worry whether his recovery was for naught. Striker might strut his power and then have him killed.

He'd been lucky up until now, Maestri thought. In the ghetto, a municipal reclamation vat would have digested his torn and paralyzed body along with other rubbish. In this instance, however, the President's patronage had originally provided a surgical team while, later, HHR's possible need for a bargaining chip had funded his recovery.

He wondered what happened out in the world. He guessed that Benjamin still lived. The hospital staff--all Achievers of course--seemed worried. They snapped at Maestri. And the other patients--also Achievers--wouldn't talk to him.

Violence had risen in Washington. The two orderlies who escorted him to this conference room grumbled about a flood of trauma cases.

Was there a message in who normally used this room? Did the doctors think him crazy, that all activist Welfies were crazy? Would Striker put him in a straitjacket? Or was this quiet chamber the only unused one, now that injuries flooded the hospital?

When Striker strode in, wearing his dark blue jacket with the Nehru collar and embroidered HHR insignia, he had a guest with him: Miss Ginny Pederson, the ex-President's daughter. Striker's bushy, frowning, gray brows and growing belly radiated the arrogance of power, while she seemed more reserved than before, her long face sober. Miss Ginny wore a conservative, gray suit and a yellow-checked scarf. She carried a handbag.

"What do you hear from my nephew?" Maestri asked as he touched hands with her.

She darted a quick look at Striker.

The executive pulled up a chair for himself opposite Maestri's and left the young woman to fend for herself. "Bjorn has fought a Corps Brigade to a standstill in northern Ontario," he said. "The Chiefs are so angry they abandoned the destruction of Bjorn's force that cut through South Dakota, finally deciding it was only a decoy. They've sent those forces to reinforce the brigades at Nakima, in Canada. They also bring in a second division."

"Ben broadcast from Winnipeg, on the net," Miss Ginny added. "He declared war on the Administration and appointed you the Welfie negotiator."

Benjamin protects me as well as he can, Maestri thought. He warmed at the thought.

"Your wretched ghetto-heads trash Achiever suburbs," Striker shouted and slapped his knee with a hand. "Even here in Washington. Our people run convoys from the suburbs through to the Corps-guarded government offices near the river in the morning, and back in the evening. People from Virginian estates around the Alexandria ghetto can't even drive to the Potomac bridges." He stood and kicked at his chair.

Maestri smelled pine needles and glanced around the psychiatric conference room. The corners had rounded, providing womb-like comfort, he supposed. The walls now changed to a green, leafy pattern and became the fringe of a forest glade. He heard the low chuckle of a thrush.

"Stop that shit!" yelled Striker, his head tilted up.

The room returned to normal.

"The Corps will finish with your nephew one way or another," Striker said as he returned to his seat. "Then they'll do what HHR and I apparently can't do. They'll tame the ghettos."

Miss Ginny pulled a chair close to Maistre. "How're you feeling?" she asked.

"Okay," he answered. "Thanks for my life. The last thing I remember was how grim you looked as you kneeled over me and fired."

"Ben thinks I caused your wounding," she said. "He believes I told John here the plan to attack Health and Human Resources headquarters. I didn't."

Striker only smiled.

"I tried John as a lover for a while," she continued, "but I never betrayed my father, or you and Ben. I swear!" She looked at Striker, her lips tightening.

"Okay, Gin," the HHR leader said. "In a fit of sexual exuberance, I guess, your Aunt told the late Captain Wallace what she had planned with Bjorn. He was my channel from the White House."

"Tell Ben what John just said, if you ever get the chance," she said to Maestri.

He nodded and then glanced at Striker. "Why'd you bring her?" he asked.

"I repay old service," the HHR executive answered. "Remember how considerate I was of you after Wagoner's rebellion? How I didn't send killers after your nephew right away? Softness is my failing." He grimaced and looked down at his clasped hands.

"I never served you, John, except sexually," she whispered. "And that was something I enjoyed, too. Tell him again that I was honorable."

Striker glanced up, his eyes now cold. "I've had enough of this," he said. "Welfies ruin Achiever suburbs; Bjorn beats up the Corps; our Achiever world falls apart; and you moon over that golden-headed stud. Grow up!"

"I believe you," Maestri told her. "I'll tell Benjamin."

Striker snorted. He waved his hand dismissively. "Neither side of your proposed conversation may live long, you know."

Thuds vibrated through the floor. Maestri frowned.

Striker, preoccupied, leaned forward and shoved his face within ten centimeters of Maestri's. "I'll use nukes on your nephew, if I have to. What do you say to that, 'Welfie Chief Negotiator'?"

Damn!

"Do you couple a compromise offer with that threat?" Maestri asked.

"Everyone eats San Angeles rations for his lifetime, but no more children. Mandatory chemical abortions."

"Of every child?"

"Yes. Punishment squads will shoot underage children on sight, then find their mothers."

"No."

"How about one child for every woman?" intervened Miss Ginny.

"China proved you can't be sure of that," Striker answered. "Besides, we want zero unproductive people. None."

Maestri sighed. Nukes, eh? Not on the ghettos, probably. That would disgust the world and poison suburbs as well as needed farmland. Only on Benjamin.

"The answer is still 'no.' Our men knew of risks; I can't surrender for them."

This time noises from below sounded like explosives, then shots.

Striker swore, rose to his feet, and turned toward the door. Miss Ginny stood, also. "Don't go just yet, John," she said. "I've something you must see."

She dipped into her handbag, walked to the frowning HHR man, and held out her hand. By this time Maestri had stood, too.

Striker jumped back. Miss Ginny followed him, still held her hand near the executive's face. "That's right, John," she said. It's my face snare. I've released the safety; all I have to do is let go of the device, maybe toss it in your direction."

Maestri slid his bare feet into slippers. This was crazy, he thought. But the noise downstairs proved she had confederates. He walked past a red-faced Striker and opened the door a crack. The Director's two bodyguards had collected down the hall with the nurses aids that'd shepherded him here. All had their backs turned. They looked and listened in the direction of the main bank of elevators, the sound channel for the gunfire.

So far, not too crazy.

"If you'll lead the way to the Wisconsin Avenue exit, Mr. Maestri, John and I will follow," Miss Ginny said from behind. "I'm sure he will tell anyone who objects to let us through."

"Have you gone insane?" Striker incredulously blurted at the woman. "You turn against your own kind and side with the dumb and squalid. What's got into you?"

"Strangely enough, I find I want to be Bjorn's woman permanently," Ms. Ginny replied. She grimaced while staring fixedly at Striker. Her face was pale. "Weird, I grant you, but there it is. This is the task he set me."

Maestri stepped outside and walked quietly away from the guards.

"Believe me, John," he heard, "if I think we're trapped, your handsome face goes."

Maestri glanced back. Miss Ginny held Striker's right arm, strode along beside the HHR director. Her right hand swung along her side and her fist held the baseball-sized snare. Striker's face was now white, also. He stumbled, while Miss Ginny seemed calm.

Maestri entered an elevator occupied by a nurse and an empty stretcher-bed. He turned at the back and watched Miss Ginny squeeze Striker's arm.

"It's all right, nurse," the executive said. "First floor, please."

"Something bad is going on down there, Sir. Welfies from across the street, maybe. We've been told to stay above the third floor."

Miss Ginny let go of Striker's arm, reached out, and pushed the first floor button. She smiled sweetly at the nurse.

The woman glared, started to speak, and then noticed Striker's rigid posture, the sweat on his forehead. She gulped and shifted her stare to the blank door.

When they exited, the hall was deserted. Maestri found a wall sign that pointed toward Wisconsin Avenue. He heard the elevator door close and glanced back. As they followed, Striker and Miss Ginny appeared the best of friends, maybe even man and wife. Anger, however, had replaced the fear in the HHR man's eyes.

Shots! Then Maestri heard shouts. He walked alongside an empty Achiever shop, turned down a short marble hallway, and stopped abruptly.

"Well, damn! You're the man!"

Maestri had found a picket of three black Welfies. They lay on the floor, held bottles and homemade crossbows. One man faced toward him, the others the other way, next to the walls. The speaker was about Maestri's own size, he guessed, had a bad face scar and a squashed nose. He lay near a burned dead man. Three other victims curled behind, clothes charred and flesh welted with blisters. The dead had been hospital guards, Maistre guessed.

"Yes, I'm the man all right," he said. "The two Achievers behind me are escorts. Don't harm them."

Under his worry and growing delight, Maestri's admiration for Ginny Peterson blossomed. The woman must have found Tracey, his dead bodyguard's mother and member of the local Residents' Council. Somehow she had persuaded the woman to intervene, and had brought along others, too. If the girl's intervention was crazy, her strategizing was first rate and her political ability great.

He gestured to where the hall apparently opened up into a lobby. "What's going on?"

"We slammed the regular Navy police when we arrived," the spokesman reported. He rose to his feet and motioned his men up, too. "But now some HHR pricks have shown up. And they've probably called for help."

The man bent and hit his half-full glass bottle on the stone floor. Three short clunks, then a long scrape.

"Run for it!" a woman screamed.

A black Welfie grabbed each elbow and hurried Maistre along. He glanced back. Ginny sprawled on the floor while Striker ran away. She threw the face snare from her prostrate position, but Maistre thought the jet from the ignited little motor faded too soon.

"Bring her along," he gasped. "She's Bjorn's woman."

Then a giant picked him up with one arm and lumbered across a large lobby toward two brass doors. Torn and bleeding bodies, mostly Welfie, littered the marble floor.

Ten black fighters dashed from farther inside the hospital and turned to fire captured Navy pistols. A Molotov cocktail suddenly exploded beyond the information kiosk. Soon he was outside in the dark night. His steed now limped; blood spilled from his side. The man collapsed. Maistre found himself standing on a marble step in his slippers.

"Follow me," shouted Tracey from nearby, her thick-lipped face strained with fear and resolve. "You others run behind and shelter him."

Maistre was tired, and his spine hurt. A strong hand gripped his elbow and helped him run. He glanced to the side and saw Miss Ginny.

#

Later that night, Will Maestri sat in one of the only two chairs in a cubby. Residents had found vegpro brew for him. A little drunk now, he felt better, believed he hadn't disturbed anything in the delicate column of bones and carbon compound castings that guarded his new spinal cord. Tracey sat in the other chair, while Ginny--he'd given up the distancing "Miss"--leaned against a dirty wall along with two of Tracey's cronies.

"My, but ain't HHR mad," reported the messenger from a neighboring net-watcher. "Punishment companies blind everyone they catch on the streets. All the hostage families of the blocks near the hospital have squeezed throats."

That information made Maistre feel sick.

"They looking for you pretty bad, Tracey," the woman said. "HHR went down the chain of contacts this Achiever lady used to find you. Their families and them are history."

The silence seemed chill.

"Rumor is that HHR quits megacities around here and brings in more punishment battalions," Tracey said in a thin voice. "That'll give our friends in the deserted cities a chance to revolt, however."

"I must speak to General Bjorn," Maistre said. "Can you find him on the Web?"

"Wait 'till he opens a node," Tracey said. "Our people are watching."

..Chapter 33

Northern Ontario in October became too cold at dusk, especially for someone used to temperate or tropical climates. Sitting against a half-meter-thick tree a day and a half after the Marines attacked his force from the air, Bjorn pulled a thin blanket higher around his chest. Smoke from small forest blazes tingled in his nose.

"Let's light a fire," he said to his little headquarters staff. "The snoopers will have a hell of a time distinguishing a body-warmer from all the hot spots left by missile strikes."

A sergeant picked up dry wood and placed pieces on an old stump. An older Welfie, a private, dragged over a large branch, and began to break it up. Two other men gathered sticks.

Carter Bryant, his media expert, stopped snoring on the other side of the stump, opened his eyes, and rolled over.

Nearby, Colonel Cardenas glanced up from the processor display that he'd attached to the radio. "A hell of a lot of RF traffic, General. More and more marine units land at Nakima. Colonel Rodriguez of our Tenth Regiment sent scouts down along the lake. They captured a marine scout, from the 3rd Division! If all of the latter drops in, we'll dance with two, full marine divisions, plus the remnants of the airborne brigade."

Bjorn pursed his lips in a silent whistle.

"Do we have many prisoners?" Bryant asked Cardenas. He sat up and disdainfully examined a vegpro packet.

"Not many. Perhaps four hundred. Lots of

wounded taking care of each other on big missile scars, where the transports came down. Maybe another hundred free marines skulk around in the woods. Most of the lurkers have leg and ankle injuries that make them harmless."

"Any new Achiever prisoners?"

Cardenas darted a cynical glance across the growing woodpile. "Considering the way our people feel, what do you think?"

"Some Achievers are on your side, you know," the old man said. "Our side, that is. 'Holistics,' they're called. They want to move away from two-nation, double standards, want everyone integrated into society. The President became a believer, and there'll be some oriented that way in the divisions here. They won't like the way the government handles things. We could use them, maybe."

Bjorn waved his hand dismissively. "What does the marine scout we captured report?" he asked Cardenas.

"The canes are out and Enforcers have raised two crosses." He hesitated and then added, "All the prisoners are scared as hell. They think they'll be killed when we go down. We'll have infected them with our rebellion."

Bjorn's operation chief, Colonel Ochoa, walked into their tiny clearing. "About a hundred men of Company C, Third Battalion, bivouac around us, General. Scattered, per your orders. Good morale, too, and plenty of anti-aircraft loads left."

Bjorn grunted.

"Damn, I wish we could tap into the net," Cardenas said. "I feel deaf and dumb, especially the latter."

"Villasenor will find us."

If the Corps hasn't found him first, Bjorn thought. The maglev line, with its accompanying optical cable, would be the first place the Corps explored. It was an obvious pathway into the forest. But Villasenor should have finished there hours before the Corps pushed in.

The sergeant held a starter to dry leaves under his woodpile; the fire caught.

Nice, Bjorn thought, but it won't warm us much.

"The Corps will burn its way into the woods tomorrow, Ochoa," he said. "You know that? No more vertical crap. Laser dragons first, followed by tanks that hose down the woods with machine guns. Marines will march beside the column to protect against any Welfies who lie doggo with anti-armor missiles. They'll blaze roads into us, maybe four or five, more the next day, and the next. Cut us into small boxes, if they can."

"It'll take the Marines time."

"Yeah. And we'll hurt them bad while they're at it," Cardenas contributed.

"Make sure our people aren't heroic," Bjorn continued. "Have them pull away from the heads of the enemy columns, drift back only after the heavy stuff goes by, then strike the sides and rear."

"Yes, Sir," Colonel Ochoa replied.

Bjorn lay down and rolled on his side so he could collect radiated heat from the little fire.

"I don't understand you, General," Bryant said. "Night before last, when we faced an airborne brigade, you couldn't sleep. Now, when a division, and maybe a second, is about to attack us, you look like you may fall off for hours."

"We've tested ourselves and our tactics, Bryant. I've confidence now."

Colonel Ochoa nodded.

"Corps officers are insanely arrogant," Bjorn explained. "They think Welfies are inferior and can be easily beaten unless Achievers tell them what to do." He laid his head back. "The Corps commander won't retract after burning his fingers. He won't abandon the airborne troops we surround in here. He'll charge into a terrain that's perfect for us. We're going to win."

#

The attack by the First Division began before dawn the next morning. Even several kilometers away, Bjorn observed through the trees an incandescent glow that accompanied thunderous noise.

"Colonel Jaime Boleros has the sector bordering Nakima and the east-west maglev line," Colonel Cardenas said. "He reports that the enemy puts in two spearheads. His northern neighbor receives another two. The way I've reconstructed General Howe's plan, he'll order two additional regiments to cut into the forest even further north. Those six regiments will try to link up with the remaining pockets of the airborne brigade. The last Marine brigade, with its three regiments, will feel for our northern flank and place most of its strength where it thinks our deployment ends."

"Yeah." Bjorn answered. "It'll try to flank us."

"Isn't there anything hot to drink?" Bryant grumbled.

#

Colonel Salvador Villasenor, Bjorn's communications chief, walked in at about noon. Two soldiers helped with the spool of gossamer optical cable, another two carried a lightweight box between two stretcher poles.

Villasenor saluted Bjorn. He grinned disgustedly. "What a wonderful time I've had, Sir!"

Bjorn returned the salute and held out his hand. "Glad you made it. I gather the bit stream's continuous?"

"It was at the last laser repeater station I made."

His men removed a photonic converter from the box, clipped the cable, and fastened the two together.

Villasenor watched, with Bjorn. "I've only one more installation left," he said. "Twisting in this forest used the repeaters up."

Cardenas's intelligence sergeant and the old private brought a transceiver and a cable. They connected them to a flat screen and a broadcasting camera. He handed them to Villasenor's assistants.

"What took you so long?" Bjorn asked as he led his communications specialist--now Colonel Villasenor-- toward the growing photonics center.

"I had to return to Nakima, break into one of the storage huts, and find repeaters and cable," Villasenor said. "On the way, I recruited these guys."

"Sorry," Bjorn said. "I should have told you earlier that I wanted access to the net. I thought you comm people carried everything you ever needed in your back pocket."

The Corps must have been hot on Villasenor's heels the second time down that maglev line. Marines maybe moved all around the communications expert while he broke into a repeater station and operated on it.

"You've done a great job," he told his officer. "You've given me a lever I can use to pry apart Achiever power."

"I'm into the Montreal Switch, Sir," Cardenas said. "Where to?"

"Here, let me." Villasenor squatted and pulled the display to him, breathed numbers, responded with letters when the screen glowed and the machine spoke. "Chicago, Sir?"

"You've thought ahead while you walked, I guess. Yes. Get me Con Wagoner, head of our revolution."

#

"General Bjorn's on the net, Sir. He wants to talk with you."

Con woke with a start and stared at the grinning Major Hata. Then he jumped up and limped to the communication center in the Chicago residents' council headquarters. He sat in front of the lit flat screen.

"Napping, Con?"

No more depression! Gone! He grinned at Bjorn, noted the thick forest background and the faint sound of distant gunfire. His general smiled back, the corners of

Bjorn's eyes crinkling on each side of and above the long nose and below the tight knots of yellow hair. That confident image told Con everything! "I thought you stood us up," he said.

Bjorn shook his head. "Sorry. Just got a line through. We've been at a party, though. What's happened at your end?"

Con passed his hand over his face, shook himself. "You've woken the ghettos finally. We've squashed Welfare King gangs all over the country. In the ghettos, an Achiever doesn't dare walk down a street without armored escort. But nobody's put together anything comparable to our revolt in San Angeles and the clean out of Chicago. We've completely taken over only one more city. And, in most places, punishment companies are slaughtering hostages."

He was quiet for a moment and then mustered a smile. "Minneapolis is free; punishment companies left as the remains of your decoy force entered. Afraid the slaughter might be turned on them, I guess."

Bjorn's face lit. "Did Brigadier General Lopez, the old sergeant major, survive?"

"No, but a lot of his men still stood when the Corps brigade they fought flew off to wherever you are. The senior Major says he's making a regiment out of them, although he doesn't have many missiles or cartridges left."

"I sent two regiments." Bjorn shook his head. "And I liked Lopez. That decoy idea of mine was one of history's cruelest brainstorms."

"You and the rest of the division live, right? Don't worry about the cost."

"How is morale?"

Con didn't feel like smiling any more. "HHR has lost control of the tenements in most megacities," he said. "Killing the hostages boomeranged. People talk freely now and build hand weapons.   They're resolute and defend their cubbies, but don't control the streets. They're too under-equipped to attack burners, lasers, and assault rifles." He shrugged. They're scared, General."

Con leaned forward. "Our hackers think HHR plans to concentrate its military strength in Washington, New York, Boston and Phoenix—the last two places are where the short range missile plants are--and in Denver and San Francisco. The bastards will send in multiple punishment battalions to clean out the ghetto leadership in each megacity, level blocks to make shooting avenues, and build bordering death strips so no one can threaten suburbs."

Con waved his hand, the depression of the past days returning. "When HHR has sterilized that set of megacities, Striker will transfer the punishment companies to another set and re-start the process."

He spread his hands. "We don't have much time before we lose our best people and become tamed."

"Lots of agony right now, I guess," Bjorn replied. "But better the agony that accompanies fighting than soul-killing resignation. Pump them up, Con! Tell our people in the target cities to snipe, ambush, and trade tenements, whole blocks, for time. They must make sneak attacks at night, poison water, and use their women to tempt HHR thugs into ambushes!" He slapped his leg. "Tell the leaders to hold on!"

Bjorn's dark blue eyes seemed to bore into Con. "As HHR concentrates, we must move into the places it abandons." He leaned forward. "Look, get on the net with the Residents Councils of those ghettos. Tell them to kick out whatever small HHR forces remain. They ought to manage that, for Christ's sake. Then have them form their own militia, turn over buses and trucks to form street barriers, assign snipers even if they only have crossbows, and make bombs out of fertilizer, oil, and scrap iron. Ask for volunteer suiciders. Prepare to fight to the death when HHR comes back."

"Everyone is afraid of Marine retribution," Con quietly stated. "The Corps is too disciplined and has too many high technology weapons. We won't have a chance when its divisions return from Canada."

"The Corps has me on my back, Con, but I have my claws in its belly. Whatever returns to the States won't be good for much." Bjorn glanced over his shoulder, smiled at someone Con couldn't see, and then turned back. "I'm about to start ripping again."

Bjorn reached out of the projector's focus. His hand came back with a broken piece of vegpro. "Listen," he continued, not taking a bite yet. "We can't worry about losing. All Welfies must take risks to win. You're the leader everyone respects. Take over. Tell our people to find retired Corps non-coms in their ghettos and put them in charge of assault platoons. In the abandoned cities, the leaders must form independent battalions."

Con felt light-headed. He had expected commiseration, received orders instead. "Your Uncle Will Maestri desperately tries to reach you," he said. He fed a slip of paper into the data slot. "Here's his didg code."

"Uncle Will's free and in hiding?" Bjorn asked, a delighted smile taking over his face.

"Yes. Miss Ginny had Washington Welfies break him out of the hospital."

Bjorn beamed. "Great!" He raised a hand in farewell. "Try to keep our people civilized, Con. We'll need Achiever support later. But step up the pressure."

#

"General Bjorn's on the monitor, himself!"

Will Maestri stood and led a procession across the hall to the cubby with the interactive, flat screen. No one in this block owned a holovision platform, Maestri had learned. The residents were the poorest of the poor.

He felt Ginny's hand under his elbow. She

probably wanted to make sure the Welfies let her come to the flat screen, also wanted him to remember her when he faced his nephew. Then he kneeled to face the display.

Benjamin looked good, Maestri thought. A little lean, maybe, but full of that sometimes-aggravating self-confidence.

"Hi, Uncle Will," Bjorn said. "Where's Ginny?"

"Here, Ben." The girl crouched to bring her head down level with Maestri's. She cried.

"Ginny put her snare to Striker's face and brought me down to the lobby of the naval hospital," Maistre volunteered. "Our friend, Tracey here, and her people held off the HHR. They led us both out."

Ginny squeezed his arm and he said the rest. "Striker told me that the Ambassador, the President's sister, was the leak, Benjamin. She bragged about your plan to Captain Wallace, who then cued the assassination attempt on me. Ginny had nothing to do with it."

Benjamin stared at the young woman. "I'm sorry I thought badly of you," he said.

Ginny stayed quiet.

"I love you, sweetheart," he added.

Damn if the woman didn't collapse. She fell on her rear next to Maestri and bawled. He shook his head.

"Striker's terms are San Angeles rations and no children, ever," Maestri finally reported. "I said 'no.'"

Benjamin raised his eyes from where Ginny must have disappeared off his screen. "That's genocide. What else?"

"He'll use nukes if the Corps doesn't defeat you soon."

"He can't have meant it," gulped Ginny, now up by Maestri's elbow again.

Benjamin closed his eyes tightly together--a childhood habit, Maestri remembered. It was a grimace that gave Benjamin a private space in which to think.

The man who had been a boy only a few years ago, opened his eyes. "Yes," he said. "That's logical. They will do that, if they can."

He leaned forward. "Take care, Uncle Will, Ginny. I must go now."

#

Bjorn sat back against the tree. "Any of you old Corps people know operations men in the Carib. Division?" he asked his team. "It's up in Vancouver now."

"The top operations sergeant of its Second Brigade is a buddy," Colonel Rafael Ochoa answered. "We were both at division headquarters behind Veracruz."

"Is he smart?"

"We always came in neck and neck on the qualfies."

"See if you and Villasenor can ring him up--privately, for his sake. I want to persuade him to do something."

"He a Carib?" Villasenor asked Ochoa. "Do we try Mex Spanish or ghetto English?"

Nukes, eh? "Then get me Fifty-two Smith out in San Angeles."

Bjorn glanced at his media expert. "And Bryant, now that we have access, I want another national hook-up."

#

"Welfie friends and Achiever enemies, good evening," Bjorn said.

He hoped Bryant delivered the networks he'd promised. Some of the marines whom Bjorn opposed here could sneak a look and a listen around Achiever backs if enough frequency bands carried his speech.

"I talk from Nakima in Northern Ontario, where Premier Saltonstall of Canada and his cabinet have marooned us." He grinned. "You Canadian Welfies

who listen, pass the word, will you? Your Achiever
politicians need a lesson. If they can screw us, who
only wanted to return home, they will do worse to you."

He held up a hand. "Listen."

Villasenor had sworn the amplifiers would deliver
far-off shots and missile detonations to people's cubbies
or living rooms. A Marine spearhead drove east on
each side of their campfire this afternoon and provided
not so far-off sound effects.

"That's gunfire you hear," Bjorn said. "Short,
dumb, underfed Welfies fight Achiever-led Marines. And
beat them, too. HHR brought two and a third, high
technology Marine Corps divisions up here to destroy
my Welfie infantry. They won't succeed."

He paused. Bryant had told him to let his
audience absorb each whack on the head before
delivering another.

"Do you know what HHR plans for the ghettos?
Extermination, that's what. Wipe out. It'll shoot children
and their mothers and gradually starve the rest of us."

He didn't have to pretend; rage tightened his
face. "You Welfies know HHR; that's why you're fighting
now. To the death, friends, to the death."

He smiled coldly.

"Maybe some of you Achievers didn't know HHR
plans," he finally continued. "If the news turns your
stomach, pick up the gun you're keeping near your front
door to repel Welfie boogey men and join us, instead."

Another pause. He eased an inch closer to the
camera. "There's one group of people I've no time for.
That's the Welfies who support those who'd kill our
parents, our families, and our friends. I'm talking about
you, Marines. I'm talking about you, Caribs of the
Rainbow Division."

He pointed into the camera's focus and wished
Villasenor had a hologram set-up that could put himself
in the laps of the audience. "Your people need you to
stand up for them," he continued. "Stop obeying their

enemies."

A surface-to-surface missile exploded nearby. At Bryant's questioning throat-cut, Bjorn nodded both to his Achiever producer and the distant audience.

Chapter 34

While Bjorn waited to challenge the attacking Corps in the north woods, Brigadier General Louis Lefko of the Corps staff met with John Striker. Lefko didn't feel like smiling at HHR's executive director. "You've waited late to ask for my advice again," he said. "This north woods grappling is madness. And I told the chief of staff the same, when the Canadians informed us where they had marooned Bjorn. Sending our troops up there to fight was crazy. We should have let him flail away, trying to escape, and concentrated forces on the rebellious ghettos."

"When I want criticism of our policies, I'll ask for it."

Lefko glanced at the security screens on Striker's office wall. HHR guards filled the building. A gun slaved to sensors would point at him inside here, too, and Striker's voiceprint could trigger the weapon. "You'll hear my opinion when I want to give it," he said.

The official half-rose and then dropped back into his seat.

Striker had gained weight, Lefko thought. Frown lines around mouth and eyes now wiped out the charming grin the man once possessed.

"That's right, Mr. Striker," he said. "Don't bother to frighten me. Less and less of the future is of interest, anyway. Death might be a better alternative. Even if we destroy Bjorn and his division now, the Welfies will have ruined us."

Striker scowled. "We can rebuild."

"The country won't economically recover fully in our lifetimes," Lefko replied. "Our Achievers and their machines will take at least fifty years to repair the damage done by the fighting that's ahead. To the transportation system, the factories, and communications. We military will sit in the ghettos, slaughtering people." Lefko twisted his hands together. "We'll be locked in at home when we should be disciplining the mid-world empires that breed more and more people and problems, that threaten Europe and, eventually, us."

"You have duty."

How tiresome! By now, Striker should realize Lefko obeyed reason, not old maxims. Whether their relationship was originally based on the linking of unique chemical bonds in their pheromones or some sort of mental joint set of prejudices, Mr. Striker and he developed rapport the first day. Now, Bjorn threatened that anchor, too.

Lefko hoped their special relationship wasn't history. Striker needed to show sense. Otherwise, the whole Achiever class was in deep trouble.

The heavyset leader of the United States gestured a half-apology. "We're in a mess," he said. "I don't deny it. But we still have a chance to quiet the Welfies. You exaggerate their unity. If we destroy Bjorn and his division, then kill the President and the Welfie leadership now located in Chicago, we'll have kicked in the ghettos' guts.

"I guarantee HHR can then pacify every megacity other than San Angeles, Chicago, and Minneapolis. Rebellion has had a chance to grow roots in those three. The Corps will have to plow and harrow them."

Mr. Striker's eyes were intent. Conviction poured from him. "Our economy will have regressed," he said firmly, "but the Corps won't have to worry domestic concerns beyond the next year. My Punishment Companies will take care of order. And we'll use most of the welfare budget to repair damage."

Maybe he's right, Lefko thought. We in the

military could then turn our attention abroad. He hoped so.

Striker still made him want to say, "Yes, Sir!" The man possessed a magnetic attraction. Charisma. Lefko remembered the morning after Bjorn's attempt to corrupt his regiment outside San Antonio, when he flew to Washington and first met this man. Both were impressed, Lefko thought.

Then, he stilled his excitement at the chance for a larger stage. Carefully and coldly he outlined what the government should do with his regiment--with the new infantry divisions, in fact. Striker should have the chiefs propose to the President--who still held the office--that the country obtains more grain by invading and absorbing western Canada. Conquest would solve the food shortage created by the President's conciliatory policy to the Welfies.

Moving each army infantry division north would also take care of loyalty problems, he suggested. Once in place, without long-range transport, the Welfie soldiers could do nothing practical to help United States megacity ghettos.

Of course, the chiefs shouldn't tell the pro-Welfie President that second motive.

Lefko sighed. Bjorn exploited his bit of cleverness to revolutionize Welfie power.

"You should have followed my tac-nuke recommendation when I recently made it," he said.

"Enough." Striker waved his hand dismissively. "That's done." He smiled. "Or not done, rather."

"Bjorn has opened Pandora's box," Lefko said tiredly. "His Welfies threaten our production facilities and our cultural centers, as well as the suburbs. They hold Achiever hostages in the depths of ghettos. His people kill more of your punishment police every day. The ghettos are bloodily awash with Welfie revenge." Lefko rubbed his chin. "Now Bjorn grips two thirds of the Corps in Canada. I don't see how he can triumph, but I never thought he could get this far. He frightens me."

        "You're the great planner," Striker interjected. "What do we do? I'll listen more carefully this time."

        "Bjorn's the center of the metastasis," Lefko said. "We must cauterize him. Same advice as before."

        "You now have my permission to use your nuclear treatment," Striker said. He stared at Lefko from under brows that seemed to shelter live coals. "In fact, you will carry my order to the chiefs. I require use of the ultimate weapon."

Chapter 35

"I thought commanding generals stayed out of the enemy's weapon range," Carter Bryant, the media expert, said as he wiped sweat off his brow while sitting on the ground near Bjorn. "This sneaking up on them is ridiculous."

Bryant told Bjorn that recent microscopic repairs to the natural wiring system which drove his heart made him feel only fifty years old again. Then, his fear aroused by the aerial pursuit, the exhaustion of his swim, and terror from the fight in the crushed forest maybe inoculated him with courage. Health and new spirit let Bryant bear this march well.

"I'd like to be as close to the Corps as possible right now," Bjorn answered. "With threats of nukes flying around, we're safer in its shadow. And I'm not comfortable sitting back when my men fight.

"Don't worry," he continued. "You and I have company. Colonels Ochoa and Cardenas, with their assistants, are only a kilometer or two away. Several battalions are nearby, also. The men sift separately through the woods; they wear blankets as ponchos to keep-in their infrared."

"'To retain their heat' is what they'd say." The hologram producer pulled his own pinned blanket tighter. "It's getting <u>cold</u>, even in daytime.

"Why are you pairing with me," he asked after a grumpy silence, "instead of with one of your staff?"

"You're my media expert, my link with the sophisticated, Achiever world. You're important. Other Welfies might not look after you properly when high explosive starts flying."

And he needed to tie the man to him.

Half the regiment around them should near the enemy column and concentrate at its middle by dusk. Another two battalions from the neighboring regiment would close in on the marines' other side.

"I hoped you walked with me to explain this maneuver to your historian."

"You'll learn in the best way, through experience."

"I'm a verbal creature," Bryant countered. "I like explanations. For instance, how can you clump together your force now, but couldn't before?"

"We've poked sticks in their aerial eyes. But even so, my move's a gamble. Their ground sensors should soon notice the thickening of our signatures. Will we be close enough to badly hurt the marines before they catch on? Or, will they have time to concentrate and clear fields of fire?"

"You're trying to squeeze all the enemy spearheads tonight, aren't you?"

"All but the most northerly one. There, Rodriguez and his regiment have a different assignment." He stood and offered a hand. "Time to trudge onward."

"This is a novel experience for me," Bryant said as he followed Bjorn through the woods. "Fantastic scenes, of course, better than I'd hoped for. The railroad station with your troops' discipline in the midst of disaster. Your pass through the ranks at Nakima as units prepared to march into the woods. How men looked at you, some crying. They knew the lives of their families as well as their own depended on what you commanded and they did. Then the enemy landing in the forest, the fight, and my terror."

Bjorn paused in a more open space and let the old Achiever catch up and walk close to him.

"I hadn't expected to become committed to your cause," Bryant went on. "I like you, Ochoa, and Cardenas, admire you all, actually. And I like your soldiers, even with their Welfie accents and their lack of culture."

"Yes," Bjorn said. "The two-nations policy kept the classes apart so that each thinks of the other as alien."

"We need to break down barriers, rather than erect more," Bryant said and then fell back as the forest thickened again.

This Achiever <u>was</u> his now.

As dusk rapidly fell, the woods ahead of Bjorn suddenly exploded with light and sound.

He guessed that the enemy column pushing forward only a kilometer distant had detected some of his soldiers. Since no shell or missile came his way, the marines must fire at the Welfies who moved closer from the other side.

He motioned to Bryant and sat on the gravelly ground between frequent trees, among browning ferns and red-leafed vines. He touched his chest transceiver, ordered-in Ochoa, Cardenas, and their equipment porters.

A squad of infantry dashed by, carrying anti-armor missiles in their arms and, over their shoulders, rifles. The armored marines couldn't move like that, Bjorn thought. Especially the Achiever officers with heavy, full suits. And they couldn't drive their weapon vehicles into the forest without first carving roads either.

Then the sound and brightness increased. A scream of tank shells and machine gun bullets chewed into the forest in front of him. The enemy column would be feeling what Bryant had called the "squeeze" from both sides now. Four of his infantry battalions tore at pieces of an enemy regiment stretched out along a narrow, new road.

Colonel Rafael Ochoa kneeled, while a technician shot a stealthy antenna into a treetop and then slid an attaché case to him. "We've cut the column behind us in two places already," the Director of Operations said.

The explosion of light and sound in front of them ceased and then another replaced it farther east. "Our boys have taken out the vehicles and burners here," Ochoa said. He swung open his display screen. "They work up the column now, using dead vehicles as shelter. They'll attack from three sides, try to disable as many as they can before the marines fortify."

"Here come their planes!" shouted Cardenas, who sat at his own communications node.

Bjorn felt the shock of air bombardment once more. The forest became bright as day for almost a full minute. Tree limbs, needles, and leaves, some of the latter bearing the yellow and brown colors of fall, cascaded to the ground. Warheads pulverized clumps of trees nearby. Anti-personnel bomblets struck the canopy like hail, and then trickled, fizzling and darting with dying energy, to the ground. Bjorn's head ached again from noise.

Most of the aerial danger was behind them, however. The pilots didn't dare drop ordnance too close to their own men in the stalled column up ahead.

He motioned to Ochoa and Cardenas, touched Bryant on the elbow, and then strode to a nearby area where boulders bulged out of the earth among meter-thick, broad-leafed trees. He sat down between two granite outcrops and motioned to his staff to join him.

The timber-harvesting machines mustn't have liked the rock, he thought. As a result, the area made an ideal headquarters. The big trees provided tall antenna masts, while the stone ridges would prevent laser burner and tank reprisal from the beleaguered enemy south of him, if his staffs' short wave, frequency hopping broadcasts were somehow triangulated.

Bryant passed out vegpro packets.

When it became full dark, Bjorn rose to his hands and knees. "I'm going to take a look," he said.

"No!" protested Colonel Ochoa. "You're the

commander. We can't lose you."

He's really right, Bjorn thought. I wouldn't let him, my Operations Director, take inspection trips right now. But I can't sit around with my thumb up my ass, cocooned from what's going on. "Only a quick reconnoiter," he said, suppressing guilt. "The rest of you stay put and keep your fingers on the pulse."

He stood and then surveyed them. Ochoa and Cardenas appeared worried, Bryant angered. "Don't shoot me when I come back," he said.

The track south of him that the marines had blazed through the woods was quiet. Bjorn felt his way in the gloom a half a kilometer towards it and then dropped to his hands and feet and walked like a big spider. Finally, he saw, through a bunch of thin tree trunks, small flames lick at a turret. He collapsed to his belly and crawled forward until he reached a mound of roots and crushed trees that bounded the carved-out track.

The turret held a burner nozzle. The round weapons box fitted on an armored naphtha and oil tanker. It had burst along the top as fuel compartments sympathetically detonated. The metal was crusted with a black, caramelized gunk.

The red and yellow of remaining fire made his pupils narrow and the rest of the scene harder to see. But he smelled the stink of burned flesh, wood smoke, and blood. The trees near the destroyed burner had been torched; farther away trunks were blotched and bare for ten meters up.

He heard no wounded. His men took them to an aid center on the other side of the track, he guessed. He hoped they found as thick tree-shelter as his staff.

Bjorn looked away from the flickering fire; his eyes adjusted after a moment. A knocked-over APC loomed to his right, the front side caved-in. He thought a large missile--or two portable anti-tank missiles, more probably--had caught it on its cab door, right behind the engine compartment. Logs--no, bodies--lay strewn in the vehicle's rear, where marines had exited, only to be cut down.

The track dipped where he lay, but he could see occasional flashes of light over its eastern and western rises. A rumbling of battle noise filled his ears.

Bjorn turned back to his command post and found his officers relieved by his return.

#

"My summary program says our air defense units have taken out a hundred and fifty-three transport airplanes as they entered or exited drop zones," Colonel Ochoa reported several hours later, after midnight.

The First Division's Air Wing must be in shock, Bjorn guessed, as traumatized as the Airborne Brigade's tac-air units were.

"We've chopped-up seven enemy columns," Ochoa continued," and surrounded pieces of two brigades and slices of an independent regiment--in addition to pockets of the airborne troops from two days before."

Most of the First Division will be incapacitated! Bjorn thought. Surrounded, many of their vehicles destroyed, unable to move forward and frightened by their officers from retreating.

"The enemy repelled our attacks on the final, northernmost thrust, however," Colonel Ochoa noted. "Since the 10th had another assignment, there was no squeeze. The Marines there have opened up fields of fire that keep the single regiment away. That enemy column contains two Marine regiments. It will likely turn south on a broad front soon and try to join up with the columns we've broken. Just as Jose predicted."

"And it'll be helped by the 3rd Division, if I'm any good at guessing," Bjorn said. "Tell the boys to expect more visitors here, too."

Re-supply would soon be a major issue, Bjorn thought. For both sides.

The enemy pockets and the marines' northern column would be expending munitions at a horrendous rate.

"What're our casualties?" he asked.

"In this regiment, our two battalions in the north each suffered over twenty-five percent dead or out of commission from wounds. The butcher bill for the rest is ten percent."

Bjorn decided not to ask about treatment for the wounded. Nothing he could do for them, whatever their state. Although the Eagle and Snake Division had a medical organization, it would be prey to air attack once its teams collected. Thus help would be scattered and unsystematic. And modern munitions tore apart unprotected men. He guessed that many wounded, out in the cold, would die before morning.

"We can't let our people's suffering bother us," Colonel Ochoa said. His eyes glinted in reflected light from his display. "Morale is high. We're Welfie infantry and we've badly hurt the Achiever-led Corps."

#

The Nakima farmer wore a turban and a beard, like the other orthodox Sikhs Colonel Fernando Rodriguez met in his ghetto childhood. Apparently Winnipeg held a large community of that minority. Some had traded ration guarantees for a piece of hardscrabble land out in the wilds.

The farmer was tall and powerful, but no match for Rodriguez's "squat and powerful," the American Welfie guessed.

Not that he distrusted the man. The Sikh had seemed suitably enraged over the destruction of his farm when a scout brought him to where Rodriguez and a couple of his fellow ex-sergeants broke their trek. He knew about Bjorn, too. The Sikh credited him with the bombardment warning that had saved his family and friends.

"I'll give you your choice of loot if you help us,"

Rodriguez said. "There'll be food, command shelters, heaters, and all kinds of vehicles. Enough to get you folks through the winter and enough to sell for big money if you know how to bring contraband into the city."

"Thank you, Sir," the man answered. He flashed a white grin in the dim dusk. "That will be suitable."

The Sikh spoke better English than most of his Welfie soldiers, Rodriguez thought. He watched the man give instructions to another farmer and wave him off into the dark woods.

Now, countless stars and a sliver of moon let the colonel study the other side of the long, narrow lake that bordered Nakima to the west. The low bluff on the western side made him grunt with satisfaction. His men could marshal on the rocks after their swim, sheltered from Corps radar and infrared sensors. He would have to form them into fighting units fast though, send companies into action before they became sick from hydrothermia.

His body shrunk at the idea of standing, wet and shivering, in shallow water for an hour or more, shouting at slow-moving Welfies.

"When your general's man warned us, we carried our people across in row boats," the Sikh said. "They're in a cove down the way. I can transport some of you and your communication equipment, blankets, whatever you've time for. My neighbors are back across already and dig fire holes in the bank. We'll put up blanket screens that hold the heat so your soldiers can recover from their swim."

Maybe this would work after all, Rodriguez thought. He followed Bjorn because the man fought. Maybe his general had luck, too.

#

"You must fly your two divisions out of Nakima, General Howe," Lefko said before dawn from his holovision platform. "And what you can salvage of the air brigade. Tomorrow. I want to bring in the tac-nukes on the day after, before Bjorn spreads out his people even more."

"Don't tell me what I must do, Brigadier," rasped the heavy Corps commander. "The fact that you're HHR's man in the Pentagon and on a ramjet career path doesn't give you the right to give orders to a superior."

Lefko bowed his head in casual apology.

"I can't do what you want, anyway," the three-star General continued. "We're in a major night battle as we speak. If I disengaged, Welfies would think they'd beaten me, that we resorted to nukes to avoid military defeat. That'd be the wrong message to give the ghetto-heads."

Lefko remembered Howe as the brutal brigade commander at Veracruz who'd crucified over a hundred men. The officer had a round face and a petulant mouth, and wore his hair cut close to his skull. He brought the ruthlessness the chiefs needed, but lacked the wisdom that was even more required.

"What's your tactical plan, Sir?" Lefko asked.

"The Welfies have concentrated around a few of my columns, as I expected they'd have to do when I went into the forest after them. Formed targets. I've just ordered the Third Division into the woods. It'll finish them off."

"How are you using the extra brigades?"

"One carries munitions to the three brigades of the first Division that have built defenses in the forest. The other three brigades are en route to join the most northern penetration, the column that has successfully maintained its cohesion. I think that's Bjorn's flank. That combined force will turn south, send fingers to the northern, stalled penetration, and comb the forest for Bjorn's Welfies. Soon I'll have four brigades, a Corps Division, that burns paths through the trees and herds Welfies into the weapons of the resupplied columns. My weight will increase as I move south."

"If you have to help your already engaged columns, they must be in a bad state. You're reinforcing defeat there."

Lefko heard some one enter Howe's projection room and speak rapidly. Howe flushed, started to rise, and then abandoned the effort. He glanced at Lefko, became even redder and shot a glare back at whoever had caused the interruption. "Take care of it!" he shouted. "Kill them!"

General Howe sat still for a moment, apparently to control rage, and then gave Lefko a false grin. "It appears there were Welfies north of my unbroken column after all. Some have swum across the lake--I'm surprised they didn't freeze to death--and attacked my headquarters guard. Don't worry, we'll send them to warm up in the fires of Hell."

"Damn!" exclaimed Lefko. "Bjorn fixes it so you can't leave, so we can't bomb him with nukes without bombing you, too. He'll take out your transport aircraft first of all."

"I told you not to worry, didn't I?"

"You also told me you sent your reserve into the woods, a quarter of it into where the enemy has already cut up ten regiments. You're attacking his vacated flank with the rest, while he's attacking your center. You'll not have time to even hurt him before he eviscerates you."

"Use that famously cold brain, sonny!" Howe shouted, his face now pale except for a spot of red on each cheek. "Quiet your nervous bladder. I've military police, air force personnel, missile people, headquarters soldiers, and God knows whom else here in the cleared area. They're more than enough to take out a few terrorists."

"I'll bet a regiment is about to overrun you."

Howe stood. "You're a goddamn planner, frightened by suspicion," he said. "I won't tolerate second-guessing by junior staff. You're finished in the Corps as of this conversation."

Lefko stood, too, and a flash of anger overcame him. "If you're still alive and in communication at the end of the day, General, I'll kiss your dumb ass. Good morning."

#

"Go! Go!" Rodriguez yelled. He slowed behind his First Battalion's line of skirmishers. Blocks of men swept by him to attack three sides of the Marine headquarters compound.

He stopped when his regimental reserve company came up, and waved them to a halt. Rodriguez shivered--and not from the cold, but from what he saw nearby--then motioned for his comm specialist.

He stood at the start of the cleared area, in front of the lake--at a high point that undoubtedly could be seen from everywhere in the Marine encampment. He noticed, off to the east, over the maglev railroad huts, streaks of flashes that flickered through the forest. He thought that violence must be from General Bjorn's other regiments taking on the Marine Corps' spearheads.

Suddenly a line of yellow and red, accompanied by a hard wave of sound reverberated from the enemy's compound! His lead battalion fell prone. Damn! He needed men to take that protecting mound from the rear.

He looked to his left, beyond the headquarters. His Second Battalion surrounded the Marine barracks, waited for its residents, woken by the sound of local firing, to dash out.

The Third Battalion must be almost at the small airfield and its parked air transports.

"Get me Major Slovinsky," he yelled at the little man who carried his radio and electronic brains.

"Hey, Polak!" Rodriguez shouted when he had his commander of the Fourth Battalion on the radio. "Roust your men out of those warm warehouses. We'll work over the loot later. Get your asses up here and help take the headquarters!"

He yelled in order to fight the cold that might slow down his mind. God, what he'd do for dry clothes! Also, of course, because the thing he refused to look at again made him sick to even think about.

"Show me a panorama," he ordered his specialist. The man unrolled a flat screen display, locked it to his computer. He bent down, set a rocket on the ground, and pushed its ignition button. In a moment, the infrared sensor kite spread its wings a hundred meters up and started rotating.

"I'm sweeping from due north," the wizened little Welfie said. "Going east."

The freezing bastard's hands trembled, but Rodriguez still could pick out the beacons of the comm specialists who traveled with each company commander.

The sweeping detail of black and white paused, and then fixed on a collection of beacons around the transports. He saw little bursts of light, too. His men threw grenades into cockpits, he guessed.

That was the General's highest priority. Done--or soon would be.

"Keep going! Show me the east!"

Hernando Salinas was to take his Third Battalion to the forest edge, make contact with the General's people. A firefight showed Rodriguez his subordinate's position. A vehicle park spread out over there, and a fuel dump. There'd be marine guards, maybe even a regiment, to block Welfies leaking from the forest.

He looked up at the cold sky. The stars and sliver of a moon seemed like pieces of ice. But Rodriguez sensed victory. Whatever enemy forces lurked on the forest fringes were now pinched between him and General Bjorn.

"Here comes Slovinsky," Sequiros, his comm. specialist said. The poor bastard's voice shook.

His Welfie staff man had trained the focused

sector to the southeast. Rodriguez saw four companies running in their direction from the tent city.

The cold is colder, Rodriguez thought, when you keep leaving behind the air your body has warmed.

"Okay," he said. "We're taking my reserve company to the comm. shelter over there, short of the command headquarters perimeter. The one with the antennae. It's bound to have a space heater."

On the way, he skirted the crucifix that towered six meters tall, its arms short stubs. What had been a man sagged from it, his shins pulled up and wired to thighs. To drag his chest down, make breathing harder.

#

"Colonel Rodriguez has taken the Corps communication center and shut down the jammers so we can hear his signal," Ochoa reported. "He's now attacking the Marine headquarters with two battalions."

Jose Cardenas beat Bjorn to the nearest tall tree.

What the hell, Bjorn thought. He needed to preserve some dignity, anyway.

"One of Rodriguez's battalions was into the supply drops," Rafael Ochoa continued. "It began to pile heaters and anti-armor missiles into captured surface fliers. Food and medicine were to be next. The battalion is off helping to take the command center, but Rodriguez says the stuff will start flowing in an hour."

Ochoa spoke code to his display. "I must alert the air defense units not to shoot Rodriguez's men," he explained.

Bjorn had decided to find another tree, when he saw, even from the ground, a yellow glow through the treetops.

"Must be a fuel dump," Cardenas yelled from above.

It was early dawn now, the sky clear and cold. Bjorn wondered what the surviving senior Corps officer, who was probably with one of the northern brigades, would do when his commander no longer responded from Nakima.

"Remind Rodriguez of the stores of scatterable hopper and jumper mines the Corps must have dumped somewhere," he ordered Ochoa. "He must quickly spread them at the passages into the woods where the undamaged Marine brigades entered. Tell the battalions you have attacking from the forest edge to help as soon as they link-up."

Bjorn thought for a moment of that marine commander's quandary. "Pull back from the enemy columns," he told Ochoa. "Set up bivouac areas and hospitals, and get hot food into the men. The new marine commander won't follow the old plan--without an air force and a re-supply of munitions. He'll hoard what he has and radio for instructions."

He picked up his blanket, draped it over his shoulders again. "The Administration has the next move," he said.

Chapter 36

That evening, John Striker, presumptive
President of the United States, strode into Brigadier
General Louis Lefko's personal quarters at Fort McNair
in Washington as if he were still in the cold rain and
gusting wind that moved up the Potomac River. He
moved heavily, his head hunched between his
shoulders.

Lefko nodded to the marine escort who brought
his visitor across the open parade from the entrance
where the executive had left his bodyguard. Then he
closed the door, took Striker's umbrella, and gestured to
a seat. The HHR executive marched to the bar, instead,
and punched a neat, double scotch. He drank a
mouthful, turned, and glowered. "The San Angeles
Welfies have destroyed the long range transport aircraft
of the Corps division that faces them out west," he said.

"They shot their entire inventory of big missiles,"
Lefko elaborated, having heard of the strike earlier that
day. "The division couldn't defend against a thousand,
very fast warheads coming down together, aimed at
one, relatively small target."

He had thought of alcohol himself when he heard
the news.

"So it can't go to the aid of the other divisions
trapped at Nakima?"

"No."

"But the division could move into San Angeles
now without being bombarded on the way, right? It
could punish the bastards."

"Yes. If we want to entangle it in a block-by-block
war that would make the unit unusable elsewhere for

months. That wouldn't be smart."

"Being smart hasn't helped us."

"That division protects the Achiever enclaves along the California coast. In two days it could drive north and hit the Bay Area if things go bad there, maybe save your Welfare Kings and punishment companies. We can also march the division to a train hub and bring it back east. It's our only free military asset. It's too valuable to send into San Angeles now."

"Free but useless. Your General Bjorn has parked the division for you where it won't do us any strategic good."

Bjorn did things like that, Lefko thought.

"And yesterday the Carib Infantry Division mutinied and occupied Vancouver," Striker said. "Welfies now control the northwest."

"Yes," Lefko responded. "To save you from reminding me, I'll also acknowledge that the rest of the Corps huddles uselessly in northern Canada."

Striker grunted.

"What military forces the chiefs have are immobilized in California and the north woods," Lefko said, "while HHR loses a city or two every time you concentrate or try to form a reserve of Punishment Companies."

"Yesterday," Striker mouthed, "Miami and Philadelphia declared independence and joined San Angeles, Chicago, and Minneapolis in acknowledging Con Wagoner as their leader. Now the bastard has Vancouver for his Free Ghettos Council, too, and probably will add Seattle soon. All over the country, our suburbs quake."

"You've come here to tell me we should nuke Bjorn no matter what," Lefko said. "The chiefs say 'no.' It's too late. If we take him out, we'd also vaporize two thirds of the Corps."

"Terrible problems require terrible remedies."

"My superiors believe Mexico would immediately

send a human wave against our death strip and take back the southwest," Lefko argued. "Canada might raid the northeast, move missile plants from Massachusetts to Ontario. We must save the Corps."

Striker stepped closer. His head was still retracted between his shoulders, like a boxer expecting pummeling. "The chiefs are idiots!" he whispered. "They will lose to the Welfies everything they want to save from Mexico and Canada, and more."

"The Welfies are dumb and capable of being manipulated. The breeding mid-world is the greatest threat to the West," Lefko replied. "We must retain the power to protect civilization from physical overrun."

"You and your 'internationalist' chiefs!" Striker looked ready to spit. "First things first."

The argument reminded Lefko of histories about the late Roman Empire, when statesmen measured the required force to put down slave revolts against the needs of the legions along the Rhine and Danube.

The temperate lands then fought to keep the north at bay. Now the north feared the warmer south. Amusing, he thought. The reversal in historical roles worked for the Orient, too. China now threatened Mongolia and the steppes, once the home of Genghis Khan.

"The Marines at Nakima are <u>cold</u>," he said. "They need re-supply quickly or nature will destroy them," he said. "We must act soon."

Striker filled his glass again. "Nukes are the answer."

Lefko looked out at the green parade ground and the soft red brick of the ancient buildings, all under a driving, black rain now. "We've lost," he said. "We must negotiate."

Lefko watched Striker's reflection in the window. For a minute he thought the HHR executive might throw his drink at him.

The man who directed American strategy stood

rigid. "I'm sorry I didn't take your advice earlier, when you recommended nukes," the HHR executive finally said. He sipped from his glass and provided Lefko a small smile. "You were right; I apologize."

He stared at Lefko as if he would engrave his own conviction on the officer's brain. "We'll use our nukes to keep off the Mexicans and Canadians also," he said. "It will only take a couple."

"Everyone has nukes now," Lefko countered. "The chiefs won't cross that threshold."

"You can't let your chiefs stop a stroke that will save our culture!"

Lefko made himself a drink also. He stared out the window as he sipped.

"You must nuke Bjorn," Striker said after a long silence. "And the independent ghettos. We'll build the Achiever militia into a dependable force and no longer use Welfies in the Corps' non-com ranks."

He touched the edge of the glass with his tongue. "I'll arrange the retirement of the chiefs tonight and put in officers who owe me. Tomorrow morning you'll find yourself head of the Operations Directorate."

He never realized how hard Striker was, Lefko thought. A fanatic almost. He returned to his seat in front of the window and closed the electronic scrolling book on the side table. Then he swiveled so he faced his guest again.

"We can't delay further," Striker growled. "After we crush this uprising, we must exterminate most of the ghetto population right away." He sipped from his drink and pulled his eyes from Lefko's. "We dare not give them a second chance."

"You're talking about killing two hundred and fifty million people overnight. That's impractical and impossible, politically. Moderate Achievers will baulk."

Striker focused on Lefko again. He frowned.

"The alternative," Lefko said, "is to negotiate a compromise, as Wagoner and Will Maestri have asked for. We'd de-escalate the confrontation. Give self-government and increase rations. Make all sorts of promises."

He waved his drink. "Our women can bring Welfie leaders into the Achiever class. We'll bribe their best with our privileges and culture. In a few years, we could start reducing the Welfie population more quietly, more cleverly. Put fertility suppressant in their water."

"No! A second postponement would follow the first."

"Some of the Welfies have Achiever-level intelligence. Wagoner, Maestri, and Bjorn, for instance. A lot of the illegal immigrants into the U.S. have, too. They'd invigorate our class."

"They stink, don't talk properly." Striker's anger was cold now.

"I don't have the stomach for mass slaughter, Mr. Striker. Let's talk to the Welfies."

The HHR executive stood. For a long moment he was quiet, but he trembled; his hands shook. "You fool!" he finally shouted. "You'd doom our civilization! We'll become a mongrel people and drown in our own effluent."

Now Striker did throw the glass. It bounced off the window. Drops of alcohol splashed on Lefko's sleeve.

"The chiefs and I have an appointment with the Vice President in the morning," Lefko said. "He'll have no option but to open negotiations."

The HHR executive shouted an expletive and turned to storm out.

"Sorry, Mr. Striker," Lefko said, and held up a hand. "You're under arrest. When you came on the base for this private talk, you provided opportunity. We can't have HHR acting wildly now."

Chapter 37

The marines who'd mutinied stood at parade rest in the forest, their weapons at their feet. Bjorn and Ochoa walked briskly up the line of vehicles and men. Bjorn stopped in front of a non-com he knew--this was his old regiment, after all. The man stood at attention, a meter in front of the files of men. "Why'd you mutiny, Sweeney?" he asked.

The blond master sergeant tightened his long lips but kept his eyes fixed to Bjorn's. "The new units brought Enforcers into the woods..." The marine stiffened as he apparently recognized his old comrade. "General Bjorn, Sir."

Bjorn nodded and waited.

"They was going to crucify some of us. To make the others fight, Sir."

"You're from Chicago, if I remember."

"Yes, Sir. They was watching me close 'cause the ghetto's free. I probably would be fruit on a tree now if I didn't mutiny."

Crushed and splintered wood, torn limbs, and scattered leaves floored the forest opening. The sun was bright, the surrounding tree trunks gray, the foliage red and yellow. About three hundred and fifty men watched Bjorn, he guessed. From four companies. This complement of marines had dwindled from the five hundred who must have entered the forest.

"Did you guys know we killed General Howe and took your supplies into the woods?"

"Yes, Sir. And, by noon yesterday, your minefields had us trapped. Our comm people spread your message about nukes, too." Sweeney grimaced.

"Seemed you were the only one who could get us out of this fix alive."

Sweeney was a gregarious man, Bjorn remembered. When he said nothing for a moment, the marine waved his arm. "Hell," he said. "We're Welfies, too."

"We may have to fight the four brigades north of here. You willing?"

"Aye, Sir."

Sweeney was smart enough, Bjorn remembered. He knew his business and was careful. But, like so many of his fellow Welfie enlisted men, he wasn't very comfortable with original thought. The rebellion he led must have made him sweat.

"Okay. Take a silver leaf from your commander's body and pin it on your collar. You're now in command of this battalion."

Sweeney swallowed.

"Appoint officers and organize," Bjorn continued. "Strip those Marine patches and name tags off the men's fatigues; otherwise our people will start shooting at you. Colonel Ochoa here will give you orders until we sweep up more Marines and can form a higher unit headquarters."

"Aye, Sir." Sweeney had to clear his throat then.

Once you all start following my orders each and every one of you is doomed if the Corps recaptures you. You'll fight like tigers for me to avoid that fate, won't you Sweeney?

Bjorn started down the line of men again, nodding here and there at a few he knew. As he passed, the marines snapped to attention and stared as if he were some natural wonder. Most wore corselets and stood behind assault rifles on the ground, although a few toed the semi-automatic short guns that identified them as vehicle and major weapon operators.

"The next battalion in this column is about to come over, too," Ochoa said. "The major commanding shot the Enforcers who walked in with reinforcements. He thought they would destroy what morale he had. He's talking to Cardenas and Bryant now."

"We completely replace the officers. No Achievers!"

"Yes, Sir. The bargaining is about safety guarantees for them, though."

"What about the rest of the regiment?"

"Jose tells me the Colonel went down. His replacement is having a hell of a time putting everything together. He probably doesn't even know that one of his four battalions on this temporary forest track has mutinied and come over to you, that another is about to."

Bjorn stopped suddenly. He grabbed Ochoa's shoulder. "Keep it that way," he said urgently. "Leave the insignia on. Bring in Bryant's tame officer-prisoners, the ones he says are 'Holistics,' or whatever. Make one of them a front for Sweeney, have him tell Regiment that Enforcers stiffened the outfit."

Bjorn bit his lip and tried to think of everything. "Tell the second battalion commander to pretend he's still boss," he continued, "even though his non-coms take over. If he acts straight, he and his fellow officers go home to mama without a mark on them."

Ochoa stared at him, puzzled.

"This fight isn't over yet," Bjorn explained. "Take over personally on this, Ochoa. It gives us a hole card."

Maybe he set up a con that wasn't needed. But the Marine units he surrounded in the woods were fragile. Maybe he could use disguised mutineers to bring others over, or to launch a surprise attack.

The commanders of the four brigades north of him, fortified in regimental porcupines, were still arrogant. They sent parties--which Bjorn had his men ambush--to cut mine-free exits from the woods. Those commanders would soon note the captured air defense missiles and guns emplaced around the airfield, and would soon realize that Corps re-supply wasn't in the cards, even if somehow they could break free. They'd see that the maglev line was inoperative. They'd soon understand that neither support nor escape was possible. The troops would soon get the idea, too.

If he put a few mutinous marine scouts up there to drop a few words to their fellows, maybe...

And south of that force, Bjorn commanded a re-supplied, although gravely hurt, light infantry division that had proved its superiority in thick woods by destroying a Corps division and an independent airborne brigade, and by paralyzing much of a second division. That Welfie force had proved its fighting merit.

He probably didn't need a hole card. Still, passing up a chance like this went against his grain.

#

"Maybe we've won a compromise, Benjamin," Uncle Will said from the flat screen. "The government wants us at the State department day after tomorrow. To negotiate a peace, they say."

In the cold forest night, Bjorn pulled the blanket tighter around his neck. "How're you feeling, Uncle Will? Don't forget you left the hospital a little hurriedly."

His uncle grinned. "I'm as good as ever. The cubby's cramped and the vegpro poor, but I'm able to deal again." Then he sobered. "I like seeing you healthy, too. For a while there I thought your odds even worse than mine."

His uncle did look spry, Bjorn thought. And, his color was good.

"The Corps has Striker in storage," Uncle Will said. "The chiefs don't want to nuke the marines you've locked up with you in Canada."

Well that's a relief, Bjorn thought. "How're you talking to the Administration?"

"By the didg comm. line. No way snoops can locate me."

God, it was cold! And the worst of the night lay

ahead. Bjorn closed his eyes for a moment. "They've got to bring all of us down," he said after he opened his eyes. "Both sides, and now. Otherwise, the Corps units up here will start dying off. We've captured and monopolized most of their blankets and heaters."

He nodded at his uncle. "They don't bring out an Achiever-led unit, however, without taking one of mine first. I sit on the maglev lines as they pass east and south through the forest.

"The chiefs will have to muscle the Canadian Premier. The bastard wants us to destroy each other. Tell Saltonstall either he energizes the maglev line, or the Air Force bombs Ottawa."

Uncle Will nodded.

"My director of logistics will move the units," Bjorn continued. "First, a Welfie infantry regiment loads up and departs, then a Marine Corps regiment, and so on. He'll work with the Canadians to schedule the trains through Toronto and into the States."

Bjorn tapped his knee. "If the Corps tries to rush, we'll shut down the maglev line where it passes through our forest. If we try to jump ahead of line, the Canadians shut down the electricity from Toronto."

"I'm with you so far," Uncle Will said. "But what about the meeting at the State Department? They want you and Wagoner there, too."

Bjorn frowned.

"I don't think it's a trap. My source about Striker being imprisoned is good."

"Tell the chiefs they've got to let me bring a regiment to the party."

Now Uncle Will frowned.

"When HHR concentrated," Bjorn said, "it stationed extra HHR battalions in the capital. Wagoner told me that some time ago. You could make the argument that a Welfie regiment can't threaten their control. We'd only protect our negotiators."

Uncle Will rubbed his nose. "If I were them, I

wouldn't buy that, nephew."

"Try. Tell them we'll put no Welfie leaders at risk unless they're accompanied by suitable protection."

"What's the fall-back?"

"Let them bring in a regiment, also. After my force. Have the chiefs post it around the White House and Executive Building. We'd stay downtown, next to the ghetto."

"How would you manage it?"

"I'll take the first train, with a Welfie regiment, into Washington. The next train will follow with a Marine regiment. The other Welfie infantry will drop off in Detroit and Buffalo. I don't care where the chiefs unload the remaining Corps regiments as long as they remain six hundred kilometers from Washington."

"You think your regiment can hold off theirs if the chiefs decide to scoop us up?"

"We'd at least make a big mess of Washington." Bjorn leaned forward. "What's our alternative? Civil war in every megacity and town for a generation? Let's take the gamble that the chiefs and the more moderate Achievers tire of this bloody shit. A peace party must be stirring in the suburbs. Everyone can't be swept up by hate. Let's give negotiations a chance."

Chapter 38

Bjorn watched Colonel Fernando Rodriguez's regiment march from Union Station toward the governmental center of Washington. The formation wound past the Capitol, where he stood on broad marble steps, to camp on the Mall.

Hundreds, maybe thousands of loiterers quietly observed from side streets. They'd be on welfare, he thought, but newly so because the Administration had been slow in this town to replace human bureaucrats with netted, talking computers. The big bosses had friends among the Washington office workers. The civil war's demand for funding, however, had spurred efficiency and increased unemployment. New claimants for welfare received rations once destined for occupants of revolting ghettos.

These unemployed would want something other than the historical descent to the ghetto of their predecessors. They might side with the Welfie rebellion and, at any rate, now appeared friendly.

"Don't worry, General," Colonel Rodriguez said from beside him. "My men will let the corps regiment and its heavy equipment through without problems. After Winnipeg and Nakima, they'll do anything you ask."

By that apparently subservient speech, Rodriguez once more expressed his opposition to Bjorn's arrangements. The colonel had complained in the train when he heard that Bjorn's director of logistics allowed the enemy to load laser burners, tanks, and other heavy weapons. Naturally he would object, Bjorn thought, since the equipment made Rodriguez's force badly inferior.

Bjorn shrugged. "There'll be no heavy fighting."

He'd learned that Congress was on extended summer vacation. Legislators didn't have much to do nowadays, anyway. They couldn't micro-manage after the twenty-sixties. Constitutional revision had limited their staffs and given the President a line item veto. Federal departments made the major decisions now.

He glanced south. Striker's headquarters sprawled a few blocks away, but he knew the HHR executive wouldn't be there. The Corps had him in their brig.

"Put the battalion with your best light colonel into the railroad station right after the Corps regiment disembarks," he told Rodriguez. "Your man and his troops protect the train carrying Mr. Wagoner and the President as it enters the station. A Welfie bodyguard battalion from Chicago will be with them."

Bjorn fixed Rodriguez's eyes with his. "Have your man take over the maglev power grid," he said slowly. "The battalion commander's to turn off all maglev energy on incoming lines once the President's train stops. He keeps it off until he hears from me personally."

A recent Atlantic storm had blown away most pollution. The bright morning was cool, but not cold like the north woods. Bjorn stood on his toes and stretched nervously.

#

Will Maestri and Bjorn stood when the President's party entered the Corps shelter Rodriguez had brought down from Nakima and erected on the Mall. Bjorn came to attention and saluted, his eyes focused on Con Wagoner. He then slipped past out-thrust hands and confronted Ginny, whom, he'd learned, had joined her father's party at the railroad station.

She wore a tailored blue suit that emphasized her thin, straight figure. Her face was solemn, even frightened. "Hi, sweetheart," he said.

She stared at him. Her hands trembled slightly.
"May I kiss you?" he whispered.
She nodded.

When he leaned forward, her reserve broke. She flung her arms around his neck, closed her eyes, and returned the kiss passionately.

Bjorn wondered what the President thought about the embrace. He gently swung her aside, kept an arm around her waist. "Sorry to ignore protocol for a moment," he said to the others, "but Ginny had priority."

Out of the corner of his eye, he saw her bite her lip, felt her stiffen with purpose. "I'm serious about General Bjorn, father," she proclaimed. "I want to marry him and have his children."

Shit!

The Ambassador broke the following silence. She stepped close to Ginny and shook her shoulder gently. "Are you sure, niece? He's a Welfie. All your friends..."

"Oh, Aunt, I have new friends now. His." She glanced at Bjorn. "I'm a Welfie, too."

Uncle Will appeared amused. The President didn't have to make a decision about his daughter's love affair, he would think. His nephew did.

The Ambassador turned to her brother. "It's good politics," she said. "The marriage will show both classes you're serious about fusing the two nations."

"Ben's important now and will be more so."

With that, Ginny seconded her aunt's declaration. Bjorn didn't doubt that the woman loved him. She had cleverly chosen the place to declare her intent to marry, however. She squeezed him, and the system, too.

"I'm a gun target right now," he said. "When the fighting is finished..."

"We'll arrange an elegant, public wedding," the Ambassador concluded for him. "We'd win massive network exposure that way."

Her father stepped forward to grasp Bjorn's hand,

the man's normal reserve even more pronounced.

Damn! Bjorn thought. Ginny started a stampede! He glanced at Uncle Will.

His uncle slowly shook his head. *Now's not the time for a blow up,* he all but said.

Con Wagoner's handshake was hearty, his grin expansive. He, also, saw the political value in a marriage, Bjorn guessed. Con believed in "wedded bliss" and all that shit, too.

"I must talk to Major Hata and our San Angeles friends," Bjorn finally said to Ginny.

She bit her lip, swallowed, and then smiled.

Bjorn walked out the shelter entrance. He admired Ginny's tactics, but guessed they were a forewarning of what marriage might bring. He couldn't see tying himself to someone who would try to manage him.

Outside, in the fall afternoon, Rodriguez's troops dug trenches along the street that divided the Mall. Across the pavement reared the Washington Monument, while the Reflecting Pool gleamed further away and, finally, the White House shimmered. The Corps regiment, across the street, that had marched past them to occupy the monument and pool grounds erected only a wire fence to hold back throngs of curious.

Red and yellow leaves from the trees on the Mall fluttered down in a swirl of wind. Regimental cooks built fires for the evening supper--meat the President had brought from Chicago in three refrigerated cars. The aroma made Bjorn hungry.

He waved his hand at nearby Welfie pickets from the San Angeles battalion and strode over to Tommy Hata.

Bjorn returned his old friend's salute and grinned. "How was the morale in Chicago when you left, Tommy?"

"Great, Sir! Although Hone was jealous you gave

me the Presidential escort job."

"As I remembered, your battalion has more combat experts," Bjorn said. "We may need those skills tomorrow."

He remembered his own frustration when past commanders kept him in the dark. He put his hand on his Veracruz buddy's sleeve. "Look, Tommy," he said. "You're to guard this shelter and the ones we've set up for the politicians. Rodriguez watches the perimeter; you kill any unauthorized people he misses. Okay?"

"Yes, Sir."

"Pull out your best hand-to-hand combat people--short guns and knives. I'll need forty of them tomorrow. You'll share guard duty with Corps officers at the conference."

"Yes, Sir."

"And don't let your people talk to the Welfies of the Corps regiment across the street, not even nod. Ignore everything that goes on over there. Understand?"

"Yes, Sir."

"One other thing."

Bjorn put his arm over Hata's shoulder and led him even deeper between the troops' shelters, where long-range collectors couldn't pick up coherent sound waves.

#

"Oh, Ben, you want to marry, too, don't you?"

Ginny's slim, naked leg touched his as she propped her head on her hand and stared down at him. Their sleeping pad was narrow, but she took hardly any space at all.

"We'll talk about it later, when we're in calmer times."

He doubted she could see his face and gain much information that way.

"What about babies?"

"Our problem's overpopulation, you know."

It was probably eleven o'clock. Almost time to get on with the night's job.

"Our problem is <u>useless</u> population. We smart people need to breed, somehow make the dummies not."

He reached up to fondle her small, firm breasts and ran his hand down her slim side. "If we married, you'd be a Welfie too, one of the dummies," he said. "You would have to set an example."

#

The next morning, Achiever officers from the Pentagon and Major Hata's Welfies guarded the interior of the Department of Agriculture building--only a block from the two regimental camps. The men stood on each side of a door, or on alternate steps, their hands close to weapons.

Uncle Will had reluctantly agreed to this armed equality in lieu of an enforceable ban on all weapons. If a gun went off or anyone shouted, however, each man would try to make sure he was the first to fire and the final one to stand. It was an explosive arrangement, Bjorn knew.

He followed the President and the Ambassador, and stepped pass the guards. Con Wagoner and Uncle Will strode at his sides down the wide hallways and up the sweeping, granite stairs. He paused to nod at Major Hata and winced at the size and apparent belligerence of the Corps colonel on the opposite side of the doorway before he entered a conference room. The Achiever officer wore no battle ribbons, however.

Administration negotiators sat on the far side of a gleaming conference table. Halfway through the door, Uncle Will glanced back at Bjorn. Striker was the central figure!

According to Uncle Will, a Welfie non-com, personally involved in the imprisonment, reported the HHR executive's arrest by the Corps. Striker had cursed and kicked his jailers before being thrown in a cell.

Bjorn rotated his head slightly and felt the firm presence of his hidden knife. None of them would have come if they knew Striker was still on top. His gut tightened.

Admiral Wolverton, the head of the joint chiefs, positioned himself between Louis Lefko, the Achiever general now in charge of operations according to Welfie spies, and Striker. Vice President Myers sat on the other side of Striker, the Attorney General on the farthest right. The room contained no one else, conforming to the protocols Uncle Will negotiated.

"So we all meet again," the President boomed. He sat down in front of the wiry, balding Vice President. He did not offer a hand. "I presume you gentlemen regret your rebellion?"

The Ambassador touched her brother as she sat next to him, opposite the bluff Attorney General.

She's the more cautious, Bjorn thought, and also probably the wiser.

"Hello, Will Maestri," Striker said and nodded across the table. "Congratulations on getting this far. I never expected to negotiate anything with you."

Bjorn slid into the seat next to his uncle and across from the heavy-set, handsome Chief. He watched as Con limped up and sat opposite Lefko.

"I don't regret our attempt to squash your idiocy," snarled the Vice President, "just our failure until now."

"You do mean to withdraw the Bill of Incompetence and have us return to the White House, don't you?" asked the Ambassador. "You will restart the election process?"

"Elections are impossible," Striker replied from the middle of the table. His eyes were half closed and a smile waited around his mouth. "We must impose order first. The country's close to total chaos after what you people have done."

"Why don't we hear your demands?" proposed

the Vice President.

"You know them!" responded the President. He slapped the table with his hand. "Repeal of the repressive sixty-six laws. Abolition of HHR. Welfie police and courts in the ghettos. Return of the old rations."

"We might agree to some of that, when we get into detail, but HHR stays," Striker said. "After all, someone has to hand out welfare."

Con Wagoner stirred. "No HHR," he said. "That's not negotiable. "I agree that some agency will have to administer welfare. We want its name to be 'The Rations Department,' however, after a complete turnover of personnel. Headed by a Welfie. Everyone, Achievers too, will receive a standard ration, and only that. No more distribution of necessities according to the ability to pay."

"That's ridiculous," blurted the Attorney General.

Con glanced coldly down the table at him. "Ghetto rations must increase," he said. "Our people starve. Therefore, others must receive less. And, universal rationing isn't ridiculous. We did it before, during wartime, a hundred and fifty years ago."

"We also require wholesale resignations," Uncle Will said, "and from those of you here. Welfies must be brought into the administration, in key posts, such as Justice, Education, and Rations."

Bjorn tapped the table. "Welfies must take command of major Corps units, too," he said. "Any settlement must result in equal military power until we're truly one nation."

"Let's stop this stupid play-acting," Striker said. "You wretches must understand something. HHR is not finished. Your insurrection is!"

He waved at Lefko.

Here comes their trick, Bjorn thought.

"Last night," Lefko said, "I ordered the Corps regimental commander out on the Mall to move his troops' heavy weapons around your encampment at noon, General Bjorn." He smiled sadly. "That'll be in an hour or so. You don't have thick woods here to shield you from our fire. Actually, our men's assault rifles alone would be enough to destroy the regiment you brought down from the north woods."

Wagoner grunted as if he'd been hit in the stomach.

"You gave a solemn, sworn-to promise!" the President shouted. "You said you'd negotiate fairly!"

The Vice President only smiled.

"Major General Lefko enticed you here, trapped you all very nicely," Striker said. "He even fooled me. This Administration has not capitulated to the weaklings who advocate compromise." His smile was savage, triumphant. "Now we'll talk reality," he continued. "Instead of fantasizing about changes in Washington, we'll discuss practical steps you will take to quiet the ghettos."

"I'll do nothing under duress," Wagoner said. "I'll not tell my people to surrender without satisfactory terms and guarantees." He folded his arms.

Uncle Will looked at Bjorn, while the President shoved his chair back and swore. The Ambassador wiped her forehead, damp now with perspiration.

"Did you talk to your regimental commander this morning, General?" Bjorn asked.

Lefko stared at him.

#

The night before, Bjorn didn't think he awakened Ginny when he crawled out of the shelter, but they were initially so entwined that he couldn't be sure. She stayed curled beneath the thin blanket, however.

Tommy Hata and his three men waited in the night then, at the road, across from the Corps regiment's camp. After Bjorn led them across, he found Lieutenant Colonel Sweeney sitting on his heels, near the cut open fence.

"Did Lefko and any other generals visit your regimental commander today?" Bjorn asked Sweeney.

"Big meeting at headquarters after chow tonight, Sir. Lots of gold braid. The regiment's heavy weapons people were called in; we infantry pukes were excluded." He smiled. "Just as well."

"You have any trouble on the way down?"

"No, Sir. My battalion was separate on the train from the other battalions and the Achiever officers you spread around us spoke up good on the radio. Colonel Ochoa, who you put in charge back in Nakima, has them tame."

Bryant was the man who did the taming, Bjorn thought. In the days of their captivity, the hologram producer motivated the officers with images of their Achiever suburbs in flames--likely outcomes if the Welfies didn't obtain what they wanted.

Two of the regiment's four battalions were already his. Once he took the headquarters, Sweeney and others would "turn" their fellow non-coms of the other battalions. Achiever officers would find gun muzzles at their foreheads when they awoke in the night.

Sweeney had promised no gunfire.

Back from the fence, fifteen men crouched between bare Japanese cherry trees. Ochoa's selected strike force of Marines wore black, night-fighting clothes, their faces and hands smeared with dead brands from the cook fires.

"None of your men, please, General," Ochoa said. "The Marines want to do this themselves."

Ochoa, too, was camouflaged. In his right hand he carried a semi-automatic short gun.

"What about the second battalion?" Bjorn asked. "Is the light colonel who surrendered reliable? Will he stand firm now that he's in Washington with his Achiever allies near?"

"Bryant says yes. The officer didn't like the threat

of nukes and felt the administration planned to sacrifice him and his men."

A touchy operation, Bjorn thought. Marines had obedience pounded into them from the first day of recruit training. If some Achiever officer...

"I've got two non-coms with cane stripes on their backs shadowing him to be sure," Ochoa added.

"Make the take-over quiet. Put Villasenor into the comm. room right away. Nothing goes out to the Pentagon."

Bjorn nodded to Sweeney, who broke off to collect his non-com "persuaders" for the other two battalions.

Bjorn went with Ochoa, behind three point men. They passed pre-briefed sentries who saluted, then stepped aside.

"Who goes there?"

"Bastard Enforcers!"

"Crucify my brother, will you?"

Two men who stood at the lighted entrance pulled hastily at their guns.

The marines in front of Ochoa leaped forward with bared knives. Bjorn heard a gurgle and the whistle of air from a slit windpipe. Ochoa and his men darted inside.

Bjorn stepped over the two bodies and followed his new men into the lighted regimental command shelter.

#

Now, Bjorn grinned at Lefko. "The Corps force I brought down for you was rotten with mutiny," he said. "I took command at midnight."

Lefko had turned pale. He bit his lip.

"I think General Lefko believes me and would agree that I now control Washington, Mr. Striker," Bjorn said. "That's your reality."

For a moment the Achievers remained silent. Their arrogance had undone them again, Bjorn thought.

They'd made the same mistake they made on the battlefield, at Nakima. After cornering dumb Welfies, they thought defeat impossible.

Striker stood and kicked a table leg. "No, you bastard!" he shouted. The admiral twisted and shouted questions at Lefko, while the Vice President leaned forward to yell down the table, too. The Attorney General's cheeks turned red and his mouth worked, but he issued no sound. On the Achiever side of the table, only Lefko maintained composure, although his lips had thinned to a white line.

Striker reached into his pocket and yanked out a gun. "I'll never give up," he said. His voice shook with emotion. "We can still escape this building and organize a government in Baltimore."

"Fire that gun," Uncle Will said from his opposite seat, "and you'll start a war in this building, one you won't survive."

Bjorn stood to confront Striker. He was very conscious of his hidden knife.

He noted that Uncle Will's hand pressed the table so hard the fingertips were white. His uncle's black eyes flickered up into his. "Patience" was the message.

Lefko shook his head. "How do you always come up with the unexpected counter-stroke?"

"Your call now, General," Bjorn answered. "Kill each other or compromise?"

From his chair, Lefko reached across the admiral, seized Striker's hand, and wrenched the gun away. He stood. "Don't be stupid," he said to the heavy HHR director. "You'd be the first to die. Look at Maistre and Bjorn. They've throwing knives. They're ready and the one you didn't immediately kill, would kill you."

He slid the gun onto the table in front of Con Wagoner.

"Give it up," Lefko said to the man who led the effort to eliminate Welfies. "You couldn't win in here." He waved toward the exit. "It wouldn't matter if you did

survive Bjorn and his uncle; we'd stumble out of the
building holding our throats together."

Striker shifted his eyes back and forth. He
perspired, and he trembled.

Uncle Will stood now, too.

"I wouldn't have slaughtered your people," Lefko
said to Bjorn. "The Chief here was prepared to
compromise, if you surrendered your forces and agreed
to some long range plan to empty the ghettos. Like a
fertility suppressant dumped in your water."

Striker pushed in front of the still sitting admiral.
He reached for his weapon that lay on the table.

"No, you madman!" shouted Admiral Wolverton,
who swung his arm and caught Striker hard in the gut.
"You'll kill us all."

The senior officer stood and wrestled with the
HHR executive. Their bodies pushed back their chairs;
they collapsed to the floor. Both heavy men, each was
unable to master the other. They cursed and gasped for
breath as they rolled and scrabbled for each other's
eyes.

Still sitting, Con picked up the gun. Uncle Will
and Bjorn stepped back from the table and the
struggling Achievers.

"As soon as the chief of staff dismisses his
officers from the guard outside," Uncle Will told the
President, "we'll bring in Benjamin's public relations
expert. You must announce your return to power."

Bjorn stepped around the table, patted down
Lefko, and then returned to the other side.

"Son of a bitch!" gurgled Wolverton from the floor.

"You're fired," snarled the Ambassador to the
Vice President. "You can join Striker and fatso here in
the Bahamas." She gestured at the Attorney General.
"If we ever catch one of you in the continental United
States, he'll die."

"Bullshit," the Vice President said in a deep,
vibrating voice. He stood. His hand held a gun he'd

hidden in his lap. He leveled it at the President. "I'm with Striker," he said.

The struggle on the floor ceased as apparently both the Admiral and Striker listened.

The Vice President glared at Bjorn and Uncle Will. "Your leader, the President, is hostage to our peaceful departure," he said. "Throw a knife and I'll kill him before I fall."

"No!" Con shouted. He was white and his whole body shook. He pointed Striker's gun down the table at the Vice President and fired. "Bang!"

Bjorn lurched back. He held his knife by the blade, but couldn't remember slipping it from his neck sheath. From the corner of his eye, he saw Uncle Will next to him, in an identical posture.

Wagoner had shot the Vice President in the chest, but only once. Blood pulsed down the man's white shirt. He braced himself on the table. "You are traitorous scum," he yelled. He fired.

His hand and gun turned.

Wagoner shot the Vice President again.

The official collapsed. His head thudded as it hit the table.

The President coughed in his seat and then pitched over onto the table also.

Shots resounded from outside the room.

"I surrender!" shouted the Attorney General. "I'm not in this." He backed against the wall, his hands raised, his eyes wide.

"Neither am I," the admiral said from the floor. He convulsively freed himself from Striker, stood, and stepped to the wall, next to Lefko. Both raised their hands. Striker kneeled on the floor, his hand bleeding from a bite. He was white-faced.

"The bastard killed my brother!" the Ambassador shrieked.

Bjorn sprinted to the door and slid the lock closed. He heard more close shots and then screams

and groans, but no one tried the handle. The noise
diminished. Bjorn still heard firing, however, apparently
from the stairwell, and downstairs, and then farther
away, at the building's entrance.

"Tommy?" he called.

"You okay, General?" his friend whispered
raggedly from floor level. "Stay tight for a while. I'm still
operative and my men control the corridor. The stairs
too, I think."

Hata's battalion now dashed toward the building,
Bjorn knew. Ochoa would throw a loyal Corps cordon
around it within minutes and move in heavy weapons.

Bjorn stepped carefully back toward the table.
The Ambassador bent across her brother's back, held
his lifeless head, and sobbed. Con held his gun on the
standing Achievers and Uncle Will returned his knife to
its scabbard.

"What a mess," Lefko muttered. He held very
still. "The speaker of the house is next in line. He's an
ideological idiot."

Bjorn sniffed the cordite. Not as bloody as many
of the actions he'd experienced, he thought, but the
results were more serious.

Con threw his gun on the table and Bjorn picked
it up.

"We might as well be honest with ourselves,"
Uncle Will said. He pulled out his chair and sat. "The
Vice President just killed all chance of a compromise
government. The Welfies in this room will run the
country now."

"I dreaded an Achiever victory for so long," Con
said in an uneven voice, "I couldn't give them another
chance. I'm going back to San Angeles where I won't
screw up everything anymore."

"No." Uncle Will stood again and caught Con's
arm. "Forget what you did. Maybe it was necessary.
Anyway, we have no more uncertainty. The next steps
are clear. You're our new President. You must unify the

Welfies." He turned to Bjorn. "And Benjamin, you must establish our authority. You must disarm all opposition."

Bjorn shivered. Why me? he thought. When I started out, all I wanted was a job. Now I must manage things. What about the Achiever-run nations in the rest of the world? Must I beat them off, maybe change their ways, too?

I'll have to marry Ginny, he thought. She was the only bridge left to the President's party of Achievers.

Uncle Will and Con stared. They waited for him to take charge, he supposed. After all, he commanded the military now. All of it.

Damn!

The End

Made in the USA
Charleston, SC
16 September 2013